CROSSFIRE

CROSSFIRE

R.D. NIXON

This edition produced in Great Britain in 2021

by Hobeck Books Limited, Unit 14, Sugnall Business Centre, Sugnall, Stafford, Staffordshire, ST21 6NF

www.hobeck.net

A CIP catalogue for this book is available from the British Library.

ISBN 978-1-913-793-35-7 (pbk)

ISBN 978-1-913-793-34-0 (ebook)

Cover design by Jayne Mapp Design

Printed and bound in Great Britain

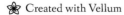 Created with Vellum

Are you a thriller seeker?

Hobeck Books is an independent publisher of crime, thrillers and suspense fiction and we have one aim – to bring you the books you want to read.

For more details about our books, our authors and our plans, plus the chance to download free novellas, sign up for our newsletter at **www.hobeck.net**.

You can also find us on Twitter **@hobeckbooks** or on Facebook **www.facebook.com/hobeckbooks10**.

For my boys, Rob and Dom. I'm insanely and embarrassingly proud of you both. Thanks for letting me nick your initials!

Prologue

Glenlowrie Estate, Fort William, Scotland, New Year's Eve 1987/8

'WE CAN'T KEEP IT, DUNC.'

The contents of the canvas rucksack remained untouched by the light of three straining candles, but Duncan Wallace stared into the depths nevertheless, feeling the satisfied smile start from somewhere in the middle of his chest. His prize was in there, tantalisingly within reach... His two companions wouldn't know such a treasure if it were illuminated in pink neon, and this rickety wooden hut, hidden away in the foothills of the estate, was hardly a worthy place for it.

'Dunc! I said—'

'Shut up, Sandy, I'm thinking.'

Duncan dipped his hand into the bag. He felt the shift and slide of velvet-covered boxes and smooth, heavy chains, and as he tilted the bag to let the meagre light dust the corners he saw where the Fury nestled, swathed in black silk. The inner smile turned into a tight thrill that was almost an ache; the fiery black

Lightning Ridge opal, so far from his reach as to have been almost mythical, was now his.

He withdrew his empty hand, and a loose earring caught in his own expensive watch and dropped onto the tea chest, giving off a muted glow as it lay, incongruously opulent against the splintered wooden base. Sandy Broughton tried again, looking to the third man for support, but Rob just shrugged.

Sandy hunched forward, his expression more worried than ever. 'Duncan, man, this is *serious*. A joke's a joke, but now we—'

'Now, my friends,' Duncan broke in, 'we're richer than anyone's a right to be.'

Rob Doohan smiled. 'We were already rich,' he pointed out, his voice calm.

'Not like this.' Duncan picked up the emerald earring and examined it in the light of the nearest candle. A gust of wind surged against the side of the hut, shaking the walls and blowing the flame almost horizontal. He glanced at his companions. Shadows flickered across Rob's features, creating hollows where none were, lights glimmering in eyes that had no depth. Yet Duncan trusted him.

Sandy appealed once more. 'This isn't just any old collection – this belongs to Mick! Our *friend*, remember? This was supposed to be nothing more than a prank. Jesus, Rob, tell him. Maybe you'll get through.'

'He'll listen to whoever he wants to,' Rob said, still mild.

Duncan dropped the earring back into the bag. 'It's quite simple, Sandy. Prank or not, I don't *want* to give it back. Mick doesn't need this. We're going to split it three ways and stash it for a while. A long while.'

There was a pause, heightening their awareness of the creaking trees that surrounded them. Sandy glanced up nervously, as if he expected to see a branch come crashing through the roof at any moment.

'How long?' Rob leaned forward, scooping up a handful of the rucksack's contents. Duncan tensed, then relaxed as he saw that his friend's questing fingers had not snared the black silk. He moved the bag closer to himself, then looked at his companions in turn, needing to gauge their responses.

'Around thirty years.'

Sandy stared, bemused. '*Thirty?* But we'll be—'

'In our sixties,' Rob interrupted. 'Think of it as extra pension credit. It'll appreciate in value, and in the meantime we've no financial worries – we don't *need* this, any more than Mick does. But Duncan's right; why should we give it back? It'd only rot in some vault somewhere.'

Duncan saw the fight going out of Sandy, and began the task of separating the spoils of their Hogmanay raid – careful to ensure that the silk-wrapped prize remained in the corner of the bag. The wind grew stronger; the candles burned low on their blobs of wax; tempers stretched, and were eased, and stretched again. But at last the job was done. Even Sandy seemed happier now; funny how hard it becomes to advocate giving something up once you've experienced the warmth of it on your fingers.

After the other two had left, Duncan stared at the closed door, frowning. Rob was solid enough, but Sandy would likely be trouble; he was just too damned twitchy. Another face kept trying to push forward in his mind, but he shook his head and watched it fly away into dust; he couldn't think about that now.

He waited a few minutes to be sure his friends had gone, before unwrapping the black silk with a reverence usually reserved by priests for the Holy Sacrament. The opal lay in front of him at last, and even the guttering candles seemed to pick up an extra source of light from its blazing heart. Duncan's breathing eased, and as his mind cleared, he linked his hands on the tea chest, bowed his head, and began to think.

———

The candles had long since burned out, and a thin, watery daylight was creeping under the door of the hut, when he finally straightened, grimacing as the cold air stirred around him. He folded the silk across the Fury again, feeling something inside him shrivel at the loss. The temptation to keep it was almost too much to resist, but he knew he'd made the right decision.

Chapter One

Abergarry, Scotland, 2nd August 1993

THE CAR CAME out of nowhere. One minute Dougie was striding along the empty road, enjoying a bit of Pink Floyd through his earphones, the next he was staring over his shoulder in disbelief at the BMW hurtling towards him. Heart hammering, he jumped for the drainage ditch, and felt a moment's elated triumph until his boots slithered on the wet grass. He went down onto his hands, yelling out in pain as his right wrist bent sharply and his tailbone connected with the stony ground.

The car purred its expensive way onward over the summit, and, as far as a stunned Dougie could see, the brake lights hadn't flashed once. His wrist throbbed, and he cupped it in his left hand as he climbed unsteadily to his feet, looking both ways on the once more deserted road, then let out an explosive, but trembling breath. *Tourists!* Just because you could see for miles didn't mean you could hammer along these roads at seventy-plus... There might not be a lot of traffic around at this time of the day, but there were other things to consider. Like people! Christ, if Floyd hadn't gone quiet at the crucial moment, he wouldn't have heard the car at all.

Feeling queasy at that thought, Dougie brushed at the bits of grass that clung to his wet hands and tried to get his heart under control again. Fifty-one was no age, right enough, but it was also no age to be leaping about like a teenager; he'd be feeling that near miss for a good while yet. He shakily removed one of his earphones and lowered the volume on his Discman, then continued his walk into town, all the while keeping a wary eye on the road ahead and behind.

Abergarry was one of those towns where businesses actually stayed shut on the bank holidays, and there was no-one around as Dougie turned into Inverlochy Court and took out the key to his shop. He saw that his hands were still trembling – that was anger, of course... He gave a soft snort and shook his head. *Anger?* Okay. Tell that to his fiercely skipping heart, which was still going nineteen to the dozen in there.

He passed through the shop without turning on the lights; there'd be no-one around to buy anything today, and there was no sense in opening up just because *he* had nowhere better to be. At least that meant he had all the time in the world to work on his next collection, and be ready for the Christmas gift-buying season.

He went through the door at the back of the counter into his workroom, and as the overhead fluorescent bulb hummed, then flickered into life, he began to feel some semblance of normality reasserting itself. A cup of tea and a custard cream, and he'd be all set. His wrist twanged uncomfortably as he filled the kettle, and he sourly wondered if he'd be able to do much work today after all, but there was too much to be done to consider taking the day off.

An array of newly carved figurines lined one edge of the work table, marble chips littered the surface, and a metal box stood open, ready for his practised fingers to select the correct tool... Usually without looking. But today he was working with paints, and although he no longer had a wife to tell him off, he could still hear her voice: *Douglas Cameron, do you think I've nothin' better to do than sponge paint out of your shirt?* It was a bitter-sweet memory, but it brought a smile to his face as he tied his apron and turned to find a tea bag.

The sound of the shop door opening made him start, then sigh. Should have locked it. An apology formed behind his lips, but he managed no more than three steps towards the work-room door before it opened. When he saw who stood there he relaxed, though his irritation remained; distractions, however welcome the rest of the time, were not part of today's plan.

'I thought you were away down south this weekend?'

His visitor didn't reply. He had a strange look about him; his colour was high and his breathing rapid, and Dougie's apprehension returned. 'What do you want?'

'You were lucky back there.' The visitor moved into the room until he was standing directly in front of Dougie, whose forehead tightened as he realised what the man was referring to.

'*You* were driving that flash car? What—'

'Lucky for a wee while, anyway. I didn't fancy running the car right off the road though, just to make sure of you.'

'Oh, Jesus...' It came out flat and far-away sounding, as realisation hit. From the corner of his eye Dougie glimpsed the tool box again, and with a speed that would have surprised him if he'd seen someone else do it, his hand flashed out and his fingers closed on one of the larger chisels. He held it like a dagger in front him, but his would-be assassin didn't seem fazed; instead of backing away, he rounded the work bench, brushing by the wavering, four-toothed tip, and reached for a box that sat on top of the cupboard.

Dougie's skin broke out in a clammy sweat, prickling along his hairline, but he still couldn't move. 'Don't,' he whispered, less an order than a plea, but the intruder ignored him and lifted the handgun from the box.

'You won't be needing this any more then,' he said. 'Pity to have wasted it.'

'Look, I won't—'

'Put the chisel down.'

Dougie tightened his grip instead. 'That thing's not loaded,' he said in a thin voice, nodding at the gun. 'The ammunition's in another box.'

'What, you go to the trouble of obtaining a gun for your own protection, but don't have it ready to use? I'm not stupid.'

'I never really thought I'd need it,' Dougie confessed. 'But aye, it's the truth.'

It wasn't, but the momentary hesitation on the part of the intruder was enough; in the split second afforded him by a glance at the top of the cupboard, Dougie lunged with the chisel.

He immediately knew he'd missed his chance. He'd have had to use every ounce of strength he possessed to drive this tool through a heavy cotton jacket, and then into flesh, and he had neither the conviction nor the faintest inkling of what it would feel like. His sprained wrist flared with a white-hot pain and lost all its strength, and a moment later he felt the iron grip of gloved fingers on his arm before the chisel was ripped from his grasp. His blood froze and he tried to take a step back, but there was nowhere to go. Even as his back came up against the work bench he knew it was over.

The blow took him low in the chest, then he felt a wrenching sensation and the spill of warmth down his apron. There was no pain yet, just a deep sense of shock, and he slumped against the bench, praying blackness would take him away before the pain hit.

He dragged his gaze back to his attacker's face, and to his bewilderment it was the face of a suddenly uncertain man, one who nevertheless knows he has gone too far to turn back, and must finish. Even as the thought passed through Dougie's mind, the crimson-slicked chisel moved again, and somehow, hopeless as it was, he brought his arm up and stopped the metal teeth from driving through his throat. The tearing pain in his forearm brought his focus back, and although he could still feel blood pulsing from what must be a grievous wound in his chest, he was wrapped in a kind of cold calm. He wasn't supposed to die. Not him. He had all the time in the world... Hadn't he just thought that?

He shoved with every bit of strength he had left, and for a second there was clear space in front of him; hope leapt, fierce and bright, before the gap closed again. His attacker's eyes glittered with a kind of barely suppressed desperation, and he was panting as the chisel slashed through the air. Once more Dougie's sluggish movements were just enough to save him, and his fingers twisted into the man's sleeve, dragging the arm downwards. The gloves were awash with blood, slick with it, and the chisel slithered out of the man's grasp.

The clang it made as it hit the stone floor was like a triumphant bell – to Dougie's increasingly confused mind it was a signal to seize this second chance. He bent down to scoop the tool up, but when he tried to rise again his chest was suddenly full of molten lava, and he found he had to fight for every shortening breath. The chisel dropped once more, and this time his assailant's boot put it far out of reach.

Dougie gave up the struggle to stand straight again, and sank to his knees, dragging in a thin, whistling breath. Terror returned in a rush, quashing his cold refusal to succumb. Mocking it. He looked up to see a strange, revolted fascination on his attacker's face, as if he were studying a creature pinned live to a dissection board. Dougie's mute appeal for mercy was met with a closing down of that expression. The floor beneath him was slippery with blood, and the smell rose rank and metallic, tightening his throat. All the strength was running out of his limbs... And all the time in the world was running out with it.

Dougie's head drooped once more, and he stared at the thick smear of his own blood between his splayed knees. Helpless tears gathered, blurring the image, and began to fall. Tiredness crept over him, turning his limbs to lead and his thoughts to shadows, and more than anything now, he wished it were over. His killer squatted opposite him, and together they waited.

Chapter Two

Abergarry, August 2018

HE WAS DEAD.

Dead in a ditch with his throat cut, or tossed carelessly onto the verge by an enormous speeding lorry, or... Charis slapped at the steering wheel of her stationary car and took a calming breath. For one thing there *were* no lorries in this ridiculous little town, enormous or otherwise, and if there were, they'd have been crawling along to accommodate the annoyingly narrow road.

Fine.

Which left the passing cutthroat... *Shut up – shut up – shut up!*

Jamie had only been out of sight for a couple of minutes. Sitting in the car, trying to ignore the swiftly descending twilight, Charis had managed a carefree wave as the boy rounded the corner of what appeared to be the local library-cum-council buildings, but the moment he was out of sight she had felt the familiar tension seize the back of her neck.

She'd reminded herself that he always carried his inhaler, and that *out of sight* was a million times safer here than back home in Liverpool, but it hadn't helped. What might have, would have been giving in to his frequent requests for a mobile phone, but she'd decided he should wait until he started secondary school. Then again, he'd probably end up getting mugged for it, unless he put more flesh and muscle on those bones before September... It was a moot point anyway; her own phone was sitting happily at home on its charger, so who could he have called?

Charis tossed her cooling chip supper onto the passenger seat next to her son's and got out of the car. She was just going to stretch her legs, nothing else. Perfectly natural. After all, she'd promised herself she'd loosen the reins a bit this holiday, and it was still light-ish, despite the miserable Scottish weather. The town was only marginally more lively than the local cemetery, and Jamie was just around the corner. This voice of reason tried to edge aside her swiftly rising paranoia.

He's completely safe.

But he's only little—

He's got to learn to stand alone.

But he needs me—

Daniel isn't here.

And there it was. Jamie's father wasn't here to rest dangerously glittering eyes on a child too young to read the warning signs, and to then turn back to her with a single, raised eyebrow that *she* could read all too well. He wasn't here to take her aside and explain, in earnest and reasonable tones, exactly what he would have to do if a misdemeanour happened twice. He *wasn't* here; he was locked up. Yet in Charis's mind phantom hands were still raised against Jamie around every corner, even now, when all the poor kid wanted was a pee against the wall, out of sight of his mother. How long did it take to offload half a can of Sprite anyway?

She walked faster. At the back of the building was a wide, flat, grassy area, with a few benches and no ten-year-old boy. By the time Charis reached the last corner of the building she was running, and as she rounded it, a small, bumpy tornado knocked the breath out of her and she stumbled, clutching at the wall. The rough stone scraped the skin from the tips of her fingers, and she sucked them, smothering her curses while a distracted Jamie apologised, flapping his hands in excitement.

'But you'll *never* believe what I just heard!'

Charis removed her fingers from her mouth and kept her tone deliberately dry, to disguise her relief. 'Try me.'

'Well, there was this American on his phone, talking about statues or something, and...' He paused, momentarily unsure. 'It was a bit muffled – I thought he said something about buying two cards.' He brightened again. 'But it was dead dodgy, I could tell. We should go to the police.'

'Jay...' Charis began, then shook her head. 'Never mind, your chips are getting cold.' She started back to the car in his scampering wake, not sure whether to laugh or scream. Thanks to Charis giving him her own stash of childhood books, Jamie was now convinced everything was either part of a master plan by a mad scientist, or a plot to abduct some foreign dignitary or other... Charis had worshipped Enid Blyton growing up, but right now she could cheerfully have strangled her.

She let her excited son into the car. 'If you seriously think I'm bothering the police with this, you can think again.'

'But he was *American*!'

Charis hid the twitch of a smile. 'Last I heard, that's not a crime,' she pointed out. 'Being born in the States doesn't mean you'll grow up to kidnap the...the...Sultan of bloody Swing.'

'Who?'

'Never mind, it's a Knopfler thing. Give it a few years.' She frowned at her congealing meal before screwing up the packet. 'Anyway, you've not told me one single thing we can go to the police with. Now, are you going to finish those or what?'

Watching her son's dark head bend over his own supper, searching for the crispiest chips, she had to resist the urge to plant a kiss on the exposed back of his neck; he was growing away and wouldn't welcome it – he rarely did these days. It both frightened and saddened her, but she had to accept it. Occasionally, however, she'd feel a wave of emotion too strong to ignore, and she'd pull him to her and tell him she loved him, trying not to let it hurt too much when he shrugged away.

Charis twisted the ignition key and settled for ruffling Jamie's hair again as she gestured to his seat belt. This time he smiled, his face showing her sweet echoes of the toddler he'd been. Intrepid detective, hungry child – sometimes you just had to cater for both.

The phone started vibrating just as Paul Mackenzie hooked his crash helmet over the Kawasaki's handlebar, and he dragged his glove off with his teeth and fumbled the phone out of his pocket. He saw the name flashing on the screen and cursed, but it was unsatisfyingly muffled by wet leather; he spat the glove out and, against his better judgement, answered the call.

'Mr Stein. What can I do for you?' He sank back down into the saddle, trying not to sound too pissed off, but the caller made no such effort.

'There was a kid here.' The American's voice was abrupt and flat.

'So?'

'So I was calling Sarah at the time, and I don't know how much he overheard.'

Mackenzie briefly closed his eyes. 'Well, what were you doing calling her out in the open anyway?'

'You have any idea how many places around this shit-hole don't have a signal? Of course you do – it's your town.' Stein's voice melted into disgust. 'I take one where I can get it.'

'Aye, right. Look, I'm about to go into a meeting.' Mackenzie glanced at the impressive old building with the inviting lights glowing at the windows. True enough, it was a meeting of sorts, and despite the outward appeal of the place it was no great pleasure to be here. 'I can't just—'

'Whatever. Check it out, okay? Find him, and make sure he's not going to be any trouble.'

'Find him? You mean he's gone?'

'Yeah, his mom just drove out of town.'

'His... So he's an *actual* kid?' Mackenzie took a deep breath and spoke again, more calmly than he felt. 'Mr Stein, *why* are you calling me, exactly?'

The voice in his ear grew hard, reminding Mackenzie who was in charge. 'If this kid convinces his mom to go to the police, we'll have to pull back. Which means we don't find what we're looking for. Your job, you seem to be forgetting, is to make sure we do. That's why you're getting paid. *That's* why I'm calling you. Now, are you going to check it out or not?'

Mackenzie lifted the phone away from his ear and long-ingly eyed a puddle in the middle of the car park. 'I'll get onto it first thing tomorrow,' he said, adopting a more conciliatory tone. 'I'll come to your hotel for breakfast, and you can give me a description. I assume you have a good one?'

'Eight-thirty sharp, Mackenzie, we don't have long.'

Mackenzie made sure the connection was broken, then glared at the phone. 'Jumped up bawbag.' He looked up at the building again and sighed. Time to get it over with.

As he walked up to the door, he felt the usual heaviness settle over him; all these years and he'd never been able to bring himself to stick two fingers up and go for a ride instead. The girl on duty smiled, as usual, and showed him to the TV room, as usual. He returned her smile and indicated his preference for coffee, as usual. And, as usual, when Mackenzie took the chair opposite his father, there was no expression of warmth to greet him.

'Hello, Dad.'

'Aye.'

'How've you been this week?'

'Right enough. For someone who can't brush his own teeth.'

Mackenzie counted to three and tried again. 'Had an e-mail from Adrian the other day. You heard anything from him?'

'No.'

A volunteer assistant arrived with Mackenzie's coffee and he took it gratefully; anything to provide a distraction. He was aware of his father trying to see round him to the television and moved out of the way, pretending it wasn't just another of Frank's ways of making his indifference obvious.

'Does he know you today, Paul?' the volunteer asked.

Mackenzie gave her a bitter little smile. 'He always knows me – that's the problem.'

'Sorry?'

'I mean there's nothing wrong with his memory. The stroke hasn't affected him in that way.'

'Ah, I see. I just thought...well, he never seems...' The assistant looked flustered, and Mackenzie softened his attitude.

'It's all right. It's no secret he'd rather I wasn't here.'

'Oh, now surely not? Big, handsome lad like you? I'm sure he's very proud of you.' At forty-one, 'lad' was pushing it somewhat, but Mackenzie gave her a look he hoped conveyed flattered modesty, combined with a polite wish to be left alone. Something appeared to be working today at least, since the woman relaxed.

'Don't mind me,' she said. 'I'll leave you to your visit. If you need anything, just ask.'

Mackenzie turned his attention to his father again, gritting his teeth as the old man feigned an interest in a pair of antiques collectors and their finds. The silence stretched until Mackenzie ended up twisting to watch the TV himself, just to ease the embarrassment.

'What does Adrian say?' Frank asked suddenly. Mackenzie turned back carefully; this was a breakthrough of sorts, but it was better not to read too much into it.

'You know him,' he said. 'Mostly talks about how great the weather is over there, and how I should have emigrated with him.'

'Aye, well maybe you should have, then you wouldn't have to put yourself out to visit me all the time.'

Mackenzie closed his eyes. *What, and miss out on all this fun?* He kept his voice steady, patient. 'I'm not putting myself out, Dad. I like to see how you are, and if you need anything. If you don't want me to come, just tell me.'

'You'd like that, wouldn't you? Leave me to rot here without a spare thought.'

So it went.
As usual.

Mackenzie found himself taking stupid risks on the ride home, but made no effort to curb them. The wet roads glistened, ribboning away into tight, dark curves, and he slammed down his visor and wound the throttle open, discarding any respect for the unpredictable camber as he leaned into the corners. By the time he got home he was breathing hard, and could feel the high colour in his otherwise icy cheeks and the adrenalin still fizzing in his blood. He glanced up at the scudding clouds overhead, and, deciding the rain had probably done its worst for now, he dropped his leather jacket onto the sofa and swapped his bike boots for trainers.

He set off into the night once again, with no idea why it was taking so long for the emotions to subside this time. Often the ride home would do an admirable job; a skip of the back tyre on wet leaves was enough to jolt anyone out of their bitterness, but tonight he felt the residual tightness in his muscles, even after a two-mile jog through town. He wasn't even really sure who the anger was aimed at: his father for all those years of heaping guilt upon shoulders too young to bear it; Adrian for buggering off to New Zealand and leaving him to deal with it alone; or himself, for not standing up to his father and telling him exactly how he made him feel. Every week he visited, every *sodding week* – never missed. And all he got was grief.

He was jerked out of his sour ruminations by the sound of a car coming up the hill behind him, and he moved in to the side of the road, aware that in black overshirt and black jeans he was hardly a poster boy for *Be safe, Be seen.* A gleaming

Land Rover Discovery, on an 18 plate, rumbled past with a familiar figure behind the wheel: Superintendent Donald Bradley, bless his shrivelled little heart. He must be prematurely celebrating his imminent promotion by getting rid of the Mondeo he'd had for all of twelve months. Should have waited; the new plate came out in a few weeks.

Mackenzie braced himself for the slowing down of the car, the electric buzzing of the window, the caustic comments... But they never came. He didn't even think he'd been recognised, which was just as well; he was in the mood to rip the overblown bastard's wing mirror off and chuck it through the window. Make a bit more trouble for himself, why not?

Back home, he grabbed the last can of cider from the fridge and drank half the contents in one swallow, then wiped his face on his shirt before flopping onto the sofa and flicking on the TV.

'Oh, for fuck's sake!'

There on the screen, Bradley came across as calm, authoritative and, above all, dependable. He had evidently been filmed several hours earlier; daylight still lit his crinkling brown eyes as he talked, with a deep concern even Mackenzie could almost believe, about the crime rate in the Highland region. The interviewer sounded as if he was talking from the muffled confines of the superintendent's arse – how the hell could so many people be taken in? Bradley wouldn't care if his own granny got burgled, but if it gave him a chance to show his caring side, he'd be on the telly demanding justice faster than you could say 'knighthood'.

By midnight Mackenzie was yawning so widely it was starting to hurt, and he dragged himself off to bed, sighing at the thought of the breakfast meeting that awaited him. He knew exactly how it would go: he wouldn't be able to hide his irritation with Stein's constant fussing, Stein would get all up himself, and Mackenzie would go away feeling like a reprimanded child. And sooner or later Don Bradley was going to discover what he was up to.

Then it would really hit the fan.

Chapter Three

Culloden Place, Abergarry

Tony Clifford watched his daughter as she, in turn, watched her son. Four-year-old Tas was solemnly building a tower out of Lego, and since his uncle Nick had gone upstairs to use the bathroom the carefully selected colour scheme had gone more than a little haywire. Maddy was grinning, no doubt in anticipation of her brother's return.

'How's business?' Tony asked, handing her a mug of coffee and putting one on the table for Nick.

'Pretty grim if I'm honest. A couple of background checks on potential employees, and I'm about to wrap up something for an accountancy firm that Gavin knows. I bet you're wishing you'd not handed it over to me now.'

'Rubbish.' Tony sank into his chair with a little grunt. Arthritis was a bastard. 'I couldn't have done any better.'

'If Arnie were still alive, you could. Brent-Clifford was his baby, so more than either of us, he had that drive to make it work no matter what. And you didn't need to retire when he died.'

'It wasn't just that,' Tony said. 'Sitting around in the cold, waiting for people to act badly, it was taking its toll on these stupid joints of mine. It's a youngster's game.' He sighed. 'I still miss Arn.'

'I know you do.' Maddy gave him a sad little smile over the rim of her cup. 'He left big shoes to fill.'

'You've more than adequately filled them, love. I always worried you'd discover it was a mistake, and go back to nursing.'

She shook her head. 'Five years was enough for me.'

'Good news for me, not so good for the NHS.' He glanced up as his son re-entered the room. 'Coffee's on the table, lad.'

'Cheers.' Nick picked up his drink and sat down cross-legged on the floor again, to resume playing with Tas. He glanced at the new colour scheme, then at his nephew, and gave an exaggerated sigh and shake of the head, making the boy giggle. Tony thought, not for the first time, that it was a shame Nick's marriage had collapsed before it had given him the chance to be a father. But that marriage had never been anything but a shout of denial anyway, to himself as much as anyone. At least the lad was happier out of it, and he was a brilliant uncle to Tas.

Tony returned to his conversation with Maddy. 'So, all pretty pedestrian then?'

'Yep.' Maddy blew the steam off her coffee. 'Our other job is only marginally more interesting; some American is trying to trace his girlfriend's inheritance. Figurines, apparently not worth much, but of *deep sentimental value*.' She sketched air quotes with her free hand. 'She's probably seen some antiques show and got all excited.'

'Sounds riveting,' Tony grinned.

'Aye.' She flashed him a wry smile. 'But it'll probably be the saving of us, for now. You know how badly those employer jobs pay, but the woman's keen enough, so we're getting a good fee off that one.'

'Is she local then?'

'Not any more. Used to be, evidently, but she moved to America in ninety-three.'

'Shit!' Nick stood up, flicking coffee off his hand. 'Spilled it in the Lego.'

'Uncle Nick!' Tas's eyes were round and delighted. 'Mummy says that's a bad word!'

'Lego? Aye, well she's right. Ever knelt on a piece?'

'Go and get some kitchen roll,' Tony said, and turned his attention back to Maddy. 'Not the Wallace daughter, is it? From Glenlowrie?'

'Sarah Wallace, yes. You know her?'

'Knew of her family, though we'd only been here a year when the house burned down and she moved away.'

Nick returned with the roll of paper, and Maddy joined him on the floor, dabbing at the plastic bricks worst hit by the cascade of coffee. 'You've got blood on your sock,' she pointed out. 'Cut yourself shaving again?'

Nick snorted as he adjusted the leg of his jeans again. 'Very funny. Picked a scab if you must know.'

'Ugh, you're so revolting.'

Tony watched them for a moment, sipping at his own drink and enjoying the little domestic scene. Speaking of which...

'How's Gavin?' he asked Maddy. 'Any sign of a wedding date yet?'

'No. And you don't have to ask that *every* time we come over.'

He smiled. 'Your mother would be spinning in her grave, you living in sin like that.'

'She'd love the bones of *him* though.' Maddy nodded at Tas. 'She'd forgive us.'

'No doubt.'

'How about you, Nick?' Maddy asked. 'How's work? Still buying the lotto tickets?'

Nick pulled a face. 'As soon as my numbers come up, I'm out.'

'That bad, eh?' Maddy returned to her chair. 'I'm amazed you're still on the force at all, to be honest.'

'I keep hoping things'll change, and then, out of nowhere, they suddenly don't.'

Tony shrugged. 'Can't see it'll ever improve, with the likes of Don Bradley at the helm. I've heard the sod's up for promotion again.'

'Aye, he'll get it too. Did you see him on the news?'

'Talking about our "precious senior citizens"?' Maddy shook her head. 'He gives good interview, you've got to give him that.'

'No doubt they'll run it again tonight, and every day for the next week.' Tony pulled a face. 'He's probably bunged them to do it. You know they think *he's* the reason I left the force?'

'They?'

'Everyone I worked with back then.'

'Well it was, wasn't it?' Maddy pointed out. 'Not that I can blame you. The constant promotions can't have helped. How did he swing that, when you were the one doing all the work?'

'Ask Nick. He's in the same boat I was.'

'Not quite,' Nick said, abandoning the Lego at last. 'I never had the same ambition as you, so it never bothered me that I didn't progress beyond sergeant.' He stared into what was left of his drink and shrugged. 'I'm forty-five now; if I'm going to make the leap, I'll have to do it soon. But I can't afford to jack it all in, so I just do as I'm told, and I keeping smiling at Bradley and that dead-eyed sergeant he hangs around with.' He picked up the sodden tissues and went to the kitchen to throw them away.

Is he okay? Maddy mouthed.

Tony nodded. *I think so.* But he wasn't so sure. For years Nick had only really come alive either at work or when he was spending time with his nephew. Now he was increasingly miserable at his job, to the point of wanting to leave, and Tas was getting older and about to start school – what would he have then?

'Bradley's just one of those who'll climb over whoever he has to,' he said aloud, 'and Alistair Mulholland is shaping up to be the same, by all accounts. Rarely with his own team, and always sniffing after whatever Bradley tells him to.'

Maddy nodded. 'Well, for what it's worth, Dad, I'm glad you weren't like that.'

'Thank God for integrity eh? Even if I don't have a big square house at the posh end of town.'

'I love this house!' Maddy finished her coffee and checked the clock. 'Right, time Tas and I were off. He's got nursery tomorrow.'

Tas looked up at the sound of his name, and his face fell. 'Five more minutes?'

'Nope, sorry. Uncle Nick and I will help you put this away.'

'Or,' Nick suggested as he returned, '*you* could put it away, while I take Tas outside for a five-minute kick-about. How does that sound, wee man?'

Tas gave a whoop and leapt to his feet, and Maddy gave

him a fierce look and appealed to Tony. 'Was that sneaky or what?'

Boy and uncle disappeared, and Tony helped his daughter pick up the Lego. Looking at her as she tucked her long red hair behind her ear, his heart lurched with one of those strange and wonderful surges of love that strike most parents now and again. She'd been a damned good nurse, and now she was a damned good investigator, but something was still missing in her; she was almost a cardboard-cut-out at times, even with him. Perhaps she'd have been different had her mother lived; perhaps he was the one at fault, and he hadn't given her what she'd needed?

And Nick too – he had always been lively and humorous as a child, but as a young adult he'd grown more and more withdrawn. Now they knew why, of course; coming out to Tony, after his mother's death, had helped a little, but it had been easier for the boy not to engage at all than to try and answer questions he'd still been asking himself.

'You know what we were just saying, Mads,' he said, his gaze going to the window through which he could see Nick and Tas getting happily muddied.

'About what?'

'Superintendent Bradley.'

'What about him?'

'I was thinking of asking Nick to help. You know, to get something on him.'

Maddy stared, and he could see at least a hundred questions flit across her face. 'What?' was all she managed.

'I think he's probably in the perfect position to help me find the evidence that'll break the bastard wide open.'

'You suspect Bradley of something in particular, don't you? What is it?'

Tony hesitated, then shook his head. 'I don't want to say yet. But if Nick can—'

'Don't you dare!' Maddy picked up the Lego bucket and stood up. 'You haven't got a hope in hell's chance anyway, but you *can't* ask him.'

'I think he'd help.'

'He wouldn't! He'd never do it before, when you ran the agency, would he? He's straight down the line, you know he is. He takes his lead from you and your reputation.' Maddy cast about for somewhere to put the bucket, and Tony half-expected her to throw it at him. 'If he gets caught helping you, particularly with anything to do with Bradley, he'll lose everything.'

'He won't get caught,' Tony said calmly. 'I just want him to find out a couple of things.'

'And then what? Anything you find will be inadmissible anyway, and Nick will be kicked off the force. It's lose–lose!'

'I'm not planning on taking it to court. I just...need to know.'

'In that case, whatever it is, just leave it. And anyway you heard him – he can't leave yet for his own reasons, so why should you make him leave for yours?'

Tony looked out at Nick and Tas again, and wished he hadn't said anything. 'All right. I'm still going to mention it, but I promise I won't try and force him.'

'Good.' Maddy sighed and dropped the confrontational tone. 'I worry for Nick, you know that. He's not nearly as robust as he seems.'

'The lad's fine!' Tony protested. 'He might be a bit quiet now, but he's a different man once he's in uniform—' Too late, he realised he'd played into her hands.

'Exactly. And you'd risk that?' She shook her head. 'Give

27

them a shout while I nip to the loo. I'll give Nick a lift home too.'

After the three of them had left, Tony sat in his chair musing over what Maddy had said about the Wallace woman, Sarah, and her inheritance. Why now, after all this time? Had Sarah only just learned of it? If so, who had told her, and why had they waited?

He told himself to switch off the police brain, or he'd never sleep that night, but that was easier said than done, and eventually, despite his determination to steer clear, his mind turned to the other major event of 1993: the murder of Dougie Cameron.

Dougie had been ten years older than Tony, but they had got on well enough. He had owned the little knick-knack shop now run by his son in Inverlochy Court, and Tony had quite often bought twee little gifts there for his wife, and then for Maddy. It was the son who had made the gruesome discovery, the day after the bank holiday, when he'd noticed the shop hadn't been opened up... Poor lad. Twenty-one years old, just back from a music festival with his pals, full of the joys of a new relationship, and then to find his father, slumped in a pool of blood on the workroom floor. Dougie had been well liked in Abergarry, and this kind of crime was rare and frightening in such a quiet town.

DI Bradley had been on leave since the Sunday before, and Tony Clifford was seconded to CID in his place. The shop in Inverlochy Court had been gone over with a fine-toothed comb, but after several weeks of intense search, all they had was the weapon. The murderer hadn't even attempted to hide it, but the only prints on the chisel were Dougie's own. Motive for the break-in was clear enough though; the place was a wreck, and the till and safe both empty. Dougie's decision to work on his bank holiday had ended up costing him more than a weekend's takings.

The time of death was an odd one too: sometime in the mid-morning, not night-time, as you'd expect for a break-in. Tony also queried this, but the DCI in charge shrugged.

'Probably didn't want to alert anyone in the buildings nearby. Noises during the day are far less likely to attract attention, even if the shop's not open. It's a workshop, after all.'

'Didn't any of the shops have CCTV running?'

The DCI raised an eyebrow. 'In Inverlochy Court?'

'Well, they probably will now,' Tony said grimly. 'Too late.'

And so the investigation remained unsolved, and life moved on. There was just that little thing. That *tiny* little thing that might not have meant anything, but had been the advent of Tony's and Don Bradley's icy relationship.

Janet Bradley had been in the front office at the Abergarry station, waiting for her husband to take her to lunch; Tony, back to his usual role, was duty sergeant. It was a quiet day; no-one else was there, and the silence had become embarrassingly acute. Tony eventually cleared his throat and asked after the Bradleys' recent Spanish holiday.

'Oh God! *Never* travel on a weekday,' she said, rolling her eyes. 'We thought once the bank holiday was out of the way we'd be fine, but it was a complete nightmare.'

He smiled politely, then her words registered. 'Weekday? I thought you were flying out on the Sunday?'

'No, Tuesday. Don was called in to the Inverness station over the weekend, covering for someone.'

Tony said nothing, but later, when he and Bradley were working in the same office, he brought the subject up again.

'Would you recommend Alicante? I was thinking of taking Maddy away for a few days.'

Bradley stopped his laboured, one-finger typing and looked at him, surprised. They didn't actively dislike one another at that point, but small talk wasn't something in which they usually engaged either. 'How old's your daughter?'

'Twelve.'

Bradley considered. 'Aye, she'll like it well enough.' He returned to squinting at his screen.

'What about flying? Was it packed on the weekday flight?'

'We flew out on Sunday. It wasn't too bad.'

'Oh.'

In the ensuing pause, Bradley's eyes narrowed. 'Oh, what?'

'Only...your wife said you left on Tuesday.'

Bradley's face froze for a moment, and Tony could see the cogs whirring. He began to get an uneasy feeling, then Bradley smiled.

'No, you're right. I was thinking of our last trip out there. We did fly on the Tuesday this time. As I recall it *was* a bit crowded, but that's probably because of the bank holiday. You should be fine.'

Tony had smiled back, he remembered now, but from that moment he'd never quite been able to trust the man. Had he lied to his wife about where he'd been that weekend, or to everyone else? The thought had naturally and immediately occurred that Bradley had something to do with Cameron's death, but even as he worked through every possible angle, he could find no connection between the two men, and no motive. Still, the niggling doubts had never gone away, and the re-ignited suspicions were burning again. There had to be a link somewhere.

Chapter Four

Inverness DHQ Police Station

FAO Superintendent Donald Bradley

Dear Sir,

As president and spokesperson of the Abergarry Senior Residents' Group, I am writing to express our concern over the way crime against the elderly and other vulnerable groups has escalated recently. It has been noted that you are one of the few high-ranking officials who actually seem to care about this, and our letter to the new Chief Constable, when he or she is appointed, will reflect our gratitude – Bradley smiled. *We would like to ask if you'd be so kind as to come and give a talk on how best to protect ourselves against...*

'No, THANKS.' Bradley tossed the letter onto his desk and checked his watch for the fifth time. Perhaps Mulholland had misread his text and was waiting for him over at Abergarry station instead, though he'd told him he was here in Inverness this week. As he reached for the phone there was a brisk knock, and a narrow face peered around the door.

'Sorry I'm late, sir, traffic on the A82—'

'Bollocks, sergeant.' Bradley folded his arms and waited until Alistair Mulholland had seated himself opposite, noting with satisfaction how the younger man kept to the edge of his chair, his hands tucked under his thighs; it wouldn't do for him to get too comfortable and forget his place.

'Right,' he said, when Mulholland had stopped fidgeting, 'first things first. Has Stein finally made up his mind to buy the figurines off us?'

Mulholland's tone was as flat as ever. 'He said he had to call Sarah. Needs her to give him the go-ahead.'

'And when was this?'

'Yesterday, around six.'

'Well, what the hell are you waiting for? Call him. Not on this phone, you numpty! Use your mobile.'

Bradley had been waiting for thirty years for this, but suddenly every minute stretched interminably. He unfolded his arms and turned to look out of the window, glad for once that the weather made his view flat and grey. He needed no distractions; he had to think. No second chances – if Stein discovered that these figurines were fakes it would all be over. He could hardly believe that, after all this time, it was resting on the report of some American lapdog who'd never even seen the originals.

Mulholland had evidently reached Stein's phone, and Bradley's fingers tightened on the arm of his chair as he listened. Funny how the sergeant could sound as friendly as the next person when he really wanted to.

'Andy? It's Alistair. I trust you slept well? Aye, it's a great wee hotel. Great prices too, eh?' A laugh. 'It's worth it though. Listen, I don't want to push, but have you decided yet? Only, these are quite beautiful pieces in their own right, and of course I've others interested. Have you no seen Cash in the Attic?' Another quick, dry laugh. 'No, of course. I'm sure you have your own versions though. Anyway, I'll look forward to hearing from you. Enjoy the rest of your breakfast. Bye then!' He tossed his phone onto the table, and Bradley waited, outwardly patient but feeling the scream building behind his eyes.

'Well?' he blurted at last.

'He's going for it. He'll call me later, let me know the details.'

Bradley resisted the urge to punch the air, and instead nodded. 'Thank you, Alistair. Now, on to other matters.' As if anything else *could* matter. Still, life went on, and he suddenly felt well disposed towards everyone. He picked up the letter he'd cast away just a few minutes ago. 'I need to arrange a visit with the A.S.R.G. to discuss personal safety issues. Send the admin assistant in on your way out, would you?'

As Mulholland left the room, Bradley allowed a smile to stretch across his face. It felt strange, as if he hadn't smiled properly in weeks, which, to be fair, he probably hadn't. Since he'd first commissioned the new versions of these figurines, he'd been checking over his shoulder, acutely aware of the vulnerability afforded by his rank. Thank God then for a willing, if dense, dogsbody.

Alistair Mulholland was basically what he himself had been thirty years ago, when Duncan Wallace had approached him with a proposition that would take thirty years to yield its rewards. Though he abhorred the knowledge that he'd in fact been nothing more than some privileged landowner's errand boy, Bradley couldn't deny he'd been paid generously for it, and here was Mulholland carrying on the tradition. Granted, the wages weren't on the same scale, but Mulholland seemed a man of simple tastes, and as such didn't have the same high expectations as the young PC Bradley. Besides, Bradley had worked a lot harder for his money; Mulholland hadn't had to kill anyone.

So far.

The Burnside Hotel, Abergarry

Mackenzie laid down his fork as Stein ended the phone call. 'You're not actually going to buy them?'

'What do you think? All I'm buying is a little time. Sarah's relying on me, and while she is, she's not going to be cheated out of her rightful property by some greasy pork belly in a uniform.'

Mackenzie began to eat again, quietly enjoying the description of Bradley, but had to ask. 'And you're *sure* these are fakes?'

'Absolutely. Sarah told me about this inbuilt flaw in the bases of the ones that had belonged to her father, so she must have known this son-of-a-bitch would try to rip her off someday. I checked these three; they're smooth as a Mercedes sales pitch.' He sat forward. 'Look, we're almost there with nailing this creep, and what I don't need is for him to get the wind up his tail and run. That kid hanging around could jeopardise this whole deal.'

Mackenzie dropped his fork again. 'Oh, come on! You're not serious about that, surely? How old did you say he was?'

'I don't know, I don't do kids' ages. I'd guess maybe eight, nine?'

'And you think he—' Mackenzie held up a conciliatory hand as Stein fixed his cool grey eyes on him. 'Okay, I'll keep an eye out. But if you want me to track down your girlfriend's *actual* inheritance, you're going to have to stop calling me to heel to deal with stuff like this.'

'Oh, I'm so sorry. Am I pulling you off a major lead?'

Mackenzie let the sarcasm ripple over him, but his insides tightened. 'Why don't you just let me do my job, Mr Stein? I'll check out the boy for you, warn him off, but your dealings with Bradley really don't have anything to do with why you hired me.'

Stein shrugged. 'Well, you never know – the threat of a word in the right ear, and maybe Bradley'll come clean on where Sarah's real figurines are. I'm not above blackmail in this. Anyway, what is it with you and this guy?' He poured himself more coffee, ignoring Mackenzie's empty cup. 'Every time you mention his name you get this look, like it's got a nasty taste. You two have a history?'

'My business is my business. I'll be keeping an eye out for the...the *child*.' Give the word enough emphasis, and perhaps he could get across how petty Stein was being, but the American didn't appear to have noticed.

'Thank you, Mackenzie. I'll be on my cell if you need to tell me anything important. Good luck getting a signal though.'

That was it then; breakfast over.

Mackenzie left the hotel with no small sense of relief. No matter how he dressed – and especially when he wore jeans and a sweatshirt like today – he always felt like a tramp in The Burnside; not the largest, but doubtless one of the most expensive hotels this side of Inverness. Nothing but the best for any friend of Sarah Wallace. He vaguely remembered her. Their parents had known each other, but at five years his senior she'd held little interest for him. His brother Adrian, however, had had a massive crush on her, and thought his life was over when he heard she'd gone off with some halfwit constable...

Mackenzie stopped dead, his mind doing mathematical somersaults. It could have been anyone, but Bradley *had* known the Wallaces for years; if he'd been that deeply involved with the family back then, it was likely he knew where the genuine figurines were.

'He'd double his profit too, making Sarah pay for fakes,' he muttered aloud, ignoring the glances of passers by. There was no way Bradley would offload anything so distinctive here in town, but a visit to a few of the local shops might yield some useful contacts. And of course there was always eBay. Mackenzie felt some of his personal cloud lifting; with any luck Andy Stein might be out of his hair sooner than he'd dared to hope.

He began walking again, remembering the TV programme that had been playing at The Heathers last night; trinkets of even questionable vintage fetched unpredictable, and sometimes crazy, prices. He took out his phone and tapped a shortcut. The voice that answered the call was smooth, professional.

'Clifford-Mackenzie.'

'Maddy, hi.'

'Hi yourself. How was the meeting?'

'Short, miserly. Bugger didn't even let me finish my bacon.'

'Probably a good thing.' Maddy sounded amused.

'Are you calling me fat?'

'Not yet, but with blokes your size it's only ever a matter of time. Now, I take it you have either information or a request?'

'Bit of both. Sarah Wallace used to knock about with a copper. Can you do some digging and find out who it was?'

There was the sound of a page flicking over. 'Okay, when was this?'

'Well, I'm pretty sure Ade was just getting into girls – she was his first real crush – so I'd have only been about eleven.'

'Bloody hell, Paul! That's, what? Thirty years ago!'

'I did say digging. I'm going to ask a few people myself. Adrian for one, Dad for another.'

'I hope for all our sakes Adrian comes up trumps, then. What was the information you had?'

'Nothing much. Stein's told Mulholland the deal's on, so it'll be all systems go pretty soon.' Something else she had said suddenly registered. 'What do you mean, "all our sakes"?'

'What?'

'Why should it bother you if I have to see my dad about this?'

'Because every time you have to go up to The Heathers you come back a proper Mr Narky Trousers, and I, for one, am fed up tip-toeing around until you've calmed down. Can I get on with my work now?'

Mackenzie grinned. 'Did you just say *Mr Narky Trousers*?'

'Think yourself lucky – I could have said worse. I'll check around and see what I can come up with, okay?'

'Thanks. I'll be back in the office around lunchtime.'

'Bring me a chicken sandwich. Brown, no mayo.'

Mackenzie was still smiling as he reached the pavement at the bottom of the car park; Maddy somehow always knew when he needed to be gently bullied along and when he needed to be left alone to let the memories win, just for a little while. He raised his head to take in the familiar shapes of the mountains, rising harsh-peaked and glowering on either side of the town. Some days, like today, he could look at those mountains and not hate them.

This short hill gave him a clear view over most of his home-town, and its quietly prospering shops and businesses. Most of the people he could see were locals who'd driven in from outlying towns; even at the height of the season tourists tended to bypass Abergarry in favour of Fort William when it came to setting up base. No need for a bed and breakfast every other building here then, just this one hotel. Expensive as it was, it was rarely full, but it kept going, and kept charging through the roof, and people kept paying. People like Andy Stein, no doubt bankrolled by his pet heiress.

Mackenzie started down the the slope, but as he took a backward glance at The Burnside, before making his way to the office, something caught his gaze and held it: Stein had left the hotel and was crossing the forecourt to his car, and he seemed to have gained a small shadow.

Mackenzie watched carefully. The boy kept his distance, but it was clear he was following the American, and he occa-sionally raised his right arm to his mouth. It took a moment for Mackenzie to realise he was talking into his sleeve – no doubt into an imaginary microphone.

He fought down a familiar ache, and retraced his steps until he was once more standing across the road from the hotel. The boy would have to be told, for his own safety as well as for Stein's peace of mind, not to mention Clifford-Mackenzie's bank balance... And now it was raining again. Perfect. Where the hell was the kid's mother anyway?

———————

In the few days since their arrival in Scotland, Charis had discovered three things: the first was that she still had a long way to go in her quest to let Jamie be the adventurous boy he was turning out to be; secondly, that as romantic and dramatic as these views were, there was a lot to be said for being able to nip down to Tesco Metro for a pint of milk and a sandwich; and thirdly, she now knew how hopeless she was at predicting what the weather was going to do. She could have sworn, or maybe it was the last vestiges of her dwindling optimism, that today was going to be brighter; last night she'd actually been able to go to sleep with the zip of the tent open and her head almost touching the grass. But this morning she'd once again had to squint to see the distant, layered peaks through the misty rain.

She'd honestly believed everyone back home had been winding her up when they told her it would more than likely be cold and wet, even in August, but the sun was up now, sort of, and it had clearly been a struggle. Clouds still had the upper hand, and although it had stopped raining long enough to cook breakfast, the air was chilly and damp, decidedly un-summery. A fourth realisation, and one she pretended had never even featured in her imagination, was that the Highlands were not, after all, populated by strapping, red-haired, gentle-but-tough heroes, as her favourite books suggested.

'Hey, lazybones, grub's up.' She shook the edge of the tent and flinched as a stray raindrop flew from the nylon and found its icy way inside the collar of her jacket. There was a grunt from the depths of the sleeping bag, and after a moment Jamie appeared, blinking slowly, his mouth puffy and still sealed shut.

'Breakfast.' Charis gestured at the camping stove at her crossed feet. She and Jamie looked at the frying pan, at each other, and back down at the pan. 'Not good, is it?'

There was a pause while Jamie unstuck his lips and cleared his throat, evidently searching for the diplomatic answer. 'Um. It's okay, I like it crispy.'

'Well, let's be honest, there's crispy, and then there's cremated.'

Jamie picked up a stick he'd been peeling the night before and used it to prod the tiny, curled black strips. 'We've got bread,' he said, ever helpful.

Charis reached into the tent and pulled out a wedge-shaped packet.' Yeah, we've got bread; it's just a pity it got used as a pillow last night.'

'That wasn't me!'

'Nope. Wasn't you.' Charis sighed, then, catching Jamie's mournful expression as he prodded the bacon once more, she gave in. 'I think a little trip into town's in order, don't you? Have you seen my camera?'

'No.' Jamie scooted back inside the tent to find his shoes. 'It's probably in the car.'

'Good, we're going to visit a blackhouse later. I'll need it then.'

Parking in Abergarry on an August Saturday morning wasn't the easy matter it had been the evening before. All the passing tourists seemed to have converged on the town on their way to

Fort William, and after driving around the tiny car park for the second time, Charis gave up and went further up the town, where she spotted a small hotel with a half-empty forecourt. It was *Residents Only*, apparently, but she manoeuvred the hired Ford Focus into a corner spot, windscreen facing the wall to hide the lack of permit, and flashed a triumphant grin at Jamie.

'Right, I'm going to get some cash.' She hesitated, then made the decision. 'You wait here for a bit; no point both of us traipsing around like lost sheep.' Another chance to prove she wasn't the paranoid wreck she had been, and this time she hoped to improve on last night's performance. 'Meet me outside that bakery there,' she pointed, 'in ten minutes. We'll get breakfast in the café before we go shopping. Ten minutes, no longer. If I'm not there, there'll be a good reason, so just wait for me.' She handed the car keys back through the window. 'Got your inhaler?'

'Yes, Mum.'

She ignored his bored tone. 'Good. Don't forget to lock the car, okay? Just press that button on the key 'til it ploinks.'

Still searching for a cashpoint fifteen minutes later, she growled under her breath. How, in a town this size, was it so hard to find what you were looking for? She'd have to go back and meet Jamie before he got restless and wandered off, and it was starting to rain again. Bugger this stupid, wet place; it might have all the dramatic splendour promised by her fifteen-year obsession with the Outlander books, but she hadn't expected the rain to be so...*sneaky*. A good, honest downpour was one thing; this was just rude.

She walked quickly back up to the bakery and stood under the awning, peering up the street past the sudden sea of umbrellas that had materialised. They must be used to it here; where else would you have to carry an umbrella in August, just in case? There was no sign of a ten-year-old boy in a red hooded top, and Charis took a deep breath, letting it out slowly to focus her mind. *Don't panic, he'll be here any minute—*

'Is this yours?'

Charis jerked around and adjusted her line of vision to take into account the height of the man who'd appeared behind her. She immediately wished she hadn't; his expression was anything but friendly. No red-haired, heroic Jamie Fraser here, but the character's namesake was there beside him, and although the boy was clearly embarrassed, he was unhurt and not at all worried.

'Yes, thank you,' Charis said. She didn't look back at that stern, headmaster-ish glare, but put her arm around Jamie, hugging him until he squirmed to get away.

'You need to keep a better watch on him then.'

Charis felt herself tightening up again. 'Well, *you* need to mind your own business.'

'As a matter of fact he *was* my business. And your thanks are gratefully accepted.' The sarcasm was so heavy, he had to be joking, and Charis glanced up at him again with a reluctant smile ready, but there was no humour in the hazel eyes that stared back down at her.

Her own irritation swept back. 'I fail to see how it's got anything to do with you, unless he ran out in front of your car, and he wouldn't—'

'Bike.'

'Bike, whatever. Like I said, thanks for bringing him back. Now if you'll excuse us, we have a cashpoint to track down...' She paused. '*Were* you about to run him down?'

'No. But a word of advice, Ms Boulton—'

'How d'you know my name?'

'I told him,' Jamie put in. Charis noticed he was staring up at the tall Scot with a familiar look that made her shrink inside.

'A word of advice,' the man repeated. 'Your boy has a curious streak a mile wide; you'd do well to take better care of him.' Just as she opened her mouth to snap at him, he added, 'End of the street, turn left, then left again.'

'You what?'

'Cashpoint.'

'Oh. Thanks.' She sighed and tried on a more grateful tone. 'Look, I didn't mean to sound rude—'

'Just take care of your boy, Ms Boulton.' There was a flash of something almost approachable in his expression, but it was gone in an instant, and he nodded at Jamie and left.

Charis watched her son, who was staring after the man with that same admiring expression he had reserved for his father, in the days before he'd learned what his father was. 'What exactly did you do, Jay? And what did he say to you?'

'I was playing detectives, and he just came up to me, and... kind of joined in.'

'Joined in how?'

'He said that I was getting involved in something I shouldn't.' Jamie spoke slowly, as if trying to remember it word for word. 'And that I might get hurt if the wrong people found out. Just like the telly! How cool is that?'

Charis didn't know about cool, but she certainly felt a chill as she made out the already distant figure striding easily up the hill, hatless, coatless; obviously, and not surprisingly, used to the rain. He didn't seem to her like the sort to join in a kid's innocent detective game; he looked too miserable to have any imagination at all, in fact. She just stopped herself from putting her arm around Jamie's shoulder again, and instead straightened his hoodie and led him in the direction of the bank.

As they walked, she managed to get the full story. Jamie had just 'ploinked' the car key, locking the Focus, when he'd spotted the American he'd seen last night leaving the hotel. Bored with waiting, he'd naturally tailed him, pretending he was reporting back via a microphone hidden in his sleeve. The man had got into a posh, silver-grey car of some kind, and Jamie had taken out his notebook and written down the number. That was when he'd felt a hand on his arm and his notebook had been taken away.

'Bloody cheek!' Charis noticed passers by staring at her and lowered her voice. 'Then what? Did he give it back?'

'Yeah, but he tore the page out, and that's when he said that thing about the wrong people finding out. He's funny!'

'No, he's not. He was out of order. Bang out,' she amended, as she recalled the way he'd admonished her in the street. It was none of his business, and although she'd felt a bit ungracious for telling him so, she was glad she had; there was no way she was going to let someone else step into the bully-shaped space Daniel had left.

'He rides a motorbike,' Jamie was saying.

'So? Does that make him Mad Max?'

'It makes him cool.'

'Don't talk cobblers! Plenty of people ride motorbikes.'

'Yeah, but—'

'I don't want to hear any more. I'm getting some cash, then we need to go shopping for more food. Plus I promised to get something for your Aunty Suze. Better check your inhaler too, while you're here, in case you need a refill. There's a chemist up the road.'

She took her cash from the machine and looked around. They were at the entrance to a small courtyard; Inverlochy Court, the sign said. Shops lined the edges, an ornamental garden stood in the middle, its plants drooping under the weight of the rain, and the wooden benches were full of puddles.

Charis shivered. 'We'll go up here a minute, see if we can find something for Suze that's not too tacky.'

'Do we have to?' Jamie sighed.

'Yes we do. And if I were you, I'd just be thankful we're not packing up and going home right now.'

'What're we doing after?'

'That blackhouse I told you about, a few miles out of town. If you stop giving me grief, I'll let you have half a glass of wine and lemonade tonight.' Jamie's face lit up, and Charis's irritation melted. Once more she had to resist the temptation to pull him close, and once more she ruffled his hair instead.

They wandered up through the small courtyard, dismissing each of the few shops until, almost tucked away at the end, they found a small, brightly lit window displaying porcelain and glass figures. The sign was simple and elegant.

Cameron and Son
Fine Porcelain

Charis wrinkled her nose as she peered in, but the figures weren't actually that bad when you looked at them properly. Suze quite liked ornaments, and there were some pretty enough pieces in there, as long as they weren't too pricey.

'Might be out of here quicker than you think,' she told Jamie, who tried to appear enthusiastic. Charis poked her tongue out at him to make him giggle, and pushed open the door.

The man who appeared from a room in the back smiled at her, albeit a little distractedly, as he wiped his hands on a cloth tucked into his belt. She smiled back, thinking how much nicer he seemed than that other bloke; around the same age, late thirties or so, but a bit of friendliness made all the difference.

'Can I help you?'

'I'm here for my sister. She likes...' she waved her hands vaguely around her, '...stuff like this. I said I'd bring something back for her.'

'Ah, your sister likes it, but you don't?' His expression was of one who had been struck in the heart, but his tone was teasing, and Charis grinned.

'Well, you know. Each to their own.'

'Okay, take a look around. If you see anything you like, just hit the bell here, and I'll unlock the case. I'm afraid I'm...uh, pretty busy in the back.'

The light in his eyes vanished, leaving him distracted and pale again. He flashed her a brief smile and gestured behind him, before ducking back through the door again, leaving Charis and Jamie alone in the shop. Charis shrugged and started to examine the figures on display.

As she'd suspected, they weren't nearly as awful as they could have been; there was a simplicity about them that made them quite attractive. She spent longer admiring them than she'd intended, and finally, catching sight of Jamie's martyred expression out of the corner of her eye, she chose a small cat that looked up brightly from a slipper it was chewing. If someone had described it to her she'd have gone green and run a mile, but the cat's eyes were so realistic, and the shape perfectly formed with its little hunched shoulders, she knew Suze would like it.

She was about to press the bell on the counter when the man appeared again, looking less harried now.

'Sorry about that, I've had a big project on. It's done and

delivered, but I've been going mad catching up with other orders.' He wiped his hand through his short blond hair and grimaced, looking at his fingers. 'I've probably just wiped green paint in my hair, haven't I?'

She checked. 'Yep. You have. All up the middle. Very stylish – all the local kids'll be copying you by the end of the week.'

The man smiled. 'Found anything for your sister?'

'Yeah, I'd like that little cat there, please.' Charis pointed, and he produced a key.

'Did you make all this stuff?' Jamie asked him.

'Aye. Every last piece. And I've more in the back. Plus some I'm working on that aren't finished.'

'So it's your shop.'

'Ben Cameron at your service,' the man said with a touch of pride.

'Where's your son?' Jamie asked.

'I'm the son.' He abruptly became very businesslike, packing the cat in a small, sturdy box and expertly tying a ribbon around it. Taking Charis's money, it suddenly seemed as if he couldn't get them out of there quickly enough; his demeanour had gone from lazy charm to unbearably tense in the blink of an eye.

Even before she and Jamie reached the door, Cameron had gone back into the room behind the counter, and Charis's thoughts were dragged back to the tall, angry Scotsman as Jamie started discussing the American yet again. She tried not to pay too much attention to the niggling worry that had taken up residence in her head, but worrying was what she did best, and something told her that this time she'd be a fool to try and ignore it.

Chapter Five

MADDY EYED her brother across the café table. He was looking at her with a faintly impatient air, but she wouldn't be rushed – she was still trying to figure out the best way to broach this. After everything she'd said to their dad about not asking Nick for help, here she was about to do that very thing herself...although actually, she reasoned, this wasn't quite the same. This wasn't going after a high-ranking police officer, over a decades-old cold case, with the intention of destroying his career. Procrastinating further, she took a gulp of her coffee that burned her throat, and for a moment she was only able to concentrate on her watering eyes, on the heat travelling down through her body, and on not swearing out loud.

'Come on, Mads,' Nick said at last. 'My shift starts in twenty minutes.'

'Right.' Maddy took a deep breath. 'Look, you know I'd never ask you to use your position to help me. Normally.'

Nick's eyes narrowed. 'Not so far, no.'

'This isn't anything major,' she hurried on. 'Nothing to do

with any ongoing police investigation, I mean. Well, it is, but not—'

'What *is* it to do with?' Nick took a sip of his own drink, squinting at her through the steam, and she sighed. This was stupid. He was a police officer, she was an investigator...they were on the same side, when all was said and done.

'Do you remember someone called Sarah Wallace?'

Nick twisted his coffee cup on the table, frowning. 'The rich girl from the Glenlowrie Estate you mentioned at Dad's?'

'Aye, that's her.'

'Vaguely. I remember hearing she'd run off with a police officer, and that her father was pretty mad about it. She moved to America, didn't she? What's this about?'

'I just wondered if you knew who the officer was.'

Nick didn't reply at first. He looked at her steadily, and she returned his gaze, hating herself for the conflict she could see in his expression. Then he shrugged. 'It was Don Bradley. Not that it lasted long. And you didn't get that from me.'

'Of course not.' She paused. 'Seems an odd kind of relationship.'

'If you say so. That it, then?'

'She must have been very young,' Maddy pressed.

'Probably. Can I go now?' The troubled look deepened, and Maddy reached across to squeeze his wrist.

'I'm sorry, Nick. I told Dad off for suggesting...' She stopped herself before she could make things worse. 'Do you know how they met?'

'No! For Christ's sake! All this was years back.' He stood up, his expression closed. 'Don't ask me to help you any more, Mads, it could get me fired. You know that.'

'It's not like I asked you to go poking around in secret files,' Maddy pointed out, a little irritated now. 'I just asked you something any one of a hundred people in this town would probably know.'

'Well, next time ask them.' He threw a fiver onto the table. 'Coffee's on me.'

'Nick!' Maddy rose too. 'Don't be so touchy. We're family, right? I'd help you if you wanted me to.'

'Would you?' Nick glared for a moment, then his taut shoulders relaxed, and so did his expression. 'Sorry, that was stupid. I know you would. And you have.' He gave her a brief, apologetic smile and changed the subject. 'Are you coming over on Sunday?'

'Sunday?' She kept her own face deliberately blank, and was rewarded by an exasperated eye-roll.

'My birthday?'

'Oh, gosh! I'd totally...remembered, *and* bought you an ace gift.' Maddy grinned at his suspicious look. 'Just ask Tas if you don't believe me; he helped me choose it. He's decided you need a Paw Patrol cake, by the way.'

'Which character?'

'You know them?'

'I've not babysat the lad for the past four years and learned nothing.'

She laughed. 'Fair point. I don't know which character, sorry. Will Max be joining us?'

A gentle flush stained her brother's cheeks, and his smile told her that the relationship was still going strong. 'Aye, I believe he might show his face.'

'Good.' Maddy leaned in for a hug, relieved to have banished the careful, mistrustful look from his face. 'I'm sorry to have put you in an awkward position. It's just that this case could make or break the agency. And it's a good thing we found out, since we're trying to stay out of Bradley's way because of... Well, you know.'

'Paul.'

She nodded. 'Thanks again. I'll not ask you any more, so you can relax now.'

'Look, I'm not trying to be obstructive. If it wasn't for my job—'

'I know. See you Sunday.'

Maddy zipped her jacket against the drizzle and turned her thoughts to another of her investigations; just a report to hand in, then a welcome payment would land in the Clifford-Mackenzie bank account. And as long as Paul didn't find out who the client really was, it might stay there. William Kilbride kept to himself, true, but his line in 'financial facilitating' was a badly-kept secret in the business world, and if Paul got a whiff of it he'd go mad. She'd wanted to turn the job down, but her fiancé had been the one to introduce her to Kilbride, and had been pretty insistent, which wasn't like him.

'He's a new client; it'd be good for us both.'

'A client? Gav, people don't need solicitors like you unless they think they're in trouble. What's he done?'

Gavin hesitated. 'There's been a question, just a *question*, mind, of fraud.'

'Must be quite a loud question,' Maddy pointed out. 'What kind of fraud?'

'Does it matter? He's ditched his old firm, and wants to be prepared just in case he has to take it further. That's all.'

'And this...*question* of fraud is totally separate from the work you want me to take on?'

'Totally unconnected, I promise. He just wants you to follow someone, and report back on movements, lifestyle, acquaintances, that kind of thing.'

'Just a report.'

'Will you do it?'

'Paul will never go for—'

'Sod Paul!' Gavin's voice was tight now. 'You're in charge, and I'm asking *you*. As a favour to *me*.'

Maddy blinked at the vehemence in his normally placid manner. 'It'll cost him,' she said at last. 'I've got to make it worth the hassle.'

'Take that up with him. I'll put you in touch.' He'd softened then, and put his arms around her, but she'd been uneasy all the same. Kilbride's methods were questionable at best, and whoever she was reporting on had better have a damned good reason for not paying the man what was owed, for their own sake.

So, for the first time since she'd taken over the agency, she was putting a job through the books using the false name supplied by a client, and every time Paul drifted anywhere near the computer she got as jumpy as hell. She'd be glad when this was all over, though her conscience had eased when it became clear that Kilbride's suspicions were well founded; the man she was investigating had two vastly different lives, and one of them was about to get very difficult.

So far, she'd managed to avoid meeting the fearsome Kilbride face to face, and conducted everything either by phone or private e-mail. With any luck she could just fire off this report, and that would be it; she wasn't easily unsettled, but some of the things she'd heard about him told her she'd have trouble looking him in the eye across a desk, and that that would not go down well with Gavin.

But as she walked back to the office, Maddy's mind kept sliding off the report, and back onto the unlikely relationship that had developed between the daughter of a local landowner and an as-yet undistinguished police officer six years her senior... It was doubtful Sarah Wallace had ever been in trouble with the police. Who might know? Who'd been around back then?

She stopped with one hand on the door, and the two unconnected investigations took a step closer together: Donna Lumsden, Kilbride's daughter. She and Sarah had grown up in the same circles, and they'd probably be around a similar age... Instead of going up the stairs to the office, Maddy turned back and fished in her pocket for her car keys.

Twenty minutes later she was drawing up outside a cunningly hidden, but enormous, house on the outskirts of Fort William. The tyres of her rather beaten up Corsa crunched on gravel, and she patted the steering wheel comfortingly as she parked next to an immaculate BMW and a muddied, but still impressive-looking Range Rover.

'Don't fret, Cora,' she murmured. 'You're still number one in my book.'

She looked up at the imposing façade of the house as she climbed out of the car. Donna was now a successful business-woman, owner of *Thistle*, a chain of fine-dining restaurants, but the odds were pretty good that Daddy had originally paid for this pile. Odds on, too, that her chain would be forming part of the case of fraud that was being built. Kilbride's own home, somewhere near Inverness, was apparently half the size of this place again, so he could certainly afford the admittedly inflated price Maddy was charging him.

She rang the bell, and while she waited she gazed around at the breath-taking views down the valley, and the wide expanse of lawn either side of the drive. One day, Maddy, she promised herself, then gave a little snort of laughter. Right.

Donna herself opened the door and frowned at Maddy, then glanced back into the house. 'No, it's just some random woman,' she called over her shoulder.

Charming. 'My name's Maddy Clifford.' Maddy held out her hand. 'I'm doing some work for your father—'

The woman ran one elegant hand back through short, streaked-blonde hair. 'My father doesn't live here.'

'I was going to add that I'm actually here on another matter,' Maddy said. 'Can I come in for minute?'

'No. What other matter?'

Maddy's hopes began to fade. 'Do you know Sarah Wallace at all?'

Donna flung another look back into the house, taut and impatient. 'I was at school with *a* Sarah Wallace. She was in the year above me. We weren't friends.'

'Your father and hers moved in similar circles though, I gather?'

'Ancient history. Duncan Wallace died years ago. What's this about, Ms Clifford? I'm busy.'

'I just wondered if you knew that Sarah'd had an affair with an older lad when she was still at school? Well, a young man really. A police officer.'

Donna scowled, and a despondent Maddy was about to apologise and leave, when she realised it was this woman's version of a thinking frown. God, she was almost as scary as her dad's reputation.

'Aye,' Donna said at last. 'Now you mention it. I think she met him during some investigation or other.'

Maddy's interest leapt. 'Investigation?'

'A burglary, I think. Her father was questioned, but it

turned out he wasn't involved. A couple of my father's other friends were, though.'

'Which friends?'

'No idea. You'd have to ask him.'

'And do you know which burglary it was?'

Donna gave a heavy sigh. 'No. Our family was going through a bit of a difficult time, as I recall, and had bigger things to worry about. Now, can you give me some news about my father's job, or were you just leaving?'

'I just have the report to file with him.'

'Good. Then don't let me keep you.'

With that, Donna stepped back into her hallway, and for the first time in her life, Maddy Clifford had a door slammed shut in her face. She stood there for a moment, not sure whether to swear or laugh, and instead settled for pulling a face at the glass-panelled uPVC.

In the car once again, she pulled out her phone, stared for a moment at the contact named *Macnab*, and eventually pressed to call.

'Mr Kilbride? Maddy Clifford. Just to let you know I'm e-mailing you the report today.'

Alistair Mulholland shoved his phone back into his pocket, irritation creeping over him again. What the bloody hell was Stein playing at? How could there be a problem now? Bradley would do his nut having to wait another whole day, and he wasn't looking forward to breaking the news.

He pressed the internal extension number on his desk phone, and blew irritably at his fringe. 'Slight hitch – I'll be in to see you in a moment.'

'Nature of hitch?'

The tone was cold, and Mulholland felt his defences prickling. 'Nothing to do with me. Problem with the bank.'

'Oh, for crying out loud, it's *Satur*—'

'I'll be in shortly.' Mulholland hung up and shook his head. After all the grief Bradley had given him about using the internal phone network, you'd think he'd know better; it was just one more sign that the man was getting desperate. And careless with it.

It wasn't as if the whole thing rested on Bradley's shoulders alone. Mulholland was in this just as deep as he was, had risked just as much, and with less chance of smarming his way out of it. Like tracking down the bloke whose father had made the original figurines, for starters, and getting him on side to make the fakes. Did Bradley think he'd just walked into Cameron's shop, smiled, and gained the man's co-operation just like that? Christ, if only! He'd put his job on the line, not to mention his liberty if the bloke had decided to blab.

It hadn't been at all hard finding the craftsman; Ben Cameron had simply taken over his father's business in the same little courtyard at the end of town. Mulholland had timed his visit carefully, late in the afternoon, and checked to see the shop was empty before ducking his head under the low-beamed doorway.

He'd expected a dingy little place with dusty shelves full of crap. He'd also expected to have to deal with some dotty old volunteer bint running the place, while Cameron worked in the back, and he was already thinking about how he'd charm his way past any pushy assistant he might encounter. Instead the shop was bright, airy, strategically mirrored to show off the best items in their glass cabinets, and it looked as if the owner himself was behind the counter. Bonus. A man in his late thirties or early forties, with dark blond hair, and dressed casually in a checked shirt worn open over a black T shirt, he was totting something up on a calculator. He looked up as Mulholland came in, a ready smile on his open, honest face.

Mulholland closed the door behind him and locked it; when he turned back, the man's friendly smile had gone. His own remained. 'Ben Cameron?'

'Yes?' The man didn't seem worried yet, but there was a wariness about him that set his shoulders square and his posture straighter. Mulholland saw the frown that creased his forehead, and noted the tension as he walked around peering at the porcelain works on display.

'Look,' Cameron said at last. 'Are you going to pretend you're in the Mafia for much longer? Only I've work to do, aye?'

Mulholland made a mental note to remember that little snip. 'I'm just making sure your work is up to the standard of your father's.'

That hit its mark, and Cameron's eyes narrowed. 'My dad taught me well enough.'

'How did your father die?'

'I'm surprised you don't know. It was a big enough story at the time.'

'Indulge me. I've only been in the area thirteen years.'

Cameron looked at him steadily for a moment. 'He was murdered. Surprised a burglar.'

'Bummer. Do you have kids, Mr Cameron? Or can I call you Ben?'

'No you fucking can't!' Cameron's voice rose, to Mulholland's amusement. 'And what's it to you if I have kids?'

Mulholland saw his eyes flick towards a photo stand beside the till, and he picked it up. 'Very nice. How old are they?'

'Put it down.' Now the voice was hard, the eyes like ice. Mulholland looked at Cameron a moment longer. This man would be no pushover, but he had the right buttons. It would work.

'I've got a proposal for you, Mr Cameron.'

'Get out of my shop.'

'Hear me out, I just—'

'Get out now, or I call the police.'

Ah, at last. Mulholland smiled and produced his warrant card, and saw the anger fade to a kind of trapped fear. It always worked.

'Now, can we go through to the back?' Mulholland gestured to a door behind the counter.

Cameron led the way, and Mulholland was pleased to note the shoulders were not so rigidly set now. The back room was a workroom. *The* workroom. Mulholland looked around at the assortment of knives and cloths, half-finished pieces and draped statues.

'Got a catalogue?'

Cameron stared at him as though he'd just halted a firing squad to ask for a cup of tea. 'What do you want that for?'

'Why do you think? You don't look like a stupid man, Ben, so don't ask stupid questions. Now, may I see it?'

Cameron took down a large folder, and Mulholland started flicking through the plastic-coated pages.

'Are these examples of yours and your father's work, or just yours?'

'Dad's stuff is in there too. Sergeant—'

'Did he photograph all his pieces? Even those commissioned by individuals?'

'Everything. Would you hand over something that's taken weeks of work, without keeping a record of it?'

'As I thought.' Mulholland halted his search at a beautifully lit collection, three figurines of delicate-featured women, each with different burdens: a child, a laundry basket and a pile of books. Each had a long, wide skirt and was painted sparingly, in pastel colours – not something that appealed to Mulholland, but he could at least appreciate their workmanship. Dougie Cameron had been a master of his art, no doubt about that; Duncan Wallace had known what he was doing when he hired him.

'Who commissioned these?'

'I don't have the records of customers for private jobs, and he never noted it in the book. Just his initials and the year. In this case 1988.'

'I want you to make another set.'

'What?'

'You heard.'

'Aye, but... *Exactly* the same?'

'Exactly.'

'Is that what all this is about? So why the hell all the theatrical crap?'

Mulholland closed the catalogue and turned to face Cameron. 'Because this is going to be our little secret. And because there's something I want you to put inside them, and if anyone finds out about it you're going to be watching from a big fluffy cloud when your kids finally stumble across your dead, rotting body.'

'Oh, for God's sake!'

Mulholland leaned closer and smiled. 'Like you did with your dad.'

'So you did know—'

'Use your brain, pal.' Mulholland's voice was almost kind. 'Are we going to be able to do business then?'

Cameron's face said it all. 'What choice have I got?'

'Oh, but you do have a choice – that's what I've been telling you. It's just not a particularly pleasant one. I'll bring in the little bits and bobs I want you to hide inside your lovely figures soon. Time is of the essence, as they say. By next weekend?'

'What? No!' Cameron looked flustered at his own response. 'I mean, to be honest there's really no chance, not so soon. I've got commissions I'm working on – people will be asking, and I've a shop to run.'

Mulholland assumed a concerned look. 'Close the shop for a couple of days – you're looking a little peaky.' He patted the counter and walked away. 'Next Saturday at the latest, okay?'

Chapter Six

MACKENZIE REMEMBERED Maddy's lunch just as he arrived at the office. He racked his brain for an excuse, but it was too late; she'd heard him come up the stairs, and opened the door before he could turn back.

'Where's my sandwich?'

'Forgot it, sorry.' He grinned at her scowl, and patted her shoulder as he passed her. 'I called Ade earlier, caught him just before he went to bed. He remembers hearing Sarah at school, banging on about this bloke—'

'Don't change the subject, you useless great lump – I want my lunch!' Maddy sat back in her chair and subjected him to her usual critical appraisal. 'You look like crap, by the way.'

'Thank you so much.' He sat down opposite her, and she accepted his thanks with a gracious nod, opening a packet of crisps from her drawer.

'Right, you were saying?'

'The lad he remembers was called Don.'

'How on earth could Adrian remember that, from thirty years ago?'

'Do you remember your first boyfriend?'

'I do, aye. His name was Simon. But that's different; he was *my* first boyfriend, not someone else's.'

'Why'd you two split up?'

She shrugged. 'We started secondary school. Things were different after that.'

'Why?'

'What does that have to do with anything?' She sighed, as he just looked at her. 'Okay, we were put in different classes. Plus there were loads of other girls there, of course. All very new, and therefore more exciting.'

'Anyone in particular?'

'God, yes. Horrible cow from Fort William. Debbie something...ah.' She smiled and shook her head. 'Point taken – Adrian remembered the boyfriend. But *you* still forgot my sandwich.'

'I'll make it up to you sometime. Can I have a crisp?'

'No.' Maddy picked up her pen and tapped it on the pad in front of her. 'Since it looks like I'm going to starve, I might as well get on with this. Adrian was right; according to my brother, Sarah Wallace *did* run away to paradise, or at least Inverness, with Constable Bradley. Evidently her daddy was none too pleased. She soon came back though. Interestingly enough—'

'So it wasn't a big deal between them then?'

'Don't interrupt, this is the good bit. I found out that they only met because Bradley was one of the officers dealing with some scandal that Wallace was involved in around that time. He and two of his friends had been arrested for burglary, only Wallace was never charged.'

'Which burglary?'

'I haven't been able to find out yet, but I'll get onto it.

Nick's told me all he's going to; I'm not asking him to risk anything else, but it shouldn't be hard to find out.' She shrugged. 'We don't have that many high-profile burglaries that we can't put two and two together from the newspaper archives. Anyway, the other two got the book thrown at them, but Wallace was let off on a technicality; apparently Bradley messed up the evidence. Then he went off with the man's daughter. A bit funny, wouldn't you say?'

Mackenzie sat forward, a tingle starting across his forehead. 'How did you find this out so fast?'

'You just have to know who to ask,' Maddy said, with a faintly smug look. 'And *how* to ask,' she added pointedly.

'Okay, so my people skills are zero, but that's why we work so well together. Who were the two blokes who got sent down?'

'One of them, the one who got them all arrested, couldn't face the scandal he'd put his family through, and topped himself in jail. His name was Alexander Broughton. The other one was Sarah's godfather, Robert Doohan. He's—'

'Doohan? I think I know him.'

'Good, that'll save me digging out his address.'

'I mean, I don't know where he is *now*, but he was a friend of the family back in the day.'

'Much good you are. Anyway, he served five years and has been reclusive ever since.'

'Why do we need to speak to him?'

'I thought, being Sarah's godfather and a close friend of Duncan Wallace's, there's a fairly good chance he'd know where to look for those original figurines Sarah's after.'

Mackenzie nodded. 'Good point. Stein would know about him too, I assume, though it's odd he's not said anything. I'll go and ask him.' He stood up. 'Well, that deserves two sandwiches at least. Maybe even triple-deckers. I'll be back in a bit.'

'How's it going with Stein?' Maddy asked. 'You still want to punch his lights out?'

'More than ever. Still, his job might just save this place.' He indicated the room in general, but noticing the cloud crossing Maddy's face, he was sorry he'd said anything. 'It's not that bad, Mads. Honest, we'll make it pay. We've got those other couple of things on that you're dealing with, but this one will help massively, you know it will.'

'I just wish we didn't have to rely on nailing Bradley to do it. Although my dad would be delighted to watch the bugger go down.'

'We don't have to nail him. I just have to track down those figurines, and basically stay out of his way.'

Maddy pulled a face. 'It's looking more and more as if you won't be able to do the first without failing at the second.'

'In which case I've got to make sure this is done absolutely right. No room for mistakes.' Mackenzie checked his pockets for phone and keys. 'He *can't* be allowed to find out I'm involved – he's got too much clout, and we know from experience he's prepared use it against me.'

Maddy's voice was quiet, but hard. 'He has to answer for what he's done.'

'He will, eventually. Did you know he's got a new car? Bloody great Discovery. Just about accommodates his ego.'

'He'll slip up. They always do.'

Mackenzie sighed. 'He hasn't so far.'

'Then he's due. Dad's got some long-standing suspicion about him, too. Something he was never able to prove, so he won't say what it is.'

'Knowing your dad, it wouldn't surprise me if he's spot on,

whatever it is.' Mackenzie squeezed her shoulder as he passed the desk. 'Thanks, Mads. I don't know anyone else who can make me talk about Don Bradley and not want to break things.'

'Good.' Her face softened, just for a moment, then she pointed to the door with her pen. 'Now go out and bring me food.'

Jamie was getting bored now. This was his holiday too, and he wanted to go back into town and find the American again, or at least be allowed to look around by himself. But no, Mum had spent all that money on a new camera, and now she had to go and point it at every old place she noticed. It was a sick camera though, and it *had* taken her ages to save up for it. Maybe she'd let him use it if he didn't whinge too much.

'Where's this black place then?' he asked, as his mother parked up and turned off the engine.

'Black*house*,' she corrected. 'It's right there.'

He peered through the window. 'But it's not even black.' He'd been hoping to see some huge, looming, scary house like something out of Scooby Doo; instead there was only this long, thin place with a roof made of grass and rocks.

He got out of the car, already disappointed. There were a few other cars around, and the house was right in the middle of the village, so they weren't alone, but if this was all there was, it was going to be a pretty dismal visit. He looked back to where Mum was rootling through the sweet wrappers and stuff in the glove box.

'I don't believe it! The bloody camera's not here.'

'Use your phone.'

'It's at home. I told you that.' She slammed the glove box

shut, took one last glance into the back seat and joined Jamie. 'It must be in the tent after all. Arsebiscuits! Come on, then, let's go in anyway.'

Reluctantly Jamie followed his mother in through the door, where she paid the admission fee: six pounds for her, four for him. A tenner, just for being allowed into this dark little room with a stinky fireplace in the middle, and not even a proper carpet on the floor!

There were some people wandering around inside, and Jamie wondered how they could really be interested. They were probably just trying to look impressive, like people who pretend they understand paintings of just blobs and lines. His eye caught the display of armoury along one of the rough walls, and while his mother started reading an engraved plaque nailed to a post, he went over for a closer look. This was more like it; one of those swords was even bigger than he was. How could anyone ever have used that?

'It's called a Claymore,' a deep voice behind him said. 'Would ye like a demonstration?' Jamie turned to see a man in full Highland dress smiling at him – the smile only just took the edge off the frightening sight of skins and plaid, and wild hair barely imprisoned by a small, feathered hat. Awed, Jamie couldn't speak, but the Highlander repeated the question to Jamie's mother, who at first frowned, and looked as if she were about to say no. Then she nodded quickly, and went back to reading those plaques. Rather determinedly, Jamie thought.

He followed the Highlander outside. In the small, grassed garden at the back of the house, Jamie saw another of the huge swords, along with a selection of smaller but equally deadly looking weapons, lined up against the wall. A few other people had come outside to watch as well, and Jamie watched eagerly as the Highlander demonstrated how to hold the weapons correctly. He mimed the same actions, and the demonstrator smiled again.

'Here, lad. You give it a try, aye?'

To Jamie's delight he was allowed to handle the wickedly sharp dirk and the heavy wooden targe, but had to have help to lift the huge Claymore over his head.

'Once it was up there, you'd wave it around in a circle, or a figure of eight, and lop as many heads, arms and legs off the mounted infantry as you could. Fun or no fun?'

'Fun!' Jamie yelled, turning around to face the smiling spectators, while the demonstrator supported the massive weight of the sword above his head.

A couple of the men in the group looked as though they couldn't wait to get their own hands on it and show they possessed just as much strength as any ancient warrior. Jamie sensed how much of the weight was being supported, and knew how badly his own arms already ached, and he wasn't so sure. His thoughts flashed towards the big Scotsman who had found him that morning, and he thought maybe *he* could do it without too much trouble.

As he turned again, Jamie's gaze fell on the cars parked on the other side of the stone wall, and if the Highlander hadn't been supporting the Claymore he would have dropped it; someone was crouching by the driver's door of their car, trying to break in!

He opened his mouth to yell, but the Highlander chose that moment to encourage the spectators to give him a big round of applause and, distracted, he looked away. When he turned back again the figure had gone. The sword was taken from him and an eager tourist stepped forward to try, leaving Jamie free to run to the wall and peer over it, half expecting to see someone crouching there. Nothing.

He went back inside where, as his eyes adjusted, he gradually picked out his mother, listening with rapt attention as another Highlander, this one lying on the floor, demonstrated how to put on the belted tartan. He tugged at her sleeve but she shushed him – for some weird reason she was taking as much interest in this as he had done with the sword and dirk outside. Impatient, he waited until the demonstration was finished and the polite clapping had started, before he pulled her jumper again.

She turned to him, still stuck in whatever world she'd been hearing about. She looked happy, though. 'You know, Jay, you should hear some of this. It'd make you really appreciate all the stuff you've got at home. I wish I'd not left the camera back at the tent. Did you know that end of the room had animals in? I don't mean guinea pigs and—'

'Someone tried to nick the car!' he blurted, and that shut her up. 'He's gone now, but I bet it was something to do with—'

'Don't you dare say anything about Americans and statues,' she warned. 'Who on earth would steal a car, somewhere like this?'

'Well, if he wasn't stealing it, he was breaking into it to see what stuff we've got.'

'Well, he'd be disappointed then. Good thing it's a hire car, but he'd better not have scratched it, or that's the insurance excess down the pan. Which way did he go?'

He shrugged. 'I dunno. I looked away for a second, then he left.'

'He can't have got far,' she said, and he recognised the sudden edge to her voice and groaned. When she sounded like that she thought she was seven feet tall and made of iron, and that nearly always meant trouble.

He followed her outside, where some of the men were

trying out the Claymore, and Jamie was gratified to see that even they needed help to lift it as high as it was supposed to go. The Highlander saw him and winked, and he grinned back, the smile vanishing as he ran to catch up with his mother; why didn't she just ask for help from someone like that? Not that she ever did, or would, ask – she was so certain that she could do everything.

'Did you see any other cars driving away?' she asked. Detective Mum... What could she do if he had?

'No. At least, I don't think so.'

'Then he might still be here.' She stared around them. That iron had disappeared and she suddenly, and for once, looked scared. The last time Jamie had seen her this uncertain and worried was when his dad had still lived with them – she'd been like it all the time then, and seeing it again made him glance around fearfully too, sure he could feel someone watching him. The feeling persisted even as his mother came over to him, put her arm around him and kissed his forehead.

'Don't worry. Probably just some chancer watching all us stupid tourists going in there, and seeing who's left their car unlocked.'

'Ours was locked though, wasn't it? I heard you ploink it.'

'Of course. But on the off chance they got into it, with any luck they'll have nicked Suze's cat, and I'll have an excuse to go back to that shop with the nice lookin' fella in charge.' She grinned when he rolled his eyes. 'Come on, let's go back in. It's actually really interesting if you let your imagination work for you.'

So they went back into the blackhouse museum, and while his mother sank happily back into her dreams of 17th century life, Jamie stayed firmly in 2018, keeping one eye on the door. Just in case.

Charis lifted the groceries out of the car, and she and Jamie made their way through the gate and around the stone wall to where they'd made camp two nights ago. The blackhouse reconstruction had been a real eye-opener, and even the uncomfortable thought that someone had tried to break into their car had taken up its rightful place in reality; the history of this area was so steeped in treachery, violence and hardship, someone trying their luck with a rented Ford Focus was hardly comparable. And they hadn't managed it anyway, nor scratched it in their attempt, thankfully.

She and Jamie had returned to their temporary home with enough bacon and bread to feed a small army, and she'd even treated herself to a bottle of white wine, which she'd been looking forward to sipping while the sun went down. It was already late afternoon, and Charis could see clouds gathering once again over the hills to the west; she reckoned they had about twenty minutes to get settled in the dry. The light patter of drops on the shopping bags, a moment before she felt them on her skin, told her she was getting no better at predicting the weather, and with a sigh she amended her evening's ambitions to sitting in the doorway of the tent, watching the mountains disappear behind a curtain of rain.

Jamie ran ahead, leaping over the soggy patches he already knew by heart; he had taken to rural life as naturally as Charis had taken to single-motherhood, and it was doing him just as much good; he'd hardly needed his asthma inhaler since they'd arrived... Charis groaned as the thought popped into her head; after all that, they'd forgotten to pick up the refill in town. That meant another fight for parking spaces on Monday when it all opened again—

'Mum!' Jamie was already running back towards her, his face a mixture of dismay and excitement. 'Someone's been in the tent!'

Heart hammering, Charis ran down the slight slope to the sheltered patch where their tent stood, its open front flapping in the wind and the poles almost collapsed. 'Shit!' The word was out before she could stop it, but Jamie was too busy picking over their belongings to notice. Charis seized the front of the tent and pulled it upright, flicking rainwater over them both as the nylon snapped into place.

'Where's the camera?' The brand new digital SLR had been the result of three weeks' overtime and an Amazon gift voucher from her sister, and was her single most expensive possession. 'Oh *hell*! Keep looking, Jay.'

They both rummaged among the piles of wet clothing, but the camera was definitely gone, although nothing else appeared to be missing. Miserable once again, almost to the point of tears, Charis started pulling muddy steel pegs out of the ground and letting the tent fall in on itself.

'Are we going home?' The disappointment in Jamie's voice stopped her for a moment; that had been the plan, but what would it achieve?

'I don't know,' she admitted. 'I just need to think. No matter what we decide though, we'll have to go back into town and find a launderette. Assuming that bloody place has such a thing.' She held up a pair of his faded jeans, now a dark, shiny blue in patches where the rain had soaked them. 'We can't wear our stuff like this. And anyway, I don't like leaving the tent out here now. Not that there's anything worth nicking in it any more. God! *Why* didn't I take the bloody camera with me today?'

'You couldn't find it this morning either,' Jamie pointed

out. 'Maybe it was stolen before?' He was looking at the pile of green nylon with a little grimace of distaste, mirroring her feelings exactly.

One nasty little act of invasion and their holiday had been spoiled, along with all the good feelings she'd been collecting, storing up for their return to the noisy, stressful life back home. His words hit home, too; if someone had been into the tent before, taken the only thing of value and then returned to do this, it was more than some random destructive act by passers by.

Who could have done it, and more importantly, why? A prickle started at the base of Charis's skull and she turned her head quickly. There was no-one behind her, but just for a second, she was sure there must have been. Her thoughts flew back to the incident at the blackhouse museum; it now seemed even less likely it had been some kid hoping for a joyride. Someone had seen the car there, knew they were out for the day, and had taken the chance to come here and leave this obvious message.

'Jay,' she said suddenly, 'the person at the museum, messing with the car – d'you think it was the same bloke who took your notebook this morning?'

'Don't think so.'

'Or you don't want it to be?' Her voice was grim.

'I don't know! I didn't see who it was; they were sort of crouching down by the door. And then they were gone. I couldn't see if they were tall, or what.'

Charis frowned. No-one knew where they were camped; this wasn't somewhere you just happen to stumble on – she'd been told about it by Suze, who in turn knew of it from a friend who'd camped here for years with the permission of the estate owner. It was a hard place to find, even on Google Maps, and she'd had to get Suze's friend to write out detailed instructions, which were still safely in her coat pocket.

'Did you tell him where we were staying?'

'I don't *know* where we're staying,' he pointed out. 'I just told him we were camping on this side of town, but not where.'

Charis peered closely around, and into the hedges behind where the tent had stood, and she could see nothing out of place and no movement. But what had heightened the appeal of a peaceful haven now only served to highlight their vulnerability.

She spoke loudly and clearly, partly to hide her own fear, partly to convey to anyone who might be listening that he hadn't won. Her voice only shook a little bit.

'Right. We'll go into town and get our stuff dried out, and then we'll find somewhere else to camp. Okay?'

'Yay, great!'

Jamie helped her pack the rest of their belongings, and together they carried everything back to the car. It was slow going over the muddy ground, but Charis was determined to manage it in one journey; there was no way she was ever going back there again. With Jamie safely in the front seat, she closed the boot and hunted around for some clue. Tyre tracks on the wet mud, or footprints too big to be hers or Jamie's...

And there they were. Her heart stuttered as she peered at the tracks on the other side of the gateway. She hadn't really known what she'd been hoping for, unless it was simply proof that she wasn't over-reacting, but this mess of tyre tracks and sliding footprints said *someone* had followed her up here, and that now, with the theft of her precious camera, that particular someone had possession of at least one clear picture of her son.

Charis fumbled at the car door and dragged it open, almost falling over herself in her haste. Only when she was in and had locked the door did she register that, though there were tyre tracks, there was no sign of the vehicle that had made them; they were safe. Then again, logic had no place in the blur of blood-freezing panic.

No-one would go to all this trouble just for a couple of hundred pounds worth of camera, so it had to be something to do with Jamie. The image flashed into her mind of a tall man, low voice, grim expression... He was dangerous, anyone could see that, and he had brazenly threatened her boy.

'Where are we going?' Jamie wanted to know, as Charis twisted the ignition key with sudden ferocity. She glanced at him briefly, then out of her window towards their abandoned campsite.

'The police.'

Abergarry Police Station

Passing through the front office as he headed for Bradley's, Mulholland was thinking over the news of Andy Stein's latest bit of heel-dragging, and how to present it. His scowl matched his sour thoughts, until he was distracted by the woman arguing with the duty sergeant. At first his interest was aroused by no more than the fact that she was a nice-looking piece – although her mouth could do with some training – but as he reached the door, something she was saying filtered through his mental rehearsal, and he stopped.

'He wasn't imagining it,' she was insisting. 'He definitely heard something about statues—'

'I'll take over here if you like, Nick,' Mulholland said. 'Would you like to follow me, Mrs, uh, Miss...?'

'Boulton. And this is Jamie.'

'Come this way, Ms Boulton. And hello to you, laddie.' Mulholland tried on a hearty smile that seemed to fit well enough, and though the boy still looked a bit nervous, he managed to give off waves of barely suppressed delight too, as he gazed around him.

Sergeant Clifford looked relieved to have been let off the hook, and Mulholland could hardly blame him. But at the same time, the thought that the man might have just pushed the woman out into the street again, without alerting himself or Bradley, gave him a little internal shudder.

He waved the two visitors through the doorway ahead of him, then turned back. 'Nick? Call the super and let him know I'll be a few minutes late for our meeting. Cheers.' Let Sergeant Stupid cope with Superintendent Snappy for a bit.

In the interview room, Mulholland gestured to the chairs and took one opposite. 'I'm sorry to make you go over everything again, Ms Boulton, but I'm sure you'd rather this was done properly.'

'That bloody copper on the desk didn't seem to think so,' the woman said. Her Liverpudlian accent was strong, and her voice was surprisingly low for someone of such slight stature. He decided he could put up with it after all; she was definitely a looker, with her short, spiky dark hair and wide apart blue eyes. And what a great little ass she had in those skinny jeans.

'Can I take your full name?'

'Charis—'

'K-a-r?'

'No, with a c-h. And one s. Charis Anne Boulton. Anne has an e. And Boulton has a u.'

'Right. And you, sir?'

'Jamie.'

'With a J?' Mulholland grinned at the woman, but she just looked at him. He cleared his throat. 'Right. Jamie Boult—'

'Thorne. With an e.'

Was she taking the piss? But again she had no humour in her eyes. He frowned. 'He's not your son?'

'Yes, he is. Thorne is his father's name.'

'Right. Of course. Now, Ms ... may I call you Charis?' She wasn't keen, judging by her expression, but he pressed on anyway. 'Now then, Charis. Start at the beginning, and tell me exactly what you were trying to tell Sergeant Clifford.'

While she talked, he wrote down the key points and kept flicking his gaze from mother to son, checking to see if anything she said surprised the boy. But he seemed in full agreement with everything she was saying; she was telling the truth, at least as he understood it.

'And what makes you so sure it was this same man who stole your camera?'

'Well, he didn't like Jamie snooping around, for a start. And when Jamie wrote down the reg number of the American's car, he ripped that page out.' Her eyes glinted with anger despite the evident fear. 'He must've followed us out to the campsite last night, after Jamie overheard the phone call, and taken the camera from the car then. You know, in case Jamie'd taken any pictures of him while he was on the phone. Then once he saw were in town again today, he must have gone back out there to leave a cowardly *message*, by wrecking our stuff.'

'I see. Now, in as much detail as possible, I'd like you to describe this man who's been harassing your little boy.'

His carefully chosen words had the desired effect, and the mother in her rose visibly to the challenge. She closed her eyes to think, then her words sketched an image that made his teeth itch; there could be no doubt about the man she was describing, and that would not make Bradley happy. Not at all.

To give him credit, Bradley sat through Mulholland's explanations of Stein's delaying tactics without comment, although it looked as if it was as much as he could do not to slam out of the room and go and find Stein himself. After all this time, they had the money in sight, but because of some so-called 'screw-up at the bank' it meant waiting until Monday at least before Stein could speak to an actual person face-to-face. They couldn't exactly call him a liar, though. No wonder Bradley was twitchy.

Then Mulholland moved on to the reason for his own late arrival, and gradually, as his words filtered through whatever angry fog was clouding the superintendently brain, Bradley frowned. 'What did you say?'

'I said the boy heard an American talking to someone on the phone. About statues. Anyway, the bloke this Boulton woman's pointing the finger at got very antsy about the whole thing, and it seems like Stein has got him involved in this.'

'This is the man she says stole her camera?'

'Aye.'

'Describe him.'

Mulholland shuffled his papers, gave him a *you're not going to like this* look, and started to read aloud. 'Probably late thirties, tall – this lass is only tiny herself, mind, so it's all relative. Um, fairly well built, but she wouldn't really call him fat. He has dark hair, and when she saw him this morning he was wearing a dark blue sweatshirt, jeans and black boots. And apparently he said he rides a motorbike.'

Bradley leaned forward, eyes narrowed. 'Go on.'

Mulholland cleared his throat. 'He was wearing a manky bit of leather around his neck, with two knots tied in it. Oh aye, and his eyes were hazel.'

'Sod the colour of his eyes! You know damn well who she's talking about.'

'Paul Mackenzie. The leather was very old, evidently.'

'Well he's been wearing it about twelve years, if memory serves.'

'Thirteen, sir.'

'Jesus!' Bradley rubbed his face with both hands. 'Odds on he's the one behind this delay. Screw-up at the bank, like hell! Where are the woman and the boy now?'

'They're planning on staying at The Burnside tonight, I believe. Moving on tomorrow.'

'Right.' Bradley sounded decisive at last. 'Bring him in.'

'Who?'

'Tyrion Lannister.' Bradley rolled his eyes. 'Who do you think? Mackenzie! Get him in here for questioning about the harassment of this child and the theft of the camera. Hopefully, that'll make Stein think twice about hiring him, and we can get everything back on track.'

Mulholland shook his head, and for the moment, kept his tone polite. 'Is that wise, sir?'

'Why wouldn't it be?'

'For starters, to let him know we're aware of his involvement? It'll just make him more careful. If we leave him to—'

'All right!' Bradley conceded irritably. 'How the hell did he ever get involved anyway? The man's poison.'

'To be fair, sir, you've been a thorn in *his* side for years.'

'I'd rather be a knife in his sodding throat.'

'So I gather. The fact remains, though, you've got to be

careful. With the promotion board coming up, you'll be watched even more closely than usual. By everyone. Better let me handle things, sir.' He shook his head. 'Beats me why you didn't wait until it was all over to do this.'

'Because it should have been sorted by now!' Bradley gathered himself and sighed. 'Okay, call Stein again. Call his bluff – tell him we're pulling out of this deal until it's safe. You don't have to mention Mackenzie by name; he doesn't need to know we know the bastard. As you say, it'll just make him more careful. Just make him aware that the...*interested parties*, I suppose, are becoming rather too many.'

That was true enough; what had started out as a simple transaction was turning into a three-ring bloody circus. And Mulholland couldn't help thinking he was looking at one of the chief clowns right now.

'Just one thing, before you go,' Bradley said, as Mulholland rose to leave.

'Aye, sir?'

Bradley stood too, but he still had to look up to meet Mulholland's eyes. 'You patronise me one more time, or question my orders, and you're out on your arse. Got it?'

Mulholland studied him in silence for a moment, noting the glisten of fresh sweat that broke out on the superintendent's brow. The man was learning. After thirteen years, he was finally coming to understand he'd got a tiger by the tail.

He kept his own voice very quiet. 'Got it. *Sir.*' He held Bradley's gaze a moment longer, and watched the super's hand come up and rub his lower chest, as if a nervous heartburn had flared there. Then he smiled, a quick, on-off flash, and left.

Chapter Seven

THE HOTEL DIDN'T LOOK like much to write home about, from the outside, but once you got in through the large glass doors it was like another world. Charis gazed around her, suddenly unsure. It had seemed like the perfect solution: one night here, then home. Jamie would take some placating, but she'd make it up to him, maybe even get him his phone before his birthday. But The Burnside looked as if it would cost a fortune, and that was something she certainly didn't have; the loss of her one extravagance, her precious Canon, still made her feel sick. She'd have to check her home insurance when she got back, to see if it was covered, but in the meantime she was going to have to watch her pennies, for sure.

The hotel tariff was tacked high on the wall behind the counter, no doubt deliberately, to bring potential customers in to a point where direct contact with the counter staff was unavoidable. She groaned at what she saw, and the receptionist materialised as if summoned by the sound.

'Can I help, madam?'

'I'm just checking prices, thanks.'

The young man shrugged, though not without sympathy. 'We do offer a lower rate for subsequent nights.'

'We're only here for the one. These prices are a bit mad, aren't they?'

'We usually find people are extremely satisfied with the service.'

'I'm sure they are; it's not the service I'm complaining about.' Charis sighed. 'As it happens, I don't have that much choice at the moment, so I'll take a twin room please.'

Behind her she heard Jamie give a little 'yes!' not quite as under his breath as he assumed, and she smiled, catching the receptionist's amused glance. Then she reluctantly produced her credit card, giving it an apologetic look, and a minute later the receptionist pushed two keys over the polished wooden surface – actual keys too, not cards, and with large, smooth, wooden fobs engraved with their room number. Very nice.

'Second floor,' the receptionist said. 'Out of the lift, turn left, and it's right at the end of the corridor, by the fire exit.'

After an early dinner, she saw Jamie into his bed and told him she was going to the bar for a quick nightcap; might as well take advantage of the fact she didn't have to drive anywhere, and at least she'd be drinking out of a glass here, instead of a plastic cup.

'Are you sure you don't mind?' she asked Jamie, for what might have been the hundredth time judging from his expression. It had only been twice.

'Of course not. It'll only be like we're at home, and you're in the front room.'

'I'll be half an hour, tops. Lock the door behind me, and do *not* leave this room, understand?' She kissed him goodnight, reminded him not to watch anything on TV except the regular channels, and went downstairs.

The bar was as beautifully decorated as the lobby and their room, and Charis wished she had something nicer to wear; the clothes she'd put through the dryers at the launderette were passable but by no means smart. She took her glass of wine and retreated to a small booth, where she could watch everyone else without drawing attention to herself and her faded jeans. She needn't have worried, really, she realised; as it was still early evening no-one had yet gone to change for dinner, and many were still wandering around in never-seen-a-patch-of-mud green wellies and new quilted Barbours. She blended in reasonably well.

Around ten minutes later she sat up straight, slopping her drink over her wrist. The man who'd stolen her camera was walking through the door... Was he still following her? Silly question, why else would a local bloke come to a hotel? She was about to march up to him and demand answers, when a figure emerged from another booth and moved into the light, crossing to the bar where the Stalking Scotsman now leaned.

Charis had never seen the American Jamie had talked about, but she guessed this was him. He moved with an assurance and a purpose that made the tall Scot seem like a shambling bear by comparison, and also dressed in classic smart-casual, in contrast to the rest of the happily mingling guests.

She watched closely, hidden by the curve of her own booth, and soon realised these two men were not the best of friends. The Scotsman turned as the other approached, and immediately he stood straighter, his brows drawing together in the same frown she had last seen directed at her. She almost felt sorry for the American, who had his phone in his hand and was clenching it tightly as he waved it at the Scot. None of their words reached Charis, but it was clear the American was reporting a call that had displeased him, and that he clearly blamed on the other.

They both looked around them often as they talked, falling silent as the barman approached their end of the bar. The Scot ordered a pint of beer, the American a tall glass of what looked like sparkling mineral water, and they moved back to the booth where the American had been waiting. Off to carry on their stupid secret conversation... Charis had had enough. She finished her drink and banged the glass down on the table, choosing to ignore the curious looks she got from a group in the corner as she stood up and straightened her baggy sweater.

She raked her boots down the backs of her calves to smooth the wrinkles in her jeans, snatched her room key from the table, and took a deep breath. He wasn't getting away with this, local or otherwise; if the police weren't going to do anything, she would.

Rounding the corner of their booth she wasn't at all surprised to see them sitting across the table from each other, glaring into their drinks and not speaking.

'Where's my camera?'

Both men looked up, startled, first at her and then each other. She stood with folded arms, key fob dangling from her fist, the key itself gripped tight enough to hurt, but she needed that small pain to help stop the trembling.

Finally the Scot spoke, his voice low pitched and insultingly bored. 'Camera?'

'I want it back,' Charis said, 'and if you've deleted any of those pictures, even one, I'll—'

'I don't have your camera, Ms Boulton. Now go away, this is a grown-up conversation.'

'I'll go away when you tell me why you're following me, and why you stole my camera.'

'*Following* you? Why the hell would I do that?'

'Oh, I don't know, let me think... No, I've got no idea.' Charis flicked an accusatory glance at the American, but, clearly embarrassed for her, he was staring fixedly at the dangling key fob and her sarcasm was wasted.

The Scot followed his gaze, and an amused note crept into his voice. 'A room key? Why, Ms Boulton, I thought you were roughing it up in the hills. What happened, did the rain get too much for you? Had to come down here to get warm?'

'As if you didn't know what happened.' Charis felt her own fury struggling to break free, but she held it in check. 'That camera was expensive—'

'And where's your little boy this time? Locked in his room while you come down here to get pissed and shout at the other guests?'

'I am not pissed!' She could have slapped herself for rising to his bait, but to hear him once again cast negativity on her relationship with Jamie was too much to take. 'He's absolutely fine. He's ten, not five.'

'Ten's pretty young,' the Scot observed, but the confrontational tone dropped away, and he looked back at his drink. There was silence in the booth, and the noise in the rest of the room seemed to rise in proportion.

The American stood up, his phone still in his hand. 'I've got a call to make. Will you guys please sort this out while I'm gone? Mackenzie, we still have things to discuss, and I'd rather not do it in front of this...*lady*.'

So, his name was Mackenzie. All right, now she had a name to give the police. Speaking of which... She slid into the seat the American had vacated. 'I've reported you, you know, Mr Mackenzie. I couldn't give them a name, not then, but I'm damned good with descriptions. And that,' she jabbed her finger at the knotted leather at his throat, 'seemed to make the nice officer sit up and take notice. Know you, do they, the local police? Seemed like it to me.'

Mackenzie didn't answer, but his hand went to the leather and brushed over the knots. A strange, hollow expression touched his eyes, just for a second, but when he spoke again those eyes bit into hers like diamond tips.

'Look, we've been through this. Number one, I didn't follow you and I've no idea why you'd want to leave your camp. Number two, I haven't got your bloody *expensive camera*, and number three, you have *really* got to learn to stay away from people like me. And him.' He jerked his thumb over his shoulder towards the door the American had gone through. 'More particularly, you've got to keep your boy away.' He shook his head. 'Don't you care what he gets into? What will it take to convince you to just leave here and go and stay somewhere prettier, eh? Go down to Fort Augustus and take the boat trips. Find Nessie. Only piss off and leave this alone.'

'The only monster around here is you,' Charis hissed back. She had liked the way it sounded in her head, but his pitying expression made her feel stupid. And she hated him for that as much as for his careless remarks about Jamie. 'You don't know anything about us,' she said, and absurdly and annoyingly she felt the hot prickle of tears. 'You have no idea what we've been through, or how much I care about him, and unless you've got kids of your own, you never will.' She waited for him to answer, but he was focused on his drink again, although he'd not taken as much as a sip. She saw a small muscle jumping in his jaw, and pressed on. 'Well, *do* you have kids?'

'No.' He still didn't look up.

'Then don't you dare try and tell me how to raise mine.'

The row was halted by the reappearance of the American, clearly still angry with Mackenzie. 'We'll talk more in the morning. I'm going to bed.' He picked up his jacket and, without any pretence at pleasant leave-taking, he strode away and left them in their booth.

Charis glared at Mackenzie, trying to figure him out; one minute he was pinning her to the back of her seat with the ferocity of his stare, making her fight for every comment she wanted to make, and the next it was as if he were defeated, unable or unwilling to fight his own corner. She didn't know if she'd won, or if he'd simply given up trying to get through. Either way she wanted more answers, and she was going to get them.

She stood up. 'I'm going to get another drink, and this time it's going to be whisky.'

'Do what you like, it's a free country. I'm going to finish my drink, then I'm away. *If* you've no objection?' Mackenzie finally picked up his pint and took a long drink. For a second Charis's guard dropped and she considered asking him to stay; she really wanted that camera back. But remembering his cold stare, she kept quiet; if he left, he'd just cement her view of him as a bully, and good riddance to him. She'd had enough bullies in her life. When she got back from the bar, however, she was glad to see he'd replaced the glass, still half full, on its beer mat.

She sniffed her own drink, blinking at the fumes. 'Did you sell it?'

'Sell what? Oh God, you're not still on about your camera, are you?'

'What do you think?' Charis drank half her whisky in one gulp, and her mouth dropped open in shock at the burning that flooded her nose and throat. 'So, did you get rid of it?' Oh great, now her voice was knackered, momentarily paralysed by the neat whisky.

Mackenzie's mouth twitched. 'Are you ever going to accept that I didn't steal it?'

'No. So you might as well tell the truth.'

'Right. Okay, I stole it. I came up to your campsite at... Where was it?'

'It's not a proper site, and I can't remember what the estate's called,' Charis said crossly. 'Glen-something-or-other.'

'Right. I sneaked up to Glen-something-or-other, by Loch-thingummyjig, and I... What did I do?'

Charis's certainty wavered. 'You went through our stuff, and stole—'

'Your camera. Of course. It's on eBay for a fiver; I'll send you the link. There, happy now?'

'Stop taking the piss. If you didn't steal it, then who did?'

'Oh, you're prepared to believe me now?' Mackenzie's eyebrows disappeared into his hairline, and he slumped back in mock amazement on the velvet-covered seat.

Charis shrugged. 'Well, I'm prepared to accept that, *maybe*, it was someone else.'

'Ah, that must be the dram you just half killed yourself with. Makes humans of all of us in the end.'

'Your American friend then?'

'He's no bloody friend of mine.'

'Then what is he? What's going on, Mackenzie?'

Abruptly the mellow humour that had been gradually

creeping across the Scot's face vanished, and he was closed to her again. 'Finish your drink, and get away to your bed and your wee boy, okay?' He stayed slumped, staring into his drink again, distractedly turning up the corners of his cardboard beer mat. Charis picked up her own drink and sipped at it, reluctant to leave until she knew more about what Mackenzie and the American were up to.

'Is it illegal? I mean, your part in it?'

'No!' He looked up, and his voice softened. 'No. It's not illegal.'

She stared at him a moment longer, assessing the truth in his expression, then, satisfied, she nodded. If she had misjudged him about the camera, perhaps she was being hasty about his treatment of Jamie.

'Goodnight then, Mackenzie. And... I'm sorry.'

'Don't be.' Now his smile was back, just a shadow, but it was there. 'You pissed my "American friend" off, and that's worth all the verbal scourging you can dish out.'

Two floors up, Charis found herself still echoing that faint smile as she stepped out of the lift, but it froze as she saw someone outside the last door in the corridor: hers and Jamie's room. The man had been bending over to call through the lock, but had looked around at the muted ping from the lift. The sight of that handsome, familiar face turned her blood to ice.

He straightened. 'Hello, love.' His voice was soft, friendly. 'Our lad in there, then?'

'What are you doing here?'

'Is that any way to greet your husband?'

'Ex.' Charis's throat was so tight she could barely get the

word out. She had to get him away from that room. 'How the hell did a nasty piece of work like *you* get parole?'

His expression darkened, but her words had worked. He came down the corridor to where she stood, and she forced herself to remain still, praying Jamie wouldn't hear them and open the door. 'Well?'

Daniel's hand rose, and she flinched, but he simply stroked her rigid jaw. 'What you did to me, love, that was wrong. Vicious and unnecessary. But you know that now, don't you?'

Fear was uncurling, snapping at her insides. *How had he found out?* 'Who told you?'

'My brief let it slip. She was gutted about that, but I'd say she finally earned her fee by that mistake alone. Because now I know who to blame for getting me put away.'

Charis's heart was hammering, and she felt sick. How could he be here? How could he have found her? She closed her eyes, desperately wishing someone would come up the stairs, but no-one did. Daniel's hand dropped away, but the relief vanished when he took hold of hers instead.

'Come on, love, I know things have been difficult. I know you think you and the lad weren't a big part of my life, but you're wrong. I was probably just a bit...heavy-handed, trying to be a good dad to him. A firm parent. *We* were good together at the start, weren't we? Hey.' He put a finger beneath her chin and made her look at him. 'Weren't we?'

She nodded, tears prickling at her eyes, and the tenderness that came over his face almost convinced her, the way it had convinced everyone else who saw it. *He's such a nice bloke, Charis! Such a great dad. You're so lucky...*

'Then why don't we give it another shot?' Daniel's brown eyes were gentle. The soft shine in them told the story of how deeply he felt about her; of course he would put everything aside to come and find her, despite what she'd done. 'Come on, love. Fetch the lad and let's go home.'

'He's not here,' Charis managed. 'He's...staying with some friend he made at the campsite.'

'Campsite?' Daniel raised an eyebrow. 'I'd hardly call it that.'

Realisation had been late in coming, but it hit now. 'So it was you,' she whispered. 'How did you find us?'

'I'll tell you all about it later. Look, come home,' he repeated. 'We'll go and fetch the kid, and then we can go back tonight. No need to hang around here.'

Charis kept her voice steady, with an effort. 'Come downstairs, we can't discuss this in the corridor.'

He tugged her hand gently. 'Let's go to your room, then.'

'No!' Charis jerked away. She forced herself to sound more regretful. 'It says on the notice downstairs that non-residents aren't allowed in rooms.'

'Does it, now?' Daniel gave her a rather too-knowing smile. 'All right then. Downstairs it is.'

On shaking legs, Charis led Daniel down the stairs and into the lounge. To her relief she saw Mackenzie still staring into his drink, and when he looked up she tried to catch his eye, to convey her distress, to make him see past what everyone else saw. But he merely registered surprise.

'Ms Boulton.'

Daniel put an arm around her shoulder. 'Not for much longer, mate.' He grinned at Charis, that sweet, endearing grin with which he'd won her heart in another life. 'Charis Thorne always sounded better – you said so yourself, didn't you?'

She somehow smiled at him, then turned back to the Scot. 'Can we join you, Mr Mackenzie? You look a bit lonely sitting there by yourself.'

'Leave him alone, love,' Daniel said, tightening his hold on her shoulder. 'He's probably just winding down after a busy day.'

'Not at all.' Mackenzie sat up straighter and indicated the banquette opposite. 'Please, sit down.'

Charis felt Daniel's fingers digging into her upper arms, and just managed not to cry out; she'd done that before, and lived to regret it. 'Just for a few minutes,' she said, as much an appeasement to her ex-husband as a promise to Mackenzie.

Daniel ushered her in first, so that she sat in the corner, pinned. He put a hand over hers where it lay on the table. 'You two know each other, then?'

'No,' they both said together. 'Not really,' Charis went on. 'I'm afraid I gave Mr Mackenzie a bit of a hard time when I thought he'd stolen my new camera.'

'This one?' Daniel dug into his coat pocket. 'Silly girl, you left it in your sister's flat. She asked me to bring it for you since I was coming up.'

Charis's chest tightened. Of course he had been to Suze's; how else would he have found out where she was camping? But how did he know about the hotel? The room number? He must have been following her for the last day, at least. And now it was obvious too, who Jamie had seen hanging around the car at the blackhouse. Was he hoping to find her with some new bloke?

Mackenzie was studying Daniel lazily over his glass. 'So, you've come to take your errant wife back home then? Good luck.'

Daniel laughed, affection written all over his face. 'I think we've worked out our differences now, haven't we, love?'

'Even after what I did?' Charis hoped the reminder might provoke him into betraying what she knew hid behind the smile, and she tried to withdraw her hand from beneath his, but he lifted it to his lips instead, and smiled at her.

'Exactly! I'm the injured party, and if I can forgive you, you've got no reason to stay hidden away up here.'

'I'm not hiding,' she pointed out tightly, feeling his breath hot on her skin. She tried not to show her revulsion; doing so would work against her later. In private. 'You know I've always wanted to come to Scotland.'

Mackenzie looked from one to the other. 'I've no notion of what you've done to him, Ms Boulton, but it seems to me you've got a very forgiving bloke there.' He took a deep swallow of his pint. 'Perhaps you should just listen to him and go back to Scouse City.'

For a second Daniel's eyes glinted at the faint distaste in Mackenzie's tone, but then he laughed. 'He's right, Charis. We'll fetch the kid tonight, from his mate's. It'll save you a packet on this place.'

Mackenzie's expression did not change, and Charis's heart beat a little faster. He knew Jamie was upstairs, so why didn't he seem surprised by what Daniel had said? Unless he already suspected that the charmer was not what he seemed. The little dig about their hometown, too, had almost achieved what she had not. She tried once more to catch Mackenzie's eye, but he was smiling at Daniel in a calm, friendly manner, and it was impossible to read him.

'So that's the elusive camera?' He nodded at it, where it sat on the table in front of Charis. 'It's a nice one, you're right.'

'Daft girl,' Daniel teased. 'All that money wasted on a gadget like that. Bet your phone takes pictures that're just as good.'

'I saved up for it!' Charis was unable to keep her old self from blurting. 'And Suze gave me a—'

'A voucher, I know. She told me.' Daniel sighed, drew her close, and kissed her temple. 'Don't be so defensive, pet. I don't mind about you spending the money. Everyone's got to have a hobby, and you were always great at taking holiday snaps. You can use it when I take you and the kid to Greece in September.'

'May I see?' Mackenzie reached out and picked up the camera.

Daniel tried to grab it, but he wasn't quick enough. 'That belongs to my wife.'

'It'll just be a few test shots though, won't it? Mind if I look?'

'The battery's dead,' Daniel began, but fell into silence as the screen flared to life. 'Well it won't last long then,' he muttered.

Mackenzie began paging through the shots. 'Ah, that must be the view from your living room, aye?' He turned the camera so Charis could see her flat's window seat, and a road beyond with a blurred car whizzing by.

'Give it her back, mate,' Daniel said. 'You'll embarrass her if they're all as bad as that one.'

'*Are* you embarrassed?' Mackenzie asked her. She glanced at Daniel and saw the old, dangerous glint in his eye. Her courage failed her.

'A bit,' she confessed. 'Don't bother with any more.'

'Oh, I'm sure they'll get better,' Mackenzie said, and carried on paging. Charis could have thrown her arms around him, but settled for shrugging at Daniel; she'd tried, at least.

Eventually Mackenzie put the camera down. Charis leaned over so she could see the whole screen; it was a picture of Jamie, shortly after they'd arrived, doing battle with the fly sheet, and with instructions on how to assemble their tent blowing around him.

She remembered being helpless with laughter as she was taking it, overwhelmed by the sense of freedom after the closeness of the city, and with their holiday stretching before them. Outlander country. Now her old life was tightening its grip on her again, and thank God Jamie had had the sense not to come out of the room when he'd heard his father's voice.

'I've only been to Liverpool once,' Mackenzie said at length, his eyes back on Daniel. 'Really nice place. I remember the docks, the statue of the Beatles, the big shopping centre – Liverpool One, isn't it? Oh, and the Liver Bird by the pier. Don't recall seeing any mountains, though.' He smiled, but beneath it Charis saw a fierce and even disturbing anger. His shoulders were set, and there was a muscle jumping in his jaw, but his tone was conversational. 'You're a lying wee bastard, aren't you?'

Daniel hesitated, then shook his head. He had no choice, after all. 'All right, so I took the camera.' He turned to Charis, his eyes pleading. 'But it was only so I had an excuse to come and find you. To give it you back, and maybe convince you I've changed, that I want you and the boy to come home.'

'His name's Jamie,' Charis said quietly. 'Why do you never use his name?'

Daniel gave her a pained look. 'Maybe because you named him after some character in a book, some big hero it was impossible for me to live up to?'

'He was actually named for my granddad, not that you were ever interested enough to ask. You didn't even have one suggestion when I tried to get you to talk about it – you couldn't have cared less, and you didn't mind letting me know it.'

Daniel looked as if he wanted to argue, but he subsided again. 'Jamie, then. I do care about him, of course I do; he's my son. I'll prove it to you both if you just come home.' He took her hand again, and although he was gentle, it felt as if a vice had her fingers and was crushing them one by one. 'Okay, Charis-with-a-c-h...' He flashed Mackenzie a quick smile. 'She always says it like that, like it's her whole name. *Charis-with-a—*'

'Shut up,' Mackenzie said mildly. 'If you so much as open that vile mouth once more, I'll plant my fist in it. Understand?'

Daniel froze, and let go of Charis's hand. She didn't know whether to cheer or to search for somewhere to hide; if this went wrong, and Daniel was somehow still able to convince Mackenzie, the last four years of her life might as well never have happened. Including the divorce.

'Go upstairs and get your wee lad,' Mackenzie said to her, not taking his eyes off Daniel. 'I'll find you somewhere safe to stay for the night.'

'Just a sec,' Daniel said, incredulous. 'Are you seriously telling me to—'

'Didn't you hear me?' Mackenzie was on his feet in seconds, and hauling Daniel out of the booth. He pushed him towards the door. 'Away and raffle yer doughnut.'

Daniel tried once more to appeal to her. 'Sweetheart, I know you still care for me. For what we had.' When that had no effect, his voice took on a harder edge. 'You're being cruel to the kid you claim to love, stealing his only chance to be part of a proper family.'

Charis's temper instantly caught alight, but before she could snap anything back, Mackenzie spoke in a low, fierce voice, directly into Daniel's ear. 'Go now, or no-one'll find the pieces.'

Daniel flinched, but threw the Scot a furious look. He ran his hands through his hair and wiped them on his jeans – Charis could see they were shaking, but she couldn't tell if it was anger or fear. And then he turned away, dug in his pocket for a set of keys, and left.

Charis stared as the door swung shut behind him, stunned and relieved; Daniel Thorne had finally met someone he'd not been able to fool.

'Thank you,' she began, knowing the words sounded thin and inadequate. 'But...*raffle yer doughnut?*'

'My partner's from Glasgow; it's one of her favourite sayings.' He gave her a brief grin. 'Go and get Jamie and your stuff. She'll put you both up tonight.'

Charis mused on that as she stepped out of the lift. If he had a partner, what was he doing drinking alone in the hotel now Stein had gone? But thank God he had been; no-one else had ever seen as quickly through Daniel's convincing act of tenderness and forgiveness. She put her key in the door, wondering what the partner was like, and oddly certain she would be the polar opposite of the grim-faced Scot: smiling and easy-going; humorous, judging from the doughnut thing; a home-making sort; used to reining in Mackenzie's temper and throwing oil on his clearly troubled waters. Well, good luck to *her*.

'Sorry to get you up again, Jay,' she said as she went in, 'but we're not staying here after... Jamie?' She gazed around, and her blood ran sluggish and chilly in her veins. The sheets of Jamie's bed were rumpled, but the pillows were on the floor and the door to the *en suite* stood open, showing the tiny bathroom was empty. 'Jamie!'

There was no response. Charis took a deep, slow breath and forced herself to think. Had he perhaps gone to find her for some reason? Maybe he was even now down in the lounge searching for her, having taken the stairs while she took the lift? What if he'd bumped into Daniel in the lobby?

Halfway along the corridor to the stairs, she was struck by another thought: the American was here in the hotel, and Jamie was still fixated on him. Mackenzie had sworn they were doing nothing illegal, but something was definitely up, and if Jamie had disobeyed her and been playing out in the corridors he might have seen the American and followed him again, determined to prove himself right. He could be out on the streets, and once out there anything might happen to him – especially if Daniel were still hanging around.

Almost tripping over her own feet, Charis took the stairs at a run, leaping down the last few. She scanned the lobby, and seeing no sign of Jamie, Daniel or the American, she pushed open the door to the lounge. Mackenzie was just pulling on his leather jacket; when he saw that she was unable to speak, he came over.

'What's happened? Where's Jamie?'

'The room's empty.'

Mackenzie's face darkened. 'Gone off with your ex, d'you think?'

'Maybe... No.' Charis couldn't believe she'd considered it, even for a second. 'Daniel's never wanted Jamie; the only reason he'd have tried to see him upstairs was to get to me.'

'Okay. Stay calm, let's check again – maybe he's come back already.'

She led Mackenzie up the stairs, to the room she'd checked into with such a sense of relief a scant hour ago. It was exactly as she'd left it, and she moved to the phone on the bedside table. 'I'm calling the police.'

'No!' Mackenzie was at her side in a second, taking the phone off her.

Charis snatched it back, astonished and furious. 'What the bloody hell d'you think you're doing?'

'Listen to me,' Mackenzie said, his tone calmer now. 'You could file a report, fine, but the police will just tie you up with questions when we could be out there searching ourselves.'

Charis shook her head. 'I don't care what you and that American are up to. I don't care if you lied and said it was legal when it's not. I just want my boy back.'

'Then come with me now, while there's still a chance he hasn't gone far.'

She hesitated, then, conceding the sense of it, she replaced the phone in its charging cradle; whatever Mackenzie's motives for not wanting the police involved, he was right about being detained by pointless questions.

'Let's go then,' she said. Mackenzie looked at her, and she could see he wanted to explain, but she turned away and dragged her jacket out of her bag.

'Does he have a mobile?' Mackenzie asked.

'No. And nor do I.' Seeing his incredulous expression, she scowled. 'I left it on the charger at home, okay?'

Mackenzie picked up the phone again and called reception, instructing them to keep their eyes out for a ten-year-old boy wandering around alone, and giving them his own mobile number to call. As he put the phone down, Charis noticed something that renewed her conviction that Jamie had gone following the American again.

'His clothes are gone. All except his T shirt, anyway. And so's his asthma inhaler.'

'And he was in bed when you left him?'

'Yeah, in his PJs. That means he probably left of his own accord, right? I mean, the lad deserves a thick ear for not staying in bed, but if he's dressed, that means no-one snatched him from his bed at least.'

'Aye, well, that certainly puts a positive slant on things.' But Mackenzie's reserved tone seemed more shadow than light, and she shook her head, exasperated and annoyed.

'And you don't want to bring in the police. Speaks volumes.' She pushed open the fire door, and Mackenzie was right behind her.

'There's a good reason—'

'Not interested, Mackenzie. If I can't find Jamie, I'm bloody well going to them whether it's on your list of good ideas or not.'

They went out through the back door, emerging alongside the river that gave the hotel its name; the air out here was damp and chilly, the night almost fully on them. Charis started down the path that led along the side of the hotel, and she kept staring down to where the river flowed. What if Jamie had fallen? No-one would have seen him, his screams would have gone unheard... He might have hit his head, then there would have been no sound at all. She stopped suddenly, the horror of her thoughts dropping icicles into her blood. Mackenzie seemed to read her mind.

'It's not deep here,' he said in a gentle voice, 'or fast enough. You can see that in full daylight. If he fell in, even if he'd been knocked out, he wouldn't have been carried away, not from here. We'd have found him by now, aye?'

Charis let her breath out, nodding slowly. They reached the end of the path, where it met the car park at the front of the hotel. Charis looked around at the suddenly terrifying shapes of the mountains pressing down on them – not graceful and elegantly sculpted, like the post cards they sold in the petrol stations, but lumpy, black and hostile.

She tried to picture Jamie, wherever he was; if he was scared, if he'd cried for her or was maybe even still crying... The thought hurt too much, and she'd be no good to him if she drove herself crazy, so instead she pictured him following the American, notebook poised, face alight with excitement. It helped a little, and she turned back to ask which way they should start walking now, but the words didn't come.

Mackenzie was staring away up into the dark mountains, and his face was bleakly hopeless; he'd already written Jamie off, already believed the worst. Wouldn't she know if that had happened? She'd surely feel Jamie's loss like the shrivelling of her own heart, with nothing left to keep it full. Wherever he was he was alive, and the moment she stopped believing that, would be the moment he died.

Chapter Eight

Los Angeles, California

THE SUN's rays ricocheted off the white stone veranda, and into Sarah Wallace's eyes, the moment she stepped out through the sliding doors. Shooting an ineffectual glare at the unrelenting blue sky, Sarah fanned the open neck of her snow-white linen shirt with a hand she could barely lift, then picked up the drink she'd left on the table and moved back into the cooler – and blessedly dimmer – lounge. She sank gratefully into the couch and pulled off one high-heeled shoe, rubbing at her aching instep, then caught sight of her phone sitting on the smoked glass coffee table, smug in the knowledge that it had done its work. Sarah threw her shoe at it. It was times like this she wished she still smoked.

Damn Andy Stein! He was a nice enough bloke, but why did he have to be so pathetically incompetent? Ever since she'd talked about this to Don Bradley she'd known she was leaving herself wide open to be cheated, but had always considered it worth the risk. Now she'd been proved right on both counts, she *should* have been able to send Andy in there and have him sort it out. It should have been perfectly straightforward. But letting some kid listen in on his conversation and then run to his mother... Just how careless was he? Jesus!

She went over what he'd said when he'd called her yesterday, trying to figure out if he'd said her name or given anything else away, and one phrase stuck in her mind like a bit of apple in the back of her throat: *I can lie to those two cops, sure. Tell them there's a problem with the money transfer.*

God, *lie to the cops?* Seriously? In front of a small boy? Talk about a red rag to a bull. Then another call from him had put the icing on the cake: Don was calling her bluff. Too many interested parties poking around, apparently, so he and his little buddy were cooling off until the path was clear. What right did *they* have to pull out? Knowing they were screwing her over made it worse, and Sarah had hung up on Andy in a dark temper. It was one thing to have him stall things until she had a chance to get over there, but to get them spooked to the extent that they were threatening to withdraw what was already on the table... No. Wouldn't happen.

Her cab was due any minute, the plane left in less than three hours, and there was only one sure way to sort this out. She retrieved her phone from the floor and called Andy back. 'I can't have them taking control,' she said, without preamble. 'Get the boy, get him out of the hotel, and get the little shit out of my hair. Then get Bradley back on side. Fast.'

'Sarah, I don't—'

'Shut up! You've fucked this up; you put it right. Listen carefully – there's this place I knew as a kid, but it's hard to find. And you'll need to fix it up so he can't get out. Got a pen?'

In the cab on the way to the airport she turned the whole mess over in her mind until she was ready to scream. It didn't take a genius, knowing what she knew now, to work out where Dad and his cronies had hidden those jewels they'd stolen from their friend all those years ago; she remembered spotting the three figurines in Dad's study not long after the robbery, and how she'd been immediately drawn to them. He'd said he was arranging to auction them on behalf of a friend who'd left the country.

They'd been so pretty she had picked one up, and, surprised at the unevenness of the weight in her hand, she had nearly dropped it. Dad had gone mad, clipped her around the ear, and sent her out of the room. Then the little statues had simply vanished; no auction, no friend. Just one day there, the next day gone. It wasn't until a few years later that it had all clicked into place, and the recent phone call from an old friend had clinched it.

Setting up this deal had been a clever move on Don's part, she acknowledged with reluctant appreciation; all he'd needed was her confirmation that the statues were still out there, and he'd offered to find them. Lo and behold, a scant few weeks later, there they were. Perfect!

Too perfect.

How fortunate then, that she remembered Don Bradley of old. Rob Doohan had done his godfatherly duty and looked out for her, which included telling her about the barely perceptible flaw Dougie Cameron had built into the bases of the figurines her father had commissioned. *Just in case*, he'd said. No-one else alive knew about that flaw, and it was odds-on Andy was right, and that Don was trying to fob her off with fakes, but eventually his greed would lead her to the real thing, and the missing part of the Spence collection. All of it, including the most important piece. And then they would have a long talk about what he deserved for crossing her.

Tom Bradley International Terminal at LAX was a seething cliché of shrieking children, harassed businessmen and women, and sunburned tourists. *Bradley...* Christ, he was everywhere! Sarah was momentarily transfixed as the iconic clock tower came to life with its hourly show, then she shook it off and made her way to the British Airways desk. She tried to ignore the noise, focusing instead on the PA system announcements; delays were something she couldn't afford if she were to make the connecting flight from Heathrow to Inverness. Time was short, and getting shorter well out of proportion to the tale told by that gorgeous clock... Thank goodness she only had cabin luggage, so at least checking in was quick and automated.

She bought a magazine, and some pills for the headache that pushed at the side of her skull, and tried not to think too far ahead in case the frustration sent her over the edge. It was all taking so long, and in the meantime, in Scotland, things were getting rapidly out of control.

Finally boarded and belted, Sarah tried to concentrate on the magazine, but it wasn't working. All she could see was Don's face, at least as she remembered it, but she had no idea how he'd fared in the battle with the last thirty years. He'd been quite attractive back in the day; six years older than her, a police officer, and therefore naturally quite exciting to a sixteen-year-old. He'd seemed such a man of the world – turned out to be more of a man in his own head, but it'd been okay for a while. Useful enough, and they'd kept their secret on-off thing going right up until she'd left Scotland. He'd probably still be handsome now; he'd had those sort of looks that would age quite gracefully as long as he'd taken care of himself. But no matter – if seduction turned out to be the key to getting back what was hers, she'd fuck a stoat if it asked nicely.

She made short work of letting the woman in the seat next to her know she was not looking for a travelling companion, and then, left blissfully in peace, found she was able to focus on the task ahead without feeling that time was overtaking her; she would lose another fifteen hours on the combined flights, but still things weren't as dire as they'd seemed. Everyone had to sleep, after all.

Once in Inverness, she would be able to collect the one item she hadn't been able to risk bringing with her, and the ammunition to go with it. Then, a hire car to the good, and armed, she should be able to make her old home by late Sunday afternoon. The little boy wouldn't be a problem now, and she'd be able to deal with Don as the situation dictated.

After that it was just a case of finding the Fury. She closed her eyes and willed the treasured image to the front of her mind. As always it took very little effort, and the glowing, shifting fire, vivid against the darkness of the stone, gradually changed to flames of a very different kind: fire that was almost as hypnotic, fire that instilled a sense of terror and awe, and that had led her to be sitting here, now, with enough money to buy and sell Don Bradley a hundred times over, with or without the missing third of the Spence collection.

But that collection, and the glowing, dark heart of it, was hers by rights, thanks to her father's enterprise, and she meant to have it. She wondered how good this private detective Andy had hired was, and if he had the local knowledge he'd undoubtedly need. Andy hadn't told her much about him, just that the office was a shambles, the place was about to fold by the looks of it, and the agency was evidently relieved to have a high-paying client to take the financial load off. Good; he'd be more likely to want to do the job right.

She pondered the name: Paul Mackenzie. The name was as neutral as it could be, but still something about it tugged at her memory. She had a vague image of a tallish kid, but he must have been a lot younger than her, otherwise she'd have paid more attention; she'd always liked them tall. Andy was tall too, and athletic – even after all this time she responded to him physically, but he was weak. As long as he did as he was told he'd be fine, but loose ends were loose ends, and Sarah was nothing if not thorough.

Glenlowrie Estate

Jamie coughed. It was a dry, hacking sound, signalling the onset of another attack, and he instinctively raised his inhaler before he remembered and threw it away miserably. This had all begun to feel like a dream, too terrible to be really happening. Even now, as he sat huddled around his knees on the cold stone floor, it all seemed removed from him in some way; as if he were reading about it, or even watching it on TV. He coughed again. That was how it had all started, back there in the safety and warmth of the hotel, a simple dry cough.

He'd lain in his deep, comfortable bed, wondering what had triggered it this time. Then he'd felt the scratchy prickle on his cheek. Feather pillows. Ugh! He sat up and reached for his inhaler, and then his T shirt, and spread the shirt on the pillow as a barrier.

The cough came again, and with it a familiar tight feeling across his chest. Wheezing and frustrated, Jamie flung his pillows onto the floor and gave himself two puffs of Salbutamol. His airways loosened, but when he looked around for something to freshen his mouth he saw the glass of water by the bed had gone cloudy, and probably wouldn't taste any better than the medicine. At least the room had a little bathroom on the side, which was pretty cool.

On his way to re-fill the glass, he remembered the vending machine he'd seen at the far end of the corridor, and his taste buds woke up; a Coke would be way nicer than warmish water. Practically feeling the fizz dancing on his furry tongue already, he quickly dragged his jeans on over his pyjamas, stuffed his inhaler into the pocket, and pulled his jumper on in case anyone saw him.

He'd kicked his shoes right under the bed when he got undressed, but he didn't need them anyway; this place had carpets posher than anywhere he'd ever seen. He patted his pockets for the last two-pound coin to his name, then padded barefoot to the door and unlocked it, hoping his mother wasn't on her way back; Coke was a no-no, even on holiday – it was water or nothing at this time of night. He considered wedging the door open with one of their bags, but picked up the key instead. If she caught him outside the room against her orders she'd be annoyed enough, but leaving the room unlocked, especially after what had happened with the tent, would send her ballistic.

There was no-one in the corridor, and Jamie carefully locked the door behind him and fixed his gaze on the glass-fronted machine near the top of the stairs. Maybe he could even spend the rest on a Mars Bar, then claim he'd lost the coin on the moors.

Suddenly sure his mother would appear on the stairs, summoned by the lie that had popped into his head, he ran to the machine. He punched the button for the chocolate first, that being the bigger offence.

His change clunked too loudly into the little tray, and as Jamie double-checked the number for Coke, he heard someone coming up the stairs. They hadn't rounded the corner yet – it could be anyone, but equally, it *could* be his mother; she'd been downstairs for at least twenty minutes and was probably getting twitchy by now, as usual. He bit his lip, glancing at the machine, then at the stairs... He'd never have time to run back to his room without being seen, and if she caught him running she'd want to know what the hell he was doing anyway.

Nothing else for it; he'd just have to wait, and if it was her, he'd sacrifice the Coke and select water instead. Pretending to stare intently at the choices, he felt his heart speed up as his gaze slid sideways and he recognised the figure who rounded the corner. Not his mother, but the American. Jamie felt the grin spread over his face; this was his chance to prove he wasn't just playing, and his mother couldn't be annoyed with him being out of bed if he were performing a public duty.

He could see it now, like they did in the old films Mum liked watching. Black and white newspapers spinning up, bigger and bigger until the headlines filled the screen:

Whizza Whizza Whizza Whizza – BAM! Ten-year-old Solves Highland Mystery!

Whizza Whizza Whizza Whizza – BAM! Villains Caught by Intrepid Young Investigator! Whizza Whizza Whizza Whizza – BAM! American Gangster Outwitted by Liverpool Boy!

Jamie checked for his notebook; it was still there in his back pocket, complete with the tiny pen he'd 'borrowed' from the Lotto station at the motorway services on the way up. He slid, without really thinking, into the gap between the vending machine and the wall, but the gap wasn't very big and the American only had to glance to his left to see him there. As he did so, his expression was a strange one; narrow-eyed annoyance fading quickly into a tight smile that didn't look at all happy.

'I'm, uh, just getting a Coke,' Jamie croaked, not even sure why he felt he had to explain his presence. The excitement of imagining those headlines was replaced by sudden fear as the American flicked a glance behind him to check they were alone, then stepped close, effectively pinning Jamie into his little corner.

'I've about had it up to here with you,' he said, 'but you've saved me a job.' The accent didn't sound at all cool any more; his voice was flat and held no expression at all. Jamie squeezed further back, and yelped as a hand shot out and seized his wrist. He tried to tug away, but the grip was hard and didn't budge.

'You're coming with me, and if you so much as whisper, I'm going to take this key and shove it right through your eyeball until it pops. Got me?'

Jamie's breath clamped off as the key appeared in front of his right eye, close enough to brush the lashes. He closed both his eyes tight, scared to nod in case the key jabbed him anyway. The notion that anyone could have been play-acting was wiped away completely; this was too real.

He grunted as he was pulled out into the corridor, and stared at the stairwell in the frantic hopes of seeing a friendly face; his mother, a comfortingly outraged fellow guest, anyone.

But no-one appeared, and the next moment he was pushed into a room identical to his own. It smelled horrible, like his dad's car used to.

Immediately the cough started up again – that smell always did it. Aftershave or something; it tickled, made him cough, and then it got hard to breathe. The moment the thought crossed his mind, it became reality. His chest locked up and his fingers found the inhaler in his pocket, but before he could take it out, the American seized both his arms and pulled them behind his back.

'No, please!' It came out as nothing more than a thin, wheezing whistle, and Jamie struggled to turn, but the man's grip was too strong.

'What did I tell you? Shut your mouth!'

The American's grip changed, and as Jamie felt something cool and rough wrapped around his wrists, he did the only thing he could think of; he let his knees buckle and slumped to the floor. It hurt his arms but it was worth it; the half-tied leather belt whipped apart, and as the American reached down to drag him up again, Jamie wriggled away, giving himself enough time to grab the inhaler from his jeans. He slammed it into his mouth, triggering relief in the same moment. Able to breathe again, his focus on the man standing over him cleared, and Jamie saw with surprise that he seemed suddenly uncertain.

'Shit. I'm...sorry. That must have been – look, I've got orders, okay?'

'I won't tell anyone anything, I promise,' Jamie said, hope propelling him to his feet, but the man shook his head.

'Like I said, orders.'

Jamie was mortified to feel the prickle of tears at the back of his nose and eyes. He gripped his inhaler tight, and the man glared at him with mounting exasperation.

'Okay! I won't tie you – you look like you're gonna need that thing again.' The tone hardened again. 'But you're coming with me, and there's a new deal on the table, okay? You make me wish I hadn't laid eyes on you, and I'll see that your mom regrets it.'

Cold swept Jamie from head to toe and he started to shake. The accent might be different, but the words might as easily have been his dad's. 'What will you do?'

'Me? Nothing. But you know that big Scottish guy you've seen hanging around with me? I guess you know he's got a pretty mean streak. He already has reason to think your mom is trouble, and he's just a phone call away. See?'

Jamie nodded, silent, but the tears spilled over as the American pulled him towards the door. The corridor was still empty, and it only took a moment for them to reach the fire door to the back stair-case. As he passed his own room, he gave it a longing look. If he'd left the door wedged open after all he would have seen the messed up bed, and the pillows on the floor where he'd shoved them in a fit of annoyance... The sheets were probably even still warm.

The door at the end led out to a chilly stairwell, and as they descended the bare concrete steps Jamie felt a cold pressure on the back of his neck, at the base of his skull.

'We meet anyone out here and you paste a smile on, okay? This key could do as much damage to your spinal cord as it could to your eyeball.'

Jamie didn't answer, but he couldn't help wondering why, if this man was such a big villain, he hadn't threatened him with a gun, or at least a knife – what was all this stupid key stuff about? He found a spark of hope in it, simply because it *was* stupid, and with that came the confidence to ask for something to drink.

'You made me leave my Coke in the machine,' he pointed out.

'I'll see what I've got when we get in the car. Now move it.' The American really sounded worried now; his voice was tight, and Jamie could tell without looking that he was checking behind them, as well as ahead, to ensure they were still alone.

At the bottom of the stairs, Jamie saw the corridor that led back in to the lobby, but the idea of catching someone's attention faded, as they went out through a side door instead and emerged onto a path beside the river. To Jamie's surprise it was still quite light, and he heard the American curse under his breath as if he were surprised too. And annoyed.

He saw their own hire car, parked slightly skewed in his mother's typical hurried way, with her favourite smiley-face air freshener and the mess of sleeping bags and clothing on the back seat; it all looked so normal he felt like crying again. His bare feet shrank from the hard ground, and he stopped still, wanting to reach down and brush the soles to loosen the gravel that was stuck in his skin, but not daring to.

Pressure from the key on the back of his neck forced him to limp onwards. He might have thought the key a stupid weapon, but it was starting to hurt – it was easier to believe now that it could do him some real harm. He still had his own in his pocket, but there was no question of reaching for it and trying to return the threat. The American hustled him across to his own vehicle, and as Jamie lay trembling on the back seat of the big posh car he'd admired so much earlier, he wondered how real that threat to his mother was.

The Scottish man had seemed okay, but tough. Jamie

remembered the coldness of his expression when he'd looked at his mother, and she clearly hadn't trusted him either. Maybe she would go to that nice bloke in the shop where they'd found Aunty Suze's present, and ask for his help; she'd liked him, and he'd seemed like he would be good in a fight. In the meantime he himself would do exactly as he was told, and it would all be okay. As soon as whatever the American was doing was finished it would all go back to normal; it had to.

The drive seemed to last for hours, and it had grown dark, but Jamie's watch was back on the bedside table in the hotel. He'd been allowed to sit up once they were out of town, but the road wound through tight bends, rose and dipped, and rose again, leaving him feeling queasy nevertheless.

The car doors were all locked, but one glance out of his window told him that, even if they hadn't been, to try and jump from the car would be the very worst thing he could do. On one side was the high, steep mountainside, where he'd be caught instantly, and then who knew what would happen? The other side fell away from them, the bottom too far down to see, the ground littered with boulders and gorse bushes; it was lit up by the car's headlights for a second, then plunged back into cold darkness.

Finally they stopped outside an old stone building, crumbling at both ends and with gaping, dark holes in the roof. There was a sound from the hill nearby, which was hard to identify for a moment, but which Jamie finally recognised as tumbling water. The thought of it, cold and fresh, made his mouth feel dryer than ever.

The American left the car's lights on and the engine running, while he half pulled, half carried Jamie to the broken front door and kicked it open. Once inside, Jamie felt his chest tighten immediately in the musty, mouldy atmosphere. He coughed, the loud barking sound coming back at him strangely from the uneven walls and ceiling. He couldn't stay here...

'I'll die,' he pleaded, beginning to cry again. He took a blast from his inhaler and tried to hang back as his captor strode to the end of the short passage, pulling him along.

'It won't be for long, and you've got your...thing that you need.'

The grip on Jamie's arm hurt badly, and he twisted to get away, but the American jerked him forward and he fell, skinning his knees even through the jeans and pyjamas. He sobbed harder, terrified both for himself and that, in his extreme fear, he would do something that would end up hurting his mother.

The car's headlights shone right into this room, and Jamie saw into the far corner where a heavy-looking door stood open, waiting to swallow him.

'No!' He pulled back again. 'You can't put me in there. Please, I won't run away, I promise, just please don't make me go in there!'

'You want to get your mom killed?'

'No!' Jamie struggled harder, so hard that he took the American by surprise and actually managed to wrench free. He stood for a second, as stunned as the man in front of him, before they both came to full awareness at the same moment. Jamie broke and ran, out into the narrow passage, his heart hammering wildly... He could actually get away! He even felt the mountain breeze from the open door brush his skin, then there was a weight on his back, and the stone floor came up and smacked him on the jaw as he was brought down from behind. The pain and disappointment were too big for him to brush away, to pretend it didn't matter, and he felt fresh tears flood his eyes.

The American pulled him to his feet, and the voice in

Jamie's ear drove the fear still deeper into his bones. 'You better hope Mackenzie doesn't find out about this – he's just itching for an excuse, and it may be you just gave it to him.'

Jamie pictured his mother, grown up, yet as vulnerable as a child next to the looming spectre of the man he now knew was called Mackenzie. His hatred for the man flared until he felt sick, and he stumbled into the tiny room, helped by a none-too-gentle shove from the American. He looked around through the heavy curtain of tears, but the American had become just a blurred shape, a darker shadow among the grey.

The shadow spoke. 'Sit down.' He did so. 'Someone will be here to check on you tomorrow. Here...' Jamie felt a plastic bottle land heavily in his lap. 'It's just water but it'll keep you going. Don't think about trying to get out; you'll just hurt your-self and get nowhere. And your mom won't thank you.'

The door slammed, plunging Jamie into crushing black-ness. He closed his eyes, trying to pretend that was the only reason it was so dark, as the chill of the long-unused room started to seep through his clothes – he'd never known such pure, heavy darkness. He wasn't even sure he'd opened his eyes again, and had to feel them with trembling fingers to convince himself.

He felt a tickle in the back of his throat and reached for his inhaler just in case it proved to be more than a normal cough. It didn't, but he still felt a surge of panic when he couldn't find what he was looking for. In rising panic, he slapped his pockets and at last found the little plastic tube, which he gripped tightly as he sat back against the wall, too scared to move any more.

Before long he felt the inevitable sensation again, and the more he worried about it, the harder it got to breathe. He held off using the inhaler for as long as he could, and when he couldn't ignore the pressure any longer, he fired off a dose, gasping it into his lungs gratefully. He breathed out, then triggered it once more to be sure, and his scalp prickled in horror: nothing left, just the faint, medicinal taste, and an empty container.

Numbed by this new fear, Jamie let the tube drop into his lap, heard it hit the plastic bottle and took a small sip of the water, barely able to swallow it for the tightness of his sob-swollen throat. The attack passed – eventually. Through the confusion of thoughts that tumbled like displaced waterfalls in his head, he found one standing out clearly; whether through her death or his own, he was probably never going to see his mother again.

Chapter Nine

MADDY HIT *send* and logged out of her private e-mails. A quick check to make sure nothing with Kilbride's name on it had found its way into the agency account, and she finally felt able to draw a sigh of relief. Lying to your closest friend was like lying to yourself, but now the job labelled *Macnab* was done and dusted, and there was no reason for Paul to find out.

She switched off the laptop and checked around to make sure the desk was as tidy as she liked it. Left to Paul it'd be permanently buried under piles of crap, newspapers and ancient letters from grateful clients; Tas had more of a sense of order, and no-one could call him a finicky child. At least on the days she worked later than Paul she could go in to a neat office the next day and actually find what she needed, when she needed it. He'd left a pile of freshly laundered, but very crumpled clothes on the edge of the desk, and, resisting the temptation to fold them, she picked them up to put them in the cupboard.

The office landline rang and she hesitated, then stifled a

groan, dumped the clothes again and answered it, grabbing a pen with her free hand. 'Clifford-Mackenzie.'

'Hi, it's Dad.'

Maddy sat back down and began to doodle on the pad in front of her. 'Hi, everything okay?'

'Fine. I couldn't get you on your mobile.'

She looked around, and patted her coat pocket. 'Sorry, I've left it in the car again.'

He gave an audible sigh, but she could imagine him rolling his eyes as he chose not to pick her up on that. 'I'm at Nick's,' he said instead. 'I just wanted to check you and the lad are still coming over for Nick's birthday on Sunday?'

'Try and stop us. Tas is already demanding advance intelligence of what kind of cake there'll be. He's put a vote in for Marshall.'

'Who?'

'Paw Patrol, Dad. Honestly!'

He laughed. 'Excellent. Right, I'll see you both then. Nick's new, uh, boyfriend, do we say? Seems wrong to use that word for a fifty-year-old. Anyway, he's coming too.'

'Nice. I've met Max – you'll like him.'

'Good. I trust your judgement. 'Til Sunday then.'

'Hang on. Before you go, I've been thinking about what we were talking about last night. About Don Bradley.'

'What about him?'

She doodled a decorative *DB* on the page. 'His name's come up in that job I told you about.'

'What, the Wallace girl and her inheritance?'

'It turns out she was seeing him at the time her dad was arrested for some robbery or other back in the late eighties. An investigation that was flawed because of a mistake he made.'

'That would have been before my time at Abergarry,' her

father mused. 'I was still based in Glasgow then. But... hang on, late eighties? She'd have been a child, surely?'

'Sixteen. Paul's older brother was at school with her, and he knew about it.' There was a pause, and Maddy doodled an equally ornate *SW*. 'Dad?'

'What?' He sounded distant, and Maddy frowned.

'Don't you think it's odd that Bradley was dating the Wallace girl, and somehow managed to mess up the evidence that might have convicted her father?'

'Very.'

'You've never said what your suspicions about him were. Was this it?'

'No, like I said, this was before we moved north.' He sighed. 'All right. You'll think this is a bit mad, but I suspected him, at the time, of having something to do with the death of Dougie Cameron.'

Maddy blinked, and the question she had been going to ask flew out of her mind. 'Really? You were seconded to CID for that, right?'

'Aye. And I know it was a so-called "break-in that went badly",' Tony went on, 'but there was something about Bradley over that weekend that bothered me. He lied about where he was, to me *and* to his wife. It wasn't until I challenged him that he admitted it, and tried to cover it as a mistake. Now you've said this about Sarah though, if they were still together—'

'He was probably off with her somewhere.' Maddy doodled *DC*, and circled all three sets of initials with a flourish. 'Well, at least now I know what kind of bee's been in your bonnet all this time.'

He let out a sigh. 'Simple explanation, after all.' There was a pause. 'Nick's said he'll help me get evidence that Bradley lied about covering a couple of shifts in Inverness that weekend.'

Maddy tensed and carefully replaced her pen. 'Is that fair on him?'

'It's nothing major, and he might not be able to check that far back anyway. He refused at first, but I remembered he was friends of a sort with young Ben Cameron back in the day, or acquaintances at least. So when I told him what I suspected, he agreed it wouldn't hurt to at least make sure Bradley wasn't doing *something* job-related when he said he was. Just as a start. Plus,' he went on, sounding surer of himself now, 'if we can shake him even a little bit, reputation-wise, it'd help your own investigation, wouldn't it?'

Maddy pursed her lips and reluctantly conceded that point. 'If we could prove he had a motive for screwing up that Wallace investigation, whatever it was...' She lifted her head as she heard the downstairs door open. 'Damn. Sounds like Paul's back for something; I'd better go before my evening's shot altogether. Don't make Nick do anything he doesn't want to. Promise?'

'I promise. But, Maddy, he's a grown man.'

'And one who'll do anything for you,' she reminded him. 'Okay, got to go. We'll see you both on Sunday.'

Paul's voice floated up from the stairwell. The voice that replied was feminine, and since they had no women on their books at present, that meant she was either a new client, when they were stretched work-wise as it was, or a female distraction that Paul could certainly do without just now. Either way this wasn't particularly good news.

The first person through the door confirmed her fears; no-one but Paul could get himself entangled with a woman like this, and at a time like this. She was clearly ten feet of trouble compressed into a tiny, five-foot frame, and all the more fero-cious because of it. Like an enraged kitten.

The kitten glared at her, then turned to go. 'I'm not here to meet your girlfriend, Mackenzie; this is just wasting time.'

'Wait.' Paul blocked the doorway, and Maddy suppressed a sigh; why not let the woman go, since she was so keen? She herself just wanted to go home and see what Gavin had cooked for dinner; it'd been a long day, and finally finishing off the Macnab report had left her drained. Her famous people skills were going to be tested to the limit on this one.

'Can I help or not?' she asked, politely.

'No you can't,' the woman snapped,' this is nothing to do with you. Mackenzie, why did you bring me here? I don't need somewhere to stay now, and you can say whatever you've got to say while we're out there, doing something useful.'

'Just sit down a minute. Please?'

It was so unlike Paul's usual gruff tone that Maddy looked more closely at them both. Paul brought the woman further into the room and, catching Maddy's eye, indicated the sectioned off area where four small sofas faced each other. He seemed tired, worried, and far too old, and Maddy tightened up in response; he'd been like this on his bad days. His worst days. The days when even she had been unable to reach him.

She sat down next to him, but he didn't appear to notice, and she could see his anxiety mirrored in the woman's pale, pinched expression.

'This is Maddy Clifford,' he said to the woman, who frowned.

'Clifford? I think I met your husband earlier.'

'I haven't got a husband,' Maddy began, but Paul briefly raised a quietening hand.

'Maddy, this is Charis Boulton. Her little boy's gone missing.'

Suddenly his expression made perfect sense. She squeezed his wrist, feeling the tension there and forcing him to look at her. When he did, she was at a loss to ease the dread she could see in his eyes, and could only imagine what was going on in his head.

The woman was a living echo of that fear, and Maddy turned to her, taking care to appear calm and positive. 'Okay. You came to the right place, Charis. We'll do our best to help.'

'What do you mean, "we"? How on earth could *you* possibly help?'

Maddy frowned, puzzled. 'Well, that's why you've come to an investigation service, isn't it?'

'A what?' Charis turned back to Paul. 'So you're... The American—'

'Andy Stein is a client, yes. But there's more to this case than I realised when I took it on.'

Charis was still fixing him with a look that clearly said: *this had better be relevant or I walk out right now.*

Paul nodded. 'Okay, simply put: Stein's girlfriend grew up near here, on the Glenlowrie Estate. Her name's Sarah Wallace. She moved to America when her family home burned down twenty-some years ago. Anyway, she's heard about some old family heirlooms that have turned up, and is negotiating a deal with the guy who's found them. Our favourite police officer.'

'The one I saw?'

'I don't know. Was the one you saw a bit overweight, fifty-ish, red in the face?'

'No, younger. About your age. Thin.'

'Right, well that's his pet sergeant, Mulholland. They don't work together, but he's in Bradley's pocket, and he'd have gone straight to him the moment you gave him my description.'

'How was I supposed to know—'

'Let him finish!' Busy with the Macnab case, Maddy wasn't clued in on all of this herself and wanted to hear it. Charis glared at her, and she glared back. Neither backed down, but when Paul spoke again Maddy was privately relieved; she'd been on the verge of caving in under that stare.

'Right, well the thing is, Stein's found out that the heirlooms, three porcelain figurines, are fakes. So he's hired me to find the originals. That's supposed to be my only involvement in this.'

'How did he know they're fake?' Maddy wanted to know.

'Who cares?' Charis half-rose to leave, but Paul gestured her back into her seat.

'Sarah says that, according to what her godfather told her years ago, there's a minute flaw built into the base of each one. Hardly more than a nick in the finish, but she told Stein to check for it in the ones Bradley showed him: no flaw. When Stein told her that, she instructed him to stall the deal until she can get over here herself and sort it out.'

'Are these things *that* valuable then?'

'Stein says they're mostly sentimental; they're all Sarah has left of her family.'

'Cobblers.'

'Quite.' He focused on Charis now. 'Stein's a twitchy wee bastard though, and he noticed Jamie sneaking around when he was on the phone to Sarah. Just playing, I know.' He held up a hand to forestall another heated interruption. 'But playing or not, he put the wind up Stein.'

'So you're saying that Stein went upstairs tonight while we

were talking, and persuaded Jamie to let him in?' Charis's voice was tight. 'How did he know which room was ours?'

'Didn't you see him looking at your key fob when we were all in the bar tonight?'

'I thought he was just...' Charis shook her head. 'Yeah, I saw him. But I still can't believe our kid would be that stupid, after all I've said about opening the door to strangers.'

'Maybe he was too excited to think about that?' Paul said gently. 'Boys being boys.'

'Maybe,' Charis conceded, 'but excited enough to go off with him? No. Not voluntarily.' She was sitting bowed on the very edge of the sofa, as if poised to leap up and run without warning. Maddy felt desperately sorry for her; she talked too much, and too loudly, but she looked worried out of her mind. Maybe if she just let Paul get on with things, he'd be able to help her.

'You think Stein's taken him somewhere then?' Charis repeated.

'I do, yes. We just need to make sure, because if he has, I'm as sure as I can be that Jamie'll be okay'

'How?'

'Stein's an annoying little shit, but I'd lay bets he's no killer.'

Charis flinched at the word, and Maddy shot Paul a glance that bypassed him completely; he was rubbing at his forehead as he always did when he was trying to think around noise.

'He needs to know about Jamie's asthma,' Charis fretted. 'Jamie might not tell him.' *Or not be able to,* was the unspoken end to that sentence, but they all heard it.

Paul nodded. 'We'll make sure he knows, somehow. Leave that to me. First we have to find out for sure if he's got him.'

'Call him now,' Maddy said.

'What, you think he's just going to own up?' Charis looked disgusted at the idea, and Maddy was about to bite back, but thankfully Paul was tuned in.

'Of course he won't, not right away. But if I can convince him I've changed my mind, that I think he was right about the boy, and offer to go after him myself, we can gauge his reaction.'

'And in any case,' Maddy put in, 'you should be able to tell by the sounds whether or not he's in the hotel. If he pretends to be, you've got him.'

Charis turned back to Paul. 'So what are you waiting for? I'll be quiet, I promise, just get calling.'

'I'll use the landline, so he knows I'm not following him.'

Paul went to the desk and found Stein's mobile number in the client index. Then he held up a hand for silence, looking particularly hard at Charis, Maddy noted with an inward smile.

'Mr Stein, it's Mackenzie. Sorry, is that the shower I can hear? Don't want to disturb you.' He shook his head, his sour expression indicating he'd just been lied to. 'Anyway, I was sitting here in the office, thinking about what you said about that bloody woman with her annoying kid.'

Charis's big blue eyes blazed fire at him. Talk about a test of keeping quiet – Maddy was reluctantly impressed.

'Well, I was thinking, maybe since Bradley's going to pull out of the deal otherwise, it might be worth sort of – removing the boy, just for a little while? You know, nothing too intense, just keep him out of the way for a bit... Oh, I see.' He paused, suddenly pale, his hand tightening on the phone. 'What makes you say that?'

He closed his eyes for a second, then looked over at Charis and nodded, his colour returning. Maddy saw Charis slump in relief, her hands gripped between her knees, her head bowed almost to her lap.

Paul was clearly growing annoyed with Stein again; Maddy recognised the way his eyebrows pulled together. 'Okay, you were right about him after all. Now I can get on with my real job then, unless you need me for babysitting duty? Right, well we'll talk it over tomorrow.'

He put the phone down and rubbed his face hard with both hands. 'There's no way he was in the hotel; that wasn't a shower I heard running, it was a waterfall. He's got Jamie up in the hills somewhere.'

Charis sat up, evidently ready to hit the mountains immediately, but Maddy saw Paul's mind turning inwards for a second, and spoke quickly to bring him back.

'What did he say to make you react like you did? Before you realised Jamie was okay?'

He stared at her, unfocused for a moment, then blinked. 'Right. When I said about taking Jamie out of the way for a while, he said "the kid won't be a problem any more." I felt sick, I don't mind telling you, and not just from the theatrical bullshit.'

'So how *do* you know Jamie's all right?' Charis was starting to sound scared again.

'Stein just said he would be kept out of the way until the deal was done. Thing is, he's got completely the wrong end of the stick; Bradley and Mulholland aren't the slightest bit worried about Jamie – they're more concerned that I'm involved.'

'Oh, naturally.' Charis scowled. 'You and your ego.'

Maddy met Paul's eyes. The woman evidently had no knowledge of the crackling hatred between him and Bradley, or its origin.

'So if *you're* the problem,' Charis persisted, 'why would he take my son?'

Paul sighed. 'Stein and Sarah still think it's him that's holding things up. We both thought he was the one Mulholland meant by "interested parties", but that was before I knew you'd described me to the police. And, like you said, they had no trouble recognising me from your description.'

'Oh great, so all this is your fault?'

'No!' Maddy broke in, rising to her feet. 'For Christ's sake try and get your bubble-head around this, okay? *This* has happened because your poor wee boy has a curiosity too big for his own good, and you've got a mouth to match. *This* isn't just about Jamie! Paul is now in danger, because *you* went whining to the police about some missing bloody camera and a wobbly tent—'

'I'm not in danger,' Paul protested.

'No?' Maddy's fear for him was spilling out as anger. 'Think about it! One word from Bradley, once he's got the slightest excuse, and *you're* going to wind up getting the shit kicked out of you, and that's only if you're lucky.' She sat back down, her entire body rigid. 'Bradley might be too soft nowadays to do much of anything himself, but that Mulholland is a nasty piece of work, and you know it. Otherwise why would you be so worried they'll find out about Jamie?'

Charis was looking from one to the other, her eyes wide and fearful. 'Is that true? You think if they find out about Jamie, they'll—'

'I don't know.' Paul reached across the gap and laid one hand over hers, and Maddy wasn't completely surprised to see she didn't pull away. 'We'll find him before they do, don't worry. When Stein last saw us, we were arguing, right?'

'No,' Charis said tartly. 'I was telling you where to get off. *You* were sitting there taking it like a big girl's blouse.'

'Good point.' Was he actually smiling? 'Anyway, that aside, as far as he knows, you and I are at each other's throats.'

'Well, we are.'

'Just shut up for five minutes, all right?'

Wonder of wonders she did, and Paul went on, 'Right. So he's got no reason to think I'd be doing anything to help you out. He'll trust me. I'll find out where Jamie is, one way or another.'

'And what does Charis do in the meantime?' Maddy asked.

The smile Paul flashed her was as wide as it was false, and she cursed him in block capitals in her head, knowing what was coming.

'I've got a little job for you and your dressing-up box,' he said, then turned back to Charis. 'Stein will expect you to call the police. Public proof that Jamie is out of the way. But Maddy is going to be your responding police officer, right? The two of you need to make a very public show of this. Stein's never met Maddy, so he'll not know who she really is, and in order to let him relax a bit, you're going to publicly point the finger at your ex-husband. Plenty of people saw him in the hotel, saw what went on there—'

'What did go on?' This much Maddy hadn't heard, and the mention of an ex-husband did little to ease her misgivings about Paul's involvement. If this ex of Charis's was anything like his former wife, things were about to get very noisy in quiet little Abergarry.

'Charis will fill you in later,' Paul said. 'All you've got to do, Charis, is tell the "constable" here all about Thorne, and that while we were upstairs he managed to get away from us. Got that?'

'Right. He went down the back stairs, and he said something nasty on the way.'

'Nice. What did he say? We need to get this bit straight in case Stein asks me too.'

'Um, he said Jamie hates living with me, and has been e-mailing his dad, asking him to get him away from me.'

'You're good,' Paul said, and a faint smile crossed Charis's face.

'Bit worrying when a private dick praises your lying capabilities.'

'Just take the compliment. Right, I'm going to find out what I can from Stein. Charis, go back to the hotel, wait 'til you get a message from me to say he's back, then put on your best performance, okay?'

While Charis used the lavatory, Maddy followed Paul to the top of the stairs. 'How're you going to do it?'

'Do what?'

She lowered her voice. 'Get Stein to open up to you. I mean, you've more or less promised you'll get her boy back, but what if...' She trailed away, seeing his face darken, then shrugged; might as well say it. 'I think you're maybe getting a bit too involved.'

'With *her*?'

'With the boy. It's unprofessional, but I do understand.'

'Don't talk crap!' He subsided, shaking his head. 'I'm sorry, Mads. I had a shaky moment earlier, but I honestly think the boy's all right. For now. And if I can get to him quickly enough, he'll carry on being all right, which is why no-one's going to stop me finding him.'

This time, Maddy silently finished for him, as the door closed.

Chapter Ten

Abergarry, November 2005

MACKENZIE ZIPPED up the bag one final time and slung it over his shoulder. Nearly time to leave; just time for a quick coffee. Finding an excuse not to attend this health and safety conference had been impossible, but then he'd known it would be, as a senior safety officer. Now it was time to go though, and he wished he'd tried even harder, though Kath had vowed the whole downstairs would be redecorated by the time he got back; she wouldn't thank him for hanging around and getting under her feet.

Coming into the kitchen, he saw she had already put down her paint roller and switched the kettle on. 'Rock star,' he said with a smile. 'You read my mind.'

'Aye, well.' She turned to grin at him. 'It's a simple enough one to read.'

She looked ridiculously young today, in her old clothes, her hair pulled back into a ponytail, and she whistled in appreciation of his own smart clothes, a notable contrast to his usual workwear. Her locket swung out and clinked against a cup as she leaned over to spoon the coffee; it got in the way constantly but she never took it off, saying that the tiny pictures inside kept her men close to her when she took her hiking parties up through the glen. She had gone through four silver chains in the nine years they'd been married, and he'd finally threaded the locket onto a leather thong and presented it to her on their anniversary three weeks ago. It made him as happy to see her wearing it, as it made her.

'What'll you be doing later? I'll call you when I get there.'

Kath pulled a face. 'No you won't; you'll meet up with your boozy friends and hit the bar the minute you've dumped your things.'

Mackenzie laughed. 'Maybe,' he admitted, 'but you know, these drunken binges are expected of us at these events. Bloody hell, *conference* – sounds a bit posh.'

'That's why it doesn't suit you.' Kath yelped as Mackenzie tugged her ponytail.

'I will call,' he promised.

Her smile softened. 'I know you will. Josh and I will probably go for a walk later, but we'll be back by four or five, so call after then.'

When she dropped him at the station, his two colleagues had yet to turn up. He bent down to pull eight-year-old Josh into a tight hug, and the boy hugged him back, kissing him on the cheek.

Surprised and touched – Josh had considered himself too old to kiss his daddy for at least a year now – Mackenzie held him tighter. 'Watch after your mother,' he said. 'Be good, and above all... This is really important, so listen hard. Are you listening?'

'Yes!'

Mackenzie stared at him seriously, then he looked over his shoulder, as if checking for eavesdroppers. 'Don't let her paint the living room pink while I'm not there. Got it?'

'Ugh, got it. No pink.'

'I was going to do the whole room and ceiling in fabulous fuchsia!' Kath protested. Mackenzie pulled a face and stood up straight, ruffling Josh's already unruly hair and resting his hand on the back of the boy's head, reluctant to break the unexpectedly rekindled closeness. It was hard, working on the rigs, being away for weeks at a time – the bond between them was too easily broken, and often hard to mend. But today it was there, and Mackenzie felt the warmth of it.

Then Kath's arms were around his waist. He could smell paint in her hair and on her skin, mingling with the soap she'd tried to scrub it off with, and he breathed deeply, his free hand pulling her close. That moment, and the memory of his son's kiss, nearly killed him.

They also saved his life.

It was late evening by the time he returned to his hotel room and called Kath. Her mobile went unanswered, and no-one picked up at home, and Mackenzie reasoned she could be in the shower, or anywhere. He waited an hour and called again. Then, becoming increasingly frantic, he began trying family and friends, but no-one had seen or heard from either Kath or Josh all day.

In the early hours of Sunday, after a sleepless night, he

called the police and started home. The weather, nasty since Saturday afternoon, had turned even worse, delaying his return; snow flurries were spinning in the air, and the mountains and many of the back roads were already white. Mackenzie unlocked his front door with a feeling of dread, and his heart hammering so fast he felt as if it would spin right up through his throat.

The first place he checked was down to his left, then up on the same side, and his vision went grey. Two of the three pairs of walking boots were gone; two of the waxed jackets, one small, the other even smaller, also gone. He turned back to stare out of his front door, up at the surrounding hills. He could barely see any defined shapes through the swirling snow.

Josh and I will probably go for a walk later, but we'll be back by four or five...

He threw off the lightweight coat he'd worn to Edinburgh and dragged on the remaining heavy-duty wax one, but his hands shook and he gave up trying to zip it closed. The front doorbell rang, and on the step was someone he vaguely recognised, flanked by two uniformed officers.

'Paul Mackenzie? DI Bradley. I've come about your wife and son.'

An inspector? For this? 'Have you found them?'

Bradley shook his head. 'Sadly, no. Or from your point of view, maybe I should say luckily no.'

Mackenzie frowned. 'I don't understand – look, will you let me pass? I'm going out to search for them.'

'I think not, Mackenzie.' Bradley smiled, but it was thin, and it cut through Mackenzie like a wire. 'If you'd be so good as to come with these officers, we'll chat at the station.'

'The car was found abandoned near the foot of Aonach Mor, and the snow is now well up around the wheel arches, so it's been there a while.' Bradley stared hard at the man opposite, willing him to break. It had to happen soon; Mackenzie was a wreck. Unshaven, red-eyed, he kept rubbing his hands viciously over his face in an effort to stay focused, to make sure he didn't slip and say the wrong thing.

'So what have you done with the bodies?' Bradley pressed on. Mackenzie's head snapped up; the veins on his neck were standing out with the effort of control, and Bradley knew just another few small pushes would send the man spinning over the edge. His exhaustion would be his undoing – the confession would be in the bag soon.

'Mackenzie, evidence suggests that your family car has been parked at Aonach Mor since Saturday morning. Where were you?'

'It can't have been. Kath dropped me off at the station in it, around lunch time.'

'Can anyone corroborate that?'

'Two of my colleagues – we travelled to Edinburgh together...' He shook his head. 'Shit, no. They didn't turn up until after she'd left.'

'Convenient.'

'But they might have seen her on the road.'

'Hmm. Names?'

Mackenzie gave them, in a low voice cracking with strain. 'Look, how many people have you got out there searching? Why won't you at least let me help? I know where she'd—'

'Forget it.' Bradley took his time writing down the names. 'Given the first opportunity, you'd be away over the horizon before we could blink.'

Mackenzie stared at him, disbelief written all over his face, and his eyes sought support from the other officer at the table. 'In this weather? I'd have to be insane!'

'But you're happy enough to send your wife and child out?' Bradley felt a certain satisfaction at the effect his words had; for the first time since childhood, he had a Mackenzie in his fist and he was going to squeeze until there was nothing left. Patience was, indeed, rewarded.

The Mackenzie family had owned the Bradleys, right up until the moment its patriarch had had a stroke, and the estate collapsed and was sold off to pay for his care. Of course all the staff had been laid off like discarded junk, including Frank's put-upon estate factor, Iain, whose son, Donald, had always been invisible to the enviable and popular Mackenzie boys.

Rejected as a companion, his envy had only grown through the years as, despite everything, those boys somehow still managed to get whatever they wanted handed to them on velvet cushions. Including, in the younger boy's case, the fresh, friendly, and captivatingly pretty Katherine Donachie, a girl Bradley had noticed around town, and who'd featured in some pretty intense dreams on occasion.

Of course their only son was as touched by the fortune fairies as his annoying, entitled, prick of a father; the perfect, sweet little family, carrying on their perfect, sweet little line. But now the gilded rope keeping Mackenzie moored to his charmed life had finally snapped. Something had pushed him to the point of violence, and a bloke Mackenzie's size could inflict a lot of damage if his fire was blazing. He didn't deserve someone like Katherine Donachie. He didn't deserve his liberty, either, for what he'd done.

The newly transferred constable who was sitting in on the interview sighed, and shifted on the hard chair, making Bradley aware of his own discomfort. He glared, but the constable – what was his name again? Hollander? – merely looked at him blandly. For once Bradley wished he had Tony Clifford in here; he might be a self-righteous turd, but he was good at his job. He would have probed and probed, until he'd found the trigger that would make Mackenzie confess.

'Interview suspended, fifteen twenty-five.' Bradley stopped the tape. 'You can stop play-acting now, Mackenzie, it's just us.'

Mackenzie raised his eyes from where they'd been staring fixedly at the table. 'Are you going to tell me where you're searching for...for my wife and Josh...' But he didn't finish; his breath seemed to be locking in his chest. Suddenly, startling both officers, he slammed his fists on the table.

'*Why* won't you let me show you where to look? They've probably gone where we always go when we go to Aonach Mor. Let me at least show you on the map!'

'And have you send us on a wild goose chase?' Bradley snorted. 'I don't think so. Your wife is a trained mountain guide, Mackenzie, well used to walking the hills. If she were really out there, she'd know what to be wary of in this weather, and she'd be safe. Stands to reason.'

'But they might *be* safe! For now anyway. They might be sheltering somewhere waiting for someone to find them, and you won't even let me—'

'We've got those not-quite-witnesses of yours to speak with; we'll continue this later.'

Bradley sat in the canteen some time later, frowning into his too dark coffee. He looked up as the constable joined him. Mulholland, that was it.

'You're sure of this bloke aren't you?'

Bradley nodded. 'He puts on a good act, I'll give him that, but Kath Dona.. Mackenzie, and her child are past help.'

'You're not even going to send out the dogs?'

'It's not worth the risk to life, not in these conditions. No, he's done something, I'm sure of it.' He looked up as Tony Clifford came in and threw a cool glance in his direction before ordering a drink. 'What are you looking like that for, sergeant?'

'Paul Mackenzie would never hurt that woman, nor their child,' Clifford said. 'You've got to stop letting old grudges affect your judgement. *Sir*,' he added, with a rare touch of insolence.

'You're a fine one to talk about grudges,' Bradley said, and had the satisfaction of seeing Clifford's face colour. He knew the sergeant hadn't for one minute believed that bollocks about the flights to Alicante, and from that moment to this, he'd felt the man's eyes on him at every move.

'So what have you actually got?' Mulholland asked, dragging his attention back.

Bradley shrugged. 'Enough to hold him for a while, but not much longer. The car was noticed at Aonach Mor in the early afternoon, rather than the morning, but that's not to say it *wasn't* parked there earlier; the snow drifts against it indicate it's possible. No-one actually saw the woman or the boy, in any case. Tourist season's over, and the weather's shit, so witnesses are a bit thin on the ground.'

'And the alibi?'

'Mackenzie could have left the car there and made his way back in plenty of time for the train. His prints are all over it, as well as hers, but then it's a family car. He was definitely alone when his colleagues showed up at the station; he told them his wife and son had dropped him off and already left – she was busy painting the house or something, and didn't want to hang around. That's been checked, and it looks like there *was* some painting being done. Who knows though? Maybe there's blood on the walls that he was covering up. When the bodies turn up, forensics'll have a field day and we'll nail the bastard one way or the other.'

'You really don't like him, do you? Why?'

The tone was conversational enough, but Bradley glanced over his shoulder at where Clifford sat nursing his tea and pretending not to take any notice. 'Don't go listening to *him*, constable,' he said in a low voice. 'Whether I like Mackenzie or not has no bearing on this. I've got to make sure it's done right. A woman and child are missing and I'm pretty sure they're not going to turn up alive. We can't afford to screw up on any details; I've done that once before and the bloke got off.'

'So I heard. Duncan Wallace and the Spence jewels, wasn't it? So what now?'

'We let Mackenzie stew. Let him think we've got plenty of people who're going to put him up at the foot of Aonach Mor on Saturday morning. The bodies will probably turn up at the bottom of a loch somewhere miles away, but we'll find them. And when we do, I'm going to see Paul Mackenzie get exactly what he deserves.'

Throwing open Mackenzie's cell door that evening, Bradley found the younger man sitting hunched over on the edge of the bunk, and felt a thread of anticipation pulling through him. One phone call, just a few minutes ago, had changed everything, and now he had an excuse to get tough. He fingered the clear plastic bag in his pocket, wondering how Mackenzie would react to it, and making a mental note to watch very, very carefully.

'Shall we?' He gestured to the door.

Back in the interview room, Mackenzie looked worse than ever, no doubt panicking by now. Bradley cleared his throat and took the bag from his pocket. He tossed it onto the table in front of Mackenzie, who stared at it blankly for a moment before focusing on its contents. Then the blood drained from his face so quickly Bradley was certain he was about to pass out. He leaned forward.

'Recognise it?'

No answer. Mackenzie reached out a violently shaking hand and touched the bag. He raised a stricken face to Bradley, whose conviction wavered for the first time; he appeared really ill, and his body seemed to hunch as if he were in physical pain.

'Kath's locket,' he whispered finally. 'Where did you—'

'Wrapped around your dead wife's fingers.' Bradley punched the words out, pulling none of their impact, studying Mackenzie's face closely. 'She was huddled around your boy's body, trying to keep him warm, but...' He shrugged and didn't finish. He didn't need to.

Mackenzie groaned in such anguish that Bradley knew he didn't have to wait for the preliminary report; much as he'd wanted to believe otherwise, this man had not killed his family – he'd have to let him go.

He glanced at Mulholland and was jolted by the unmis-takeable light of enjoyment on the constable's face as he stared at Mackenzie. He'd felt a certain satisfaction himself, granted, but then he'd hated the man, and everything he stood for, for years. Mulholland had no cause to dislike Mackenzie, and yet he was watching as if he owed him a lifetime of pain, and was relishing the payback. Bradley filed this away in his mind, under Interesting, and Potentially Useful.

Two hours later, Mackenzie appeared close to collapse. He answered the questions in a bleak monotone, his story never wavering. Bradley had taken back the bag containing the locket on its leather cord, but Mackenzie couldn't stop looking at it.

'Can I have it?' he asked suddenly. Bradley shrugged. It couldn't hurt – after all, it wasn't exactly evidence; Katherine and Josh Mackenzie had both died of hypothermia, but Bradley was holding on to that bit of information for just a little while longer.

He took the locket out of the bag and slid it across the desk to Mackenzie. The man fumbled to catch it and his face paled further, his eyes barely more than dark smudges filled with red lines. Finding a grip at last, he ripped the locket from the leather thong, and it bounced and skidded over towards Bradley, who opened it and saw the two almost identical faces, father and son. He felt the same twinge of guilty sympathy he'd felt before; no matter how deep Bradley's hatred of that ancient family ran, Mackenzie wasn't guilty of murder. He didn't deserve this.

But Mulholland was still studying Mackenzie's reactions to every single word, and Bradley took his lead from that; there was still the question of how the man could have sent his wife and child off alone; he was culpable even if he hadn't killed them himself. He was twisting the thong in his fingers – at first Bradley thought he was aimlessly working out his confused grief on the leather, then he saw the two freshly tied knots, one smaller than the other, heard Mackenzie whispering the names of his wife and son as he rubbed his thumbs over them, seemingly heedless of the tears that fell from his bowed head.

Enough was enough. Bradley gestured to Mulholland to remain where he was and stepped outside the door. While he waited for a convincing time to pass, he pondered what he'd discovered about Mulholland; the man had a mean streak a mile wide, and that was something Bradley could always use.

He considered the possibilities; Duncan Wallace hadn't entirely trusted him, he knew that, but he had ensured Bradley's slow but steady rise through the force nevertheless, knowing Bradley would be forever, and demonstrably, grateful. He could do worse than cultivate that kind of loyalty for himself, and of all the young officers with that kind of potential, this one was showing the most favourable signs. Yes, worth serious consideration certainly, but right now there were other matters to put to rest. He pushed open the interview room door again.

Mackenzie had tied the shortened thong around his own neck, the knots resting in the hollow of his throat, the locket discarded on the table. His hand covered the knots instinctively as Bradley came in. Protectively, even, as if he were prepared to argue the right to keep them close.

'Right, you can go,' Bradley said. 'Cause of death was hypothermia.'

Mackenzie lowered his head and dragged in a deep, splintered-sounding breath. 'Hypothermia.'

'Pity no-one found them sooner, eh?'

Mackenzie looked at him, expressionless, yet his hatred struck Bradley full in the face. Bradley held it, returned it, and from that moment on the two men were in perfect harmony.

Chapter Eleven

The Burnside Hotel, August 2018

CHARIS WATCHED, tight-lipped, as Maddy came in, now changed into a police uniform. A really convincing one, complete with hi-vis vest and stab-proof padding. Wasn't it illegal to impersonate a police officer? Would she herself be in trouble if Maddy got caught? She dismissed that thought almost immediately; she didn't care. Whatever it took to get the message across to Stein that he wasn't a suspect in Jamie's disappearance, she'd go along with it. She wanted to shrink under Maddy's cool gaze, but was determined not to admit her sense of inferiority; the woman had been looking down on her, literally and figuratively, from the moment she'd arrived in her office.

Charis sat in the window seat and tried to settle her rising impatience. They had a while yet before they went downstairs to put on their show of interview witnesses, since Stein wouldn't be back, and he was the only audience they needed. To avoid thinking about Jamie, she turned her thoughts to

Mackenzie instead; much as she disliked admitting it, there was no denying the flicker of envy she felt at the obvious bond between him and his partner. At first she'd put it down to not having anyone in her life with whom she felt that close, but pretty soon she admitted to herself that sharing this frightening and uncertain experience with Mackenzie had turned him from an angry stranger into the closest thing she had to a friend up here. His dry manner and rare, unexpected smiles had begun to ease some of her panic, and she was even starting to say and do things to try and prompt them. He steadied her. And that was all secondary to the way he had seen through Daniel's façade, and shown her she had allies, and choices, for which she would never be able to adequately convey her gratitude and relief.

Maddy picked up the phone. 'I just want to ring my fiancé.'

'So that one I met at the station, is it your brother?'

Maddy nodded, checking her mobile for the number she needed, and Charis frowned. 'Why don't you just use that to make the call?'

'Can't risk tying it up, in case Paul phones.' Maddy gave her a tight smile. 'Don't worry, I'll pay for the call.'

But that only raised another question; was Charis expected to pay for the services she'd had thrust upon her? And how much did investigation agencies cost anyway? She had vague pictures from TV in her head: people shoving brown paper packets at shifty-looking sorts, and the recipients shuffling through wads of unidentifiable notes. Nowadays it'd probably be PayPal or BACs transfer – either way it was going to take a long time to raise it. But she would, if only—

'Gavin, it's only me.' Maddy drew her feet up to sit cross-legged on Jamie's bed. 'Aye, sorry I will be, yes. I finished the report and sent it off, so Ki...Macnab should make the payment soon.' A pause. Then, 'Don't know, maybe another couple of hours if I'm lucky. Thing is, this might turn into an all-nighter. At the moment? In The Burnside. A woman's lost her little boy...'

There was another pause while Maddy listened again, her gaze returning to Charis, who shivered a little at the expression on her face. 'Yes, he does. Actually he's the one who brought her to the office. Well, what do you think? Frankly, he's a mess. No, she's just a tourist. Aye, I will. Kiss Tas for me. Love you too. Bye.'

'A mess?' Charis said tightly. '*He's* a mess? Why is everyone so bloody concerned about how Mackenzie's feeling? What about Jamie? What about me?' She could hear her own voice rising, but didn't attempt to stop it. 'I didn't drag anyone into this, least of all you, so why don't you and your precious Paul let me tell the police the whole story? Maybe they can actually do something instead of just sitting here.'

'Do you want to get both Jamie and Paul killed?' Maddy's voice was calm, and the contrast made Charis feel like a screaming fishwife.

She fell back onto sarcasm. 'Yeah, that's obviously exactly what I want. What kind of a stupid question is that? You two have no *idea* how I'm feeling right now, so—'

'That's just it. We do. Or at least Paul does.'

Charis had started to get up but, startled, sank back down and waited for Maddy to continue.

Maddy took a deep breath. 'Paul was married before I knew him,' she began, 'and he had a son.'

Had... Charis shrivelled inside. She sat in silence while Maddy told her about Kath and Josh. No wonder he'd looked at the mountains with such a bleak expression, or that he'd lost hope for just a moment back there, and even less wonder he'd been so judgemental about her parenting skills.

She turned to stare out of the window at the blackness beyond, where the mountains stood guard over the town. Out there, where Jamie was.

'It *was* winter though,' Maddy said. 'The snow came early; they were caught out. It happens, more often than you'd believe. Then again, Kath was an experienced mountain guide; she'd have known how to keep them safe for a while. They'd probably have been okay if the normal rescue procedures had been followed. I gather Bradley was none too gentle when he broke the news either. It was that so-called investigation that finally persuaded my dad to leave the force.'

Charis shook her head, unable to speak for a moment; she remembered the discussion in the bar, when she'd grimly pointed out how the local police knew Mackenzie. The look on his face had been indecipherable at the time, but now she thought she'd learned enough to understand it.

'What's the leather about?' she asked at last, remembering how he'd touched it. Maddy explained about the knots, and as she spoke Charis saw it all unfold behind her closed eyes. How it must have been in that little room, knowing his family desperately needed him and unable to do anything. She had an inkling of how he'd felt, but at least she knew something was being done for Jamie, whereas the opposite had been true thirteen years ago.

'Paul lost it, totally,' Maddy said. 'Went looking for the place where they died, but the weather forced him back until he collapsed. It was touch and go with him too, for a while. That's where we met, in the hospital where I used to work.'

'Oh, Christ...'

'Aye. All he could talk about when they brought him down

was how Josh had kissed him goodbye.' Maddy's voice was distant as if reliving it rather than recalling it. 'But in the end he turned it around; used that same feeling as a reason to go on. We became friends, and later partners in the agency.'

'And that's when you got together?'

Maddy looked searchingly at her. 'What makes you think we "got together" at all?'

'It's obvious you're closer than friends.'

Maddy chewed her lip for a second, her expression going distant again. The faint smile of memory made her seem younger. 'Aye, we *were* more. For a while...' She visibly came back to the present, with a long, slow blink. 'But not any more. I think we were each what the other needed for a little while, but we're not suited. He wasn't really ready to let go, even after a few years had passed, and I'm engaged to someone else now.

'With a child?'

'Aye. Tas. He's four.' Maddy cleared her throat, clearly uncomfortable talking about children to Charis. 'Anyway,' she went on, 'from that day on, Paul and Bradley were set on a road of mutual destruction. Paul was an idiot – he wound Bradley up every chance he got, while Bradley's jealousy just got worse when our business took off. But,' she shrugged, 'that didn't last, and to cut to the end of a very long story, Paul's now a partner in a failing business, and Bradley's a superintendent, somehow, and heading for even greater things.' Her disgust was apparent in her voice. 'Luckily he spends most of his time in Inverness now, but he has his fingers in so many pies it's frightening. And he still has offices here too; some kind of district liaison thing he has going on.'

'So if I'd gone to the police *anywhere* around here, Bradley would definitely have found out about it?'

'Oh, he's paranoid about anything to do with Paul, always

has been. He'd have heard all right. And that would put Jamie at risk as well. You both did the right thing.'

'But it's twisted lines right the way through! Bradley doesn't have the faintest idea about Jamie. Yet.'

'And nor will he. Don't worry, Paul will stay below their sight-line now he knows they're aware of him, so they won't find out about Jamie through him, and Stein won't want them to know either.'

'This is such a mess.'

'Aye, it is.' Maddy's mobile whistled. She checked the new message, fired off a quick response, then swung her legs off the bed and stood up. 'Right, Stein's just come in. Time to put on a show, I think.'

'Break a leg.' Charis couldn't resist the dry tone, and Maddy looked at her, one perfect eyebrow raised.

'I believe ballet artistes use the term *Merde*,' she said pointedly, and straightened her uniform.

They went downstairs.

Stein watched the action unfold from the lobby, but as he was about to follow it into the lounge bar he saw the tall shape of his private detective pushing open the glass doors, and he bit down on a sigh. Didn't the man have a home to go to?

'We need to talk,' Mackenzie said. 'Outside.'

Stein shushed him without taking his gaze off the open door into the lounge, but Mackenzie persisted, a note of urgency in his voice. 'For God's sake, Stein, that's the *police* in there! If Bradley knows I'm sniffing round it'll mean no deal for you, and no payment for me. I knew I shouldn't have taken this case—'

'She's telling them it was her ex,' Stein threw back over his shoulder, amused.

'Why him?'

'Apparently he was here this evening, and they argued.'

'Well that makes sense.' Mackenzie shrugged. 'She's bound to think it was him who took the kid, then. That's a good thing, aye?'

'Yeah, quite a bonus. Wish I'd thought of it myself.'

'Plus, now the police *are* involved, Bradley'll find out the kid's off the scene, right?'

'See? Perfect.'

'So now can we get out of here? We really need to talk – you've crossed a line tonight, and if you want my help, you're going to have to tell me everything. *Everything.* Right?'

Stein looked at him steadily and came to a decision. 'Sure. I'll see you in my room in ten minutes.' He handed the key to Mackenzie and went into the bar.

He took a tall stool, watching the striking policewoman; she'd evidently done well to ease the mind of the boy's mother, who was red-eyed and shaking, but talking calmly enough. When the officer caught sight of Stein she pressed the mother's arm and left her to join him.

'Good evening, sir. Are you a resident guest here in the hotel at the moment?'

'Uh huh.'

'I'm Constable McClure. I'd like to ask you a few questions if I may?'

'Sure. Want to sit down?'

He led her over to a booth and spelled his surname for her, watching as she wrote carefully in her notebook; she was certainly stunning, cool as a peach, her red hair tied neatly back... Sarah had red hair too, though hers was paler, and the comparison gave him a sharp pang. How long before he could put this whole thing to bed, and he and Sarah could go back to being normal together? To being uncomplicated, loving partners, instead of him feeling like her lackey? Willing or not, it wasn't a nice feeling.

Constable McClure was studying him curiously. 'You're American? Or Canadian perhaps?'

'American. California actually.' He studied her to see if she was impressed, but she gave no sign. Cool lady; they mostly started right in asking about beaches and movie stars at this point. Well, maybe cops didn't.

'Were you in the bar earlier this evening, sir?'

'I was, for a while.'

'Do you remember seeing that woman?' She gestured to where the Boulton woman sat, staring at him with dislike.

He blinked slowly. 'Yeah, she was in here. What'd she do, try to abscond without paying?'

McClure frowned, clearly not appreciating the joke. 'Her son's gone missing, presumed abducted.'

'What?' He looked suitably shocked, glancing around their plush environment in a convincing: *from here?* 'Well, that's terrible... Uh, there was no-one with her when I saw her.'

'And what time did you see her?'

The questions went on. Stein answered them all, mindful not to mention Mackenzie; the last thing he needed was to wind Bradley up further, now that the boy was gone. When she'd finished, Constable McClure smiled, touched his arm and thanked him warmly for his help. 'I hope we find this wee boy, Mr Stein; he's asthmatic you see, and stress can do terrible things to someone with that condition.'

'Yeah, I...uh, I hope you find him too. If I can help any more, I'll do what I can.' Stein was horrified at how close he had come to admitting he knew of the boy's condition; it was that confidential smile, that touch. But McClure didn't seem to have noticed anything amiss and thanked him again, returning to where Boulton sat. With one last glance at the police officer, Stein went upstairs to his room.

He found Mackenzie lying on the bed, and fought back a sharp comment. He was in charge, sure, but sometimes the big Scot looked at him in a way that actually frightened him – something in him fell short of the 'gentle giant' label, despite his quiet manner. So he kept quiet, and instead went to the *en suite* to rinse his face.

'Just spoke to the police downstairs,' he said. 'Thought it was better than hiding away 'til they came looking.' He towelled his face dry, and came out to face Mackenzie, who hadn't moved.

'What'd they say?' Mackenzie asked the ceiling.

Stein found himself peering up there too, and lost his temper. 'Never mind what they said. You find out where those damned figurines are, Mackenzie, or you're fired, okay?'

'That *was* the idea,' Mackenzie said, and sat up. 'Then you raised the game by taking it on yourself to kidnap a little boy. Well done, you.'

'I didn't take it on myself! I took advice.'

'From your girlfriend? Nice girlfriend. Great mother instincts.' That grit was back, and Stein tensed as he studied the man's calm face; that stillness was evidently a thin covering over a deep, icy anger. Stein determined not to let him have the upper hand – he was still the boss here.

'You have no idea about Sarah and me,' he said coldly. 'I'm *trying* to help her.'

'You're just following orders then. Like me.'

'Listen, Mackenzie, this part of it has nothing to do with you. The kid'll be safe enough.'

Mackenzie frowned. 'He's still a threat. To you and to Bradley. What if he escapes?'

'Hardly likely, and if he does, where will he go? He won't be able to see a hand in front of his face up there.'

'Up where?'

'And he's asthmatic, so he won't be up to a lot of running.'

'Asthmatic?'

'Yeah, I found out for myself, but the police just told me, too.'

'Found out for yourself? You mean he had an attack?' Mackenzie's tone sharpened, but when Stein looked at him his expression hadn't changed.

'He's got his meds; I saw him use them. The officer seemed worried about that, but I could hardly tell her I knew he was okay, could I?'

Mackenzie shrugged. 'Fine. I can take the bike out, or up, or whatever, and make sure he's not trying to get away.'

Stein recognised the not-too-subtle digging for information, but he wasn't about to give away Sarah's hiding place. 'Not yet. Not until I check in with Sarah. Your job is to tail Bradley, and find out where those damned figurines are.' He paused, then added softly, 'I'm gonna do this for her, no matter what it takes.'

There was a long silence. So long he'd almost forgotten Mackenzie was in the room, until the Scot spoke again.

'You're really doing all this just for her?'

'I'd do anything for her, anything at all.'

Mackenzie's direct stare didn't waver. 'But you're eyeing up the local talent.'

'The police officer? Looking at her means nothing – I love Sarah.'

'And she's a good person?'

'The best,' Stein said quietly, and cleared his throat of the sudden lump. 'She just wants what's rightfully hers.'

'Then good luck to you both.' Mackenzie stood up and held out a hand. Stein took it, a little nervously, but the grip was cool and firm, and held no untoward hint of the strength he knew was behind it. This was not some subtle show of power, it was one man acknowledging, albeit reluctantly, the deeper feelings of another.

'I'll do what I can for you, Andy, and that's the truth. I'll call you, okay?'

Stein looked at him levelly and nodded. For the first time it felt as if Mackenzie really was on his side, and he had to admit it was a good feeling.

It seemed they'd waited hours, although it was barely ten minutes, and when the soft knock came both women moved fast. Charis got there first.

'Who is it?' she called, keeping her voice light. She could feel Maddy tensing beside her.

'Mackenzie.' At the sound of his voice Charis felt surprisingly safe. Comforted. She opened the door and he smiled briefly at Maddy, then turned back to her.

'He won't tell me where Jamie is, not yet, but I'm positive he's going to be okay. Stein's irritating as hell, but he's no monster; he won't have left him overnight without some comforts. We've sort of...reached an understanding. He knew about Jamie's asthma too, but good job on getting it in anyway,' he added to Maddy.

Charis's heart skipped. 'He knew? Did Jamie have an attack?'

'I gather just a small one. But Stein saw him use his inhaler. I don't believe he'd do anything to put your boy at risk.'

'Thank God,' Maddy said. 'Right, I'm away home to see what state my dinner's in. Gav will think I've left him.'

Mackenzie grinned. 'You treat that car the way you normally do, and he'll be wishing for it.'

She punched his arm. 'It's fine now! And it was only a wee scrape. Nothing wrong with *my* driving, pal.'

'No, you're fine right up until you let the handbrake off.'

'I can drive a car better than you, biker-boy!'

But it was late, and Mackenzie caved in first. 'You're a star, Mads,' he said, squeezing her shoulder.

'Just bathe in my light, sonny – it's all you can do.'

Charis saw that warmth again, in the smile that passed between them, and turned away, an intruder in her own room. A movement caught her eye, and she looked back to see Maddy's hand, held out to her.

'Whatever I think about you, Charis, you're going through hell, and I'm sorry I gave you a hard time. You did an amazing job downstairs, considering.'

'Oh. Thanks.' Charis shook the proffered hand. 'And so did you, of course.'

'How sweet,' Mackenzie observed drily. 'Looks like it's a night for making friends.'

'So you and Stein really don't hate each other any more?' Maddy asked.

'Best buddies now, Christmas card list and all.'

Maddy pulled a face. 'Somehow I doubt that, even of someone with your people skills.'

'Aye, well maybe an exaggeration. Gobshite still kidnapped Jamie after all.' Mackenzie shrugged. 'But I'm starting to get a sense of what makes him tick. Or rather, who.'

'Sarah Wallace? She must still have whatever it was that drove your poor brother to distraction.' Maddy kissed his cheek. 'I'll see you both tomorrow. Try and sleep, okay?'

Charis retreated to her window seat while they exchanged a few murmured words, keeping in mind the good things Mackenzie had said about Stein, the positive things. Jamie would be all right.

When Maddy had gone she suddenly felt awkward again and stood up, unsure why except that sitting down seemed to put her at a disadvantage. Mackenzie's past seemed to stand between them, a dark barrier that set him impossibly distant. Jamie's disappearance had left her raw, ragged, and while she couldn't know exactly what the Scot had gone through, she was starting to have some idea. She studied him closely as he congratulated her on keeping a cool head, but the words barely skimmed the surface of her hearing. It was the hollowness of his appearance that struck her now, the way his cheeks were pulled taut, and the lines carved deep into his forehead.

'Does it still hurt just as badly?' she said, unaware she was going to say it until the words were past her lips.

Mackenzie flinched. 'She told you, then.'

'Yes.' She looked up and reached out to touch the tips of her fingers to the knotted leather around his neck.

His hand closed over hers and, shocked at the tightness of his grip, she tried to pull away, but he held her fast. 'That's my wife and child you're touching,' he said, his voice suddenly flat.

She spoke as gently as her racing heart allowed; his fierce

154

grip was too reminiscent of another. 'No, it isn't. Let go of the guilt. It'll kill you, and it's not even yours.'

He seemed to be struggling for an answer, and then he released her hand. When she raised her eyes again, she saw a faint, wary smile on his face.

'You're a wee bit of a mystery, aren't you, Charis-with-a-c-h?'

Disturbed by an unexpected intensity of feeling, she moved away. 'No mystery here,' she said, sitting back in the window seat. 'What you see is what you get.'

Mackenzie's smile faded slightly. 'I can think of worse deals.'

Charis looked away, not sure how to respond. 'How do you get through?' she asked at length, needing to know – just in case, as unthinkable as that was.

'One hour at a time. Sometimes it's harder than others. Sometimes I go back to coping one minute at a time, like before. But it's been thirteen years now, and there are days when I can go breakfast 'til bedtime without thinking about them. And that in itself makes me feel terrible, and the whole cycle starts over again.' Mackenzie sat down on the bed, his hair sticking up where he'd run tired hands through it.

'How about you?' he continued. 'How do you live with...with someone like your ex-husband, once you know what he's really like?'

'Are you saying I shouldn't have put up with it?' Charis's defences prickled, but Mackenzie held up a hand.

'No, I'm not saying that, not at all.'

Charis subsided. 'He never hit me. Nor Jamie as far as I know, so a lot of people found it hard to understand.' She closed her eyes to block out the way Mackenzie was staring intently at her. 'But physical violence isn't always the worst thing.'

'No.'

'The early days were normal,' Charis said. 'Fun, even. We were both pretty young, he was nice looking, and he fancied me. All my mates were dead jealous. We just sort of...fell into marriage, really. Then we talked about having children, and Daniel said he wanted a family. He chose the best moment to tell me he'd changed his mind though; I was seven months pregnant when he admitted he'd only said he wanted a kid because he knew I did. He thought we'd break up if he told me the truth. Bit late to back out, at that point.' Charis gave a laugh that was as lacking in humour as the situation she'd found herself in.

'Anyway, he started drinking, then the...the physical side of things went wrong. Bound to, I suppose – he was permanently hammered, I was permanently knackered, but I was managing. Let's face it, I've been a single parent since the night Jamie was born.'

'Coward,' Mackenzie said, 'to put you in that position and basically run away from the result.'

'I wish he *had* run away. If only. He went the other way, and started...controlling me. It was like, if he couldn't dominate me in the bedroom, he was going to make damned sure he dominated every other part of our life together. I couldn't go out, not even on a lunch break with my work colleagues. He'd turn up at the office at random times, just to make sure I hadn't taken a sneaky day off and not told him.'

'Did you ever do that?'

'Once.' Charis started to shake. There were no tears yet, but this strange inability to control the shaking was worse. Staring at her hands in a kind of remote fascination, she went on, 'I never did it again. He waited 'til I got home, then got me in the car and locked all the doors, and then he began to...to *scream* at me. The worst bit was that I could tell he wanted to hit me, but he wasn't letting himself. That's when I knew he had total control over himself, and he wasn't just jealous because he loved me.'

'Christ... I never thought of it that way.'

'Yeah, well.' Charis nodded, feeling the tears climbing up her throat despite her determination not to let them. 'He said he'd never hit me. Ever. Because I'm a woman, and a real man doesn't hit a woman, you know? But he said Jamie was going to grow up to be a man, and a man needs to learn how to take pain.'

She remembered holding the little boy tight, whenever he and his father were about to go out alone together, and in her mind the little chant, over and over, as she'd gently swayed him from side to side before letting him go: *Please, love, just do as he tells you...*

'The bastard,' Mackenzie murmured.

'You're not kidding. That was when I crossed the line.'

'*You* crossed the line?'

'Oh yeah.' Charis looked at him through the curtain of tears that shimmered, her voice turning hard. 'I hit *him*, you see. I gave him the ammunition he needed, by punching him in the head.'

Mackenzie blinked, and she couldn't tell whether his expression was one of admiration or dismay. 'What did he do?' he asked quietly.

'Nothing, at first. He just smiled and got out of the car. But pretty soon he began using Jamie against me like a weapon, and...I'm not one hundred per cent sure, but I'm fairly certain he did the same thing to Jamie, with me. In public he was kind, funny, the old Daniel, with tons of friends. And people I've known all my life were forever telling me how great he was, and every time, I wanted to believe them. Every time, I hoped it wasn't an act any more, that he'd changed.'

'People like that don't. They just find new victims.'

Charis nodded slowly. 'I know that now. Our lives weren't our own. Every penny of the weekly shop had to be accounted for – even though I earn my own money – and every little luxury, or what he considered one, went in the bin. The waste... You'd never believe it. I'm pretty sure he'd have fished the best stuff out later, when he took it out to the wheelie bin. Jamie couldn't go to his mates' birthdays, or school trips. He turned into a little shadow. A ghost...'

Her own words choked off as she realised what she was saying, but she felt Mackenzie's hands rest gently on hers, and went on, 'If I put a foot wrong, spent too long on the phone to Suze – that's my sister – or even our mum, he'd think of some cruel way to punish Jamie.' She shook her head. 'I hated myself, Mackenzie. I was so weak, I couldn't leave him. I was too scared of what he'd do. I had no control over my money, but what I did manage to save, from birthdays and stuff, he found. Spent the notes on a new jacket, and made me watch him feed the coins into the machines down the local pub, and buying drinks for our friends.'

Mackenzie gave a low whistle. 'How about your family? Did they know about him?'

'Mum did, she kept telling me to leave. But it wasn't that easy; I had nowhere to go, and no more emergency money. Mum and Dad only had a one bedroom flat so we couldn't go there. And we were never actually hurt, so it wouldn't have been fair to take a refuge place from someone who really needed it. We just sort of...drifted through life, waiting for an opportunity that never came.'

'What finally made you leave?'

'I found out I was stronger than I'd realised.' Charis brushed the persistent tears from her cheek as she recalled the day. 'I got breast cancer.' She felt Mackenzie's fingers tighten. 'I went through some proper nasty treatment, but I survived. It taught me a hell of a lot, including what a shocking waste of a precious life I was living. But now I knew I owed it to both myself and Jamie to change things.'

'How did you manage it?'

'Luckily for me, while I was messing up Daniel's life, and cramping his style by puking and losing my hair, he'd got into some car-thieving circle. A violent one, as it turned out. When they were...caught, he was given eight years.'

'Caught?' He gave her a narrow-eyed look, evidently noticing the tiny pause, and she shrugged.

'Can I help it if I've got a big mouth? He never knew it was me, though. He didn't know I even knew about it. At least I thought not. That was when I got the divorce, the injunction, and then the all-clear. What a red-letter time that was.'

'Is that what he was talking about downstairs earlier? About forgiving you?'

She nodded. 'His brief let it slip, apparently.'

'And are you okay now?'

She nodded. 'Lopsided, boob-wise, but happy to be here.'

He squeezed her hand again. 'So, you divorced him. How did he take that?'

'Not well, but there wasn't anything he could do from inside. He's only done four years of his sentence, but I suppose since he'd already been on remand... I don't know.' She shook the questions away. 'Why was he trying to get at Jamie though, not me?'

'That would still punish you, wouldn't it?' Mackenzie looked uncomfortable. 'I suppose you should know; some of the pictures he'd taken on your camera were, well, I think...' He hesitated, then pushed on. 'I think maybe he wants to make up some lost time with you. Prove something.' He lowered his voice. 'I was flipping through faster than I let on. There were a lot of pictures, and none of them were of Jamie except that one with the tent that you took.'

Charis stared. 'Photos of me, you mean? And you *let him go?*'

'I've marked his card; he won't be back.'

She struggled for a moment with the anger, but remembered the look on Daniel's face and conceded the point. 'He's a wimp when it comes right down to it. All mouth and no trousers. Besides, the minute my hair fell out he lost interest in even pretending to try. That's partly why I keep it so short now. No, he'll have gone scuttling back home to find another doormat to wipe his feet on. I just want to know why Suze told him where we are.'

'Was she one of the ones who believed the show he put on in public?'

'No, she knew what he was like by then. I had to tell her during the trial, 'cause she kept urging me to help him.'

Mackenzie's voice was grim. 'In that case I'd check on her. Now.'

But Charis was already moving. She had no idea of Suze's mobile number off the top of her head, but she had punched the entire landline number in before realising she needed to obtain an outside line first. Almost screaming in frustration she hit 9 and tried again. At last the connection was made, but it seemed to ring out forever, as Charis imagined her sister stumbling sleepily into the sitting room.

Finally a groggy voice answered, 'Who still uses these things? This'd better be good, whoever you—'

'Suze! Two things; first, are you okay? And second, why did you tell Daniel where I was staying?'

There was a long silence, then, as her sister burst into tears, Charis gripped the phone and met Mackenzie's concerned gaze across the room.

'I'm going to kill him.'

When she hung up a few minutes later, Mackenzie was looking at her with a silent question on his face.

'He went round there a couple of days ago,' she said dully. 'She knew he'd never hit me or Jamie before, so she let him in, thinking she'd fob him off with some story or other. He didn't give her the chance to think of one though – blacked her eye the second the door was shut.' She folded her arms tight across her chest. 'It seems he's changed since he's been inside. A lot.'

'Is she okay?'

'Not really. Physically, I think so, but she's really shaken. Now she's scared she's put me and Jamie in danger, but she couldn't reach us because I left my stupid phone at home.'

'And now he's here, and he wants you back.'

'I don't care what he wants.' Charis stood up and went to the door. 'Suze knows he's on his way back, so she can at least go round to mum's. Jamie's the important one now.'

'Where are you going?'

'Nowhere.' She opened the door and gestured to the hallway beyond. 'Bugger off, Mackenzie, I need to try and get some sleep if I can.'

Mackenzie pulled on his jacket. 'You'll be safe here now, and tomorrow we'll get the answers we need.'

She nodded, not trusting herself to keep looking up at him; his manner was gentle, and so were his hands as he pressed her shoulder. The swift change in her opinion of him was making her uncertain of her own emotional state. Kindness was likely to tip her over the edge.

'What will you do?' she stammered.

'I know this isn't what you want to hear, but Stein's never going to tell me where he's taken Jamie. All we can do now is find out where the figurines are, so he can let the lad go.'

Charis started to protest, but he held up a hand. 'He just wants to do it right for Sarah. He's not a...' He swallowed the word she knew he'd been about to say again. 'He's not a bad bloke.'

'How will you find the statues?'

'I'll text Maddy first thing, see if she's found the address we were looking for. If I can talk to Rob Doohan, we'll hopefully know where to start. Then Stein will get what he wants, and we'll have Jamie back to you safe and sound.'

'Thank God,' Charis breathed. She closed her eyes briefly, and only when she realised he hadn't released her shoulder did she allow herself to ask, 'And what do we do with...this?'

'This?' His voice was rough, and his fingers gripped her more tightly. He looked down at her, his face set in the harsh light from the hallway. 'So, I wasn't imagining it?'

'I don't think so. But we can't think about it. Not yet. I don't even want to sleep, really. I know I should, but I can't stand to not be doing something when he's out there at night, all alone.' Her voice cracked, and he pulled her close.

'Stein wouldn't have put him somewhere dangerous,' he told her, his chin resting on the top of her head so she felt the low vibration of his voice. 'I know it's easier said, but try not to worry, Jamie'll need you to keep your head together.'

'Like you did when Josh was missing?'

He froze, then released her. 'I'd do things differently if I had another chance.'

'I didn't mean—'

'I know.' He checked his watch. 'It's late. I'll be on the road first thing.' In the doorway he looked back with a faint smile. 'So, does this mean you're going to start calling me by my first name?'

Charis, who'd been kicking herself for her thoughtless comment, was surprised into a short laugh. 'Shouldn't think so. Anyway Paul doesn't suit you. I think it means *small*, doesn't it?' She looked him over critically, taking in his height and breadth of shoulder, and shook her head. 'Nope, you're not a Paul. What's your second name?'

'Stuart.'

She thought about that for a moment, then shook her head again. 'It's better, but all I can think of is Stuart Little. Mackenzie'll have to do, until I come up with something that suits you.' She darted a quick glance up and down the corridor. 'What will I be doing while you're out looking for these figurines?'

'I'll get Maddy to come back over here soon as she's up and about. See if she can work some more magic on Stein. You'd better lie low in here for a bit. Soon as I hear anything, I'll either come back, or call you.'

'If there's a choice, do the first one. Please?' While he was here, she somehow caught his optimism that Jamie would be okay, but as soon as he was gone all her fears would pile in on her again.

'I will.' Mackenzie touched her cheek, and though he smiled there was a determination in his expression. 'Wild Scousers couldn't stop me.'

Don Bradley knew he was dreaming. Knew it but couldn't stop it. The flames were spreading, licking painlessly around his ankles as he tried to identify the shadowy figure in the distance. The flames were crawling higher. Bradley began to run – he was much younger in this dream; there was no way he'd be able to move this fast now. He was starting to feel the heat, but still he knew he wouldn't burn – he would lose something in this fire, but not his life.

He followed the figure, now no more than a blurred shape, as it pulled open a huge door, and realised for the first time that he wasn't in his own home, but somewhere bigger, older – a place full of corridors and hidey-holes, and rooms off rooms. Not like his own large, but plain new-build box.

The figure paused in the doorway, looking back – Bradley saw a pale face, lit by flickering flame and shimmering heat haze, and he almost recognised the fleeing figure. He ran faster, dodging a flaming beam that crashed beside him, sending sparks spinning high into the domed front hall, momentarily distracting him as the snaking lights shot ceiling-ward. So pretty, just like...something else. Something he desired. But it was gone. He cast about, trying to understand what he lusted after so violently, and trying to remember, too, where he was. What this huge hallway was, that seemed to stretch forever as the figure in the doorway vanished.

'Don!'

The voice pulled him back from his quest for cool air and safety. It was the owner of the house, a woman, the voice becoming more and more urgent as Bradley struggled with his conscience. He should try to help, but he needed to know who had started the—

'Don!' Then it came to him, the name. It was...Mary, Mary, Mary...

'Wallace!' he shouted, and woke, beating at his hair where the flames had finally taken hold. A firm hand gripped his arm as he struggled to sit up.

'For God's sake! That again?' Janet sank back on her own pillow. 'That's the fourth time in as many weeks. What was it this time?'

'The fire,' Bradley mumbled, lying down again. He glanced at his wife; time was when she'd have taken him in her arms and soothed him, reminding him over and over again that he'd not even been there that night; he could neither have prevented the fire nor saved Duncan or Mary.

Now she just sounded bored; she even yawned. 'The lodge burned twenty-odd years ago – what's brought all this up again?'

'Don't know. Maybe something on TV, maybe nothing at all.'

'Well try and get some sleep.' She yawned again and settled back down.

Let you *get some sleep, you mean...* Bradley glanced at the clock: nearly four am. There was no way he'd sleep again now, and even though it was Sunday he had to be up at six-thirty to sort out that bloody Stein and his delaying tactics.

He got out of bed and pulled on his dressing gown. He could do with a bit of peace and quiet anyway, to think things through, and, unable to completely shake off the dream, he went downstairs and switched the kettle on. It was getting harder to leave the dreams behind these days, and more and more often it had been the one with the fire. The fire and the Fury. He gave a short, dry laugh. Maybe it was that book about Trump that kept linking the two in his mind; he couldn't hear the title of it without shuddering. Bad enough that they shared a first name.

He poured the coffee, still in a semi-daze, and took the cup into the living room. As he reached to switch on the light, the central heating kicked in and he jumped at the sudden, dull boom. His hand shook, and shadows made the room appear unfamiliar in the limited light from the kitchen – he might have been back in his dream; in Duncan Wallace's house twenty-five years ago.

He switched on the light, and as normality reasserted itself the roar of the heating returned to its usual, barely noticeable level. Why the hell did Janet insist on having the heating on in August anyway? She'd bankrupt him at this rate. Although to be fair it was cold for the time of year, and more rain was fore-cast – still the chill in his bones was not from the temperature in the house. He sat down on the sofa, cupping his hands around the mug to warm them.

The crazy thing was, he *hadn't* been anywhere near Glen-lowrie, the Wallaces' estate, the night it burned down. He'd arrived late the following afternoon to see the dark shell that was all that remained of the once grand lodge, the smell drifting heavy and acrid across the glen, but his familiarity with the house had forced him to endure it as if he'd been there.

His first thought had not even been for the Wallace family, and that guilt had hung with him for a while; his initial concern had been for the stunning black opal that Duncan Wallace had shown him over and over again, before putting it away one last time, refusing to bend to Bradley's oh-so-casual questions: where could he possibly hide it that was safe? Wouldn't he at least tell *him*?

'In time, laddie, in time,' Duncan had said, smiling. Bradley had believed him; he'd known that Duncan couldn't possibly keep that mesmerising stone to himself, but still it irked him that he was keeping its whereabouts secret from the man who'd worked in his service for five years.

The evidence that might have convicted Wallace had been easy enough to render inadmissible, but that didn't mean it had been no risk to himself or his career, or that he deserved anything less than his share of the spoils. And he'd not stopped there, either; keeping Wallace's name out of the scandal that had ensued had been no trivial matter. Well known as a good friend to the now-deceased Sandy Broughton, and to Rob Doohan, Wallace was bound to be kept under the spotlight until everything was cleared up. But Bradley had managed it.

The question of what had happened to William Kilbride, on the same night, was one that had been quashed with such ferocity that Bradley knew there was more to it than an accident, but he'd learned not to mention it. It had no bearing on the robbery anyway, and the man had been unlikely to come out of his coma, so where was the use in pursuing it?

Wallace's daughter, Sarah, was the only person left who knew the true origins of Bradley's connection to her father. Pillow talk, of course, and he regretted it later, but at the same time there was the possibility that he might have been able to use her, albeit unwittingly, to find out where the stone was. She could easily ask her father about the Spence collection without knowing what comprised the lost part of it.

Being Daddy's girl hadn't worked this time though. Even when she told him she knew of his part in the robbery, her father had stubbornly refused to budge, raising an anger in Sarah that was as unexpected and astonishing as it was white hot...

Bradley put down his cup and swore softly to the empty

room. He'd been a police officer all his adult life, for Christ's sake, so how had it taken him this long to figure it out? Was Sarah that convincing an actress that even he'd believed in her grief, her inconsolable sobbing? Had he really been that gullible? If she *had* been acting the part, then Hollywood was definitely the right place for her to have gone.

He brought his clasped hands to his mouth, chewing on his knuckles as he thought it through. He'd never be able to prove her involvement in the fire, and if he told her what he knew, his career would be over. He was dealing with a whole different animal than he'd realised. Someone who could cold-bloodedly murder her own parents in what amounted to no more than a fit of pique, was someone to watch very closely. He couldn't help comparing Sarah to Mulholland, and thinking what a very good, if frightening, pair they'd make.

It would all be worth it, all of it, if only he could get his hands on the Fury. And if the other jewels were safe, wherever they were, then the Fury was too. Did Sarah know about it yet? Chances were she did; her father had been unable to resist showing it off to selected and trusted individuals at every opportunity, and if it had worked its dark, mysterious magic on her as thoroughly as it had on him, she would have been equally under its spell. She was already keen enough on the Spence jewels, so if he were to dangle the Fury's continued existence in front of her...

Bradley picked up his coffee cup, smiling against the rim as the confusing spirals in his brain began to arrange themselves neatly again.

Chapter Twelve

THERE WAS no moment of sleepy adjustment to his surroundings; one minute he was in Tesco, filling a trolley with Mars Bars, the next he was wide awake and all too aware. Jamie looked around him, only half-registering the fact that this was actually possible now. The stone-built room was windowless and small, about big enough for a single bed and a wardrobe, he supposed, though it contained neither. Instead of a window there was only a small vent, high up where the wall met the ceiling, and through which struggled a feeble, grey light.

Daylight. But what would today bring, when only yesterday morning he'd been laughing with his mother over burnt bacon and squashed bread? He closed his eyes, determined not to cry, but the tears leaked out anyway; what if this was the day she died? Or the day he did? Jamie rubbed his eyes, angry with himself; this wasn't the way an intrepid detective got things done. He wasn't going to be a baby about this – his mother's life depended on him. He stood up on legs that not only shook but ached from hip to ankle with the cold, and from sitting hunched in the same position for hours at a time.

He couldn't reach the vent, but after a moment of walking around the tiny space and stretching, he gave a few experimental jumps and found the aches melting away. He shouldn't exert himself – one glance at where the useless inhaler lay in the corner reminded him sharply of that – but if he could just *see* the outside... The tumbling water sounded tantalisingly close, and he could imagine its spray on his face, and how it would feel to be out there beside it. In all that fresh air.

Standing beneath the small rectangular hole, he bent his knees and jumped as high as he could, his hands flat against the wall as if, Spider-Man like, he might be able to grip there long enough to see what lay beyond his prison. A glimpse of sky, a breath of cool air, and he was back down onto the stone floor again. It had been a mistake. That tiny glimpse of *out there* made his situation seem even worse, and he began to cry again. Furious, he kicked at the wall with his bare heel, crying harder at the pain as the skin broke on the rough stonework. It was all Mackenzie's fault. If he hadn't been so mean to his mum, and wrecked their stuff, and then gone blabbing to that American about him... Maybe he was out there now, standing guard.

'I hate you, Mackenzie!' Jamie yelled up at the vent. Despite his warning to himself, he was breathing heavily with exertion and anger, and the bravado went out of him in a rush as he felt his throat close up. He forced himself to count slowly in his head, banging a closed fist against the wall in time, and trying to slow his heart down. He *would* get out, somehow, and if anything had happened to his mother, he would find Mackenzie and, and... Well, nothing better have happened.

Listening to the waterfall was having another effect on him as well, and this one was growing uncomfortably urgent. He bit his lip, trying to distract himself, but it was no good, and eventually he stood up, went to the corner farthest away from where he'd been sitting and let the hot, stinky stream go. The smell wasn't too bad at first, but he knew it would get stronger over time; he only had to remember his mother's complaints about bathroom splashes to work that one out. He hoped it was the worst he'd have to do, but if he was stuck here for much longer things might take an even nastier turn... He'd better not think about that.

He didn't know how much time had passed, but the close call of that last attack had been frightening, and now he was moving slowly around to keep warm, trying not to breathe the chilly air too deeply. He felt his stomach gurgle, and whereas it had always sounded funny before, for the first time he was aware that being hungry could actually hurt. This wasn't like at school; in a quiet classroom during the period before lunch, one whiff of chips could turn peckishness into the noisy, pleasant feeling of anticipation. But although his slight pangs were not really painful yet, he was starting to get an idea of what it would be like when they were.

He fished the now misshapen Mars Bar out of his pocket and broke off the end of it, feeling saliva squirt into his mouth, but winced as his jaw stretched to accept the chocolate. He rubbed at the spot where he had smashed into the floor last night – there was probably a really good bruise there, but a few prods told him that the pain wouldn't get any worse if he opened his mouth a bit wider.

He could see a piece of chocolate hanging free, suspended in caramel like a tiny chocolate ice floe in the most delicious sea imaginable. Fascinated by that idea for a moment, he pushed out his tongue and watched, slightly cross-eyed, as the caramel stretched and stretched, the chocolate starting to slide downwards towards his waiting tongue. *Mustn't eat it all. Just a nibble, just a bit.* Somehow, he ate only a quarter of the sticky chocolate, and managed to get the wrapper back on before shoving the rest of the bar out of sight back into his jeans.

His feet ached. There was nothing on the floor to hurt him here, but they were so cold. He rolled back the legs of his jeans and found the wrinkled bottoms of his pyjamas underneath. Pulling them out as far as he could, he quickly pulled the jeans cuffs back down and covered his feet with the blissful warmth of the pyjamas.

He tried trapping the material between his toes to keep it there, but it kept sliding back. In the end he gritted his teeth, removed both jeans and pyjamas and put his jeans back on. Then he was able to wrap his feet properly, the body warmth from the pyjamas stealing into his chilled skin.

For a while it was enough. He sat with his back to the wall, breathing slowly and calmly, telling himself what a great time he would have recounting all of this to his friends at home, but now and again he felt his lip tremble. He'd think of his mother, all those times when he'd resented her protection of him, and how one act of disobedience had put them both in such terrible danger.

'I'm sorry, Mum,' he whispered, forcing his eyes wide so as not to give in to the tears he could feel there. If he closed his eyes, he wouldn't be able to help crying, and then anything might happen. The empty inhaler in the corner mocked him and only made it harder. But as he stared at it, hating it, something else caught his attention. He kicked the wrappings off his feet and, keeping his gaze locked on the corner of the room, crawled over for a closer look. He frowned; he was blocking his own light now and had lost the image that had seemed to stand out. He sat back, then checked over his shoulder at where the light fell and moved to the side. There!

The uneven stone floor rose in bumps in various places, leaving gaps in several areas, but right there by the wall someone had made a point of plugging one of the gaps up. The others were left, dark little spots where you could see right through to the packed, peaty earth on the other side, but this one, right in the corner...

Curiosity drew a temporary but comforting curtain across his fear, and he reached out and touched the jagged stone that had been pushed into the gap. Not a perfect fit, but still a snug, deliberate placement, out of place in this old wall. He pushed at one side of it, hoping the other side would pop out enough to be able to grab hold of it.

What if this was a secret passage? In his mum's old Famous Five books there was *always* a secret tunnel activated by a stone like this. And look at Indiana Jones, and the guys in the Mummy movies... Maybe a section of the wall would slide to one side, and he'd be off down the inside of the mountain in no time. Suddenly convinced, he shoved and dug at the stone, now and again putting his sore fingers into his mouth, sucking blood from the tiny cuts the sharp stone inflicted on his cold skin.

After a while he remembered the hotel room key in his pocket, and had one of those moments where you want to slap yourself on the forehead. He pulled the key out and set to work again, and at last he did it. The stone finally lay at an angle where he could take hold of one side, and he did so, drawing it out, holding his breath while he waited for its secret to be revealed – whatever it was.

Nothing happened. The wall stayed as solid and unmoving as ever.

Bitterly disappointed, Jamie threw the stone at the far wall, where it struck hard and broke into two. He pressed the heels of his blood-slicked hands into his eyes to hold back the fresh, hot tears and then, still sniffing, turned an angry, betrayed glare on the gap. As the light wriggled pale fingers under there, he saw something that might have once been white, but was now a dirty grey-brown. Gingerly he used the key to lever it out, and saw it was a loose piece of cloth, wrapped around something about the size of a cricket ball but flatter.

He reached in and tugged at it until it rolled free. It lay in his hand, filling his palm; a weighty object wrapped in now-bloodied cloth. It didn't look too impressive, but someone had made really sure it was kept hidden – that loose stone would have been hard for anyone to notice, never mind shift. So what was it? A spare key in a box? He began unwrapping it, bit by bit, rolling it over as the wrappings gave way under his fingers, revealing another cloth underneath, this one black and soft. He was starting to get irritated by the whole 'pass the parcel' feeling, when the last piece of cloth fell away and there it was. He blinked. A stone. Another stupid, pointless stone.

He tried to take a deep breath to scream in frustration, but his airways narrowed alarmingly and the breath started to whistle as he dragged at it. He tried to count again, to force himself to use the small amount of air he was getting in order to relax, but it wasn't working well this time. In fact it was getting harder and harder to breathe at all – and it was all the fault of this ugly little stone; angry and scared, he lifted it to throw it after the one he had pulled from the wall, and stopped, eyes wide.

He looked again at the stone. Lying in his palm, shadowed

by his eager, bowed head, it had been just a dark piece of rock, another disappointment to be smashed against the wall of his prison. But as he'd moved, he'd been struck by a sudden, fiery beauty that flashed from it, and the peace that stole over him at the sight slowed his panicked breathing and his racing heart until he barely noticed them.

He turned the stone in all directions; the colours, mostly reds, seemed to roll out at him from its depths however he held it, and when he held it up to the thin light coming through the vent, he found he could actually see right through it. He stared at it for what felt like hours, turning it, holding it, its warmth seeming to seep into his hands when he cupped it, as if it were a living fire protected by dark crystal. The longer he stared, the more vibrant the stone seemed to be, like a friend, sharing that dancing brilliance, but only with him. He clutched it tightly to his chest, suddenly certain that someone would come and take it away from him. Then he looked again, worried he might have dimmed it somehow by smothering it, but the fury of the colours only seemed brighter, and he smoothed it with one trembling finger.

'Keep me safe,' he whispered. 'Keep me company. Help me breathe.'

Although his voice sounded strange there in the echo of the stone room, the dark gem in his hand sent out soothing shafts of comforting fire, and Jamie held it tight.

Abergarry

A text from Maddy confirmed that the electoral register had come up trumps on Doohan's address, and Mackenzie grabbed his bike keys and helmet and headed out, slamming his front door behind him. Shivering as he looked up at the hills, for once his first feeling was not the yearning for a child forever lost, but hope for one who might yet be saved. In the nine years since he'd taken over Maddy's father's job in the partnership, he'd dealt with a number of missing persons, but none of them had been children, and that was probably down to Maddy's protective instincts.

This time, though, she'd not been there at the start of it to deflect his attention, and he could tell she was worried about him, about how he'd deal with a parent's worst fears without transmitting his own. This boy must be reunited with his mother, and only then could Mackenzie begin to explore which part of his heart Charis Boulton had sneaked into: the sympathy, the obligation, the curiosity... Or a much deeper part, that had been locked for thirteen years. In the meantime there was work to be done.

The road seemed endless, with no sign of the landmarks he'd been searching for, and eventually Mackenzie stopped, flicked the bike into neutral with the toe of his boot and pulled out his phone. Balancing the bike between his legs, he pushed his visor up and opened the text again, grateful for Maddy's dislike of abbreviations and text-speak.

Robert James Doohan,
Aonach View,
Spean Bridge,
Fort William,
PH34 8NF

When you get to Spean Bridge, take A86 for about two miles, then turn right onto minor road (unnamed, far as I can find out).

Doohan's cottage around three miles down on the right. Just over bridge crossing River Spean. Sheltered but can just see from road, apparently. Don't get lost!

Maddy xx

NOW will you invest in a new Satnav?

He gave a soft snort; this would teach him for putting it off. Probably. Well, he'd followed Maddy's instructions to the letter, turning onto this narrow road about a million miles back, crossing over the tiny, humped bridge, so where was the bloody house? He felt a low tingle again as he thought about the name of Doohan's home: Aonach View. Anticipating the familiar ache, he looked across to the imposing slopes of Aonach Mor. He stared for a long time, distantly aware of precious time ticking away, but also of a strange diminishing, inside. He took a deep breath, realising what had both surprised and liberated him.

'I don't hate you any more,' he said aloud. The mountain stared down at him, unmoved, and Mackenzie smiled; what had he been expecting – music? Choirs? Beauty and colour to spring forth and bathe everything in golden light? He touched the knotted leather with his gloved finger, staring up as far as he could see through the swirling mist, trying to encompass all of it. It was just a heap of rock – Kath and Josh were no longer there. They were here, with him, where they belonged.

Now it just remained to get the boy Jamie back where *he* belonged. He caught a flash of white as he moved his head, and peered through the trees again. As his eyes adjusted to the need to filter out the spiky branches and leaves, he saw the cottage and, squinting closer, the roofs of two cars. Neither one appeared abandoned or particularly old. Mackenzie's right thumb hovered over the ignition button, but something made him hesitate; why would one man, living alone, need two decent cars?

He took off his helmet, heeled the bike over onto its stand and climbed off. Still trying to peer through the tangle of branches to the clearing a hundred yards away, he clambered into the hedge to get a closer look. Immediately he identified the larger of the two cars – his heart skipped and he hissed a curse. Talk about mixed blessings; that was Bradley's new blue Discovery, which at least was a pretty good indication that he was in the right place. On the other hand, if Bradley took the figurines now, the chances of finding them again were close to zero. And if Bradley saw Mackenzie following, he'd go straight off and demand answers of Stein. Which meant he would then find out about Jamie.

Then again, if Bradley *didn't* have them with him, precious rescue time would be wasted while he himself backtracked all the way out here and tried to succeed where the superintendent had failed. Mackenzie was as certain as he could be that they were here; if not, they might be literally anywhere in the world, and that didn't bear thinking about.

He looked around for somewhere to stash the bike. Reluctant to start it up again, he pushed it back up the road until he found a place where the rain ditch was crossable. He wheeled the bike round into the trees, as far out of sight as possible, then chucked his helmet after it, and after a moment's thought followed suit with his creaky leather jacket. The sweat of exertion quickly chilled, leaving him shivering as he crept through the heavily wooded area around the back of Aonach View.

The damp from the ground started to creep up his legs as he stopped by the barn. The long grass brushed against his calves, leaving cold trails on his jeans, and he was glad of his bike boots, even if trainers were better suited to this creeping around. He leaned against the rough wall of the barn and cursed under his breath; how much longer was Bradley going to be in Doohan's cottage anyway? And was Sergeant Rottweiler with him? Mackenzie had a good view of the Discovery, but couldn't risk going any closer to the cottage itself; too many windows. Still, he'd be able to tell if Bradley had found anything useful, and he'd soon be able to catch them up on the bike. At that point it would be worth the risk of being seen.

The door clicked open; Mackenzie jumped, and pressed himself tighter against the side of the barn. The voices he heard were raised in anger, but even if they hadn't been, they'd have carried clearly through the still air to where he stood.

Mulholland spat his words out. 'I told you he'd be no fucking use to us!'

Mackenzie narrowed his eyes; he'd not had much to do with the skinny officer since that day, but something was different about him now, something about the way he carried himself. He seemed less sulky than usual, more belligerent. Even Bradley seemed to be keeping a deliberate distance between them as he pointed the key fob at the Discovery.

'And I'm telling *you*, he knows the bloody things are still out there.'

Mackenzie slumped again, fighting bitter disappointment. This had been a wasted trip after all. He'd have to go back to Charis and tell her, and the thought of that... But Mulholland was speaking again, and Mackenzie strained to catch the words over the smooth clunks as the two officers opened the Discovery's doors.

'We'll just have to watch him then, see where he goes.'

'Fat chance! Thanks to you the poor bastard'll be lucky if he's out of hospital before Sarah gets into the country. And if she gets to him first it'll be—'

The doors slammed in unison, drowning out the conversation, and Mackenzie stared at the cottage, torn. He couldn't just leave if Doohan had been hurt. But then, from the sounds of it, there was no point in following Bradley anyway, so he waited until the jeep had disappeared up the lane and, hoping he'd hidden the bike as well as he'd thought he had, he left the shelter of the barn and pushed open the front door.

He stared around the sitting room in shock. This must have happened before he'd arrived outside, or he'd certainly have heard; the place had been torn apart. Furniture had been thrown aside and crockery smashed; on the floor in the corner, he saw a shadow move. Mackenzie took a step forward, but stopped as the man held his hands in front of his face.

'I'm tellin' you, I don't have them!' His voice quivered, but not with fear, as Mackenzie had expected. With rage.

'Robert Doohan, I take it?' Mackenzie said. He moved back and waited, and the man dropped his hands.

'You take it right.' After a moment's consideration, and evidently accepting Mackenzie as friend rather than foe, or at least non-violent, the anger faded from Doohan's voice and was replaced with a certain waspishness. 'Well? Are you just going to stand there and leave me on the floor?'

Mackenzie reached out again and helped the man into the one chair still standing on its four legs. 'I believe you were just entertaining Superintendent Bradley. Champion of the elderly of his community.'

'Aye, wee gobshite that he is. Him and his weaselly buddy.' Doohan grunted as he settled himself, and Mackenzie switched on the light to get a better look at the damage to both man and home. The room would easily be put right; beyond the crockery breakages and a crooked fire surround it wasn't as bad as it had first appeared. Doohan, however, was looking pale and sick, and Mackenzie could see a nasty thick seepage of blood running from behind one ear to the collar of his neatly pressed shirt. He wasn't nearly as old as he'd sounded, probably early sixties, no more.

'Are you badly hurt?' he asked, reaching to put the phone back on the coffee table.

'I've no idea, lad. I'm a bit numb, to tell the truth. Who are you anyway?'

Mackenzie lifted the receiver and put it to his ear. Nothing. 'My name's Mackenzie. Your phone's not working, by the way. I'll use my mobile.'

'Oh aye? Good luck to you, the signal out here's non-existent.'

Doohan was right; Mackenzie's phone refused to connect to a network, which meant he'd not be able to call Charis either – on the plus side, it also meant Bradley probably wouldn't be able to get hold of Stein yet. He crouched beside Doohan's chair to check the injury to the man's head. Doohan's expression was alert, studying him with sharp interest, which was a good sign, but Mackenzie wasn't convinced.

'I'm no doctor,' he said at last, 'but I'd say you could do with some attention. I'm going to leave now, but I'll send an ambulance out to you soon as I get a signal, okay?'

Doohan nodded, but still looked suspicious. 'What are you doing here, anyway? It's not that tired old good-cop-bad-cop thing is it? They come in here and smash the place up, and then you come along and try to win me over with kindness?'

'Kindness is it? You've been beaten up; I call an ambulance. Seems like common decency to me, nothing more. Besides, I'm not a police officer.'

'But you *are* after the collection.' It wasn't a question, and Mackenzie shrugged.

'If you mean the one belonging to Sarah Wallace, aye, I am. Her friend's paying me to find them.'

'So you're a private eye?'

'Not an expression I'm fond of. I provide an investigation service, and she wants this investigating.'

'No doubt. Time was I'd have told her, too, if I'd known.'

Mackenzie frowned. 'But not now?'

Doohan shook his head, and his expression altered. Now he seemed confused and unhappy. 'Duncan Wallace was my best friend; his family was my own, since I had none. They even asked me to be godfather to their only child, and I was happy to accept. When Duncan and Mary died, the same year I was released, I swore over their graves I'd protect and look out for wee Sarah.'

'Hard to protect her when she's on another continent,' Mackenzie observed.

Doohan nodded again. 'True enough, but when she left, I believed it was for the best. And all these years I've kept an eye out, even from here. Sent letters, gifts... Not that she sent much back, but her life was different from mine, aye? I had more time.'

Mackenzie glanced at his watch, mentally counting Bradley's head start. Doohan appeared not to notice his impatience, and Mackenzie was about to say something, but Doohan's words stopped him.

'I don't know how reliable Bradley is with his information, but I believe *he* believes it. I'd bet on it, too.' He looked calmly at Mackenzie. 'She's the one set the house afire and killed Duncan and Mary.'

'Christ!' Mackenzie felt his eyes widen. 'Murder or accident?'

'Oh, it'll have been deliberate,' Doohan said, matter-of-factly. 'Duncan would never tell her where he'd hidden the collection, and she'd a vicious temper on her when she didn't get her own way. When she was a wee girl it was quite funny...' His voice tailed away, as if losing himself momentarily in the memories of a small girl stamping her foot, to the indulgent smiles of her parents and their friends.

'Not so cute now, eh?' Mackenzie said. 'Listen; I've got to be away. I'll call that ambulance, and see if I can find out where Bradley's—'

'Och, I don't need an ambulance. Don't bother yourself with that.' Doohan suddenly stared harder at Mackenzie. 'What did you say your name was, lad?'

'Mackenzie.'

'Can't throw a stone without hittin' a Mackenzie out here – what's your first name?'

'Paul. Mr Doohan—'

'I thought you had a familiar look about you. I knew your mum and dad, you know.'

'Aye, I remember you, a bit. You used to come to the house.'

'It was a shame about your mother. And I always liked your dad.'

'You can visit him anytime you like; he might even be pleased to see you.'

'Visit?' Doohan stared at him. 'He's not dead?'

'Dead? No.' Mackenzie shook his head, realising he shouldn't be surprised; Frank might as well have disappeared off the face of the earth to everyone except his younger son, and, if he had his way, even to him. 'He's in a place called The Heathers. It's a nursing home. You knew about the stroke though?'

'Aye, I did, Duncan wrote to me in prison. But he also told me the man had gone the way of your poor mother.'

'Well, he hasn't,' Mackenzie said shortly. He stood up. 'Mr Doohan, I'm sorry to hear your Sarah isn't the shining angel you always thought she was, but there's a child missing and I need to find him, even more than I need to find those stupid bloody statues.'

'Hardly "stupid bloody statues," lad.' Doohan paused, then added quietly, 'Thank you for coming in. You're your father's boy all right.'

Mackenzie swung back, suddenly angry. 'If you liked him so much, why did you never try to find a grave to visit, like you did with your precious Duncan and Mary?'

There was a heavy pause.

'Guilt,' Doohan whispered at last, and raised watery eyes to Mackenzie, who frowned.

'Guilt? What the hell are you saying, man?'

Doohan didn't answer at first; he just kept his eyes on Mackenzie's, then smiled. 'Frank Mackenzie's boy, eh? Who'd have thought? You know, I'd almost forgotten his real name – we never called him Frank. To us, he was always Mick.'

Chapter Thirteen

Glenlowrie Estate, New Year's Eve 1987/8

'WE CAN'T KEEP IT, DUNC.'

The rucksack lay protectively close to Duncan Wallace, on the upturned tea chest between the three men, its contents hidden from the feeble light of three candles. Rob saw the panic on Alexander Broughton's face as he leaned closer.

'Dunc! I said—'

'Shut up, Sandy, I'm thinking.' Duncan reached out and dipped his hand into the canvas hold-all. Rob knew that somewhere in there nestled the hypnotic Fury, the Lightning Ridge opal of such fiery intensity that Stephen Spence had found no other name that could come close to describing it. Duncan also had no idea Rob even knew it existed, and that was the way he wanted to keep it; Mick had only let a few people into his confidence, and kept them ignorant of one another for a reason. Rob wondered if William Kilbride knew about it, but decided not; he would have been a lot less scathing about the way Mick went on about the collection if he'd known the Fury was part of it.

Duncan withdrew his hand, and an earring dropped onto the tea chest. Rob wanted to pick it up, but there was always this feeling that, although equality coated the surface of their group, Duncan Wallace was very much in charge. He saw Sandy look to him for support, but he shrugged, refusing to be drawn. All he wanted to do was get his share and get out; this had been too close for comfort. After all, he'd been the one to actually take the damned things out of Mick's safe, the other two were supposed to have put them back, and failed spectacularly when the police had arrived and scared them off.

But Sandy was pushing it. 'Duncan, man, this is serious. A joke's a joke, but now—'

'Aye. Now, my friends, we're richer than anyone's a right to be,' Duncan said.

Rob smiled. 'We were already rich,' he pointed out.

'Not like this.'

The wind gusted as Duncan picked up the emerald earring from the table, shaking the hut and almost blowing the candle out. Shadows and light created the illusion of animation on the still faces around him, but Rob kept his own features steady as Duncan looked at them in turn, gauging their trustworthiness.

He felt a twist of guilt as he thought of their friend; Frank Mackenzie – Mick – would normally have been with them that night, joining in whatever childish excursions and dares Wallace had dreamed up for Hogmanay, but since he was at some big family function in Inverness he'd instead been selected as the target. A sort of punishment, even, for shunning Duncan Wallace's big party. And yes, Sandy was right; it *had* initially been a challenge, a joke, but now things had got serious. Thank god Will hadn't been involved as well; things would have taken a very different turn, no doubt.

Sandy kept on at Wallace, the idiot. Rob felt a little sorry for him, but knew he was digging himself a pit of bother in the long run. Better just to shut up, take his share, and bugger off. But of course he wouldn't.

'This isn't just any old collection – this belongs to Mick. Our *friend*, remember? This was supposed to be nothing more than a prank. Jesus, Rob, tell him. Maybe you'll get through.' He sat back in his chair, rubbing his jaw.

'He'll listen to whoever he wants to,' Rob said calmly.

The wind shrieked around the hut as Duncan told them what they would do with the Spence jewels, a plan that would take years to come to fruition. Sandy kept flinching and looking up, as if he could see the dark, heavy branches dipping ever closer to the roof of the hut; perhaps he was expecting to be struck down for his part in the robbery.

Rob leaned forward and felt inside the bag, letting the loose chains and rings pass through his fingers, and surreptitiously hunting among the velvet covered boxes for one that might contain the Fury. All the while, the arguments went back and forth, but of course in the end Duncan had the say of it. He began the task of separating the spoils of their raid, and Rob strained to catch a glimpse of the opal, but not knowing how it was packed, and short of seizing Duncan's own pile and sorting through it, there was nothing he could do. Still, there was time yet. Thirty years, in fact.

Rob and Sandy took their shares, left Duncan in his shed, and walked in silence down to the entrance to the Glenlowrie Estate.

Before they went their separate ways, Rob touched

Sandy's arm. 'You'll be careful with your share now, won't you?' He kept his voice gentle, and Sandy nodded.

'Aye, of course. I'll find somewhere to hide them, and try to put it out of my mind.' He looked miserably at Rob. 'I just wish I could give it all back, honest to God I do.'

'We'll still be arrested for breaking and entering,' Rob pointed out. 'Mick'll not take this lying down, not now. We'll do time, and what'll that do to your family?'

'Maybe when it's all died down, we can go and see Mick, and let him have what we've got?' Sandy sounded hopeful. 'We can keep Duncan's name out of it, but Mick'll probably *thank* us. After all, he'll get the insurance—'

'Bollocks he'll thank us!' Rob's voice hardened. 'You know him as well as any of us! You do what you feel you have to, but if you can keep Duncan's name out of it, you'll damn well keep mine out as well.' He leaned in close. 'Friend or not, if I go down for this, you're going to wish to Christ you'd kept your mouth shut.'

They went to their respective homes, and when, the following morning, they learned of Frank Mackenzie's shock-induced stroke, Rob guessed it was all over. He was right.

Faced with a possible charge of involuntary manslaughter, and riddled with guilt, Sandy Broughton had panicked and tried to return his share of the Spence collection. It was only a matter of hours then, before the police came knocking at his, Rob's, and Duncan Wallace's doors.

Aonach View, August 2018

'So your little prank cost me my home, my family, and my father's health,' Mackenzie said in a hollow voice, and the truth of his words cut Doohan deep.

'It was never—'

'Don't.' Mackenzie shoved himself away from Doohan's chair and stood up. 'You and Bradley, between you, have taken *everything*. And you sit here calmly accepting my help? You're no better than he is.'

Rob looked away. 'I've no idea how Duncan managed to swing it with young Bradley,' he said quietly, 'but you know what it's like; one *i* not dotted and the whole bloody case falls apart. Whatever it was, it worked. Duncan was released, and I served five years even though I gave up my share of the collection.'

'Nowhere near what you deserved.'

Rob couldn't argue with that. 'I didn't say a word to anyone about Duncan's involvement – how could I? He was my best friend. Plus he was always one for rewarding people he'd put his trust in. He told me he'd had those *stupid bloody statues*, as you called them, made up by a local craftsman, with his share of the collection split up and sealed inside. That man, Dougie Cameron, was under his protection from then until the day Duncan died. Dunc told me he'd got Cameron to put the flaw in the base of each one, so he'd know them, and I told Sarah. To protect her against people like Bradley.'

'And presumably you'd know them too.'

'I would, if I ever saw them again, but we both know it's unlikely now.' Rob took a deep breath and could hear it shuddering in his chest. 'I don't know about Superintendent Bradley, what he may or may not have done since. I've wronged you though, and I'm sorry for it.' His eyes met

Mackenzie's mistrustful glare without flinching. 'But you need to put that aside now and find the boy.'

'Easier said.' The hopelessness in Mackenzie's voice made Rob look away again, feeling wretched. His gaze wandered the room, surveying the wreckage with a bubbling outrage at the way his life had been reduced to this. A framed photo lay face down by his feet, and he bent with difficulty and picked it up. He turned it over to see a picture of Dunc, Sandy, William Kilbride and himself, back in the eighties judging by their clothes, squinting against the sun and ready for a shoot; some glorious twelfth or other...

He looked up at Mackenzie again, his heart skipping and his fingers suddenly tight on the photo frame.

'I think I might be able to help.'

Charis finished her shower and found a towel large enough to wind around herself twice and still leave room for potentially tripping up. This was definitely no cheap travellers' hotel. She sat down and rubbed her leg where she'd banged it on the corner of the bed; bending down to see if the skin was broken, she saw trailing laces under the bed. With a small moan she reached under and pulled out one of Jamie's trainers.

At the sight of it dangling from her hand, she hitched a sharp breath that hurt her chest. Poor, lost boy with nothing to keep his feet warm and dry... Please, God, let that be the worst of his worries.

She'd heard nothing from Mackenzie. And as for Maddy, the truce of last night seemed a million miles away now that emotions had had chance to cool off, and they'd all, presumably, slept at least a little. She herself had lain awake for most of what had remained of the night, but she knew she'd slept towards dawn because of the vivid dream she'd had, where Jamie had returned and slipped quietly into his hotel bed. She had been so speechless with anger at him for frightening her, and so frustrated when he laughed, that she had smacked his legs and made him cry. But it was her own eyes that were wet when she awoke.

Charis clutched the towel tighter. Unable to stop herself, she let her mind wander, finding her boy and picturing him as she'd last seen him; sitting up in bed, waving as she'd left him to go down to the hotel bar. So trusting, so defenceless, so heartbreakingly precious. She closed her eyes to hold onto the memory, until a door slamming somewhere down the hall brought her back and she jumped, a chill brushing her skin as she moved; she must have been sitting there for ages.

She reluctantly got up to find a clean set of clothes from her bag. It was all badly creased, but she shivered in relieved warmth as she pulled on a dark green sweatshirt. Her spare jeans were clean and dry now too, after their trip to the launderette. Was that only yesterday? How long had this weekend been going on for?

Her heart leapt as she heard a knock at the door. Mackenzie, thank God! She opened the door, but her smile became fixed as she saw the cool beauty on the other side, dressed in full police uniform once more. Maddy glanced downwards, and Charis realised the button on her jeans was still undone, and her sweatshirt was rucked up where she had been fighting with the newly washed jeans zip.

'They've just come out the dryer,' she began, then stopped; she didn't need to justify herself. 'Is there any news?'

Maddy shook her head. 'I just came for a progress report. Have you heard from Paul yet?'

'No, have you?'

'No. Can I come in?'

'Can I stop you?' Charis flinched at her own rudeness, but the frustration of waiting around and swapping pointless chat was starting to wear her down. Maddy gave her a thoughtful look and came in anyway. Charis closed the door behind her, hating her for not being Mackenzie, wishing she could turn around and see his kind face, filled with compassion and warmth, instead of those clear green cat's eyes that appraised her and doubtless found her wanting.

'If I've heard nothing,' she said, more harshly than she'd intended, 'there's nothing I can tell you.'

'The longer we go without contact, the less time we'll have to wait for it,' Maddy pointed out reasonably. She sat on the edge of the bed, ostentatiously averting her attention while Charis did up her zip.

'Did you see Stein downstairs?' Charis asked, yanking her sweatshirt back down.

'Yes I did.'

'And?'

'And what?'

Charis snapped at last. 'Do you always have to be so bloody snotty?'

Maddy blinked. 'Am I?' she said, frowning. 'I don't mean to be. I'm just a bit preoccupied, I suppose.'

'And you think no-one else can possibly have anything on their mind as important as what's on yours? Did it not occur to you that I might be sitting here out of my mind with worry about my little boy, and you come marching in here, giving me those...*looks*, and assuming I want you here? No, it bloody didn't. Now if you've got nothing to tell me, why don't you just get out?' She pulled open the door again and glared at Maddy, who was staring at her in amazement.

Charis gave her a tight, unfriendly smile. 'Yeah, the little pain in the arse has teeth. Now are you going or what?'

'Look, I understand you're scared.' Maddy stood up. Her police uniform, with its padded body armour, made her seem taller than ever, and her eyes shot bolts of ice. 'But I still don't believe you have *any idea* of the danger you've placed everyone in. Even Jamie.' She closed her eyes briefly as Charis started to protest. 'Just shut up and listen!' She reached out and slammed the door shut again, and her Glaswegian accent grew stronger as her voice rose. 'Those police officers are not comic strip bad guys. One of them is a psycho in all but certificate, and the other would like nothin' better than to tie concrete blocks to my best friend's feet and drop him into the middle of the nearest loch. Are you *getting* this? Now I'm going to help out where I can, but understand this: my loyalty is not to you, it's to Paul. No matter how desperately I want to help you find your son, I will do everything in my power to make sure that *your* paranoid interference does not hurt *Paul*. Got it?'

'Got it! And you understand something, too.' Charis felt the pressure building up behind her forehead, knowing she was within seconds of striking out. 'I feel exactly the same way about my child. And no matter how much I care for Macken-zie, Jamie comes first.'

Maddy stepped back, startled. 'You what?'

'What?' Charis echoed, thinking quickly back over what she'd just said.

'You *care* for Paul?'

'He's been...very kind.'

'Aye, he's kind to everyone.' Maddy softened slightly. 'Charis, listen. I get that you've been thrown together, and this situation is pretty intense, but you only met him yesterday. You can't make the mistake of—'

'I didn't say I was in love with him,' Charis pointed out, her voice tight. 'But whatever it is, or isn't, it goes both ways. He said so.'

The taut silence was broken by the warbling of the bedroom phone. Both women turned to it, but Charis got there first, despite Maddy being closer. 'Yes?'

'...enzie.' His voice was distorted, crackling, but still managed to carry a wave of comfort.

'Have you found them?'

'No, but I think...where Jamie is—'

'Oh, thank God!'

'Hard...describe, and...gnal keeps—' Right on cue his voice cut out altogether. She heard a car whizz by, and then he spoke again, fragments buzzing in her ears. '...A82...back towards Aberga...lowrie Estate, part of Wallace prop... Just got...call Stein, but going up to it now. Tell Mad...keep Stein occup...strong, Charis. ...soon. Okay?'

The line went dead, and Charis held the phone against her chest, unwilling to break the contact at her end. She bowed her head, and barely even twitched as she felt the phone gently plucked from her hand. She heard it set back into its charging cradle, and when she raised her eyes she saw Maddy was looking worried sick.

Charis shook her head. 'He's going to get Jamie,' she said, and burst into tears.

Chapter Fourteen

ANDY STEIN ENDED THE CALL, and with trembling fingers he tried to shove his cell back into his jeans pocket but gave up and just held it, suddenly hating the feel of it; Mackenzie's words, broken as they were, had nevertheless come through, too loud and all too clear. Hearing that Sarah had lied to him for so long was one thing, and that really hurt, but deliberately setting the fire that had killed her parents?

He felt ill. Disbelieving. Maybe the whole story had been concocted by this Doohan guy, or even Don Bradley, to justify keeping the statues to themselves. Maybe Sarah genuinely had no idea her inheritance had such a dark history. Mackenzie must have gotten it all wrong; she couldn't have done such a thing. Not his Sarah.

He tapped the image of her on his home screen and automatically checked his watch, mentally counting back the eight-hour time difference; she wouldn't have left Cali yet – it would still be early morning where she was. But he had to know. To his surprise she answered immediately, sounding alert and wary.

'Andy, are you all right?' The sound of her voice made his heart beat more heavily, as it always did, and he closed his eyes, holding on to the memories of her – the softer side, the vulnerability behind the social animal, and the unpredictable passion that had kept him hooked for the three years they'd been together. The hotel lobby faded away as he sat down in a corner seat.

'Sure. I'm good.' He took a deep breath. 'Listen, I have to ask you something. About the statues.'

'What about them? Have you found them?' She sounded more Scottish than usual; she must be more tired than she was letting on.

'Not yet. It's just that...I heard that maybe there's, I dunno, a little more to them than maybe you realise?'

'Such as?'

He could hear traffic in the background. 'Honey, are you in the cab already?'

'Just tell me what you're getting at, Andy.'

He sighed. 'Did you realise that your father had hidden something inside them? Something he didn't ought to have had in the first place?' He waited for her surprised reply, his fingers tight on the phone. *Please, babe, don't be in on this...* The pause was longer than he could take; she must be furious with him for suggesting it, and he opened his mouth to let the apologies spill, but she spoke first.

'Well, I suppose you had to find out at some point. My father and his friends stole a few little trinkets belonging to a friend of theirs. They split the pile, and Dad was the only one sensible enough to keep his share hidden all this time.'

'And that's it?'

'Yes, that's it. They happen to be quite valuable trinkets, that's all. One in particular.'

Stein closed his eyes again. The next question growing too big; he had to spit it out. 'And the fire?'

The pause was longer this time, and when she spoke again her voice was flat. 'You shouldn't have asked about that.'

Stein felt the pain go all the way through him, and unable to reply, or even to cut her off, he lowered the phone and walked out to his car.

Mulholland watched Bradley, who was shovelling the pub steak pie down him as if he'd been starved for days. He pointedly pushed his own plate away, eyes narrowed, as Bradley swallowed a mouthful of beer along with his latest forkful, one great rush of cholesterol and alcohol swirling down his gullet like a filthy mountain flood. He himself had barely touched the plate of food Bradley had ordered without asking; his appetite was sharp but not for food, particularly this fat-filled crap.

He just needed to find out what private little deal was going on with this socialite ex-girlfriend, and when he did, he would be in a position to blow every whistle he could find. Bradley's career would be over, and his own would be given the space to grow at last, freed from the barbed wire fence in which Bradley was keeping it prisoner.

Bradley finished mopping up gravy with his third piece of bread, and the plate looked as clean as when it'd come off the rack. Mulholland didn't bother to hide his disgust, but chose the more important battle. 'When are you going to let me in on what's going on?'

Bradley glanced around them and adopted a jocular tone, though it was clearly an effort. 'Hush now, sergeant, walls have ears. Particularly pub walls.'

'Then let's go somewhere else.'

'When I've finished.'

'You have finished, surely?'

'I ordered dessert. They do an amazing trifle here—'

'*Leave* the fucking trifle!' Mulholland hissed, leaning across the table. He noted, with satisfaction, the way Bradley instinctively moved back, and saw uncertainty cloud the man's features. Maybe he'd better tone it down; it wouldn't do to antagonise him, not yet.

'Besides, trifle is an abomination to good taste.' He sat back, forcing a small smile. 'Whoever thought of mixing sponge with jelly deserves to be hanged.'

Mulholland saw uncertain relief flickering in the super's muddy brown eyes. 'Well, maybe I've eaten enough, for now. Who knows where we may have to go walking later, eh?'

'Indeed. Shall we then?' He rose, gesturing for Bradley to lead the way.

Bradley finished his pint and stood up. He glanced back nervously as he sidled past, as if he expected Mulholland to shove him in the back like a playground bully. Mulholland just smiled, but he knew it hadn't reached his eyes by the way his superior looked away. *Oh, the times they are a-changing...*

Outside in the car park, Mulholland led the way to Bradley's Discovery. 'This is a pretty good place for you to fill in a few of the details you...*forgot* earlier,' he said. Bradley seemed unhappy about it, but nodded and unlocked the vehicle. By the time he had climbed behind the wheel and switched his phone on again, he had evidently come to terms with giving up his ace card.

'The jewels aren't the main thing,' he said. Mulholland just looked at him, expressionless; not demanding, urging, or requesting, just waiting. It always worked with suspects, and it worked now; Bradley cleared his throat, keeping his eyes fixed on the dashboard as if the array of buttons and dials helped him concentrate.

'There's one more item that both Sarah and I are determined to have. It was part of the Spence collection, and it's worth at least three times as much as the rest of it put together.' He turned to Mulholland, suddenly intense. 'But it's not just the money, you have to understand that.' The earnest look on his face was almost comical, as if he actually believed what he was saying, and was willing Mulholland to understand too. Mulholland didn't, but he nodded anyway. *Whatever, let's just have the story.*

Bradley pursed his lips. 'This stone—'

'Stone? I thought the entire collection was in settings already?'

'Not this one. It's called the Fury. A Lightning Ridge black opal worth hundreds of thousands...as much as a half a million perhaps, even back then. God knows how much now. But there's something else about it, something that gets under your skin. I hate clichés, but—'

'Pretty then, is it?' Mulholland knew he sounded bored, but he didn't care; he was locked into the possibility of a half a million pounds 'split' one way instead of three.

'I only saw it a few times, and it was a long time ago, before Duncan died. But there's something about it that grabs hold of your mind and doesn't let go.' Bradley became more animated, as if in direct reaction to Mulholland's boredom. 'It's the, the...*riot* of colour. It's alive, Alistair!'

'Oh aye, very poetic. So where is it? Inside one of the original figurines?'

'No. It wasn't among the pieces Duncan gave me to take to Dougie Cameron, or on the itemised list he showed me. I suppose he didn't trust me with it – or Cameron either, come to that. But it's more than likely stashed in the same place, wherever that may be.' Bradley looked away again, but before he did, Mulholland saw his eyes darken as his view turned inward, evidently seeing something other than the plush interior of his treasured new car.

He was growing impatient. 'So what was all that about with Sarah Wallace, then? Does *she* know where it is?'

'No.' Bradley's voice was distant, and Mulholland resisted the urge to punch him in the side of the head. Instead he kept his voice even.

'If we're going to find this wee stone, sir, you're going to have to let me in on a bit more of what's going on.'

His deferential words seemed to have the right effect, and after a brief pause Bradley looked back at him, all business once more. 'Right. Here's the deal. Sarah wants the Fury *and* the missing part of the Spence collection, of course. She thinks we have the original figurines – you knew that – but she also thinks we have the Fury. I've just offered the rest of the collection to her, in exchange for us keeping that one item.'

'All of it?'

'No great hardship for us, since we're not losing anything. Plus it'll buy us time to find the real thing.'

'And you think she'll go for that?'

'She's got no choice.' Bradley shrugged. 'She's getting off lightly at this price; she's just found out she's got a double murder charge hanging over her head.'

'What?' Mulholland sat up straighter; this was finally getting interesting

'When Sarah and I were—'

'Shagging?'

'*Together*, I was going to say.' Bradley scowled. 'Anyway, I told her what I knew about the collection. His voice took on the shadow of the past as he mused, 'I'd never seen her so angry, even had me worried.'

'Angry?'

'That I'd been protecting her father, when he'd kept the collection to himself. She blamed me for being part of the reason she never saw a penny's profit from it.'

'So?'

'So a few nights later she went to Inverness for one of her mad society parties, and – *coincidentally* – that was the night the Glenlowrie Estate burned down. Mary and Duncan both smothered in their beds. Poor Sarah, dutiful daughter, wound up the estate, collected her inheritance, such as it was, and pissed off to America with it.'

'And what makes you think it was her?'

Bradley shrugged. 'Early-morning thoughts. Pieces slotting into place. No-one else suspected, and nor did I until this morning.'

'Wasn't there an investigation?'

'Of course. The cause was discovered to have been a cigarette left burning in Duncan's study, and catching the sleeve of a nearby jacket. Sarah had an alibi: that party, and then some bloke she spent the rest of the night with.'

'And that's not enough for you?'

Bradley shook his head. 'I'm telling you, it was her. Somehow. Maybe she even got someone else to do it.'

'All right, say that was the case – you can't prove it was anything but an accident, so she's nothing to fear.'

'True. But she doesn't know that.' Bradley gave him a tight smile. 'I'm in the running for promotion, you know that, and the next chief constable already knows I'm shit hot. Sarah will find out how our contacts and acquaintances compare, if she bothers to look.'

Mulholland nodded. 'So we give her our collection at a reasonable price, on the understanding that she fucks off back to America and that we – you – say nothing about the fire. Right?'

Bradley nodded. 'Meanwhile, we've bought ourselves a bit of time to track down the originals too, now we know they're definitely out there. With the help of old man Doohan of course, if he's capable of anything after you got your great mauling fists on him. I told him what I thought about Sarah's part in the fire, while you were washing his blood off your hands.' He shot Mulholland a mildly reproving glance. 'There was no need to be quite so brutal, Alistair.'

'He's fine.' Mulholland waved it away. 'Wasn't as bad as it looked. What happens when Sarah finds out they're fakes? Because you know she will.'

'Of course she will, but not until she gets back to the States. She'd never risk breaking open the figurines here, then trying to get the collection back through customs. By the time she finds out, she can do her worst. I'll have what I want.' His phone buzzed, and he pulled it out of his pocket and glanced at the screen. 'It's her.'

Mulholland heard clipped female tones from the earpiece, and Bradley didn't say anything, but his expression changed from satisfaction to something a little like fear. When he ended the call, he turned a pale face towards Mulholland, and with a visibly shaking hand, twisted the ignition key.

'The deal's on, but we have a little job to do first; it's time for you to earn your part in this. You never really liked Andy Stein, did you?'

Rob Doohan couldn't suppress the worry that maybe he'd sent Mick's son on a fool's errand, but he was sure in his bones that if Sarah had anything to do with it, that cottage was where the boy would be. And maybe the Spence jewels too. He paused in his tidying, wincing at the headache that threatened to force his left eye out of its socket, and pictured the dirty white-washed place, tucked in its little hollow in the hills.

During grouse season, the child Sarah had regularly accompanied her father and the other guns, but usually cried off beating duties, preferring to wander alone. Rob had followed her once, concerned that she was roaming the hills during such a dangerous time. But as soon as he saw the old crofter's cottage he'd relaxed. She'd vanished in through the crooked front door, and for the half hour at least that he remained there watching, she didn't come back out.

He understood; she would be left alone there, as she never was in the grand home her parents provided, and, more to the point, she could be in charge in whatever games she concocted. She'd always been an angry child; Rob had witnessed furious tantrums, above and beyond the expected childish outbursts, but here at least, she seemed at peace. He never told her he'd seen it; a secret shared was a secret broken. But eventually Duncan had found out anyway and turfed her out, stressing the danger of the place and forbidding her from going there again.

From that day she had been icy-cold to everyone connected with her family, except Rob. They had instead become closer over the years; godfather and goddaughter, and the thought that she might have killed her own parents – and his best friend – made Rob curl up inside with grief.

And what of William Kilbride's 'accident,'on the night of the robbery? Duncan had sworn, in confidence, that it had been a fair fight, and that he'd been protecting himself; Kilbride had fallen as he'd tried to wrestle Duncan into the water, and Duncan had tried to save him. Rob had believed that, too, especially when Kilbride had recovered without pointing any accusatory fingers, but now it seemed certain Duncan had offered him something to keep his silence. Or threatened him. All this, resulting from one bitter little prank.

Then there was the craftsman who had created the original figurines too, supposedly killed by an intruder in his workshop, although Rob had a pretty good idea of who had wielded that chisel, and the greasy, red-faced little turd had been in this very house today. Not to mention poor old Sandy Broughton. Rob was only now realising how lucky he was not to have been added to the dark, and growing, death-list.

He sighed, and the thin, shaky sound of it brought him up short in dismay; what had he turned into? Some frail old man who could no longer cope with real life? Well, what did he expect? He wasn't twenty-five any more, nearer to sixty-five, although he looked and felt older. He looked around his wreck of a home once again. The skinny officer clearly enjoyed picking up furniture and throwing it, while his boss just kept on with the same question: *Where are they?* Talk about brutish, unrefined tactics.

His sadly travelling gaze brushed past overturned chairs, fallen lamps and displaced sofa cushions, and finally lit on the fire surround. Home-made, its beautiful wooden shelving was now knocked crooked, and scarred across the top where an angrily hurled coal shovel had scraped it. Duncan had helped him build that – how long ago now?

Rob remembered that afternoon as if it were last week. It

had been just like the old days. Their guilty secret pushed to the backs of their minds, if not totally forgotten, they had worked on it together, playing loud music and making their mellow way down a bottle of Talisker. The work never suffered for it though; it had been solid, strong... Like the two of them, they'd said, mushy with sentiment and whisky. Built to last, unlike Sandy and Mick. They'd raised solemn glasses to their two friends, now lost – or so Duncan had said. He must have known the guilt would prevent Rob from wanting to pay his respects; the lie twisted inside him, and he wondered what other untruths Wallace had told him.

He moved, with aching slowness, over to where the scratched mahogany shelf had been ripped free of its stone resting place, and leaned on it with his slippered foot to push it back so it would at least look right. It slipped, and his foot sheared off the side, scratching his ankle and halfway up his calf on the square edge.

He howled in fresh pain and angrily seized the nearest object, the poker, swinging it around and smashing it against the woodwork. The shelf moved again, and Rob stopped. He started to smile, and the smile turned into a chuckle, then a full-blown laugh, tinged with more than a touch of hysteria. Kneeling, he wiped a tear away, and he wasn't even sure what that tear was made of: pain, mirth or just a jumble of emotions that needed an outlet. He reached out and pushed the shelf away from the wall a bit more, then reached into the gap and pulled out a piece of newspaper packing. Voices rebounded off the aching walls of his head, playing like a scene from a film:

What's all the old newspaper for, Dunc?

Insulation. Can't beat it. Why don't you go and make some coffee while I start packing the cavity with this? Could do with diluting some of that Scotch.

'Ah, the old I'll-fill-the-cavity-with-newspaper-while-you-make-the-coffee trick,' Rob whispered, reaching further into the two-foot square base. Sure enough, as he rummaged among the newspaper his fingers touched something with more substance. He glanced over his shoulder at the door, and then the window, before he pulled out what he'd found.

It felt heavy in his hand, solid. He sat back on his heels, ignoring the fiery pain that flared along his injured leg, and let the paper unroll so its contents fell into his palm. There it was, the first of what he knew would be three, astonishingly beautiful, pieces of porcelain.

About eight inches in height, with a full skirt, the woman stared back up at him with wide, painted brown eyes, her mouth tilted in a perpetual smile, her smooth arm raised to support the child at her shoulder. Rob turned the figure upside-down to check the wide base. The flaw was there; near the edge of the signature, only noticeable when tilted so the light slid off the smooth edge and caught in the hollow of the tiny dig mark.

Rob placed the figure on the floor beside him. A minute later all three stood together, all with the tell-tale flaw, all containing part of Frank Mackenzie's lost fortune. There was no hesitation in his mind when he considered what to do next.

Maybe it wasn't too late to make amends after all.

Chapter Fifteen

MACKENZIE GLANCED up at the sky. It would rain again soon, and Doohan had told him the cottage was hard enough to find in good weather; in poor conditions the turnoff would be even easier to miss. He set off again, snapping his visor shut as he went, his heart beating hard and fast with the mixture of anticipation and urgency. Back towards Abergarry, the A82 flying away under his wheels, familiar enough that he rode by instinct, letting his mind reach ahead and work through Doohan's rather confused directions.

The Wallace estate. Glenlowrie. That was easy enough; Mackenzie knew where it began, but there were many small, un-named roads that led up into the hills from there, and even having grown up on the neighbouring Drumnacoille, the Spence Estate, he'd have a job making sure he took the right one. If he wasn't careful, he'd end up wasting precious hours following a ribbon-track that led nowhere.

'It's been a few years since I saw the place, mind,' Doohan had told him, his rheumy eyes worried. 'I remember that once you get up past the second turnoff there's a steep hill with a...a what do you call it? Blind summit. Then it curves down to the left towards the cottage. Sharp, like. If you miss that bend, you'd be all right though; the rough land ahead is a fairly flattish bit of ground. That's where we gathered for the shoot during the season, and Sarah would slope off down the hill to her wee ruined cottage. Until her father took it over for himself, that is.'

Mackenzie opened the throttle further as the road straightened out temporarily. Traffic was light this Sunday lunchtime; this kind of on-off drizzle usually persuaded most tourists of the appeal of a pub lunch. The route led through the middle of Abergarry, and as he reached The Burnside, at the far end of town, he remembered his promise to Charis and swerved into the car park. He got as far as pulling off his helmet before he paused to think, and reluctantly acknowledged that it was a bad idea; she'd only want to come with him, and that might prove dangerous; he had no idea what he was riding into. Mackenzie hesitated a heartbeat longer, but quickly pulled his helmet back on and started the bike up again, leaning hard out of the car park, out towards the lower boundaries of the Wallace lands and Jamie Thorne.

With his visor up, for clearer vision against the drizzle, he was aware of the loose strap beating its rapid tattoo against the side of his helmet; he'd forgotten to fasten it again in his hurry to be away. The rattle was annoying, and loud, but he heard the car over it long before he saw it, somewhere back along the road, roaring and coughing like an old tractor. He glanced behind, but saw only the bend he'd just negotiated; the steep side of the mountain, rising away to his right, stole his view of the road.

Dismissing it, he took the bike faster, dipping into the bends, riding much as he had ridden home from his visit to The Heathers just a couple of nights ago.

The car roared closer again, and he cast another look over his shoulder. Now he could see it; faded red and with a dented wing, one glance had shown him no more than that. It wasn't Bradley then, nor was it Stein's expensive hire car – so who else could be headed up here at this kind of speed? Even Mackenzie had to slow down for this road more than he'd liked, particularly since it had started raining again and the little-used route was becoming close to treacherous already. This wasn't some Sunday afternoon sightseer, but someone with a darker purpose.

He slowed down to risk another glance, and this time trained his eyes on the windscreen for the precious second he could spare: just a shadowy outline, broken by the swish of the wiper blades. He jerked his head round to the front again, frustrated and more than a little angry. The car was inching up behind him again, and he snapped down his visor and accelerated out of the next bend as hard as he dared on the wet road. Snow markers flashed by on his left, faster and faster; still the car kept pushing at him.

Up ahead there would be a passing place; they were dotted every quarter of a mile or so on these roads. He'd pull over there, although what would happen then he had no clue – he just had to make it to the cottage, somehow. Maybe the car would simply pass and go on its way; he'd take the mild embarrassment with gratitude. As he approached the expected passing place he eased off the throttle and headed into the cutaway – but with a surge of horror he realised the car had increased speed and was almost touching his back wheel; if he slowed down any more now it would be game over.

Another hurried glance over his shoulder made him twist the throttle open and swerve back out onto the main road, leaning forward across the tank, willing the bike faster. Where he gained, the car lost, and vice versa – this game of cat and mouse was becoming deadlier with every passing mile.

The back wheel skipped on a loose stone, and Mackenzie's heart took flight, but the danger was already past by the time he'd felt that nanosecond of loss of control. The car revved hard, pulling up alongside him, falling back, then closing in again, so close that Mackenzie could feel the heat of the engine on his leg. Hands slick with sweat inside his gloves, he flipped open his visor again, sucking in cold damp air to try and open his fear-clamped throat.

His mind chanted Jamie's name over and over, and he forced himself to think straight; to do otherwise would be to give in to panic and risk never reaching the boy at all. The hill rose ahead of him, and Doohan's words echoed in his memory:

'... *If you miss that bend...the rough land ahead is a fairly flattish bit of ground...*'

If it was as flat as Doohan had hinted, he could keep left, then change direction at the last moment to head straight for that old meeting place, while the car would carry on through the left fork.

The climb was steep, but his bike was in better shape than the car, and more manoeuvrable; he edged ahead, trying to force himself to steady his breathing, to slow his heart down. The top of the hill came into sight, and as he gave the bike a touch more throttle, he saw the sign: 'blind summit', and steeled himself. Keep left, keep left, hold your nerve...

Too late – as he came over the top, he realised the road did not dip away to the left as he'd expected; instead it veered off in a tight curve to the right.

In the split second it took to realise it was the wrong hill, Mackenzie fought to keep the bike on the road as he touched the brake lightly with his boot, resisting the urge to stamp down on it. If he lost it now, he'd be lucky to escape with his life.

Daniel Thorne's face tightened with a grimace of annoyance as the bike pulled smoothly away up the hill again; the bastard could ride, give him that. And this car was nothing more than a heap of shit held together with duct tape and hope, which didn't help. Back at the hotel car park he'd not been able to believe his luck when Mackenzie had turned up. He himself had only arrived back in town only ten minutes ago, and settled down for what might be a lengthy wait for Charis to appear; he'd looked with distaste up at mountains that didn't even look like proper ones. Just ugly lumps of rock. Charis didn't belong here – she was a city girl.

The low, throaty roar of a big motorbike coming up the main street had broken into his pondering, and instinctively, idly, he turned to look: nice machine, old-ish, but powerful; be worth a bit, if he was up here working for the lads again. The bike pulled into the car park, and the rider climbed off even before he'd switched off the engine, clearly in a hurry. He pulled off his helmet, and Daniel straightened in his driving seat. The Scottish boyfriend. He must be here for Charis too.

But Mackenzie had clearly already changed his mind and was getting back on his bike. If Charis wasn't here, the chances were he would know where she was. Daniel twisted his own ignition key and followed; his old car had a job to keep up with the far more nimble bike, but the speed limit through town slowed Mackenzie down a bit, whereas Daniel couldn't give a shit if he was ticketed, since it wasn't his car anyway. Besides, a bit of distance between them couldn't hurt, so, once out of town he hung back, just keeping the bike in sight, and wondering where the hell Charis had gone.

Pulling up this hill was hard going, though. The Kawasaki leapt ahead despite the wet surface of the road, and Daniel pressed his foot down, yanking on the heavy steering wheel to drag it round the bends. At the summit he saw the bike's brake lights flash, then bike and rider vanished from sight. Seconds later, coming over the brow himself, he saw the lights come on momentarily once more, as the road twisted into a series of tight S bends, and Mackenzie was thankfully forced to slow down to avoid the water that lay in gleaming puddles on the road surface. The car hissed through them without hesitation. Swings and roundabouts.

They were climbing again, but Daniel was bored now; it would be more fun to spook Mackenzie, riding his back wheel like a panting dog, then easing forward so the front bumper almost brushed the blue-jeaned leg clamped tight to the bike. Mackenzie couldn't risk glancing back, and Daniel grinned; any second now the arrogant fucker would lose his nerve, tip the bike the wrong way and he'd wind up with so much road rash he'd look like raw burger meat.

But it didn't happen that way.

They'd still been bumper to back wheel as they hit the top of the hill. Mackenzie should have given up, let the bike go, but he hadn't. He'd kept right at it, until the very last second when Daniel had taken a hand off the wheel to wipe his eyes free of the rain that had gusted through his open window. The front of the car – wheel, bumper, wing, he had no idea which – had clipped the back of Mackenzie's bike, and the next moment the

Kawasaki was skidding off the side of the road, vanishing as completely as if someone had erased it from the grey, drizzly picture.

Heart hammering, Daniel pulled the car into as straight a halt as he could without following the bike into the void. A hurried, unnecessary glance in the mirror told him there had been no witnesses, and he shoved open his door and ran around the back of the car, staring back and down.

The bike lay halfway down the steep slope, too far away for Daniel to be able to see the extent of the damage. But where was Mackenzie? Not pinned under his machine; they'd become separated immediately. No, there he was. Lying twisted and broken-looking on his stomach, facing down the hill, one arm bent under him, the other flung over his head. He wasn't moving, and Daniel could tell by the way his helmet lay that his head was impossibly twisted; there was no way his neck was intact, not in that position.

He felt at once sick and thrilled. Not happy-thrilled, exactly, but the adrenalin was coursing through him. His extremities tingled; he could feel every pulse point in his body... He had killed someone. Okay. That was weird. It was scary too, but on the plus side there was no way Charis would stay here now.

Daniel kept his eyes on the motionless form down in the valley, but Mackenzie wasn't going to move, he knew that. 'How does it go, Mackenzie?' he said softly. '*No-one'll find the pieces?*' The smile spread across his face, and he stepped away from the edge and slid back into the car, his fingers shaking as he started the engine. He pulled away, keeping hard to the right, mindful of the ease with which he had despatched Mackenzie to the Great Beyond. It was only around a hundred yards to the top of the hill, and as the road dipped smoothly down to the left he saw a flat, grassy area straight ahead, where he was able to turn the car around to head back towards Abergarry. As he passed the spot where Mackenzie had plunged to his death, he checked the road carefully, but there were no tyre marks, and neither bike nor body was easily visible from the road. Looking back as he drove away from the scene, Daniel realised with a flicker of reluctant respect that Mackenzie hadn't even touched his brake. He shook his head. What use was courage if it ended up killing you?

The Burnside

Charis's nerves were stretched to snapping point. She and Maddy were sitting in the lobby, ostensibly deep in discussion and note-taking, while Maddy kept one eye on the door and Charis sat opposite her watching the stairs for Stein. He was their only hope of finding the cottage now, and Maddy already had her car keys in her hand ready to follow him, the moment it was safe to do so. But if she thought she was going alone, she was hugely mistaken; Charis was determined to hang onto her belt no matter how annoyed it might make her.

'Why don't you just go and knock on his door?' she asked at last. 'That get-up would frighten anyone into telling the truth. And it's obvious he likes you.'

'He can see me, that's no problem, but he can't know we suspect him. That'll just send him into hiding, and we'll never find your lad then.' Maddy was clearly as tense as hell, but trying not to sound too impatient. 'Just leave this to me, okay? I've done it a hundred times.'

Charis fell silent. Mackenzie's continued silence was

causing her fingers to knot and twist, unable to relax, and she forced herself to focus on the low table in front of her, examining each streak in the wood grain as it curled into whorls, tracing the smoothly blended shades with her eyes until they stung. Maddy had persuaded her to eat some kind of breakfast, but she'd only managed half a piece of toast and a cup of coffee, and now they churned uneasily in her stomach.

The door opened and she twisted to see if it was Stein, but it was that pig of a sergeant, and a shorter, fatter man who had to be Bradley. Remembering how that man had treated Mackenzie, she clenched her fists in an effort to stop herself flying over there and tearing his eyes out, but she couldn't allow Mulholland to see her. And definitely not Maddy, in her high-vis clobber.

She looked back but Maddy had vanished, presumably around the back of the booth next door to their table, and she breathed a sigh of mingled admiration and relief as she sank back in her seat. Mulholland had taken the stairs three at a time, while Bradley spoke with the young woman on duty at the desk, and after a moment he reappeared, shaking his head. The woman shrugged an eloquent *I did tell you*, gesturing to the key rack behind her.

Were they searching for Stein too then? Charis strained to hear the conversation as they headed for the bar, but all she caught was, '...cottage already,' from Bradley, and, '...here first,' from Mulholland. Shrinking down into her seat she half turned away, as if searching for something she'd dropped on the floor beside her, and they passed by her again without a glance, pulling open the big glass door and heading purposefully for the gleaming Discovery on the forecourt.

'Shit, shit, shit,' she whispered, and looked frantically around for Maddy.

Just to be sure, she went over to the desk. 'Excuse me, were those two men looking for a Mr Stein?' she asked. The receptionist hesitated, but that was enough. 'Never mind.'

She reached the door in time to see the Discovery pulling out of the car park, turning onto the main street, and she hissed in frustration.

'Bloody hell, Maddy, where are you?'

'Here,' Maddy answered, appearing at her elbow. 'I'm sorry, it was too risky letting them see—'

'Look, Stein's already gone, and they know where he is, which means they're about to find Jamie. We'll never catch up now; there's no point trying.' Despair crept into her voice. 'What are we going to do? Mackenzie could only tell us it's on the Wallaces' estate.'

'Which is massive.' Maddy chewed the inside of her lip. 'Have you tried calling him back yet?'

'I've got no phone, and I don't know his number anyway.'

'I'll do it now.'

But after a moment she ended the call. 'Not answering. Not gone straight to voicemail either, so he must just be out of signal.'

'So what now?' Charis knew she sounded whining and helpless, but her re-awoken fears for Jamie, and now for Mackenzie, were getting in the way. She literally couldn't think straight; it was all tumbled and twisted, and all she wanted to do was hide until it was all right again.

'Doohan,' Maddy said, suddenly decisive. 'We call him, and get him to tell us whatever it was that he told Paul. Come on, the number's at the office.'

'Well why the hell didn't we do that before?' Charis followed her out to her car at a run.

'There was no need *before!*' Maddy shot back. 'Just shut up and get in.'

While Maddy searched among the papers on her desk, Charis borrowed her phone and kept trying Mackenzie's mobile, to no avail. Maddy found Doohan's number dialled it on the desk phone. 'Recorded message,' she reported. 'Currently a fault at the number, and engineers are working to correct it. We'll just have to go out there ourselves. The address is in my phone. Wait for me then!'

Maddy grabbed her car keys and caught up with Charis on the stairs. She took back her phone, and found the message in her sent folder before passing it back. 'That's the address.'

'Ayonatch view, Spean Bridge,' Charis read aloud, hurrying to catch up again as they went out onto the street.

'We generally say *Annock*, but that's it.' Maddy slid behind the wheel of a grubby and dented Corsa. 'Paul had a fairly good start on Bradley and his mate, so there's a good chance he's already reached the cottage, found Jamie, and set him free.'

Charis felt a flare of hope. 'D'you think so?'

'Well, we don't know how far up in the hills the cottage is,' Maddy pointed out, 'but Stein made it back to Abergarry in pretty short time last night.'

'Yeah, he did.' Charis buckled her belt with trembling fingers. 'God, I hope you're right. It does make sense, doesn't it? I wish Mackenzie'd call though.'

'He'll be in touch soon enough. I just hope he's out of danger himself.'

The road went on forever, and Charis's eyes strained past Maddy in the driving seat, through the trees on their right. 'There!' She saw Maddy jump and the car slowed. 'Behind those trees. I can just see the chimney. There must be an entrance just up here – slow down!'

'I can't go much slower!' Maddy shifted down another gear, and after a moment they turned in to where a small gateway led into a larger yard. There was no car parked outside; maybe he kept it in the big shed? He'd certainly need some kind of transport, living all the way out here. Charis looked at the wet ground and her spirits slumped; there were two sets of tyre marks in the muddy yard – one set was doubtless the usual resting place for whatever vehicle Doohan owned.

'Maybe someone else took his car out,' she ventured. 'Family?'

But the hope was short-lived. Maddy knocked loudly on the front door, and then louder still, calling Doohan's name and getting no response. Charis grew restless and went around to the back, peering through the old-fashioned sash window into a kitchen that looked as though a rhino had been let loose in it. She selected a sharp-edged stone from those scattered around, just as Maddy came around the side of the house, her eyes widening.

'Don't you dare!'

'Sod this pussy-footing around.' Charis shielded her eyes in the crook of her elbow. 'If he knows where Jamie is, I'm getting in there.' She smashed the glass and just managed to hold on to the rock, with which she began knocking out ugly shards that stuck out from the wooden frame.

'Don't be stupid! What good will that do if he's not there?'

'And you the intrepid detective?' Charis gave a derisive snort as she tossed the stone away. 'He might have got a map out to show Mackenzie, or drawn a quick plan to describe the area, anything.' She fumbled inside and released the catch, and ran the broken window up on its cord. 'You stay here if you like.'

'Bugger that,' Maddy said. She stepped forward and made a stirrup to boost Charis up.

There were no maps, no hurriedly drawn plans, nothing at all to see except total devastation. Charis stared around in dismay; what had happened here? She pushed at some twists of newspaper that littered the floor near the fireplace, evidently from inside the decorative fire surround that had pulled away from the wall. The only thing that appeared deliberately placed, in the entire room, was a phone directory that lay open on the one chair that remained upright.

'Who still has these?' she mused. 'More to the point, why's he looking up numbers, when his phone's not working?'

Maddy crossed to the book and put one hand on the open page to stop it flicking closed again. Then she crouched beside it and studied the page.

'He wasn't,' she said at last. 'He was looking for an address.'

'What address?'

'He's been checking out nursing homes, look. He's an old friend of Paul's dad, so I found out the other day, and The Heathers is listed right here. This looks like too much of a coincidence to be one; Paul's being here must have sent him to

Frank for some reason. Now we know where to find him, if we're quick.'

Following blindly, Charis felt hope propelling her onward again. She and Maddy raced to the car, and Maddy had pulled away before Charis even got the strap of her safety belt across her shoulder.

'Why's he in a home?' Charis said, holding on to the door and closing her eyes as Maddy swerved along the lane.

'Stroke. Years ago, when Paul and his brother were very young. The lads went to live with their grandmother since there was no other family.' Maddy hit the little hump-backed bridge with a jolt, and Charis swore under her breath, but saw the light of determination on Maddy's face and decided to keep quiet about the woman's driving skills; at least they were moving, and fast.

The Heathers was midway between Doohan's house at Spean Bridge and Abergarry, and as they turned up the long driveway Charis felt herself tensing up, ready to leap out the moment the car stopped.

The house was large, and seemed more like a hotel than a hospital, with its beautifully maintained gardens and wide, sweeping entrance.

Inside was plush and quiet; only the occasional glimpse of a white coat gave away the underlying medical nature of the place. Maddy went up to the desk, and a moment later she returned, accompanied by a nurse, who regarded at them both with interest.

'He's got someone with him at present. Nothing wrong, I hope?'

'No,' Maddy said briskly. 'Is the visitor a Mr Doohan?'

'I can't tell you...' The nurse checked herself, looking at Maddy's uniform. 'Aye, that's him.' Her curiosity clearly roused even further, the nurse nevertheless forbore to ask any more questions and led them through the halls for what seemed like miles, then tapped gently at one of the doors.

'Well now, Frank, here's someone else to see you.' She stepped aside to allow Maddy and Charis to enter, and her reluctance to leave might have been amusing under different circumstances.

'Well, just press the buzzer if it all gets too much,' she said at length, and drifted away as Maddy and Charis went in. The two men were not friends – that much was clear; maybe they had been once, but the tension in the air now was thick enough to taste. Mackenzie the elder, recognisable immediately by his broad stature, sat up straight in his chair by the window. Rob Doohan was at the far end of the room with a canvas bag at his feet, an angry kind of desperation twisting his face and making him look far older than he probably was.

'We don't need the police,' he said, at sight of Maddy. 'I've done my time, aye? So you can—'

'Shut up, Rob.' Mackenzie shook his head irritably. 'It's just Paul's...friend.'

'Mr Doohan?' Charis crossed the room quickly to stand directly in front of him, commanding his full attention. 'I need your help. Please.'

Doohan had jerked as she spoke his name, and when he turned she was alarmed to see his collar stained with blood, and a large white pad behind his left ear. 'Help? How can I? I don't even know you.' But she saw something in his expression that told her things were clicking into place in his mind, and that while he might not know her personally, he definitely knew who she was.

'Yes,' she said, trying to control the shaking in her voice.

'It's my son who's been...taken. You told Mackenzie where the cottage was, and we—'

'He's told me nothing!' Mackenzie protested. 'What the hell's going on?'

'Not you, Mr Mackenzie,' Maddy put in. 'Paul.'

Mackenzie senior glared at Doohan. 'You've been here hardly two minutes, and so far all you've done is babble your filthy apologies and bring this rabble of screeching women with you. You've done your worst; you've stolen my life and left me alone these past thirty years. Now get out.'

'Listen, Mick—'

'Don't call me that!' Mackenzie went white, and he gripped the arms of his chair. 'Nobody calls me that any more. You think you did your time? You didn't. *I'm* doing your time for you! You put me here – you stole what was mine. I've got nothing left. Nothing!'

'Hush, Mr Mackenzie, please,' Maddy said in what Charis assumed was her best soothing tone. 'Don't excite yourself—'

'Don't excite myself? Don't *excite* myself?' Mackenzie turned on her, his colour returning. 'Don't you dare come into my room and tell me how to behave!'

'Shut up!' Charis turned on him furiously. 'You have no idea...' She stopped, realising she was shouting at a helpless old man. But he didn't look helpless, not at all. Maybe he couldn't walk, maybe the stroke had rendered him dependant in a lot of ways she couldn't see, but helpless? Never. The eyes fixed on hers were hard and bright in the suddenly hushed room.

'Who. The hell. Are you?' Each word clipped off through tight lips, a jaw set like iron. She closed her eyes briefly, fighting the frustration, and prepared to explain, but she didn't get beyond a deep breath.

'Glenlowrie.' Doohan said in a low voice. 'The Wallaces' place.'

'Duncan?' Mackenzie looked puzzled now. 'What's anything got to do with him? He's been dead twenty-odd—'

'He was the one who had the third share of the collection, Mick,' Doohan said. He picked up the bag at his feet and came closer. 'He was the one kept the Fury.' He turned to Charis. 'There's a cottage on the estate, where Duncan's daughter Sarah used to play...'

Charis seized a much-thumbed atlas from the pocket in the car door and searched the index. Maddy had torn off her high-vis jacket and body armour and thrown it into the back seat, and now she followed it with the distinctive black and white tie. 'Can't risk getting stopped in that get-up.'

'Haven't you got a sat-nav?' Charis asked, her eyes crossing as she tried to make out the tiny lines on the map.

'The agency has one, but it's broken. Wouldn't do any good where we're going anyway; most of the smaller roads aren't mapped yet, and these estate roads definitely not. Maybe Google maps on my phone will help though, if we think we're going adrift.'

They headed out of Abergarry again. Maddy's driving still frightened the life out of Charis, especially once they got onto the narrow road that wound up into the mountains, but it didn't seem to matter now; very soon she would see Jamie again. The atlas open on her lap, she tried to follow with her finger roughly where they were going, and with the other hand she held onto the car door for dear life. They had left the two old men finally talking to each other in a more civilised fashion, and she realised now that Doohan was risking a great deal just by being there; there was no way he'd have been able to prove he hadn't known—

'Bloody tourists!' Maddy slowed down to crawl past a car, parked haphazardly by the side of the narrow road and taking up half of it. 'What the hell?' She slammed on the brakes as a loud hammering on the roof made them both jerk in shock. Charis gasped and clutched at the seat belt as it pulled suddenly tight across her chest and clamped off her breath. She released it, allowing herself to move again, and with a remote feeling of disbelief, she recognised the 'tourist'.

'Daniel!'

'Your ex?'

'Just drive on,' Charis urged. 'God knows what he's doing up here, but we haven't got time to find out.'

Daniel crossed to stand in front of the car, and Charis lowered her window an inch so she could shout through it. 'Don't hold us up, we're going to get Jamie!'

'I hope you're not expecting to meet your biker boyfriend as well, because it'd be such a waste of time if you were.' Something about the way he said it made Charis go very still. She exchanged a glance with Maddy and lowered the window further.

'What are you saying?'

He came around to lean into the car. 'I can tell you where he is though, if you like?' Charis didn't trust herself to speak, but she didn't have to; it was clear from his expression that he couldn't wait to pass on his news.

'Right at this moment,' Daniel looked over his shoulder and then back at Charis, 'at this *very* moment, Mr Mackenzie is lying at the bottom of a very steep hill, with his head on backwards.'

Charis's vision clouded. 'What?'

'He had a nasty accident on his big boy's bike, and took a bit of a tumble. I saw the whole thing, and I was honest to God *just* on my way to report it.' He flashed a grin. 'He went too fast on a bend and wheeeee...' Daniel mimed graceful flight, then clapped his hands together. Charis heard her own wordless moan; she felt dry, hollowed out with disbelief, but Daniel's face held no hint of a lie, cruel or otherwise. He had seen it. He knew. Paul Mackenzie was dead.

Daniel jerked her door open, and she cried out in shock as it wrenched at her fingers. There was no time for an equally stunned Maddy to floor the accelerator before Daniel yanked Charis out of her seat. He grabbed her arm and pulled her towards him; too close for her to raise her knee and ram it home, even if she had possessed the strength to do it. She dimly heard Maddy's car door open.

'Stay where you are!' She couldn't be responsible for anyone else being hurt, and Daniel wouldn't think twice – she knew that without any flicker of doubt. 'Don't get out!'

Daniel's hand slipped around the back of her neck and gripped tight, sending flares of pain right down to her feet. 'I know it's a rotten shame about the biker boy, but now there's nothing to keep you here, you can come home with me, can't you?'

'Aren't you forgetting your son?' she managed, through lips that felt as if someone were working them for her.

'The kid will be okay. He's just off adventuring. The police will bring him home to us. *Home,* Charis!' His voice took on a persuasive urgency, almost wheedling. 'Liverpool! Not here, not in this fucking stupid...*wilderness.*'

'Are you lying about Mackenzie?' she whispered. She'd hate him for it, but at least her heart would beat again.

'No, I'm not lying. I'm actually sort of sorry for him. Look, I didn't like the bloke, but I didn't want him dead either. Still, when your time's up, you—'

'You *bastard*.'

'Hey, I just report the news.'

Charis stared at him in bewildered fury; she had shared this man's bed, his life, borne his child, and now she would have given anything to be holding something, anything, to strike with. She'd kill him. Her expression must have conveyed this, and his eyes narrowed, glancing quickly over her to make sure she had nothing she could use as a weapon. Evidently seeing no threat, he relaxed a little, and now the old Daniel was back. He smiled, and it looked real. He touched her face, and it was gentle.

'Charis?' Maddy's voice held a warning note.

'Stay *there*, Maddy!'

Daniel's smile softened. 'Come home, Charis-with-a-c-h. You don't belong here.' He started to pull her towards his own car, and for a split second she acquiesced, but only until his grip loosened in surprise. Then she jerked her arm out of his grasp and flung herself at him, catching him off guard; she heard the low panting as she struck him time after time, and dimly she wondered why she wasn't screaming. But her hate was too bright, her grief too sharp to allow that kind of relief – she wanted to hurt Daniel, and all her energy was going into that.

He was starting to fight back, the shock worn off now, and a punch caught her along the jaw. She didn't even feel the pain, but she stumbled under the impact, knowing he'd not pulled the blow. It would hurt later, but later was something that happened to other people. Now was all there was; this moment, and her desperate need to tear this man apart. She reached for his eyes, trying to dig at them, to rip them from their sockets, to gouge, tear and destroy.

And then he had her. He caught at her wrists and pushed her up against the car, slamming her body against it hard enough to snap her teeth together. He got a knee in between her thighs, forcing them apart.

'Come home with me, Charis,' he breathed again, his eyes bright and fierce. 'I don't have a problem any more. See?' He rammed himself against her and she felt the iron-hard shape of him through his jeans and hers. 'I'll bet your bit of kilt couldn't do what I can do for you. Remember this? Remember how you cried out? *My* name, not—'

His eyes glazed over, and his face went slack. Then he crumpled to the ground. Charis stared at him and then up at Maddy, who stood behind him, white-faced, the steering lock clutched to her chest.

'Was he lying? Please, God, tell me he was lying...'

Charis's stomach lurched before she could reply and she turned away, clutching the car door as her sparse breakfast splattered onto the tarmac, hot and acidic. Eventually she sank to her knees, breathing hard, trying to push Mackenzie's face out of her mind, but it wouldn't go. She turned to find Maddy sitting cross-legged in the road, staring straight ahead, into a distance only she could see. She too was breathing rapidly, taking short little gasps of air, her lips parted to force each breath out, concentrating like a woman in labour. Controlling the pain.

Charis scrambled over and gathered the unresponsive woman into her arms. Maddy remained stiff for a moment, then hugged her back. After a minute she pulled away and looked beyond Charis, following the stretch of wet road as it wound away into the distance. Charis felt the pain swell in her heart – each beat was agony. It was all her fault; she had brought Daniel here, she had got Mackenzie involved in this whole business, and... Jamie!

'We still have to find him,' she gasped, wondering how a mother could, however momentarily, forget her own child.

Maddy nodded. 'Yes. He...he can't just stay out here in the cold—'

'Not Mackenzie!' She saw the look Maddy turned on her, and tried again. 'Of course him, but right now we have to get to the cottage. Find Jamie, before it's too late for him too.' She steeled herself for a grief-fuelled attack, but it never came. Instead Maddy stood up, her expresssion set and cold now.

'First we'll have to get rid of this.' She nodded at Daniel's inert body, and Charis kicked him in the thigh, hard enough to hurt her own foot, wishing he were conscious so he could feel it too. Together they dragged him to his car and managed to get him behind the wheel. Charis folded his legs in, terrified of feeling him move at any moment, then she plucked out the keys. She let the handbrake off and scrambled clear, and she and Maddy got the car rolling a short way before it teetered briefly on the edge of the road, then rolled smoothly down the wide wall of the valley, smashing through shrubs and over rocks as it went.

'He'll wake up soon enough,' Maddy said as they watched the car gather momentum, and then slow again, finally rolling to a stop when it reached the uneven valley floor. 'He'll have an almighty headache, but I think he'll be okay.'

'Unfortunately.' Charis's voice was bleak. She closed her eyes and folded her arms tight across her chest, as if she could stop the pain that way. 'How will we know where it happened?'

'Your ex wouldn't have hung around at the scene; he'd have

driven for a bit before he dared to stop. It probably didn't even...' Maddy paused, as if the reality of what *it* was had hit her all over again. 'It probably didn't even happen on this road. More likely up towards the estate, where it's steeper.'

Charis put a hand on her arm. 'I never said thank you,' she said softly. 'I don't know how far Daniel would have gone if you hadn't been there and...done what you did. So thank you.'

Maddy nodded briefly; Charis might as well have been thanking her for the loan of a book. 'Let's just go,' she said, turning back to her own car.

Charis took a last look down at where Daniel's car lay, dented but otherwise undamaged, and wished with all her heart that it would catch fire like they did in the films, right there in front of her eyes; that Daniel would wake up and feel the heat of flames, and not be able to escape. That his last vision in this world would be of her, standing impassive and watching him die.

Chapter Sixteen

Glenlowrie Estate

JAMIE'S FEET and legs were aching badly now, and the hunger was a hollow howl in his belly that was only going to become worse. Still, he didn't give in to the temptation to finish his Mars Bar. He clutched at the treasure he had found, looking away from it now and again, but always finding his gaze drawn back down within a few minutes. It focused his attention, helped him to stay calm – and besides, what else was there to look at? The walls were bare, and the two halves of the stone he'd pulled out were now pushed back in, so no-one would realise it had been disturbed at all unless they looked closely.

He made a sound that was almost a laugh – *no-one would realise?* And who was there to see? The almost-laugh turned into a sob, and he bit his lip, staring hard at the shimmering, living fire he held in his hand. Outside, a bird called, and faintly, somewhere out there, Jamie heard the cracking echo of a gunshot. He stiffened, folding his fingers over the stone and holding it against his heart as he stood up and crossed to the air vent. Another shot, and another...far, far away.

He remembered his mother talking about the way they hunted animals up here. Deer and peasants and stuff. No, not peasants – he'd read about those in history and they weren't birds...pheasants, that was it. And the little fat, famous ones, like on the whisky adverts at Christmas.

Then he heard another sound, and this one made his heart triple-beat. A car! Breathing heavily, he stared around him in panic, then shoved the stone into his jeans pocket where it lay against his leg; the pressure was comforting, and he patted it, hoping it didn't stand out too much.

Jamie went to his accustomed place against the wall, under the air vent, and sat down. He tried to still the fierce hammering of his pulse, feeling it in the bruise on his jaw, in each one of his fingertips, even in his frozen feet. Before long he heard the car stop outside, and the door slammed. Whoever it was seemed to be in a hurry, and Jamie swallowed the trembling fear that fluttered in his throat. He was unable to help whimpering though, as the door opened and the American appeared, for the first time looking dishevelled and urgent.

'Get out. Now!'

Jamie stared in numbed incomprehension. 'Huh?'

'I said *go*,' the American urged. 'Listen, I'm sorry, I've been...misled, stupid. Get out of here, kid, before it's too late. Go hide in my car, just like you did on the way up here.' He cocked his head. 'Shit, too late. Okay, forget the car – go around the back of the building, out that way, up across the hill. Stay low. Do it! NOW!'

With a surge of mingled terror and relief, Jamie came to life. He dodged beneath the American's arm where it was braced in the doorway, now hearing what the man had already picked up; another car somewhere down the road, not yet in view through the broken windowpane. He skidded across the slippery stone floor of the cottage and through the tiny side-room. A second later he stepped out into the cool drizzle, gasping as the fresh air struck his skin. Behind him he heard the American slamming the door, and then the car was closer. Really close... He could hear it crunch to a halt on the loose stones at the front.

Keep low, the American had said. Jamie dropped to his knees and scrambled away up the hill towards the waterfall, hearing voices; a Scottish voice, raised against the American's smooth tones. He wriggled on his front until he was over the next rise and then slid down the slight slope on his haunches, wondering whether to wait it out or to make a run for it and risk being seen. He decided waiting was the better plan; they'd have to go, eventually.

It didn't take Stein more than a moment to realise that he was staring at a seriously unbalanced man. The shouting had begun the moment Bradley and his sergeant had got out of the car; proof enough that Bradley had lost control of the situation, but now things had taken an even more sinister turn.

'Inside,' Mulholland ordered, his faded blue eyes blazing with something that looked frighteningly like anticipation as he levelled the handgun at Stein's chest. Bradley stood behind him, staring at the surrounding mountains as if they could possibly hold the slightest interest for him, disassociating himself from the scene. Stein desperately hoped the boy was out of sight by now.

He looked back at Mulholland, whose eyes were wide,

questioning Stein's hesitation and marking its stupidity. Stein turned and went back into the cottage, his mind spinning through all the reasons why this should be happening, and coming up with only one.

'Look, about the bank problem,' he said, as calmly as he could as the two men followed him into the gloom, 'I'll fix it, and have the money for you tomorrow.'

'No, you won't,' Mulholland told him.

'Oh, right, is this where you say; "for you there *is* no tomorrow"?' Stein scoffed lightly, but when he saw Mulholland's face, he wished he'd said nothing.

'I wouldn't be so predictable.'

Stein took a deep breath. 'Okay, but aren't you supposed to at least tell me why you're pointing that thing at me? And how you found this place?'

'Duncan Wallace was an old friend of mine,' Bradley said.'What are *you* doing up here, Mr Stein?'

Stein switched his attention to him: Sarah's shiny-faced ex-lover. 'Sarah told me about it, and what it meant to her as a child. She wanted me to check it out before I leave the country.' It had sounded plausible enough in his head, but aloud it struck a false chord that rang off the old stones and had clearly not convinced the two men.

'How sweet. And Sarah cares that much about you, does she? You know, sending you to run her errands and all?'

The question burned as Stein recalled her coldness on the phone. 'She just wanted me to do this thing for her. I wanted to help.'

'Well, lucky you, she's on her way here. In fact, she should be here any time now.' Bradley glanced at his watch, and despite this further evidence of Sarah's lies, Stein's spirits rose a fraction; there might be a chance to square things after all, to understand why she'd done what she had. No matter what had gone wrong with the deal, she wouldn't let him be killed; they'd shared too much. All he had to do was keep them talking until she got here.

'So, these figurines,' he said, feigning continued ignorance. 'Are they worth a huge deal or what? I mean, I'd thought it was just sentimental, but it seems like maybe there's more to them than that.' He nodded at the gun, trying to control the sweat that he could already feel prickling on his brow. 'They real valuable antiques then?'

'It doesn't matter really, does it?' Mulholland gestured to the door Stein himself had mended, on Sarah's instruction, and to which he'd fitted the heavy bolt. 'On you go, Mr Stein.'

'What do you mean? Why do you want me in there?'

'Look, I'm actually quite enjoying all this,' Mulholland said, 'so don't do anything to make me lose my temper and spoil it, okay?'

'Just go in, lad, and stop being so dense,' Bradley said, sounding bored now.

Stein crossed to the door, eager to appear co-operative. He stepped into the back room and shivered, and it wasn't even pitch black like it had been; to think he had shoved that poor kid in here. That poor *sick* kid... What had he turned into? It had made sense when Sarah told him what to do; the boy would have the adventure of his life, be the envy of the kids at school, and he'd never be in any real danger.

Well maybe she was right, at that. These were civilised times; you couldn't just kill someone and get away with it, not any more, no matter how tucked away out of sight you thought you were. He watched in profound relief, as Mulholland lowered the gun and started to prowl the tiny room, kicking at the walls.

'What are you looking for?'

'Shut up.'

Stein caught sight of the kid's crumpled pyjama trousers, and his breath caught. If they asked who those belonged to, he'd have no idea what to say – he'd be bound to give something away. But Mulholland didn't seem to have noticed; he was too busy poking around the other side of the room, thank God.

And now it seemed like the search was over in any case. Mulholland gave an exclamation and bent lower, peering at the bottom of one of the walls. Reaching out with his gun he prodded a broken stone, then looked back at Bradley.

'This has got to be it,' he said, and the superintendent, a strange look on his face, crossed the floor and knelt down where Mulholland pointed. Mulholland turned the gun back on Stein again, and Stein stiffened, desperately listening out for the sound of another car, one that would signal Sarah's arrival and his deliverance.

Bradley was grunting as he worked at the wall, but Stein couldn't see what was happening, nor did he want to focus on the muzzle of the gun. Instead he closed his eyes and thought of how Sarah must be feeling; betrayed, angry, desperate to reclaim some control – she'd always been happiest when she held all the cards, and when Sarah was happy, Stein was happy.

A volley of swearing broke through his thoughts and he opened his eyes. Bradley had stood up again and kicked the half-stone across the floor. Behind, in the wall, there was only an empty space, and in his hand lay a limp, black rag that looked like silk.

His voice was bleak. 'It's gone.'

'Is that what *you're* here for?' Mulholland stared hard at Stein, who blinked in confusion, his mind fatally distracted.

'The originals were here?' He froze as the words crossed his lips, but it was too late to take them back now.

'What do you mean, *originals*?' Bradley asked softly. 'Are you claiming that the figurines we're selling Sarah are fakes?'

'How would I know if—'

'You're lying. You've already told Sarah as much, haven't you?'

'No! I swear—'

'Not nearly as much as she did, I'll bet.' Bradley stepped aside and spoke to Mulholland, but kept his bland gaze fixed on Stein. 'I'm away outside, Alistair. Come out when you've finished here.'

Stein watched Bradley's shadow retreating and wished desperately for the power to reverse time. He heard the door bang open, and prayed again that the kid was long gone – there were still no sounds of an approaching car, and time was running out. Mulholland was grinning now, the gun travelling across Stein's body, pausing now and again while the sergeant considered.

'Now, where's the best place?' he murmured. 'Head? Heart? Balls?' The deadly black eye hovered over his groin for a moment, then moved on.

Stein's muscles loosened in terror. 'You can't just *kill* me! Sarah will be here anytime, you said so yourself.' He was babbling now. 'She won't let you do anything, and if she got here and found you had, she'd—'

'Oh, relax! I'm pulling your pisser.' Mulholland sighed and lowered his weapon. 'You're such a coward, I was hoping you'd shit yourself. I heard that can happen, but I've never actually seen it.'

Stein laughed shakily, as relief flooded through him. 'You're one cruel son of a bitch, you know that?'

'I am a bit, aren't I?' Mulholland laughed too, a little reflectively. Then he brought the gun up once more. 'I've got a message for you from Sarah.'

Jamie heard the gunshot, and whimpered, pressing his head down into his folded arms. He wondered if it was Mr Mackenzie who'd come and shot the American, and his chest tightened even further. He felt the grass scratching at his bare feet and the rain soaking his jeans; then, worst of all, his throat closed up and he hitched breath after broken breath, reciting his seven times table to focus his mind. But that only made him remember his mother, and their frequent arguments about homework. Jamie bit down hard on his arm to keep from crying out in miserable fear – what if she was already hurt, or worse?

He had to get down to the town and find someone to help, but he was too dizzy to see straight, and halfway down the slope his foot his a rock and he stumbled. He put his hands out to break his fall, but they slipped in the wet grass and he landed on his thigh, the impact making him flinch and shout in pain. He reached down to bat the obstruction aside, then stopped and dug down into his pocket instead; his fingers were shaking so hard he could hardly make them close over the black stone, but finally he had it in his hand, and concentrated on the shifting, glowing colours deep inside it.

Eventually, breathing steadily again, he put the stone away and started back down the hill. His bare feet frequently plunged into boggy holes; pretty soon they'd become numb, and the fear then was that he couldn't sense the undulating terrain. But whenever he stood on a stone it brought his skin to life again in the worst kind of way, and every step promised discomfort of one kind or another.

Spotting a small river away to his right, he followed it with his eyes for a moment. It twisted away out of sight, but he didn't know whether this river joined the waterfall, or was made by it. No matter; either way he'd be heading for lower ground. With a last, terror-filled glance back up the hill, he started down the path.

Up ahead, through the thinning trees, he saw the water churning into white foam, carving its way deep into the valley floor. With a mixture of terror and fascination he crept up to the point where it disappeared, and drew a sharp, excited breath as he watched the wall of roaring water crashing away below him. But, fascinating and awe inspiring as the sight was, realisation quickly robbed him of the euphoria of escape; the next level of the valley seemed impossible to reach without climbing back up to the road, and there would be nowhere to hide up there. It might take hours, and it would be dark before he was away from the cottage again. Plus there was at least one person with a gun... But what choice was there?

As Jamie turned miserably back, the sun made a brief re-appearance despite the continuing drizzle, and although it was a sticky warmth he welcomed it and renewed his scrutiny of his surroundings, searching for a way down that he might have missed.

A gleam caught his eye as he scanned the lower valley, and as his vision adjusted, he recognised the twisted metal shape of a smashed motorbike. Jolted by the discovery, Jamie's gaze went to the top of the hill, mentally following the bike as it must have plunged off the side – it was a hell of a fall. He wondered how long it had been there, and if there was anything he could grab off it to use as a weapon in case he was captured again. There was no sign of the rider, which was a relief, but they might have dropped a phone, or food, or anything. Maybe even left a bag behind.

His determination rekindled, Jamie began to pick his way down the least terrifying part of the slope. His feet slipped on the damp grass, and there were tiny stones embedded in the rough path, but he welcomed the softness of the occasional mud patch against his stinging skin. His mind plundered the bike as he went, trying to remember which bits might come off. Maybe he could manage to get the chain off, if it had one – that would make a good defence if someone came after him.

Not against a gun, though... His blood chilled at the memory of the shot he'd heard, and he stumbled, falling with a heavy thump as his feet struggled for purchase on the muddy path; someone back there was dead, probably the American. Actually *dead*-dead, not like in a film or a game, or even a book.

Sitting, alone and trembling, on the path, Jamie took a moment to try and get the notion fixed in his mind; someone who had been living and breathing had actually *gone*. Couldn't see, couldn't hear or feel, didn't care that it was raining, would never walk or talk again. The hands that had gripped his own, back in the hotel, would never hold anything else... And all that could all happen to him, too. Or his mother.

Jamie started to cry, softly at first as fear settled into his bones, and then harder as he heard his own lonely voice swallowed up in the roar of the waterfall; it would be just as easy for the rest of him to disappear. Knuckling tears from his eyes, he started down the side of the valley again, terrified of slipping and falling into that wild cascade. He had to work his way closer to the waterfall as the meagre path dictated, and the spray drifted across the side of his face and made the ground under his dirty feet even more dangerous.

He breathed hard as he went, concentrating on the ground directly ahead, his hands behind him acting as brakes when he slid. He resisted the temptation to look ahead and see how far he had to go, but was vaguely aware that the spray on his face was lessening; he must have curved away from it again.

At last the moment came when he realised that the ground was levelling out. His questing foot came up short and he risked a glance ahead. He had reached the valley floor – thank God, he was no longer in danger, and he'd made it away from the cottage... Now his tears came again, but they were tears of relief and he didn't try to stop them. At his his right, the waterfall crashed down into a wide pool, and as his gaze scanned the ground ahead he stopped breathing.

Some distance away from the bent and twisted motorcycle, a man lay horribly still. Jamie felt his knees unlock and almost pitch him to the sodden ground. He had to take a half-step forward to fix his balance, and then he remained in that position, just staring. It was the Scotsman, the one who had given his mother such a hard time... He'd been so sure the man was invincible, too.

He took another step, knowing he shouldn't look any more closely; it was one thing to acknowledge the murder of someone up at the cottage, where he couldn't see him, but quite another to come face to face with that same, terrifying emptiness in a man he'd known, however briefly. But Jamie was cold, the man had a jacket on and, well, he had *boots* on. And he might have a phone, which could be the one thing that saved Jamie's own life. One thing was certain: death was stalking these mountains and Jamie had no idea who would be next to feel its icy touch.

Chapter Seventeen

CHARIS SAT in the still-motionless car. Beside her, Maddy was white-faced and tight-lipped, both hands gripping the steering wheel so hard that her already pale skin seemed transparent, shrunk onto the bones with none to spare for movement. She hadn't done more than switch the engine on and fasten her belt, and they had been sitting here in agonised silence since they'd disposed of Daniel's car. Despite the urgency, Charis couldn't push her on.

She looked back out of the window. Jamie. Focus on Jamie, the only thing left that mattered. She wondered how far it was to the Wallaces' estate, but as she opened her mouth to ask, Maddy suddenly pushed the clutch in. Charis felt her heart speed up in anticipation, but Maddy simply reversed until she found a wider place in the road, then tucked the car against the hedge and switched off the engine.

The silence was heavy between them now, the only sound was the faint clinking of the keys as they hung from the ignition and brushed against Maddy's leg; there were no adequate words, so it seemed easier not to say anything. For something to do, Charis grabbed the first thing she could find in the side door, an old envelope, and shoved it in the atlas to mark the place. Then, as the silence stretched, she carefully put the atlas away in the door pocket, and sat with clenched fists. Waiting. Had Maddy simply given up?

Say something, do something...

Finally Maddy moved. 'We're leaving the car here,' she said, unclipping her seat belt.

'Why?'

'Because I don't know if there'll be anywhere out of sight up on the estate. Left here, this could be any car, going anywhere. Won't look too much out of place.'

'But how far do we have to walk? We need to hurry, and we've wasted—'

'Do you think I don't know that?' Maddy got out and slammed the door. 'It's up to you, but if you want to announce to whoever's holding your son that you've come to rescue him, then *you* take the fucking car.'

Charis watched in dismay as tears began to pour, unchecked, down Maddy's face. Maddy stared at her a moment longer, then turned and walked up the road a short way, before turning left and vanishing from view. Charis followed, feeling her own emotions frighteningly near the surface, but she had to control them for Jamie's sake; she wasn't as strong as Maddy – if she thought she'd lost Jamie too, she'd be unable to take a single step.

The place where Maddy had disappeared turned out to be a surprisingly wide concealed entrance, leading to a rough lane. It was steep and hard going, and Charis was exhausted, but she kept her thoughts on Jamie and soon caught up with Maddy's longer stride.

Eventually the road levelled out a little, and Charis found enough breath to talk. 'This is the beginning of the estate? Isn't there a sign or something?'

'Yes. And no.'

'Then how is anyone supposed to know—'

'The only people who know are the only ones who care. This estate is just ruins; nobody's lived here for twenty-five years. Now shut up and save your breath.'

'You blame me, don't you?' Charis said, trying to keep the wavering out of her voice.

'For what, for Paul's death?'

'For all of it. Yes, for...for that.'

Maddy didn't reply, and Charis too fell silent, lost in her own dark thoughts and leaving Maddy to hers.

The mist was low by the time they crested the next hill. Maddy kept to the right-hand side of the narrow road, and advised Charis to do the same. 'The valley drops away in places,' she warned. 'If you keep right, you'll always have the mountain at your side instead of the drop.'

Charis blew a drop of rain off the end of her nose and wiped her hair away from her eyes. She had been staring at the ground, feeling each footstep like a blade up through the bottoms of her feet; only the thought that each step was bringing her closer to Jamie kept her going.

Maddy's words struck a solid blow to her resolve, however, knowing that somewhere out there, on the other side of this track, was the place where Mackenzie had ridden to his death. She couldn't let Jamie down by falling too. She shivered and bowed her head again, watching her feet rise and fall, rise and fall, in a steady, mindless rhythm.

'Actually I don't,' Maddy said suddenly, and Charis stopped.

'Don't what?'

'I don't blame you. Not entirely.' Maddy turned to her, but although they were no more than twenty feet apart the mist made it hard to see clearly.

Charis resumed walking. 'I do.'

'I know. But it was always going to come down to either Paul or Don Bradley. You and your boy just got caught in the middle.'

They crested another hill, and the road tipped away sharply to their right; Maddy had pulled ahead again now, and Charis was halfway across the road in the mist before she realised she was walking straight towards the swerving drop-off into God only knew what below. She gave a cry and lurched back to her right, the shout echoing dully back at her off the hillside, mingling with another sound: water. Mackenzie had heard the waterfall on the phone, a big one, loud enough for Stein to have had to pass it off as the sound of a shower... They had to be close.

She wondered what she would have fallen into, had she carried on walking straight without looking up. There were snow markers on the bend and a few small, white-painted boulders to act as a crude barrier, but anyone could walk right through them and be stumbling into empty air before they'd even realised what had happened.

She bent over, breathing deeply to control her heartbeat, and an image flashed into her head: a bike, spinning off the road, seemingly motionless in mid-air until she saw the background blurring behind it. Before the bike could impact, she snapped her eyes open and stood up, the pain smashing into her again no matter how much she tried to deny the knowledge that he was gone.

With renewed resolve Charis started to run. She caught up with Maddy, and only then did she slow to a walk again, but this time she matched the taller woman stride for stride, and the pain in her feet faded – so did the pain in her heart, leaving only a hard, bright anger that fuelled every step.

Jamie reached across the dead body towards the discarded crash helmet. It would be another layer of protection if he had to go climbing waterfalls again, at least—

A hand shot out and gripped his forearm, and Jamie uttered a breathless shriek. A voice rasped, barely audibly, 'That's my property, aye?'

Jamie stared through the fast-falling drizzle as Mackenzie released him; his mouth worked soundlessly, and he thought his heart might burst out of his chest. Mackenzie's face had gone blank and paled further, and his reaching hand dropped instead to his shoulder.

'Shit,' he breathed, then smiled, but it didn't seem to sit right on his face, though he sounded a little stronger. 'Sorry, but this hurts like a bastard. Are you okay?'

'I'm... Yes,' Jamie managed.

'Your feet look like they might need some attention.' Mackenzie's mouth tightened in momentary anger, and he shook his head. 'I'm so sorry—'

'Why?' Jamie shouted in sudden panic. 'What have you done?' He clenched his bare toes, fully prepared to kick Mackenzie right where it would hurt the most, but the Scotsman's eyes fixed urgently on him.

'I've not done anything, that's the problem. I was trying to get to you, to the cottage, but... Jamie, listen. Was someone killed up there?'

It took a moment for Jamie to comprehend that if Mackenzie had been lying here for some time, he couldn't have been involved in the death of whoever it was who'd died. 'Some people came. The American let me go, so I ran away.'

'My phone's in my jeans,' Mackenzie mumbled. 'Try it, the emergency number might work.'

Jamie carefully drew the phone out of Mackenzie's wet pocket, but it wouldn't connect to any network at all. 'Says "no coverage".'

'Doesn't it say, "emergency calls only"?'

Jamie shook his head. 'Nothing else.'

'Shit.'

'The people that came to the cottage were Scottish,' Jamie said, putting the phone down. 'I thought it was you.'

Judging by his grim expression, it seemed Mackenzie knew exactly who it had been. 'Did they kill Stein, the American, do you think?'

'I don't know for sure, but I think so. He didn't have a gun, anyway.'

'Are you sure?'

Jamie nodded. 'He had to use a key to make me come with him. Said he'd put it through my eye.' He shivered at the memory. 'He was your friend, wasn't he? But he said you were...' *That big Scottish guy you've seen hanging around with me? He's got a pretty mean streak.*

'I'm what?' Mackenzie asked, but Jamie didn't think he really cared any more; he had gone a greenish grey. Jamie could see how close he was to either throwing up or fainting, and tried to be pleased about it, but he couldn't. 'He told me you'd hurt Mum if I tried to get away,' he said, suddenly bold. 'He said you were itching for an excuse.'

'What?' Mackenzie's head came up and he fixed Jamie with a stare that was as incredulous as it was horrified. 'He said *what?*'

'Well, he told me you had a mean streak and you thought she was trouble...' Jamie let the comment tail away, taken aback by the look on Mackenzie's face.

'Trouble? I'll say she's trouble, but... God, Jamie, no.' He reached out to touch Jamie's arm, and his voice gentled again. 'Your mum and I understand each other a bit more now, lad, we're friends.'

'You wouldn't do anything to hurt her?'

Something flashed deep in Mackenzie's eyes, behind the pain. Something just a little bit scary.

'I would rather die than hurt your mother,' he said, his voice so low that Jamie had to strain to hear him over the distant rumble of the waterfall, 'But before I did, I'd kill anyone who so much as threatened her. Or you. Do you believe me?'

'But Mr Stein said—'

'I said do you believe *me?*' Mackenzie's voice was hard, but the grip on Jamie's arm was faltering.

'Yes,' Jamie said, feeling tears start to burn again. He moved to wipe them away, embarrassed, but Mackenzie shook his arm gently.

'Let them go – you'll feel better. And I'll not think the worst of you, not after, after what...'

As Jamie watched, Mackenzie's eyes fluttered closed and his head slipped to the side. For a panicked moment he thought Mackenzie really was dead this time, then he saw the pulse beating just above the knotted leather he wore around his neck.

As the rain fell harder, he moved closer, sheltering against the Scotsman's side. After a while he wrapped an arm across Mackenzie's waist, and as he felt the creak of the wet leather jacket against his cheek and the rise and fall of Mackenzie's breathing, he finally let go, and sobbed until he fell into an exhausted sleep.

Chapter Eighteen

MACKENZIE STIRRED ONCE OR TWICE, shivering violently, before fading back into a semi-delirium, where he re-lived the moments when he'd come back into a world that had already discarded him and moved on.

There had been a strange, fuzzy darkness. Something at once firm and soft, pressing hard against his mouth and closed about his head, shutting him off from the clean air he knew must be there somewhere. A roaring sound in his head, blocking coherent thought. He moved, just one hand twitching into life, somewhere a million miles from the rest of him. He felt coolness, damp, something loose-scratchy under the semi-numb pads of his fingertips... He strived for bigger movement and felt his wrist respond as he moved it briefly from side to side, examining blindly. Grass, brushing the gloveless hand, leaving wet trails snaking across his wrist, cold against his skin. He tried to move the other hand but couldn't feel it.

Gradually, as sensations became sharper, Mackenzie realised the hand he could move was stretched out above him, that he was lying face down, and that the heavy darkness was not receding. He felt his breath coming back at him, not lifting away but huffing warmly back over his own lips, making them tingle. He tried to turn his head, and groaned as pain speared through him from the base of his skull to halfway down his back. He didn't try to move again for a moment, but instead turned his mind inward, trying to untangle the confusion.

The car. The bike, still vibrating from the brief, deadly contact. He had no memory of the fall, or of the landing, but he knew he was lucky to be alive, however long that might last. He didn't want to move again, but the need for fresh air was becoming more and more urgent, and the roaring sound was not abating at all.

Wincing in anticipation, he brought his functioning hand back towards his head – he met a solid obstruction and had no sensation from his face beyond the increasingly harsh breathing and the damp condensation of his own breath on his skin. He was aware that he was moaning softly as he patted around, desperation mingling with frustration, and it wasn't until he gritted his teeth and moved his head again that he realised what was keeping him from the cool air: his helmet, twisted so that the open visor lay somewhere around the back of his head, the fuzzy interior mashed against his face, absorbing his breath for a second before throwing it damply back at him.

He lay still for a second, silently thanking every force in nature that had made him neglect to fasten the strap before riding out again; if he'd tightened it he would probably be lying here with his head twisted at the same angle as his helmet. And he certainly wouldn't be alive to enjoy it.

He hesitated, momentarily unsure. Was he certain he was lying face down anyway? Yes, he had to be; he was starting to feel wet grass soaking through his jeans, and his knees were coming back to full sensation in response to the chill. As he became more aware of his body, he realised why he couldn't feel his left hand; it was pinned under him. He could feel the faint pressure against his stomach, through his jacket, although the arm to which it was attached remained dead.

He gave the fingers of that hand an experimental wriggle, and as they started to tingle, he acknowledged that this glove had stayed on at least. God alone knew where the other one had gone – probably still wrapped around the throttle of his bike, he thought with a flash of grim humour; never let it be said he bottled that particular chicken run.

Carefully he began to ease his left hand out, but as he did so a deep and shocking pain sank into his neck and shoulder and he screamed, the sound muffled against the interior of his helmet. The same pain that had speared down his back now centred on his shoulder, concentrated with all the ferocity of a blow torch. He breathed as slowly as possible, dismayed to hear each expelled breath as a trembling moan, and after a long while the pain had lessened enough to allow him to reach up again and begin to ease the helmet around.

It must have taken at least ten minutes of slow, inch-by-inch progress, but finally he could see daylight out of the corner of his eye, and he began to feel the touch of cool air on his temple. Spurred on, he began to work faster until finally, with a shout of mingled pain and triumph, he was able to drag the helmet off and fling it to the side, resting his sweating face against the cold wet grass.

How many times have y'heard not to remove the helmet after a bike accident? Idiot! He reached behind with his ungloved hand and pressed gently at the spot just below the base of his skull, experimenting with the pressure, and decided with a hot sweep of relief that his neck wasn't broken. He could still hear that sound though, a hollow roar that worked its way into the centre of his head and wouldn't go away; he wondered if it were even real, or generated by the sick dizziness. Then he heard something else, something far easier to identify.

A gunshot echoed flatly across the valley, and he jerked as if he himself had felt the impact of the bullet. The pain in his shoulder seemed to reinforce that notion, and brought with it a rush of nausea which he desperately fought back; he could only begin to imagine how badly it would hurt if he were to throw up now.

Instead he focused on the sound; this was the height of the grouse season – there were shoots all over the hills at any given time – but this had been different. A single shot, no dogs; the sound hadn't been like that of the sporting rifles the paying guns usually favoured, but more like the crack of a small handgun. He began to shake as he thought of the direction the sound had come from; further up the valley and echoing past him, repeating itself, lost among the more accepted sounds of the small game hunters on adjoining lands.

The boy, the cottage, the gunshot. The three factors spun and mingled in Mackenzie's aching head as he struggled to turn over, and he found himself whispering Jamie's name under his breath, forcing it out through gritted teeth. It gave him the strength he needed, and at last he lay, panting, on his back, staring up at the grey sky, the drizzle falling faster now, covering his face with a welcome coolness. He blinked away the drops that landed on his eyelashes, then lifted his left hand and ripped the glove off with his teeth. Gratefully he let his hand fall to the wet grass, where the rain washed the sweat from his fingers.

Finally he could put it off no longer and, wincing at every

movement, unzipped his leather jacket. He took as deep a breath as he could manage and placed his right hand over his collarbone. The jagged ends shifted and grated under his tentative touch and he went cold from head to foot, his heart speeding, lifting up through him, hammering until he felt as if it would pop out through his forehead. He closed his eyes against the dizziness, and the darkness was deeper than it should have been out here, with the sky so close...

When he awoke, water was running in tiny streams down his face, and pooling in the hollow of his throat and in the creases of his jacket. Every sensation was heightened; he felt as if he could identify every nerve ending in his body, and every one of them wept. Each hair on his head had its own needle, securing it to his scalp; each millimetre of exposed skin felt the passage of the air moving over him like an abrasive cloth.

His hands lay open on the ground beside him – he wondered how long he'd been unconscious for, both immediately after the crash, and since falling into the void again. And was he hurt anywhere else? His legs were stiff and ached horribly, particularly his knees; likewise his hips: sore, but not broken or dislocated. He flexed his chilled fingers and began to check his upper body, biting his lip in anticipation of the discovery of further injury, but relaxing a little more with each touch. His chest and ribs ached, but with a dull throb rather than the worrying, sharp agony of a fracture. The only serious pain, other than that of his broken collarbone, was from the savage wrench as his helmet had whipped around and twisted his neck.

He rolled his head gingerly to look at the surrounding area.

Only clumps of heather and tufts of grass dotted the side of the valley; it could well have been a different story otherwise. He must have landed hard on his left side – from waist to shoulder flared when he moved – but apart from that he was sure there was no serious damage. And as much as he did hurt, at least he was alive.

And now he knew Jamie was, too.

***

The rain had stopped. That was the first thing he noticed. The second thing was that there was a wet warmth against his side, and an uncomfortable weight across his stomach. Mackenzie moved his head and groaned. Both warmth and weight twitched, and then vanished as the boy sat up, blinking and frightened, and shuffled away.

'Relax,' Mackenzie tried to say, but it came out as a croak and he cleared his throat and tried again.

But Jamie had already remembered where he was. 'I'm sorry, Mr Mackenzie.'

'For what?'

'Well, for...' he gestured helplessly. 'For sleeping on you.'

Mackenzie smiled as best he could, but the pain in his neck and shoulder was starting to wake up and creep down his side and across his chest, and he had the feeling he'd see some pretty good bruises there too, if he ever got out of here. Breathing hurt.

He could see he'd been unsuccessful at allaying the boy's concerns and gave up trying to smile. 'You did the sensible thing, lad,' he said. 'Better you're as warm as you can be, aye?'

Jamie nodded, biting his lip as he looked at Mackenzie. 'How did you end up down here?'

Mackenzie frowned; he remembered the car, the feeling that it was deliberately running him off the road, but still had no idea who was driving it. It wasn't Bradley's car – he knew that.

'I was in a hurry,' he said at last. 'There was a car coming up behind me, and I lost it on the bend.'

Jamie nodded sympathetically. 'What did you do?'

'Seems I broke my collarbone.' Mackenzie felt the sick heat sweep across his face, remembering the horrifying grating of bones under his hand, shifting loosely beneath the flesh. Not just broken; shattered. He lay very still, breathing as calmly as he could manage, but all he wanted to do was roll onto his side and throw up until he passed out. Or died.

'Did you break anything else?' Jamie was asking.

'Like what?'

'Legs?'

'No. Nor arms, nor ribs, I don't think. Nor, thanks to my own laziness, my neck.'

'Ah. Not too bad then.'

Mackenzie stared, wondering if he was taking the piss. Jamie looked back at him, but he seemed honestly relieved and Mackenzie didn't know whether to laugh or scream. 'Not too bad,' he agreed. It was easier that way.

'Are you hungry?' Jamie asked after a few minutes silence.

'Aye, a bit.'

'D'you want some of my Mars Bar?' The boy had dug a misshapen mass of paper and chocolate out of his pocket, and although saliva flooded Mackenzie's mouth at the sight of it, he shook his head. It wasn't entirely selfless; the thought of chewing and swallowing anything at all just now made him shudder, but in any case, he couldn't take the lad's last bite.

Jamie shrugged and finished the chocolate, licking his fingers clean and wiping them on the grass.

The evening crawled towards dusk. Mackenzie lost track of time as the mist fell over them, and he knew he'd started to drift – long passages of time seemed to be spent somewhere else, some*when* else. One minute he was a boy, scrambling over the hillside with his brother and their friends, getting under the beaters' feet as they roused the game from their heathery hiding places, the next he was facing Bradley across a scratched table.

A breath-taking switchback, and he was upstairs on the landing with Adrian, at Hogmanay, watching the grown ups kissing each other with all the enthusiasm bestowed on them by an evening of heavy drinking. Women in neat dresses, tartan scarves pinned by ornate silver brooches; men in kilts and dress shirts, with dirks in their pristine white stockings, and leather brogues. From a distance they all seemed relaxed and magazine-glamorous, but up close Mackenzie knew they'd all be sweating and pink, breathing hard from the reels, which were often more athletic challenge than dance. All in all he preferred to watch from a distance.

At some point he was paging through pictures on a camera screen; at first he didn't recognise the sleep-flushed beauty, one delicate arm flung over her head, the other hand lying carelessly over that of the small boy in the sleeping bag next to her. She looked tiny, defenceless, open faced and so relaxed in her dreams it hardly seemed possible it could be the same person who'd caused him nothing but aggravation. One was so close up Mackenzie could even see her breath condensing on the chilly night air, and individual eyelashes resting on her cheek. Even in his semi-delirium he knew he was going to let her down.

There followed a period of blessed nothingness, and then Mackenzie was holding Kath at the station, feeling the warmth of Josh's kiss on his cheek...and then they were gone, and he was empty, hollowed out. Bradley was grinning at him across the table again, tossing him the locket...

'No!' In his mind it was a scream, but it emerged from his tight mouth as a whisper, taken by the mist and swallowed whole.

'Are you all right?' the boy asked. Mackenzie's eyes were still closed, and it could so easily have been Josh sitting there next to him, the accent barely noticeable in the boy's hushed tone.

'Aye,' he said in a shaky voice, and looked over at Jamie. 'I was just somewhere else there for a moment.'

'Wasn't somewhere good, was it?'

'No, it wasn't,' Mackenzie admitted, 'but it's not somewhere I ever need to go again.' He touched Jamie's sleeve. 'You're soaked, lad.'

'I'll dry out. It's stopped raining.'

'This mist is heavy enough to keep you wet. Let me see your feet.'

'Why?' Jamie nevertheless waggled his feet at Mackenzie, who caught at one of them with his right hand. The movement jarred him horribly, and he went still for a moment, feeling the blood drain from his face, leaving him light-headed.

Then he studied the foot he held. 'Which way did you come? Along the road?'

'No, through the valley, and down beside the waterfall.'

Of course, a waterfall – that was the roaring he kept hearing. It was up behind him somewhere and he couldn't turn to see it, but now the sound made sense. It was a relief to know that it had a natural origin, and wasn't something screwed up in his head.

'It's a good thing you came that way; your feet are pretty scratched up but at least you'll be able to walk on them.'

'I was coming to take your boots,' Jamie said in a small voice. Mackenzie had to smile at that; the boy sounded contrite, but it was probably the oldest instinct in the world to take what was no longer needed and use it to preserve what was. And after all, the boy had been convinced at the time that Mackenzie had meant to do God knows what harm to him and his mother.

At the thought of Charis, the smile dropped away. If she was on her way up here, she could be heading straight into danger. Maddy knew where Rob Doohan lived – between them they'd have been able persuade the old man to give them the same information he'd given Mackenzie...

'Where's the phone?' he asked sharply.

'It doesn't—'

'I know! You need to go. Get up to the road. Find a signal, and call Maddy.'

'Who? Shouldn't we call the police?'

'No! Christ, no.'

Jamie looked confused and frightened. 'An ambulance then?'

'Do that after. First you need to call my partner – it's more important.' Mackenzie began to gingerly work his right arm out of his sleeve. 'Take my socks and put them on, aye? Then...' he broke off and swallowed hard, 'then you can help me with this; I'm buggered if I can do it on my own.'

He lay back while Jamie tugged at the sodden laces of his boots. Each pull seemed to ripple up through his leg and into his chest with the speed and ferocity of a snapping wolf, and he had to fight not to cry out; the last thing he needed was to frighten the boy. Finally his boots were off. His socks followed, and for a moment he welcomed the coolness of the air on his feet.

'Can I try the boots too?' Jamie asked.

'You can, but they'll be a hindrance when you're climbing.'

He was right, and Jamie soon pushed them back onto Mackenzie's own feet. At least his socks were dry and warm, and he saw the bliss cross the boy's face as they enveloped his freezing feet. Mackenzie chided himself bitterly for not thinking to give up the clothing sooner.

But now came the hard bit. He finished wriggling his right arm out of his jacket, and Jamie knelt awkwardly beside him. Mackenzie took a couple of shallow breaths, braced himself, and then rolled onto his right side, freeing up his left arm. He mentally counted backwards as pain sent dizzying spirals of fire up through his neck and into his head, then he felt small hands on his back, easing his arm away from his body, sliding the warm jacket away from him and rolling him back down into dampness. The shock of the cold ground through his shirt made him catch his breath, and some of the pain abated, leaving him with a dull, grinding ache. His stomach roiled, and he struggled against the ever-threatening nausea.

'Thanks, Mr Mackenzie,' Jamie said. 'Promise I'll look after it.'

Mackenzie raised a hand in acknowledgment, waiting for the watery sensation in his mouth to fade. When he could move again, he looked over at where Jamie sat wrapped in the huge jacket.

'You look ridiculous,' he whispered, hoping for a smile, but Jamie just stared at him with huge, frightened eyes, and in that moment Mackenzie would have given anything to be able to embrace him.

'Which way do I go?' Jamie asked, peering around at the steep valley sides. Mackenzie remembered the phone call he'd made to Stein the night before, from his office. There was a signal up near the waterfall, where Stein must have stopped to take his call, but the risk was too great to send Jamie back that way, even if his own network also functioned up there. It was unthinkable to send him anywhere near the cottage, knowing Bradley might be waiting.

They both jerked as a short cry echoed down the valley.

'What was that?' Jamie asked in a trembling voice. An image of Charis flashed through Mackenzie's over-wrought mind, and he blinked to clear it.

'I don't know. Maybe a fox. The Glenlowrie Estate's named for them.' Some strength returned to his voice, and he fixed Jamie with a firm stare. 'Look, the important thing now is to do exactly as I say, and go where I tell you to go. Nowhere else, you understand?'

'Yeah.' Jamie waved the phone in the air. 'I have to find a signal, right?'

'Aye. But also, there's a chance maybe your mother will be on her way to find you. She *mustn't* get to the cottage – it's too dangerous. I've not heard a car go down yet, have you?'

'No, but we were both asleep for a while.'

'Even so, we'd better assume Bradley is still up there, and—'

'Who?'

'The man who'll have come up here after Andy Stein.' It could only have been him, and presumably Mulholland too. 'He and his sidekick are police officers, which means you can't trust *anyone*. Got it? I know Stein set you free, but if he told them about you they could be out here right now, trying to track you down.'

Mackenzie studied the boy closely, needing to be sure he was aware of the danger. Jamie looked serious and scared, which was fine by him; scared was far better than over-confident and careless. 'Right, go up the side of the valley there.' He pointed to the slope directly to their left; the bottom of it still bore the flattened evidence of his unremembered slide, and he suppressed a shudder. 'It looks like the easiest climb. When you get to the road, turn right, *downhill*. Okay? Down. Keep checking the phone; you may have to go a long way, or you may get a signal right away.'

'Okay.'

'While you're on the road, make sure no-one sees you. Any car that approaches – probably none will, not up here – but if they do, they'll be moving dead slow in this mist. Keep low until you've checked out the driver. Could be your mother, or it could be my partner Maddy. She has red hair. Pale skin. Very pretty in a scary teacher sort of a way.'

The boy still didn't smile, and Mackenzie went on, 'Soon as you see her, flag her down. Anyone else – keep right out of sight.'

'Right.'

'And mind how you go in those floppy socks,' Mackenzie reminded him. 'Last thing I need is you down here with a broken leg. Although the company would be nice.' He was relieved to see some of the strain leave the boy's face and a smile finally tremble on the pale lips. 'You'll be fine, lad,' he said, and Jamie's smile formed properly as he stood to leave.

'I'll try.'

He started off up the slope, and Mackenzie watched him, trying to decide whether the sudden cold that swept over him was real or imagined; a turn in the weather, the descent of night, or simply regret at the loss of his companion.

Jamie had now reached the place where the slope became steeper, and he leaned forward onto his hands in readiness for the hardest part of the climb. Then he glanced back over his shoulder. Mackenzie raised his hand in farewell, and the unthinking movement jarred him so badly that the low cry had broken loose before he could check it.

He closed his eyes and breathed through the sharp pain that radiated outwards from his collarbone, and when he opened them he groaned again – this time in despair; Jamie had turned and was running back down the slope towards him. As his last chance of survival threatened to disappear in the mist, Mackenzie looked closer at what the boy was holding in his hand and felt the years peel away, leaving him breathless for an entirely different reason.

By the time he was alone again his mind tumbled in bewilderment, but as he slipped into a confused sleep, hope had begun to unfurl tentative shoots once more.

Chapter Nineteen

Inverness Airport

SARAH FLUNG her overnight bag onto the passenger seat of the hire car and took a moment to gather her thoughts. It was roughly a two-hour drive, and the first stop was Abergarry, to pick up the gun and a few spare rounds. It shouldn't be necessary to use the bloody awful thing, not if Don had done the job right, and as a deterrent it would be all she needed; Don had never been the most courageous of men, and according to him this sidekick of his was apparently just a lanky streak of yessir-whatever-you-say.

Driving out of the airport and back towards Inverness, she found herself looking around with an unexpectedly strong sense of homecoming. She barely spared this place a thought usually; LA provided all she'd ever wanted. Life there was fast, exciting, and even her dull job at the museum had shown her that an aristocratic manner and an accent could get her miles further down the road. Here, in her own homeland, she was commonplace.

That hadn't always been the case though. For a while she had been the toast of the young set, with plenty of hangers-on of both sexes, and Glenlowrie had seemed a thriving estate, welcoming visitors from all over for grouse shooting and stalking. The guns would gather in the lodge in the evenings and toast her father in fine single malt, when really it was the gillies and the hardworking beaters who should have been thanked. But who would even think of the gillies when the laird was laying on the spread?

Rebelling against the tradition of the whole thing hadn't prevented Sarah from inviting people up to the estate and laying on parties of her own; might as well reap the benefits. In return she had been invited to every event going, and on that particular night...

Sarah took a narrow exit off the A82 and tried to remember how she had felt that night, but she couldn't. She could remember what had happened, but not how it *felt*. She never could; it was as if someone had sliced that part of her life away and replaced it with a typed list of events. Her father, straightening his tie in the hallway mirror, squinting through his cigarette smoke; his shocked face when she'd told him what she'd learned from Don; his refusal to tell her where he'd hidden his share, and most importantly the Fury...

He'd shown it to her once, when she was about six and throwing a tantrum over something. She couldn't remember what she'd been so furious about, but he'd taken her to his study and golden back black silk to reveal the stone; he'd even let her hold it, examine its blazing colours and watch them merge and twist into strands of glorious fire. Then, just when she'd been sure he was going to give it to her to keep forever, and she'd felt a huge rush of love towards him for it, he'd plucked it from her hand and she had never seen it again.

Then, the night of the party, *that* night, Mum and Dad had been going to some shindig somewhere down the glen. Dad had been standing in front of the hall mirror, she remembered, and the label on his tie had been wrong side out. Funny how little details stick.

'Don told me about what you did,' she'd said, out of nowhere. She hadn't even realised she was going to say it, wasn't even sure if she'd believed Don when he told her, but Dad was so distant and dismissive lately, she just wanted a rise out of him. His eyes barely flickered towards her in the mirror, and he spoke around his cigarette.

'What who did?'

'You and Uncle Rob, and the one who died in prison. To Frank Mackenzie.'

His fingers stilled on the knot of his tie, and she knew now that Don had been telling the truth.

'Not now, Sarah. I'm going out.'

'Later then? Will you show them to me?'

'I don't know what you're talking about.' Dad went back to his tie, but the way his fingers were shaking betrayed him.

'Please?' Sarah sighed. 'All right, I'll make a deal with you. I'll say nothing about the Spence stuff, if you'll just show me that black stone again. After all, it'll be mine someday anyway.'

The face he turned on her was suddenly pinched tight with anger and a closed, possessive jealousy as he snatched his cigarette from his mouth.

'I wish to God I'd never shown you that bloody thing,' he whispered harshly. 'If you'd not been screaming like a wee banshee, fit to give your mother and me migraines... Now away and let me finish getting ready.' He glanced down the hallway in both directions, to ensure they were still alone. 'And if I hear you've breathed a word of what that bloody copper has said, then both of you will find out what a *fucking* big mistake he's made.'

So Sarah drove off to her house party, where she got very, very drunk, but no matter; it was a sleep-where-you-fall-down party, the best kind. Glittering with good cheer on the outside, brittle with hatred and resentment on the inside, she eventually wandered out of the house into the snapping wind, hoping it would clear her head of the growing anger.

Her head did clear, but only of the fuzzy blanket that the alcohol had draped over everything, and it allowed a chink of light through, and an idea with it. The stone was sure to be in Dad's study, and since he was out, what other chance would she get to turn the place upside-down until she found it? She glanced over at where her car sat, with around twenty others, on the field adjacent to the house. She was clear-headed...all right, a wee bit tipsy perhaps, but not completely jaked. Besides, she was used to driving these roads, and it was late; hardly anyone would be about. She could be home within the hour, allow another hour or so for searching, and still be back here before Mum and Dad came home. Teach the bastard to hide something like that from her. Teach him to bloody keep it to himself, when it was her own inheritance!

Slipping away from the party was easy enough; everyone was either giving it everything on the 'dance floor' – *Girl, I wanna make you sweat* – or lip-locked with someone else. That tart Donna Kilbride was wrapped around Craig Lumsden, and just wait 'til Craig's girlfriend found out... Sarah hoped she'd be back to see the fallout from *that* one.

She free-wheeled down the dead-straight drive with her lights off, picking out the edges only by the occasional lurch onto grass, and when she reached the gate she switched the lights on, pulled her fags out and lit up, grinning into the night as, unnoticed by anyone, she started towards home.

An hour and a half later she was no longer grinning, or even smiling. There was nothing here that she could see, and not really anywhere else to look. There just literally wasn't anywhere the Fury could be hidden; Dad wasn't one for towering bookshelves or sliding panels in the walls; the house itself might be a sprawling mess of cubby-holes and ante-rooms, but the study was a square little box with a desk – all the drawers of which were accessible – an ashtray, and a never-used blotter purely for show. On top of the filing cabinet were a few lever arch files with dates written on their curling-stickered spines. That was pretty much it.

Hung on the back of Dad's chair was his everyday woollen jacket, the one he wore around the estate, and Sarah felt a surge of renewed anger at the sight of it; no-one knew Glen-lowrie was in fact falling into ruin, or that the staff they brought in for parties were only hired for the night. Only the agency staff themselves knew, and were fed the line that it was the regular staff's night off. To hear Dad speak you'd think he dined on quails' eggs for breakfast, and was piped in to a ten-course dinner every night. He still swanned about the place like the lairds of old, complete with beat-up wellies and this patched jacket, as if he actually *did* anything. Throwing his weight around along with his money. By the time Sarah inherited the place there would be nothing left. Unless... Sarah's heart thumped suddenly hard. Mum and Dad were out. No-one had seen her arrive...

Calmly, as if watching someone else, she fished out her

cigarettes and lit one, but instead of replacing the matches in her own pocket she slipped them into the breast pocket of her Dad's jacket. Then she pulled the chair a bit closer to the desk, then closer, until it was drawn right in so the back touched. She didn't do anything else for a moment, just smoked and thought. Smoked and thought.

Eventually, dreamlike, she pulled the ashtray towards the edge of the desk and balanced the half-smoked cigarette on it. Burning end facing outwards. Wool would not ignite, she knew that, but matches would. She glanced at the clock: only eleven-ish; by the time Mum and Dad got home in the small hours the house would be too far gone to save. For a heartbeat she considered getting a few things from her room, but just as quickly discarded the notion; it would only look suspicious, and she owned nothing precious enough to risk that. Thanks to her dad.

In the end she just took a bottle of wine from the cellar and left. By then the matches in the jacket had caught, the nylon lining was starting to melt down over the chair, and the desk was beginning to smoulder. She could actually hear crackling, and as she pulled the front door carefully closed behind her she wondered why she wasn't fearful, or regretful, or any of the things she'd expect from anyone else.

The rest of the night had passed in a weird kind of a blur, she remembered now, as she turned in to Abergarry's main street. She'd gone to her friend's house, this very same friend who was helping her today, and he had agreed to provide her alibi for the night; as childhood friends the same age, growing up together, no-one would think it surprising they had finally spent the night together. But in truth neither held the slightest attraction for the other, though their friendship was long-lived and solid.

They had drunk the wine, and speculated about what might be happening now up at Glenlowrie, and at some point during that long, strange, disjointed night, he had said something that drew together everything she knew and remembered, and gave her a sudden flash of insight into *how* her father had hidden his share of the Spence collection, if not precisely where.

It was only the following morning that she'd learned, with a hammer-blow of shock, that Mum and Dad's dinner party had been cancelled. They had retired early instead, and consequently perished, overcome by the smoke that had risen directly up through two floors into their room. Abruptly all thoughts of the jewels, and even the Fury, had been blasted clear out of Sarah's head, and all the missing emotions had tumbled back: crushing guilt, terror at discovery, grief for her mother, regret for her father... But, she had been interested to discover, simmering beneath it all was anger.

Now she would never find her inheritance. If there *had* been anything of that nature in the house, it would surely have turned up during the fire investigation, the same one that had so quickly laid the blame at Duncan's feet... Or rather, his fingertips. His yellowed, nicotine-stained fingertips. But the estate had yielded nothing bar some small parcels of land, which were sold for development, and a few ruined crofters' cottages. So Sarah had taken what was left, and run.

Two phone calls, that's all there had been, between old friends locked into conspiratorial silence. Just two. After twenty-four years. One from him to her, with the news she thought she'd never hear, and a little later she'd returned it to say she was coming back. Now she was here, and she wondered if he would recognise her immediately, or if both of them had changed too much in the intervening years.

She was surprised to find the door unlocked, but she pushed it open and stepped inside, and was relieved when the man who looked up and smiled was as instantly recognisable as her own face. 'Hello, Ben.'

'Sarah.' He came over and drew her into his arms. 'Welcome to Cameron and Son.'

She hugged him back, suddenly feeling trembly. 'I can't believe it's come to this,' she mumbled into his shirt. 'Have you got it?'

'Aye. Come through to the back.'

He led the way into his workshop, and Sarah looked around, oddly comforted by the sights and smells. 'Remember when you and I would watch your dad making his wee models and things in here, in the summer holidays?'

Ben reached down a box from the top of a cupboard and laid it on the worktable. 'I was surprised you had the patience back then.'

'I only stuck it because you kept making me laugh,' she pointed out.

He opened the box, though with some hesitation, and drew out his father's handgun. She eyed it a little apprehensively.

'Ammo?'

'It's loaded now, but I've no spare. I've no permit, so I couldn't get any.'

'That's fine.' She took the gun, and studied it while she

searched for a way to ease the awkward silence. 'I suppose nowadays you're making your kids laugh, instead of me, while *you* work.'

'I have different memories of this place now,' he said quietly, and she bit her lip.

'Of course. I'm so sorry. Finding your dad like that... I can't imagine how awful it must have been.'

'What a way to ruin a perfectly good holiday weekend,' he said, but the shadow in his eyes belied the jokey tone.

'Ben, I'm so sorry—'

'The festival wasn't that great anyway though. Would have been better if you'd been there, but I suppose you were off with your officer friend. The one that's currently trying to screw you in a whole other way.' He looked embarrassed, suddenly. 'Look, you must be knackered. Are you sure you won't stay awhile, maybe have a cuppa to give you a boost?'

She shook her head. 'And you're not to ask me anything about this. Promise?'

'I don't think I want to know.'

'Thank you.' She put a hand on his arm. 'For telling me about Don, I mean, and what he's up to.'

'Aye, well, when that DS Mulholland came into the shop, I remembered what you'd told me, the night of the fire.'

'You were the one who helped me make that connection,' Sarah said. 'I'd never have guessed where the jewels were.'

'You still don't know,' he reminded her. 'Not exactly.'

'No, but at least now I know what I'm looking for. And it meant I was ready when Don called with his so-called *deal*.'

'How did you know there was supposed to be a flaw though?'

'Rob Doohan told me. Between you both you've saved me from making a huge mistake.'

'Have we though?' He looked at her, concerned. 'All this really does seem a bit...extreme. Even for you.'

'Even?' Sarah laughed; she couldn't help it – he'd always brought out the lighter side in her. 'Ah, why couldn't we fancy each other, Ben?'

He shrugged. 'I suppose because Justine was always out there waiting for me, whether I knew it or not.'

'Are you saying you believe in a higher power?' she teased, slipping the gun into her bag.

'Just fate, I suppose. And you're with the American, so it's all worked out.'

Sarah fought down a stab of guilt, with the best weapon at her disposal: justification. If Andy had only done as she asked, and hadn't gone digging and learned about the fire... 'All worked out,' she agreed. 'Justine's a lucky lady.'

'You're going to be careful?'

'Of course. I told you, it's a deterrent, that's all.'

'Then why ask for more ammunition?'

Sarah sighed. 'Ben—'

'No, you're right. None of my beeswax.'

'It's protection, okay?'

'Then let me come with you.'

'And do what? We've got one weapon between us, and you have a business and a reputation at stake. Look, Don'll fold just as soon as he knows I'm aware of his stupid little game. Then we'll draw up a new deal, and he'll have a better measure of me.'

No mention of a kidnapped child, or a murdered boyfriend... That was the kind of thing that would tip even Ben Cameron's scale from earnest, helpful friend right over to appalled citizen and father; he would never condone what she had done in the name of her inheritance, even if the boy emerged unscathed. Which she couldn't guarantee either. She wished she had some of Ben's faith in fate.

'I've got to go,' she said, with real regret. 'Thank you so much for this.'

'Don't bring it back. I've wanted to get shot of it for a long time, but haven't dared hand it in.'

'I don't just mean the gun.'

'I know.' He came back around the counter and put his arms around her again. 'Just watch out for that Mulholland bloke, okay? There's something about him.'

'Like what?'

'Something's...missing. I don't think he'd think twice about putting a bullet in you.'

'Then it's a good thing I've got this.' Sarah patted her bag, hoping her smile hid the sudden lurch of nervous queasiness. 'Right. I'll be away. You finish up here and get back to Justine. I'm sure she's wondering why you're working on a Sunday.'

'I sent her and the boys away for a few days,' he said. When she raised an eyebrow, he added quietly, 'I told you; I don't trust that Mulholland one inch.'

Chapter Twenty

BRADLEY FOLLOWED Mulholland back into the cottage, unsettled by the new light in the sergeant's eyes; if he had seemed unnervingly cold before, now he looked like glittering danger wrapped in the tall, thin frame of someone Bradley barely recognised. The gun was tucked away out of sight, but he knew it had not finished its work today, and for the first time, he questioned his decision to make Mulholland carry it. It was all very well not wanting to risk his career, but everything seemed to have taken a sinister side-step into a world where careers were the last consideration.

The way Mulholland kept glancing at the door at the back of the room pulled Bradley's own reluctant gaze with it, until finally he strode across and dragged the bolt back. The waning light from the open front door washed only limply over the threshold, but it was bright enough to illuminate the sticky crimson pool on the stone flags. The lumps of greyish matter distributed throughout the mess brought nausea up into Bradley's throat, and he gagged and swallowed it, and turned to spit on the floor behind him.

He heard the soft sound of Mulholland's derision and felt spots of humiliation, like burn marks, on his skin. He wiped his mouth on his sleeve, scrubbing at the acid taste that coated his lips until pain replaced it. He made an effort to control the shaking in his voice, not altogether successfully.

'Come on then.'

He stepped over Stein's outstretched legs, trying not to look directly at the mutilated skull as his eyes adjusted to the gloom. When had he turned so soft? He'd killed before, and although he hadn't taken as much pleasure from it as Mulholland clearly did, he'd certainly not shied away from it either, knowing the rewards. And speaking of rewards, if that stone *was* still up here in this cottage, as Stein had seemed to think, he'd bloody well keep searching until he found it.

It was not the opal he found, however; it was something far more unsettling. He worked his way along the wall, kicking at the stones near where he'd found the silk wrapping, and tried not to become infuriated when they yielded nothing more. As he made his way around the room, he saw something lying on the floor; crumpled cloth of some kind. Not one piece, but two... How had they slipped his attention before? Bradley kicked at the little pile, some part of him still six years old and convinced a rat would come scurrying out if he touched it with his hand.

'What's that?' Mulholland said at once.

'No idea, but it's making me wonder,' Bradley said. Satisfied they were devoid of vermin, he bent down and picked up the two pieces of cloth. He looked at the smaller piece; smudges of red indicated someone had recently used it to wipe blood from a cut. He pocketed it, thoughtfully, then shook out the larger piece and held it up. A worried anger started to worm in his belly; this was not something that had lain in this cellar for years – the cloth was modern. New, even.

'How old did you say that kid was, the one who came in with his mother to report Mackenzie?'

'I think they said he was ten. Looked smaller to me, though.'

'Uh huh.' Bradley turned back the waistband of the pyjama trousers to reveal the label: *George at Asda. Boys. Aged 7/8*. Shit. He took his phone out of his inside pocket and flipped open the leather cover.

'Dream on,' Mulholland said. 'You'll be lucky to get a signal. Who're you trying to call, anyway?'

'Sarah.' Bradley put the phone away. 'She must know about this; why else would Stein bother to bring the boy up here? That bolt on the door is brand new. Thing is, how much does he know about what's going on? Not that it matters. Even if he only knows about this,' he jerked his head towards the cooling cadaver, 'we'll have to find him; he's a loose end. Maybe hurt, too – there was blood on that cloth.' He saw his chance at last, and put a little superiority into his voice. 'Right, I'll wait here for Sarah. You get out and start searching.'

'No, I think I'll wait here. We can find the lad later.'

The shift in power wasn't even subtle. Although Mulholland didn't need to resort to theatrics by drawing his weapon, the hard light in his eyes was enough; Bradley had finally lost whatever edge he'd held over the younger man – if he'd ever really had any at all.

Jamie stopped in the road, straining to listen against the wind; he could hear a car in the distance, he was sure of it. Mackenzie's words flashed through his mind:

Keep low until you've checked out the driver. Could be your mother, or it could be my partner Maddy...

He'd said any car would be moving pretty slowly, but this car was really motoring up here. Maybe it was moving so fast because whoever was driving it was in a hurry to rescue him? The mixture of panic and wild hope was making him feel a little sick. He kept walking down the hill, turning his head so he could hear better, keeping an eye on the side of the road to make sure there was somewhere he could duck out of sight if he had to.

On his left the side of the mountain rose away, littered with rocks of varying sizes. He pulled the big leather jacket tighter around him, then slipped in behind the largest of those rocks, at the top of a short, steep part of the hill. From there he could see the car coming around the corner at the bottom, and if he concentrated really hard, he should be able to tell if the driver was a woman or a man. And he'd recognise his mother right away, even if her face wasn't clear.

He stared until his eyes burned, the jacket sleeves gripped tightly where they fell over his fingers. His breath became shorter, his chest tightened... Not now! He breathed more slowly and felt his airways loosen. False alarm then – just normal, everyday panic.

The car was still a fair distance away, but finally the faint glow of headlights lit up the mist and he knew, with a lurch of despair, that he wouldn't be able to see past them until the car was right in front of him. There was no time to waste weighing up; the risk was huge, but worth taking, and he scrambled out from behind the rock and halfway down the slope, keeping half-curled and relatively sure he wouldn't stand out in Mackenzie's black jacket, as long as he kept still.

He squinted past the lights as the car drew level and the driver took shape; it wasn't his mum's spiky-haired outline, but there was no way that was a man. Mackenzie had described his partner as red-haired and scary-looking, and she fitted the description exactly. He gave a small cry of relief and leapt up, waving, as the car pulled slightly ahead, but the woman had seen the movement and glanced back towards him, her mouth open in surprise. It was Maddy, for sure.

The car came to a sudden, sliding halt, and as Jamie ran the few feet up the road, the woman pressed the button to lower her window, staring at him in amazement. Her hair was definitely a light, reddish blonde.

'You're Maddy, aren't you!' he said, unable to keep the grin from his face. 'Where's my mum?'

The woman suddenly smiled and looked a lot more friendly. 'Thank God, it's you! She's waiting for you. Hop in, quick!'

Jamie climbed into the back and Maddy put her window back up. Then she put the car smoothly back into gear, and Jamie sat back as they pulled away, already thinking about the fame this adventure would get him when he started comp school next month. Mackenzie had seemed really ill, but now everything was going to be all right, and he himself would be the hero, just like he'd thought back in the hotel, with newspaper stories, maybe even TV news—

His door locked with a muted clunk and he looked up, catching Maddy's eyes on him in the rear-view mirror.

'Just to be safe, sweetie,' she said. 'Can't have you falling out, eh? Seat belt on, too.'

'Oh. Yeah, I suppose so,' Jamie said, but he felt uneasy all the same. 'Why are we still going this way?'

'Can't turn around here. I need to find a wider space.'

'Okay. Then I'll show you where your friend is, so you can pick him up. I'll have to help you though, 'cause he can't stand up.'

Maddy's head whipped around in surprise, then she turned back to the road. 'He's not dead?'

He was pleased he'd been able to deliver the good news. 'No, but he's quite bad. He's down in the valley – I'll show you.'

She shook her head. 'We'll send an ambulance back for him.'

'But—'

'I said we'll send someone!' Her voice lowered again, sounding calmer, but still a bit tight. 'Better to let the professionals do it. Now hush, these roads are dangerous enough without being distracted by chatter.'

He looked at her again; her focus was entirely on the road ahead. He could see in the mirror that she was angry now, and he felt a tremor of fear. 'Where did you say Mum was?' he ventured. She didn't answer. Jamie's heart fluttered again, and he reached out to try and pull the lock up with his fingers. It wouldn't budge. A sudden certainty flooded over him, and his voice came out hoarse and thin.

'You're not Maddy, are you?'

She ignored him, but then it hadn't really been a question anyway; whoever she was, he was sure no friend of Mr Mackenzie's could be this horrible. He felt a sick wriggling feeling in his belly, and unclipped his seat belt – he still couldn't escape, but it felt a little better.

'Who's in the valley? This friend of Maddy's?' she asked at last.

Jamie hesitated, but he caught her quick, knowing glance in the mirror again and couldn't think of a fake name fast enough. 'Mr Mackenzie,' he muttered.

'The investigator? And he can't walk? What's he done, broken his leg?'

'No.'

'What then? Has he been shot?'

'No.'

'Not very forthcoming with information, are you? Tell me this at least: the American who took you, is *he* dead?'

'Yeah, I think so. I think one of the policemen shot him.' Jamie could bear it no longer; he lunged forward in his seat and caught at the woman's shoulder. 'Where's my mum?'

She jerked away from him. 'I haven't the faintest idea. Which you can actually take as a good sign. Now tell me about the policemen.'

'I didn't see them, just heard them; Mr Mackenzie told me who they were. They were talking to the American, and then I heard a shot and ran away.'

'So the American had already let you go?' The woman's voice was hard, and Jamie's fear grew. He clung to the news that she really seemed to have no idea about his mother at all; maybe, as she'd said, that was a good sign. He sat back again, trying not to acknowledge what he knew in his heart; they were going back to the cottage.

Chapter Twenty-One

CHARIS HEARD the smooth engine coming up the hill behind them, and her heart thudded painfully against her ribs. It was impossible to tell how far away the car was; the mist distorted the sound until she wasn't even sure she'd really heard it at all, but Maddy cast around frantically for somewhere to get out of sight.

'Here!' she hissed and scrambled up the slope off the road. Charis heard the shift of gears and followed, her hands stinging as they scraped over rough rocks. Maybe it was the police? But summoned by whom? Doohan wouldn't have alerted them; it would put him straight back in prison.

Somewhere over to her left she heard Maddy moving about, and then the car was on the road below them and they could only see the gleaming, rain-wet roof and the muted glow of headlights. Maddy was already starting to climb back down, but Charis was first to reach the road again and took off up the hill, hearing Maddy's regulation black shoes hitting the road at a run behind her. Before long, the taller woman overtook her, and there was little sound then except for harsh breathing and pounding feet. Just when Charis thought her heart was going to burst with exertion, Maddy turned a white face back to her.

'It's stopped!'

Charis had to hold her breath to listen, but Maddy was right – and in that moment they both heard the unmistakeable sound of a car door slamming.

'We're there!' Charis said in a rush of relief.

'No, listen,' Maddy said bleakly, as the car took off again. 'They've gone.'

Charis felt ill and a little faint. 'Do you think they found Mackenzie?' she ventured. 'Maybe they saw him, or his bike, and stopped to look.'

Maddy hesitated. 'If...I see him I don't know if I can just—'

'Just walk past him?' Charis said gently. 'Me neither. But Jamie's up there and I've got to go to him. I understand if you want to stay with Mackenzie.'

She started forward again. She didn't know what she would do if she rounded the next corner and saw Mackenzie lying in the valley, but thank God for the mist – it obscured almost everything, and as long as she kept her focus on the road she *couldn't* see him, not even by accident. After a moment she was relieved to hear Maddy following her; she'd told the truth when she'd said she was prepared to do this alone, but it didn't mean she wanted to.

The road veered down to the left, just as Doohan had described. Charis and Maddy stopped and looked at one another.

'It's down there, isn't it? The cottage.' Charis said quietly. 'Jamie's down there.'

'And so's whoever drove past us back there,' Maddy reminded her. 'They don't know we're coming, so that's in our favour at least. About the only thing that is though. Keep to the side of the road and follow me.'

She took a small handgun from her pocket, smoothly in control once more, and Charis stared at her in mingled dismay and relief, and with a growing sense of unreality.

'Don't worry,' Maddy said, seeing her face, 'it's legal.'

'Why didn't you threaten Daniel with it?'

'I didn't want him going back and reporting me. I could do without being arrested right now, aye? Now come on.'

Hunting around for a weapon of her own, Charis found only a smoothish, hand-sized rock among the scrubby bushes at the side of the road, but she pushed it into her jeans pocket anyway; it was better than nothing, and would probably give someone a hell of a headache if she used it right. She met Maddy's incredulous look with a defiant one, and Maddy looked as if she wanted to say something, but in the end she just turned away.

There was nothing around them except swarming midges and a rapidly darkening sky; the mist had lifted a little, but the day was drawing its last breaths, and the poor weather meant night would not be long in coming. Struck by the sickening realisation that Mackenzie would never see another sunrise, she reminded herself that, unless she did something about it, neither would Jamie. It took everything she had not to push past Maddy and take off down the lane by herself.

The roof of the cottage came into view and Charis stopped, her heart suddenly beating too fast. The place was a wreck, with ragged holes in the roof, and the one window she could see had only two panes left in its frame. How could Jamie have been kept up here, with Stein down in the town, if there was nothing to stop him escaping? Oh God, if he'd been tied up all this time and unable to get to his inhaler—

'Slow down,' Maddy whispered, her voice harsh in the quiet evening air. Charis realised she had almost run into her, and hung back with an effort. There were three cars down there: the posh car the American had been driving, that had so fascinated Jamie; a smart, four-door saloon, with a Hertz sticker in the back window; and Bradley's dark blue Discovery. She briefly wondered who had been driving the hire car, but the question was wiped from her mind as she saw a movement by the window. A darker shadow in the already dim room. She heard a crash and a familiar, unmistakeable cry, and all reason left her.

She tore loose from Maddy's restraining hand and started to run.

Going back into the cottage had robbed Jamie of the last of his courage. The cold from the stone floor seeped through the wet, borrowed socks, chilling his feet again, and it was gloomy inside, but he could see there were two men there now. As the woman pushed him in too, Jamie's legs suddenly couldn't hold him up any more. He stumbled and fell to his knees, but no-one seemed bothered; in fact it was almost as if he weren't there – except for the gun now pointed at him by the same police officer he and his mum had seen about their camera.

He watched and listened, terrified beyond comprehension as the three people in the room bit and snarled at one another, snapping questions, not listening to answers, shouting each other down. Jamie felt despair creeping over him as he realised that, while they were fighting amongst themselves, Mackenzie was waiting for him to bring help; he'd probably die out there by himself all night, soaked through.

'What the hell are you wearing, boy?' It was as if the big officer had read his thoughts.

'It's a jacket.'

'I can see that. Am I allowed to guess who it belongs to?'

'Don't care.' He kept his voice sullen and, trying not to let the sudden fear show in his face either, he stared at the floor.

'How do you know Paul Mackenzie?'

'Who?'

The officer gave an impatient sigh. 'That jacket belongs to Mackenzie. How did you get it?'

'Dead body.' Jamie looked up in time to see a strange expression cross the man's face; sort of a hopeful, but wary one, as if he couldn't believe what he'd heard, but he wanted to. *Really* wanted to. If Jamie hadn't already hated him for killing the American, that look sealed it.

'Dead? You're sure?'

'Of course I'm sure. Took his jacket, didn't I?'

'The investigator?' the woman broke in. 'I thought you said he was still alive?'

Jamie watched the officer carefully; the expression had turned suspicious again. He remembered the misunderstanding in the car, and seized on it. 'I thought he was your friend. I didn't want to upset you.'

'So he *is* actually dead then,' the officer insisted.

'Crashed his motorbike.'

'Always thought that'd be what did him in,' the officer said with satisfaction. 'Did he die right away, d'you think?'

He seemed almost cheerful now, and Jamie decided to keep his mood up by telling him what he clearly wanted to hear. 'No. He was alive when I found him, but he died a little while ago. Broke loads of bones and stuff.'

It worked; the man's face went pink as he suppressed a laugh. Jamie wished he could get hold of that gun so he could shoot the man's ugly, mean head right off.

'Happy now, Bradley?' The skinny officer was still holding the gun pointing at Jamie, but it seemed more relaxed. Jamie wondered if he would have a chance to rush at him, like they did on TV, but deep down he knew he wouldn't.

'Where's Andy?' the woman wanted to know. The man called Bradley nodded at the door to Jamie's former prison, and the woman raised an eyebrow. 'And *he's*—'

'As a dodo.'

'I'll just check, if I may?'

'Be my guest.' Bradley stepped aside and allowed the woman to pass. Jamie was glad he couldn't see what was in there, but the woman was clearly satisfied, though she was even paler now.

'Right. Next issue then. Where are they?'

Bradley picked up a bag from the corner and passed it to her. She unzipped it and took out a package wrapped in newspaper. Then, shockingly, she held one end of the paper and let the package roll open. The contents hit the floor with a smash, sending shards of china spinning to all four corners, and Jamie cried out and shielded his eyes.

Bradley stared. 'What the hell are you doing?'

'Come on, Don. We all know these aren't the real thing. Now, I'll ask again. Where are they?'

'You *believed* that fuckwit?' Bradley waved at the door behind which the American lay. 'You didn't even check!'

'I believe him because he always told me the truth. Unlike you.' She took another out of the bag, but this time, Jamie noticed, she opened it and checked the base of the pottery figure, tilting it this way and that in the light from the window, before letting that one, too, crash to the stone floor. He looked closely at where they had fallen, seeing that they'd held something inside, but it was hard to tell what, wrapped tightly as it was in old, yellowed newspapers. Maybe drugs? It was usually drugs.

The woman was poking around in the rubble, with a thin little smile on her face. She picked up one of the packages and opened it to reveal a handful of smallish grey stones. 'Wow. Priceless gravel.'

'Oh aye. Very clever of you. So now what?'

'Now you hand over the Fury. Then you take me to where the originals are.'

'Sorry, Sarah.' He sounded anything but, to Jamie's ear. 'I don't have the Fury. Or the originals.'

The temperature in the room seemed to drop to freezing point.

'You don't have it?' Sarah's voice could have cut glass.

'Nope. But if you think hard enough, you're bound to come up with a few suggestions as to where we might find it.'

'And if I do?'

'Original deal stands. You piss off back to America with the bulk of your precious collection, and we just keep the Fury. In return for which, we protect your dirty little secret.'

A sound outside the window halted all conversation. Jamie's heart sped up so much he could feel it through Mr Mackenzie's jacket. Running footsteps, a voice sobbing his name...

'Mum!'

Forgetting the gun, he leapt to his feet just as she burst through the door. She stopped dead, as he had, at the initial darkness, then a second later she had seen him and was on her knees, holding him tight, her hands moving across his back and into his hair, as if checking he was real, and unhurt.

'Jamie! Oh, God, Jamie...'

And then he was crying too, and the rest of it stopped mattering for a while. Gradually he became aware of the silence in the rest of the room, and he pulled away and turned, suddenly sure he was going to be staring down the barrel of that gun. The others were staring at him, and in bafflement at his mother, but at least they didn't look like they were about to shoot them.

His mum stood, but held him close. 'What are you going to do?' she asked their captors, in a voice that trembled. It didn't scare him to hear how frightened she was, although he'd thought it would; it just made him want to protect her. The thin officer levelled the gun at them again, and she moved in front of him, still holding his hand tightly as if she were frightened to let him go.

'Listen,' she said desperately. 'We won't say anything to anyone; we've got nothing to do with all this. Why don't you just let us go? We'll go straight back to Liverpool tonight, honest—'

'How many more of you are going to come crawling out of the woodwork?' Sarah interrupted. 'This was supposed to be between me and him,' she added, gesturing towards Bradley. 'It's all getting a bit crowded, don't you think?'

Bradley looked sulky, and Jamie thought it was odd how the childish expression seemed to fit so easily on a grown man's face.

'This has nothing to do with us,' the officer said. 'Look, you just told us to get rid of the problem and we did.'

'How can you say that? The little shit was out roaming the

mountains! I hardly call that getting him out of the way. Yet again I'm left to pick up the pieces. And now his bloody *mother* has turned up!'

The two officers clearly had no idea what she was talking about. 'But...*Mackenzie's* dead,' Bradley ventured. '*That's* what you wanted, right?'

Jamie felt his mother's hand tighten until he gasped in pain. 'You didn't kill him though,' she said, her voice cutting across the room, small and broken as it was. 'So you can't claim brownie points for that, can you?'

'Who killed him then?' Sarah wanted to know. 'Don't tell me there are even more incompetents out there? I actually *needed* Mackenzie, for Chrissake!'

'My ex-husband did it,' Mum said. 'He...he ran him off the road.'

There was an exasperated explosion of breath from Sarah, and she started yelling at the two officers again, but Jamie didn't hear what she was saying; his head was full of the words his mother had just spoken. His father had tried to kill Mackenzie... *His father*. Dad. Who was supposed to be in prison. He shook his head, but it didn't make the truth sink in any further.

What did click though, was that his mother believed Mackenzie was dead, and he could tell she was crying. He wanted to tell her the truth, but remembering the satisfaction on the fat police officer's face, he knew he couldn't say it out loud; the man might decide to go down there and finish the job.

His mother suddenly turned to him. 'That's his jacket,' she said in a strange little voice. 'You...you saw him?'

'I found him in the valley, before that lady picked me up,' he told her, trying to make her read his mind: *Mum, he's alive...*

But her eyes were blurry with tears and she just kept

touching the jacket, then his face. She looked as if she had a hundred questions but could speak none of them aloud. He remembered how Mackenzie had reacted when the subject of Mum had come up – they were friends, he'd said; he'd die before he hurt her... Suddenly it was more important than ever that he tell her, and he was about to risk a whisper when she was pulled away from him.

The woman had dragged her across the room and pushed her to a far corner, where she stood with her arms wrapped across her chest and her head bowed.

'What are you going to do?' Jamie asked. 'Are you going to shoot us?'

'Probably,' the skinny man said. He glanced over at Jamie's mother then, and gave a nasty little smirk. 'Although I think we might be able to find a wee diversion first, don't you, sir?'

Bradley followed his look and scowled. 'You bloody well will not. Just shoot them and let's have done with it. The bodies can stay here until we get Cameron up here too, then we'll set fire to the whole lot in one go.'

'You'll leave Cameron alone,' Sarah said sharply. 'You can trust him; he'll not say anything. And about the Fury,' she went on. 'You seemed pretty confident you'd have it to use as a bargaining tool. How do I know you're not lying about not finding it?'

'I'm out of ideas,' Bradley admitted. 'It's not here. You tell us where to start looking, we'll do it.'

'I'm telling you right now; if I don't get that stone, you're going to be joining the barbecue in the back room.'

'What the hell is it about this fucking stone?' the thin one broke in, irritated. 'It's valuable, okay, I get that, but anyone would think it had magical powers the way you two're going on.'

A lurch of recognition brought Jamie's focus onto the other officer. *Could it be?*

'You've never seen it, Alistair,' Bradley said. 'If you had, you'd understand,'

The woman nodded agreement, and as Jamie watched, her face sort of...drifted, like she wasn't really here at all. God, how he wished she wasn't. Her voice was only halfway there too.

'It draws you in,' she murmured. 'You're hypnotised and it's, sort of – well, you can scoff,' she said, more normally now, 'but I'm not so sure it *doesn't* have some kind of power. Over the mind, at least.'

Jamie decided it was time to speak up. 'Stone?' he said hesitantly.

'Shut up.' Bradley threw the words over his shoulder, barely acknowledging that Jamie and his mum were still in the room. 'It's no good trying to explain to him, Sarah, he's a philistine. He won't believe it until—'

'I found a stone,' Jamie went on. 'Is it black, but a bit see-through, with very bright colours in it? Sort of...*inside* it?'

Four pairs of eyes fixed on him; he met them all in turn, starting with his mother and finishing with the other woman, whose piercing gaze he held the longest, sort of like a test. Her face was the clearest, even though the room was getting darker now; she was standing right by the broken window.

She took a step towards him. 'Are you telling me you know where the Fury is?'

'If that's the stone, then yeah. Well, sort of.'

Sarah's hand whipped up and struck the side of his face, and through the shock of the pain, Jamie heard his mother's furious shout. He looked up in time to see her being shoved back against the wall.

'Don't play stupid games with me, sonny,' Sarah said in a

hard voice. 'Now tell me where that stone is, or your mother's going to know what it feels like to have her kneecaps shot off.'

'Leave her alone!'

'Then tell me. Now.'

Jamie struggled to swallow the tears that tightened his throat. 'I dropped it, outside. But I think I know where.'

'Well?'

'By the waterfall. Near the top.'

The woman threw up her hands. 'It'd be like looking for a needle in a whole bloody field of haystacks!'

'Wait. You say you know where?' Bradley demanded, glaring at Jamie. 'How?'

'I was sitting on a rock to get my breath back. I thought I might get lost, so I built a little... What's it called, when you pile up little stones to mark a place you've been?'

'A cairn.'

'Yes. One of those. It'll be somewhere on the ground there. I can take you tomorrow.'

'You'll take us there now,' Sarah said.

Jamie's heart leapt again; they were going to be outside where there was more chance of escape; his mother could do something too, to help them get away; she could do anything... But that hope was immediately dashed as Sarah turned to her.

'You. In the back room.'

Bradley pulled her over to the door, then hesitated. 'Someone get that body out of the way.'

No-one moved, and he glared at them, before letting go of Jamie's mum and doing it himself, grunting and puffing as he pulled the American's corpse away from the doorway. Jamie tried not to imagine it, but he couldn't ignore the slithering, bumping sounds.

Jamie's mum put up a struggle, but Bradley's grip on the

back of her neck made any real fight impossible, though she still tried to twist to look at him. 'Don't try anything brave out there, okay? I'll be all right.'

'Mum!' Jamie's eyes burned and flooded as he watched the officer push her into the room. The door remained open while Bradley wrestled with the American's long legs, which were still in the way, and Jamie met his mother's terrified gaze over the top of the dead man. He once again tried to tell her about Mackenzie without speaking; he tugged at the collar of his jacket and gave her a tiny nod, but saw her eyes brighten with tears... It was hopeless.

'You,' Sarah nodded at the one called Alistair. 'Get Don's car down to Abergarry and establish an alibi. Don and I will take the boy out and find the Fury.'

'I'll, uh, I'll get the big torch first then, shall I?' Bradley said. For someone desperate to get hold of that stone, he didn't seem very pleased that he was going out to try and find it.

Sarah took her own gun out of her bag and aimed it at Jamie, but she didn't look very comfortable holding it. 'Right. You, me and Uncle Don are going for a wee walk in the moonlight. But if you get any ideas—'

There was a sudden smashing of glass, and Sarah lurched and tumbled forward, her gun falling from her hand. Through the fog of disbelief, Jamie saw his own hand reaching out to grab it, but a boot slid in, kicking it away from his fingers as they hovered over the barrel like little white ghosts, not belonging to him at all. A heavy thump in his side from the same boot sent him crashing to the floor and he looked up, straight into the wide-eyed horror show that was Sarah. Her screams rose, foul and frantic, and Jamie's breathing shortened as, behind him, he heard the door finally slam shut on his mother.

Chapter Twenty-Two

CHARIS FELT a surge of savage elation as she heard the gunshot echoing off the hills outside. *Maddy! Thank God!* But the screams were terrible, and relief quickly gave way to trembling horror. Another shot rang through the ancient stone of the cottage, and she jerked upright, holding her breath. The woman had fallen silent. There were mutterings, and then raised voices; Bradley's rose loudest.

'No! I'll do that. You find whoever did this, then never mind what she said, you're to get back down and sort out Cameron. I'll take the kid out, and we'll find this fucking stone if it takes all night.'

The door opened again, and Charis pressed herself against the back wall as Bradley dragged the limp body of Sarah Wallace in, leaving her sprawled like a broken puppet, arms and legs impossibly twisted. Just before the door slammed one last time, Charis saw the woman's bloodied face, twisted to the side, and the glistening emptiness where her left eye had been.

She sat down against the wall, her knees pulled up to her chest, her arms locked around them. Jamie's sobs faded as he was taken out into the night once more, and as she listened to him Charis realised she was swaying gently from side to side, as she had when he was little and she was holding him. And the same mantra passed through her mind too, but now with more urgency than ever before.

Please, love, just do as he tells you...

Outside, through the small hole near the top of the wall, she could hear footsteps as Mulholland rounded the corner, searching for whoever had fired the first shot. She told herself Maddy was professional, and careful, but still she felt her heart speeding up as she listened, dreading what she might hear. Eventually though, it was nothing more frightening than a car door, the starting of an engine and the crunching of wheels on chips of stone as it turned in the small space.

As the headlights briefly touched the dark room, through the vent, Charis saw the horrific injuries inflicted on Andy Stein, and she almost threw up again. His corpse seemed to come briefly back to life in the jumping shadows, and even after the Discovery lumbered away up the slope to the main road, plunging the room into a darkness deeper than before, she couldn't banish the image. It seemed he'd turned away from the gun as it fired; one side of his head had been blasted away, the rest of his face sagged and distorted, his skin hanging in shreds over a gaping wound that let her see right through to his shattered teeth. His one visible eye was open and fixed right ahead, his mouth twisted in a grotesque, silent scream.

She tried to remember the slim, graceful man she'd seen in the hotel bar – arrogant and annoying, but still whole, living – but her mind was flooded with this hideous wreckage of humanity; she knew she'd never forget the sight, however long she might live. She was suddenly, sickeningly aware of the rank, metallic smell of warm blood, and of the revulsion of sharing this dark cell with the cooling remains of these two, who had loved one another once. It took a moment before she was aware of her name being called in a loud whisper. It was coming through the vent.

She scrambled to her feet. 'Maddy?'

'Aye. Mulholland's gone. Is there anyone else in there?'

'No.'

'Okay, I'm coming in.'

Charis crawled towards the door, feeling her way ahead in the darkness. Her foot knocked something that skittered away from her. Something light sounding. Plastic. Crouching, she fumbled after it, and her fingers closed over a familiar shape: Jamie's inhaler. He wouldn't have thrown it away if it had been of any use. She squeezed her eyes tightly shut against fresh tears and, breathless, waited for the sound of the bolt being drawn back. When it came, she gave a little sob of relief. A faint light crept in from the main room, just brushing the floor.

'Get the woman's car keys,' Maddy said. 'Quick!'

Charis fumbled in the woman's back pocket, and reluctantly realised she was going to have to turn the body over. She reached higher up Sarah's back, and her hand slapped into a patch of stickiness in the back of the arm, near the shoulder. She swallowed the acid saliva tht flooded her mouth, and then took a firm grip on the woman's clothing. It was harder than she could have imagined, turning the body, and she strained, feeling the tendons in her neck pop with the effort.

Finally Sarah was lying on her back, and Charis found the single key, with its chunky fob, tucked into a front jeans pocket. She passed it to Maddy, who vanished, and a minute later headlights flooded the front room of the cottage, spilling in through the window from Sarah's car.

Maddy returned and stared down at Sarah's body for a moment, then walked away, leaving Charis to follow, stepping carefully across the dead woman. There seemed to be far too much blood, considering she'd already been dead when she was pushed in here, but most of it was probably Stein's. In case she had missed a potential weapon, she glanced back into the room, and instead saw a familiar piece of cloth; her heart contracted painfully as she recognised Jamie's pyjamas. She bent to scoop them up, and pressed them to her face, but they only smelled like damp cotton.

'Does Bradley have a gun?' Maddy wanted to know. She kept looking at the door, eager to be away, and her voice was oddly light. Charis had the feeling she was holding in some kind of scream, and belatedly realised why. 'Maddy, you didn't kill her—'

'Does he have *gun?*'

'I don't think so. Mulholland had one – I think he took it with him.'

'Right. I'm going after Bradley then.'

Charis's heart leapt. 'Yes! You can show me where the waterfall—'

'No, you're staying here.'

'What? Sod that for a game of soldiers.' Charis was already heading for the door, but Maddy grabbed her arm.

'Whether they find what they're searching for or not, they're going to have to come back here. Now what do you suppose Bradley's going to do to Jamie when he discovers you gone? You reckon he'll be pleased?'

'Stop talking to me like I'm four!'

'Then *think* like a grown up!' Maddy sounded more in control of her emotions now. 'Since Bradley isn't armed, I'd imagine he's relying on the fact that Jamie's just a kid and won't take much guarding. I also think he's a fat twat who couldn't fight his way out of a wet paper towel.'

'So?'

'So if I miss him, and he comes back, he's going to find you waiting for him. With this.' She handed her gun to Charis, who almost dropped it; aside from the shock, it was heavier than she'd imagined, despite its small size. She didn't know what she'd expected a gun to feel like, but she was sure it hadn't been like this – so cold and greasy feeling, and the weight was strange and uneven in her hand.

'Am I supposed to kill him?' she whispered.

'Up to you. If you don't have a choice, just bear in mind it's either him, or you and Jamie. You said they'd gone to the waterfall?'

'That's where Jamie lost the stone, but I don't know where the waterfall is.'

'If it's any size at all, it'll be the Linn of Glenlowrie. I'll have to kill the car lights now, so brace yourself.' Maddy ducked out through the sitting room door into the short hallway. 'Wait here, and don't make a sound. Better we don't telegraph the fact that something's changed; we don't want to make him twitchy. Wait. Have this, too.' She came back in and gave Charis her phone. 'If I don't come back in an hour, call for help. You'll have to go outside to get a signal, though. Remember Stein was somewhere we could hear water, so go over the slope at the back and follow it down until you get within sound of the Linn, but don't go any closer.' She hesitated. 'Was that Paul's jacket that Jamie was wearing?'

Charis nodded. 'He found him in the valley.'

Maddy looked as if there was too much to say, to say anything at all, and Charis understood her completely. Two minutes later, plunged once again into darkness, only the phone, and the gun in her hand, convinced Charis that Maddy had ever been there. And the fact that she could now stretch out a hand without brushing a dead body.

She started to shake and had to sit back against the wall, clutching the gun to her like some kind of deadly comforter. How would she feel when Bradley walked in? Would she have to shoot him, or would the threat be enough to make him let her go? What if she missed him and shot Jamie instead? She moaned at the thought, and fresh, hot tears stung her eyes. With a mighty effort she got herself under control again, wiped her eyes, and thought how much better off she was than she'd been half an hour ago: free, armed, and with the element of surprise on her side.

Minutes passed, surely no more than twenty, and she sat rigidly against the wall, but even that discomfort was no competition for the utter weariness that rapidly began to creep over her. Her chin kept dropping towards her breastbone, her eyes felt as if they were filled with grit, and the hand holding the gun was growing numb. She changed hands and practised aiming with her left hand, and that revived her briefly, but it wasn't long before she felt her neck droop once more. She knew, absolutely *knew*, that Jamie's life depended on her alertness, but to her utter despair even that knowledge wasn't enough. It couldn't hurt to close her eyes for just a moment, surely?

With a grunt of anger and frustration, she forced herself to stand. How could she even contemplate sleep when Jamie needed her? What kind of mother was she? For a second she was transported back to the sleepless nights when he'd been a baby; bone weary for years, and in her fitful sleep she had got up to attend to him time and time again, only to wake and realise his crying had become more strident and she had never left her bed at all.

Now she pinched herself on the back of her hand, bit her tongue, and then forced herself to walk from corner to corner of this pitch black room, only knowing she was passing the window when she felt the gusty rain on her face through the three empty frames. She deliberately stood there, breathing in hard through her nose, hoping the freshness would keep her alert, and for a while it did, but then she became as accustomed to it as she had the discomfort of the rock hard floor. She supported herself on the lintel and drew another deep breath, holding it in, and that was when she heard the first sound. Footsteps, scraping and dragging a little, coming down the roadway towards the cottage. Bradley was back.

Fully alert at last, Charis backed into the corner. Why wasn't he using his torch? Had he lost it? She'd been planning on using that as her target; how else could she fire at him and know she wouldn't hit Jamie? Her heart hammered, and there was a roaring in her ears that threatened to drown out Bradley's approach. She realised she'd only heard one set of footsteps... Where *was* Jamie? After a moment's panic she remembered he had no shoes, so of course she wouldn't hear him. They must have found that stone already, so maybe Bradley would be more likely to let her go now...

But no, she realised with a sinking heart – he wouldn't. He had it all to lose, and both she and Jamie had seen and heard far too much. Maddy would have known, of course, that it wasn't up to her at all, that there *was* no choice; Bradley had Jamie, and could snap her child's neck with one twist of his hands.

Her hand was shaking, and she tried to take a deep breath, to focus. She'd never understood why people on TV always looked so scared when they were armed, and therefore invincible, but now she understood; the gun might save hers and Jamie's lives, but with the potential to destroy the wrong target she had never felt more like throwing something away.

The footsteps came closer. Bradley was breathing heavily, like he'd been running, and Charis fixed her mind on Jamie. She thought of what this man had done to him, and what he had done to Mackenzie all those years ago. Maybe he was pathetic, as Maddy had said, but he had that lethal combination of pettiness and extreme greed, and the authority to give both a free rein.

She stood still, pointing the gun in the direction of the sounds, following the progress across the stony yard to the front door, terrified her reflexes would over-rule common sense. But she couldn't fire right away; he'd be bound to shove Jamie in ahead of him. She wasn't confident enough of her aim to raise the gun higher, and she couldn't shout a warning to Jamie; as far as they knew she was still in the back room, and the surprise element might mean the difference between life and death.

She heard a high, distant keening sound – she recognised it, with horror, as her own voice and bit down on it. The sounds outside paused, then continued with more urgency; he'd heard her. The door opened, creaking back on its broken hinges, more pieces of wood falling off, splintering. She saw the outline of an adult, and her finger tightened on the trigger, her trembling arms outstretched. *I can do this, I can do this, I can do this...*

With a scream of mingled fear and rage, she pulled the trigger. The figure cried out and stumbled against the door jamb, and she pulled the trigger again, hearing the low thwacking sound as the bullet punched through the door.

'Get out, Jamie!' she screamed, preparing to fire once more. 'Run!'

'Stop! For Christ's sake, Charis, it's me!'

Once again, she almost dropped the gun in shock. She was imagining it, surely... As fiercely as she hoped it was real, it *couldn't* be. She shook her head, unable to speak, and the shadow came closer.

'Have you finished trying to kill me now?' Hoarse, barely recognisable, but it was him. She felt the word building up behind her lips, but it took a moment before she was able to force it out.

'M...Mackenzie?' Then she gasped in horror. 'Oh shit! What have I—'

'Nothing! You've done nothing – you're a lousy shot. Come here.'

Charis took a shaky step towards him, then another, and she felt his hand touch her hair as if he could scarcely believe it either. But he pulled back as she put her arms around him, and she realised what she'd cost him. It was no wonder she'd lost his trust.

'Daniel told me what he did to you,' she said quietly. 'I'm so sorry—'

'You've nothing to apologise for. Just let me get my breath back a minute, then we can go.'

'I can't, not yet. I have to wait for Jamie.' She told him, in as few words as possible, what had happened, while she helped him to lower himself until he sat propped against the wall. 'Do you want to lie down? I'll find something for a pillow.' She began to take off her sweatshirt, but he stopped her.

'You need that. Besides, it hurts less if I sit.'

'What have you done?' She knelt beside him, her fingers darting lightly over him while she checked for injuries. When she got near his left shoulder, he seized her hand and held it away.

'No, don't. Collar bone's knackered.'

'And that's all?'

'What is it with you two?' he protested. 'It's bloody horrible.'

'Well, you're going to be all right now,' she said firmly.

There was faint amusement in his voice now. 'That so?'

'I have spoken, and it shall be so.'

He laughed softly. 'I'll not dare argue.'

Charis smiled, and spoke more gently. 'How on earth did you get out of the valley like that?'

'It took a long time to get onto the road, but once I did it was a bit easier.' His voice was growing fainter. 'Jamie gave me something—'

'*Jamie* did?'

'Aye, he found me in the valley.'

'Of course,' she muttered. 'And he took your jacket.'

'Anyway, it calmed things a bit – looking at it distracted me. I even went to sleep. That did me a little bit of good, I think; when I woke up, it felt as if I could maybe move a bit, so I tried.'

'That must have half-killed you.'

'It was pretty nasty, I'm not gonna lie.'

'What Jamie gave you.' Charis felt wonder stealing over her at her son's ingenuity as realisation dawned. 'It was the stone they're all after, wasn't it? The one he's taken them out there to try and find.'

'They're all after it?'

'From what I can gather it's been the main prize all along, both Bradley and that Sarah woman thinking they're the only person to know about it, and both equally obsessed.'

'There's something compelling about it, true enough. The weird thing is, and Jamie couldn't have known it, but it's mine.' He gave a short, disbelieving laugh. 'It's always been mine.'

Before Charis could respond she heard more footsteps, and, looking out of the window, she saw a torch that kept flickering out and being banged against its owner's palm to make it work properly. She scrabbled for the gun again, and stood waiting, with a heavily tripping heart, to see who came in.

The Linn of Glenlowrie

It wasn't nearly as dark outside as it had been in the cottage. Even before his eyes had adjusted, Jamie realised it was quite easy to see his way, despite the heavy clouds. It wasn't moonlight, nor the beginnings of daylight, not yet. It was more of a sort of...absence of total dark. Maybe escaping wouldn't be as easy as he'd hoped. Added to that fear, hunger was a constant ache now, and Jamie wished he'd not been so quick to finish the Mars Bar down in the valley with Mackenzie... The thought brought him up short; Bradley had been horribly glad, gleeful even, when he'd thought Mackenzie was dead, which meant Jamie must keep him at the top end of the waterfall, or he'd find out the truth. He dragged his feet as much as he dared, now and again stopping to pull Mackenzie's socks higher against the evening chill. Someone must have called the police by now, he reasoned. The good police. He had to give them time to find them.

'Get a shift on,' Bradley grunted, flashing the torch back at him. 'We've not got all night.'

Jamie picked up his pace for a few steps. Bradley, marching

ahead towards the sound of the rushing water, aimed the torch at his own feet, leaving Jamie to stumble along behind him. It was just like before, where the rocks seemed to relish making him sidestep them and plunge instead into deep, icy puddles. He had twisted his ankle quite painfully, somewhere along the way, and now his slow progress was genuine, but it also meant he wouldn't be able to run very fast if he eventually broke for freedom.

The noise grew louder, and all too soon they were coming to the brow of the hill, from where the water gushed down over the rocks.

'Right, lad!' Bradley shouted over the roar. 'Where's this cairn of yours then?'

Jamie shielded his eyes from the glare of the torch Bradley shone in his face, and turned this way and that, peering into the gloom. 'I think it's just down there,' he said at last. 'See that rock sticking out? That's where I was sitting, I'm sure of it.'

Bradley followed the line of his pointing finger. 'Right. You go first.'

Jamie had just moved past him when another voice cut across the grassy hilltop.

'Not found it yet, then?'

He recognised the voice as being that of the one called Alistair, and Bradley hissed a curse. Alistair's own, smaller, torchlight bobbed into view a second later. 'Well, have you?'

'No. What are you doing here anyway? Did you get whoever shot Sarah?'

'*I* shot her,' Alistair pointed out. 'Short memory.'

'You know damn well I meant the first time.'

Alistair shook his head. 'No-one there that I could see. Whoever it was legged it pretty quick – I didn't even hear a car. Might have been Cameron, I suppose. He knows the area well enough to have parked somewhere else.'

'Seems a shame we have to fix him, if so. He's done us a favour. Wasn't that your job, by the way?'

'He can wait; we'll sort him together.' Alistair came closer, and Jamie saw he still held his gun, but now loosely, pointed at the ground. 'Let's get the stone first. Six eyes are better than four.'

'You don't trust me, do you?' Bradley said, and there was amusement in his voice. '*That's* why you're here, to make sure I don't do a runner.'

They both looked eerie and alien in the wavering light of their torches, and with the thunder of the waterfall now directly behind them, they had to almost shout to be heard.

'Teamwork makes the dream work, right?' Alistair called, his tone mocking.

'I've always hated that phrase.'

Alistair turned to Jamie. 'Come on then, lad, let's get searching.'

His cheerful tone sounded all wrong, and Jamie looked at him with deep mistrust, only moving when Bradley shoved him in the back and sent him stumbling down the path. The rock loomed larger, and Jamie grew more frightened with every step; the moment they reached it and found no cairn, the game would be up. There was only one thing he could think of that might work, and it all hinged on him not having underestimated Bradley's obsession with the stone.

He stopped dead, hearing Bradley scuffle to a halt behind him, and began to breathe hard. 'Asthma,' he gasped between dragging breaths. 'Can't bre... Help me!'

'Shit,' Alistair said, and Jamie flinched away from the light that hit him full in the face. 'What now?'

Bradley grabbed hold of Jamie's shoulder. 'Show us! Just...*point*, for Christ's sake!'

Jamie waved one hand away from the path, towards the rockier ground at the edge of the waterfall. 'Please!' He dropped to his knees, wondering what he would do if they didn't believe him, frantically trying to think of a way to make it seem more real.

But it worked, and he'd been right about the officer's desperation. Bradley shoved him aside and bellowed for Alistair to follow, and then they were gone. Off the path, scrambling down over the rocks towards the non-existent cairn. Jamie kept gasping loudly, and waited as long as he dared, which didn't feel long enough even so, before he began to inch his way down the path.

They were still shouting at one another. Their voices, and the sound of the water, masked any sound Jamie made, and he slithered and slid on his socked feet, once again feeling the bite and scrape of tiny stones and rough grass. His confidence grew with every metre he put between himself and his captors.

He was almost at the bottom of the path when, to his dismay, he heard movement behind him – they'd discovered his deception. The familiar wheezing began as he stumbled faster, away from his pursuer, trying to fight the panic that was only making it worse. From phony attack to real one... He had brought this one on himself, and knowing that made it no easier to fight; he heard the awful, high, whistling sound in his own ears as his airways constricted.

Bradley or Alistair, whichever it was, was coming closer; Jamie could hear boots slipping and sliding, knocking stones down the path to bounce off Jamie's ankles. No-one shouted at him to stop, they must think he hadn't noticed how close they were, and hoped not to scare him into running faster. As if he could. He was nearing the end of his endurance now; his arms felt weak as he used them to stop himself from falling. He wanted to cry out, but his chest was too tight to draw enough breath...

'Jamie!' A harsh whisper, and a hand reached for him. He pulled away, but the hand caught at his oversized jacket again, and this time managed to seize a handful. He lashed out, panic-stricken, and felt his fist connect with flesh.

'Stop! It's all right!' He belatedly realised it was a woman's voice, and Scottish, but that woman was dead. Was *this* Maddy? He subsided, still fighting for breath, and the woman drew him close.

'Don't worry, I've got you now,' she murmured. 'We'll go and get your mum, and then you'll be all right.'

She must have thought she was soothing him as she held him, but she was only making it worse. With the last of his strength, Jamie pulled back, fumbled for her hand in the darkness, and laid it on his chest. She uttered a savage curse and swept him up into her arms, sliding down the last bit of the path with him clutched tight against her once more.

'My car's up on the road near here somewhere,' she panted. 'Hold on... Breathe slow...'

He must have blacked out, because when he came to she was running on flatter ground. The valley floor? Mackenzie was down here... But he couldn't speak, to tell her to look for him, and soon enough they were climbing again, but a gradual slope this time, not the horrible steep place where he'd climbed before. The air was barely getting through now, and the muscles in his chest hurt... His thoughts were becoming jumbled, and for a while he drifted in and out of a strange, disjointed world.

The road. They were on the road now. His head was

heavy, and there was a clamp around his chest that was growing tighter with each laboured breath. The woman held him close; he could hear her own gasps as her shoes slapped down on hard tarmac instead of grass. She kept muttering *hold on* to him, as if he weren't trying. But then she said something else, and at last there was a flicker of hope.

'My car's just down this hill. We'll get you to hospital. You're going to be all right.'

He tried to reply but could only wheeze, and then she stopped, so suddenly that he felt himself sliding from her grasp, and he almost crashed to the ground. In a dizzy haze he heard her moan softly, 'What? No. No, no...' Then she screamed the word, and Jamie went away again.

Chapter Twenty-Three

BRADLEY KNEW he should have stopped to help the boy. Knew it from the toes of his boots to the last hair on his head, but thirty years of desire was about to be satiated; and the kid would be all right – there was plenty of air out here, it wasn't like he was still locked up. They'd see he was taken to safety, but first...

He'd pushed past the wheezing child and started down the slope towards the flat rock a few feet away. 'Come on!' Behind him he saw the flickering light, as Mulholland obeyed for once. His heart was thudding faster the closer he came to his goal; his feet lost their purchase time and time again on the loose stones, and he kept scraping the skin from his fingers as he pushed himself on.

When he reached the rock, he hunted for the cairn the boy had said he'd built. Just a small one, apparently, but there was nothing. Not even a few stones pushed together.

'It must be here somewhere.' Bradley played the torchlight over the area around the rock. Through the roaring sound of the waterfall he heard sobbing and hesitated again – was he doing the right thing? The boy was distraught, terrified, innocent—

'Half a mil. At least.' Mulholland broke into his thoughts, stooping to check a dark-coloured rock he'd found near his feet. 'Damn.' He tossed the rock into the path of the rushing water and bent again.

Bradley didn't reply; Mulholland *still* didn't get that it wasn't all about the money. He kicked dull, grey stones aside in growing frustration. 'Where the hell is it? Do you think he got the wrong place?'

'Get down here, boy!' Mulholland yelled. 'Show us!'

Bradley flashed his torch back up the path. He frowned and swept the beam from side to side, expecting to see the child on his knees, or even lying flat out, but... 'Shit!'

'What?' Mulholland's own beam found the same empty hillside. 'I'll be damned. The little sod!'

Bradley turned away. 'I'll get him later. He'll have gone back to his mother. He can't be moving very fast, not with that—'

'Don't be an idiot all your life,' Mulholland growled. 'He was obviously faking it.'

Bradley felt an unexpected flash of admiration for the kid, despite the situation he'd left them in. 'He'll still not get far. Come on.'

'Look! What's that?' Mulholland directed his torch towards the edge of the path. 'A wee cairn, look!'

All thoughts of the missing boy vanished as Bradley peered with growing excitement along the beam of light. He couldn't yet see what Mulholland had found, but followed the younger man as he scrambled across to stand next to the waterfall.

'Where?'

'There!' Mulholland pointed again. 'Ah, give me the decent torch, y'fool!'

Heart thumping with anticipation, Bradley did, and a moment later he realised Mulholland was right. He *was* a fool. There was a flare of light behind his eyes as something hard connected with the side of his head, and the ground disappeared from under one of his feet. He landed on one knee and grabbed at the wet grass to stop himself from slipping, but it tore loose, and to his terror he felt himself going over. With one last surge of strength he lunged back and seized hold of something: Mulholland's ankle. He felt Mulholland's leg bend reflexively, but it did not give way, thank God, and the sergeant stood firm, stopping them both from plunging into the waterfall.

'Help me!' Bradley heard this echo of the little boy's plea, bursting from his own numbed mouth, and hated himself. He spat out the mouthful of water he'd taken as he cried out, and repeated his plea, but Mulholland didn't move. 'Jesus, Alistair!'

Mulholland's voice lifted easily over the sound of the waterfall. 'I always knew your greed would get the better of you.'

Bradley's clothes were soaked through, and the weight was pulling him backwards, away from solid ground and towards the churning white water. 'Please...'

'All this, for a *stone*?'

'We'll talk! I'll explain... Alistair, the rocks... Please, just pull me up.'

'You made me risk everything, for *your* obsession.' Mulholland bent down, and as he stretched out his hand Bradley felt a surge of blinding relief. But Mulholland was not offering his hand in help after all. He was holding something. His gun. Bradley flinched, expecting another blow and bracing himself for it. But before he could form the question in his mind – *why doesn't he just shoot if he really wants me dead?* – Mulholland surprised him by shoving the gun down inside Bradley's wet coat. Then he began to prise Bradley's white fingers off his ankle. Bradley's terror flared once more; his free hand was grasping at more grass, but it was a token clutch, just the screaming instinct of a man in his final moments.

'Just tell me what you want!'

'I don't care if you survive this or no,' Mulholland said. 'I've got no feelings about you one way or the other. But I'll not be your puppet any longer.' He released Bradley's grip, and in the split second before he fell, Bradley's anger towards the escaped boy turned to envy for his freedom.

Just don't let him catch up with you...

Then the water was over his head and he was crashing over rocks both rough and smooth. There was burning pain in shattered limbs that was soon echoed in his lungs as he swallowed and swallowed, trying to get past the water to find air. His last coherent thought was of a black stone with a fiery heart, but as his dying fingers closed on it, it blew apart in a shower of dust.

———

Maddy stared in mute horror at the place where her car had been. Her throat hurt from the anguished and disbelieving scream, and she was only partially aware of the weight of the boy in her arms. He moved a little, and she lowered him gently to the ground and slapped at her trouser pocket before she remembered she'd given her phone to Charis. How had he done it? You weren't supposed to be able to hot-wire these cars any more, so had she dropped her keys in her hurry to be away? If so why hadn't she heard them land on the road, and—

'Shit!' She remembered sitting in silence after she'd stopped and turned off the engine, then telling Charis why she was leaving the car and walking. Getting out in a temper, and slamming the door... Leaving the keys dangling from the ignition. She'd been crying, she recalled that, but how could she have been so stupid?

Jamie was breathing, but it was thin and desperate sounding. They were closer to the town now than to the cottage, and certainly closer to passing traffic; there was no question of going back for Charis – Maddy would stick to her plan to get Jamie to hospital. She turned to explain to the boy, and saw his hunched little shadow move. A moment later he had pressed something into her hand, and she recognised the feel of a mobile phone. She pressed a random button and the screen lit up; when she saw the lock screen photo of a long-dead woman and child she didn't know whether to sob with relief or despair – Paul's phone.

'Where did...no matter.' She touched his face in mute gratitude and used the emergency call function to call for an ambulance, telling them only that she was on the Glenlowrie road, and had a child who needed urgent medical help.

'We'll get them to come for your mum too,' she told Jamie as she hung up. 'As soon as they arrive. But it would have only complicated things if I'd tried to explain now. We need to save your strength, so we're going to wait here, okay? Hold my hand and sit here with me. Don't try to talk.' She thought back to her nursing days. 'Sit up very straight,' she urged. 'Breathe slow, and as deep as you can.'

Jamie's small hand slipped into hers, and she clutched Paul's phone tightly, trying not to give in to the fresh waves of grief that wanted to drown her. She had to stay calm for the boy. He was breathing in tiny, shallow little hiccups that seemed to be getting shorter and higher as the night crept past them, but finally she heard the blessed sound of an approaching car, and she stood up, lifting Jamie into her arms once more. As the headlights of the rapid response vehicle swept over them she saw that the boy's lips were grey-looking in his white face, and just as worrying was his lack of expression; he looked as if he simply no longer cared what happened.

While one paramedic administered carefully regulated puffs from an inhaler, the other was speaking to the police, relaying Maddy's information about Paul and Charis. 'Body in the valley just off the Glenlowrie Estate road...'

Body. Maddy closed her eyes and tried to shut out the image, but Jamie tugged at her hand and she opened them again. He was still breathing shallowly, but some colour had come back into his face, and she tried on an encouraging smile. 'Good lad.'

'Not dead,' the boy managed. He patted the over-sized jacket, and accepted another puff from the paramedic's inhaler.

Maddy's skin tingled. 'What did you say?'

The driver twisted in her seat. 'Who isn't dead?'

'He means Paul, I think,' Maddy said, mystified. 'God, *did* you?' Her heart began to race, but she couldn't hope. Not yet.

The boy nodded wearily. 'He broke some bones, but he could talk.'

'Christ! I'll hurry things up,' the driver said, and picked up the radio again.'

'Get the police, too,' Maddy said. 'The crofter's cottage on the estate. You'll see it from the air – there are cars there. This boy's mother's...' she hesitated and glanced at Jamie. The last thing she wanted to do was frighten him. 'She's waiting there,' she finished. She tried to catch the eye of the paramedic over

Jamie's head and convey her fear. The medic gave a barely perceptible nod, and Maddy could only hope the police arrived before Bradley and Mulholland returned. Or that Charis's courage would not fail her.

'They're despatching the 'copter,' the driver said. 'Don't worry, lad, they'll find him. And your mum.'

Jamie slumped in his seat, and nothing Maddy said could coax any more from him. She too fell silent, but her fingers clenched and unclenched on her thigh as she began scouring the sky for searchlights although she knew it was too soon yet.

They drove through Abergarry on the way to Fort William, and as they passed the Clifford-Mackenzie offices, Maddy glanced idly out of the window and froze; her car sat outside, parked haphazardly, half on the pavement. And the office light was on.

'Stop!' she said. 'Let me out here.' The car pulled in, and Maddy took Jamie's unresponsive hand in hers. It lay there like a stunned mouse. 'Jamie, I've just seen my car, so I'll drive it to the hospital to meet you, okay? That way I'll be able to drive you back again when you're all fixed up. In the meantime these people will carry on taking good care of you.'

She waited until the car had rounded the bend at the top of town, and then pulled out Paul's phone and made another emergency call, this time to the police. Then she leaned on her car and waited. Only one person could have left it here, but how had he known who she was, or where she worked? What if she'd just gone up into the office? After what she'd done to him she'd have been lucky to get away with her skull in one piece; as reluctant as she was to involve the police, she was more reluctant to leave that animal on the loose in her home town.

A glance into the back seat made her blood run cooler,

and she just stopped herself from yanking on the driver's door and destroying Thorne's fingerprints. Instead she ran around to the passenger side, praying he hadn't bothered to lock up, and to her relief she was able to open that one instead. She seized the discarded police uniform and cast frantically about for somewhere to hide it before the real police arrived, settling on a large, lidded recycling bin in the alley below the offices. She finished stuffing the uniform inside it with moments to spare.

Checking through the car window for anything incriminating she might have missed, she saw the answer to her initial question, now lying on the passenger seat. The road atlas, and the envelope Charis had shoved in it to mark the page. Clifford-Mackenzie's address, as clear as you like.

'Fucking hell, woman,' Maddy breathed. 'You're a liability even when you're not here.'

The door to the cottage creaked open on its rusted hinges, and when she heard footsteps in the passageway Charis felt the gun slipping in her sweaty hand. This was it. She would finally have to take a life for real. That it was to save other lives didn't matter; she was going to become a killer, and nothing could ever be the same again.

A flare of light at the doorway drew a low cry from her, and she raised the gun until she hoped it was pointed at his chest. But once again it wasn't Bradley. This time it was Mulholland. Taken by surprise, she wavered; this man might be a weasel, and a criminal, but he hadn't actually hurt anyone that she knew of, and he was alone. He seemed puzzled, but not dismayed, to see her free and armed.

'Put the gun down, lass,' he said mildly. 'I've got no weapon, see?' He raised his hands.

'Where's Jamie?'

'I've no idea,' he said reasonably. 'He's not returned from the waterfall yet, then?'

'What do you think?'

'And Bradley?' He looked past her to the locked door. 'How do I know you've not put a bullet in him and shoved him in that room?'

'You don't.' Charis renewed her grip on the gun. 'But you can get in there anyway.'

Mulholland blinked. 'What? I've come to help you!'

'Have you bollocks,' Mackenzie whispered. 'Don't trust him, Charis.' His breathing was laboured now; the last of the strength that had driven him out of the valley was fading.

Charis jerked the gun, indicating that Mulholland should cross to the bolted door. He obeyed, crossing the room past the window, but he had seen something in the path of his torch-light, and he bent swiftly and snatched it up.

His face alight with triumph, he now mirrored Charis's stance, and the barrel of the gun he held was aimed directly at her. 'Nice of Sarah to leave me a wee gift,' he said. 'Now, as I asked nicely before, put the gun down.'

'Get knotted,' Charis said, hearing the words as if they were coming from someone else. Mackenzie made a faint sound; a mingled murmur of surprise, admiration and despair, and it gave her a strange feeling of pride and, with it, renewed confidence. 'Why should I?' she demanded. 'You put yours down.'

Mulholland considered her for a moment. Then he moved, slowly, across the room towards them. Charis tightened her grip, every nerve alive and tingling. Everything depended on her ability to squeeze this trigger, and stop this man in his tracks; even if he fired first, she'd still get a round off, and the odds were pretty good that it would hit him.

But all bets were off a second later, as the muzzle of the sergeant's gun swung from her to Mackenzie. 'Put the gun *down*, Ms Boulton-with-a-u.' He looked down, and his bored expression changed to one of interest. 'Oh my! What's this?'

He leaned down again and pushed the muzzle of the gun against Mackenzie's shoulder. Mackenzie's cry of pain tore through Charis like a blunt-bladed saw.

'Stop it, you *bastard!*'

Only then did she realise what Mulholland had seen: the Fury, resting loosely in Mackenzie's weakening grip; Mulholland had not seemed consumed by the same obsession as Bradley and Sarah, but he clearly had a healthy appetite for a valuable stone. Instinct kicked in, and Charis moved like a snake, wresting the opal herself from Mackenzie's hand.

'Give it to me,' Mulholland said tightly, and to Charis's relief, he lifted the gun away from Mackenzie and pointed it back at her.

'No.'

Mulholland whipped his gun around, and it cracked against Charis's cheek in a burst of pain. She stumbled and fell, and as she hit the floor another pain, unexpected and dull throbbed in the top of her thigh. She remembered what was causing it, and, her heart pounding, she seized on the only thing she could think of that might work.

'All right! I'm putting the gun down. Here.' She laid it on the floor and shoved it away with her foot. As Mulholland's torch followed its path, Charis dug into her pocket and pulled out the stone she had put there earlier. No good as a weapon, perhaps, but beyond value now. She waved it quickly in front of Mulholland's face. 'Here's your precious Fury!'

She threw it, as hard as she could, and Mulholland instinctively lifted his arms to shield his face, but Charis had thrown it at the window, where it hit the last remaining pane and sailed out into the night beyond, amid the tinkling of broken glass. At the same time she heard a low thudding sound from the direction of the valley; she couldn't place it, but Mulholland had heard it too. He stared at her in shock and indecision, and Charis was certain he was going to shoot them both. Then the noise from outside slotted into its recognised place; it was a helicopter.

Mulholland took one last look at her and Mackenzie, and turned to run outside. It was the only sensible thing for him to do; at the moment he could still claim to be on the right side of the law. The helicopter was coming closer, but underneath the sound Charis could hear Mulholland scrabbling around outside, searching for the Fury before it became too late and he'd have to run. She tucked the real thing into her pocket and knelt beside Mackenzie, where for the first time she felt the terrifying heat of him through his shirt. He shouldn't be this hot... She could only see the vague outline of his form, but when she tentatively placed a hand at his injured shoulder she felt the sharp edge of bone beneath her fingers and smelled the rich, metallic scent of fresh blood. His shirt was drenched in it.

'Hang on, Mackenzie,' she whispered, not even knowing if he could hear her. She scrambled across to where she thought Maddy's gun had come to rest, and groped around the floor until she felt it, hard and icy, and no longer frightening to touch. If Mulholland came back in she'd be ready.

But he didn't. Instead, the heavy chopping sound of the helicopter's blades grew louder, and a moment later light flooded the cottage and a calm, dispassionate voice urged everyone to come out with their hands raised. Charis willed her feet to move but they wouldn't. She had nothing left. Her cheek throbbed, and she could feel it was slick with blood where Mulholland's gun barrel had torn the skin. Besides, how could she leave Mackenzie? She ached all over; her heart was cramping with fear for him and for Jamie, and even for Maddy, and although she was taut as a zip wire and her nerves jumped with every new sound, she was utterly drained.

The voice came again, and the hovering machine sent tiny stones pinging off the cars outside and in through the broken window. Charis finally found the strength to pull herself to her feet, and to leave Mackenzie where he half-sat against the wall. She emerged into the artificial light, blinking, her hands above her head, and only realising she still held Maddy's gun when the voice ordered her to place it on the ground and lie down. To her horror she saw a tiny red light dancing across her sweatshirt, and dropped hurriedly to her knees. As she stretched out on the wet, stony ground she heard feet scuffling nearby.

'Is anyone else in there armed?' a voice demanded.

She tried to shake her head, but she was too frightened to raise it, and her cheek burst into fiery new pain as it rubbed the ground.

'Where's Paul Mackenzie? He's not in the valley. Where is he?'

'Inside!' she sobbed. 'Please help him!' The downdraught from the helicopter was tugging at her short hair, and she could feel the uneven, wet ground pressing into her as she tried to push herself flatter against it. Where had the help come from? Had Maddy found Jamie and called the police? Perhaps they were all safe back in Abergarry now...

She heard a voice, closer now, and a hand on her back

urged her to stand. The voice was kind, but the cuffs were real, and as they clicked shut she wondered bemusedly if they thought she was the one who'd hurt Mackenzie, and how long it would be before they realised their mistake and set her free to find Jamie. It was only as the officer's words sank in that she remembered the gun.

'Charis Boulton, I'm arresting you for the murder of Sarah Wallace. You do not have to say anything...'

Abergarry

An air of unreality still enveloped Charis as she entered the police station, but it was quickly dispelled by the sour smell of vomit and stale beer. Weekends in Outlander country bore a striking resemblance to those back in Liverpool, it seemed.

'Interview room three,' the desk sergeant said. 'I'll call through for Sergeant Clifford to sit in.' A moment later he hung up. 'Right, apparently he's called in sick.' He sighed. 'Put her in a cell then, while we arrange for someone. Do you want a solicitor?'

Charis blinked, confused. Should she ask for one? Didn't they always assume that that was an admission of guilt?

'Charis!'

'Maddy?' Charis looked around, suddenly frantic. 'Where's Jamie?'

'He's safe. He's going to be fine.' Maddy, pale and tired, came over. 'What happened to your face?' The arresting officer, seeing Charis's silent plea, and evidently recognising Maddy, gave a brief nod. 'Be quick. And I'll be listening.'

'Jamie's at The Belford. The hospital in Fort William,' she

clarified, as Charis looked blankly at her. 'He faked an attack to get away, but it turned into a real one, so they just want to keep him overnight to be sure.' She smiled. 'He's sitting up and asking for a Coke as we speak.'

The relief was almost too much for Charis, and she swayed slightly and steadied herself on the countertop. 'Did you hear about Bradley?'

'Aye, they fished him out from the river at the foot of the Linn of Glenlowrie. What about Mulholland though?'

'No idea. Hiding? Waiting for them to finish up at the cottage so he can go back to hunting for that bloody rock?'

'Or going after Ben Cameron,' Maddy said grimly. 'Seems he's the other loose end.'

'What do we do about that?'

'I've told the police; they've put a guard outside Cameron's house.'

'They think I murdered Sarah Wallace,' Charis began, but at those words the police officer cut her off.

'That's enough. Come on.'

'Do you need a legal rep?' Maddy called after her.

'I don't know!'

'I'm going back to The Belford, but I'll call Gavin.'

'That'll do,' the officer insisted, punching a code into the lock. 'You'll have to arrange a visit once you've been processed.'

Beyond the bustle of the front office, Charis felt that veil of unreality descend again. She was no longer handcuffed, but the walls seemed to press in, separating her from the world, from Jamie, from Mackenzie... The confidence of a few minutes ago was starting to dissipate. What if they didn't believe her after all?

A door banged at the far end of the corridor, and Charis's fearful musings were cut short as she recognised the voice drifting down to meet her. 'Ah, there's the one who'll tell you. Charis-with-a-c-h!'

She stopped, her heart slithering with revulsion and a resurgence of fear. 'What are you still doing here, Daniel?'

'A big misunderstanding. Your friend seems to think I'm the one who gave you that bruise. Tell them I'd never hurt a fly.'

'Good news for flies.' Charis fingered her jaw and wondered if, between his blow and Mulholland's, she even looked like herself any more. 'I could do you for assault on top of everything else.'

Daniel's tone was reasonable, as ever. 'Love, be sensible. Think of what it'll do to the...to Jamie if we're both arrested.'

'He'd survive.' Her cold tone was clearly having an effect now; the last vestige of his false charm fell away, and he gave her a tight smile as he was drawn past her down the corridor.

'I saw your friend's little dress-up kit on the back seat of her car. That's up to six months.'

'I don't know what you're talking about.' Maddy wasn't stupid; she'd have whisked the incriminating uniform out of the car before she called the police in. 'I won't lie to protect you any more, Daniel. You're a coward and a thief, and if I've learned anything off the telly, you've just broken your parole conditions.'

The officers exchanged an interested glance, and Charis smiled. 'Yes, he's out on licence for car theft, fraud and three counts of aggravated assault. Probably destroyed a police tag, too. Call Birkenhead, they'll tell you everything.'

Restrained as he was, Daniel could only glare at her with impotent anger, but she shrugged. 'I've beaten bigger and scarier things than you, Thorne.'

'Yeah? Surrounded by coppers and private dicks, you're all

talk. But I won't be in prison forever, and what about when life goes back to normal?'

'Normal?'

'When you come home.'

Charis found the words slipping out before she'd even thought about them. 'I am home, you berk.'

Chapter Twenty-Four

Tony Clifford's phone buzzed on the bedside table, vibrating its way to the edge. He grabbed it just before it fell off, and blinked at the screen before answering, then at the clock. Just after three am. Instantly his blood started pumping faster and he sat up in bed.

'Mackenzie?'

'No, Dad, it's me.'

'Maddy! Are you okay? You never turned up for Nick's birthday.'

'I'm sorry. I'm fine – don't worry about me.'

'Why are you using Mackenzie's phone? Is *he* okay?'

'I don't know. I think he will be, but he's pretty bashed about. He...' she hesitated, 'he came off his bike. Look, I'm at The Belford with him. I wondered if you could do me a favour?'

'Aye, of course.'

'I should probably have waited until a more sociable hour to call, but I'll have to go back to the police station in a bit so this might be my only chance—'

'Police? What the hell's going on?'

'Long story. I'll explain later, as much as I know, at least, which isn't a lot.' Her voice lowered until it was almost a whisper. 'Look, Bradley's dead, but I've—'

'*Dead?*'

'Drowned. I'll explain later, but I've found out which investigation he sabotaged.'

Tony pressed the phone closer to his ear. 'Go on.'

'It was before we moved here.'

Tony listened to the story with growing interest, and a great sense of relief. 'I knew he was dirty.'

'We all did, we just didn't know how far he'd go to protect Wallace. Look, the other reason I'm calling is that Paul's going to need some clothes – his are pretty ragged after the crash, and they've had to cut them off him anyway.'

'I could lend him some of mine until I can get into his place.'

'It's okay, there's a set of his things at the office. You've still got your key, haven't you?'

'Aye, but—'

'Good. Later on, when you can, will you fetch them over here for him?' She sounded tired. Drained. And no wonder.

'Okay. If you need me or Nick to help out, just call.'

'I will. Thanks, Dad.'

'And you're sure you're okay? You weren't on the bike with him?'

'No. Look, I've got to go. The doctors are ready to let me know what's going on.'

'Okay, love. Keep me in the loop.'

She murmured something unintelligible and broke the connection, leaving Tony staring at the screen. He replaced the phone on the bedside table, and lay down again, but kept looking at it, daring it to glow and buzz with more strange news. Eventually he abandoned any attempt to find sleep again, and threw the duvet back; he'd get the stuff now, and then get some bloody answers.

At the Clifford-Mackenzie office he spotted the pile of crumpled clothes on the edge of the desk, and as he picked them up his glance fell on the notebook page filled with Maddy's neat handwriting, and an ornate set of doodles. He stopped, frowned, looked harder. Three sets of initials: DC, DB, SW. All together inside a circle. DB and SW were at the front of his mind and easy to connect, but DC?

Maddy's words: *Wallace hid his share in some little statues...*

Tony's forehead tightened. There it was. The connection: Dougie Cameron, locally renowned for his beautifully crafted gifts; murder unsolved. Don Bradley lying about his alibi for the time of the murder... Christ, he had been right about that all along. He almost laughed aloud, but it turned into a growl of fury against the smug, self-serving officer who'd ruined so many lives. It was time to put an end to it all, which meant a brief but vital detour, before heading out to Fort William with Mackenzie's clothes and his giant bombshell.

The little housing estate was still draped in night as he pulled up outside Nick's house, and Tony wondered whether he oughtn't to wait after all. Max's car was no longer parked outside, so he must have gone home; he and Nick had had words during the birthday tea, and the atmosphere had turned pretty sour without Maddy there to defuse things. Nick had begun to drink a bit too much as a result, and was likely in a pretty deep sleep by now.

But the knowledge of Bradley's crimes was burning holes in Tony's patience, and he had to know whether Nick was prepared to confirm or deny that flimsy tale of working at the Inverness office on the days before Cameron's death. They were within inches of serving up the superintendent's just desserts, albeit posthumously, and after twenty-five years the moment couldn't come soon enough.

He'd got out of his car and was halfway to the front door when he remembered Nick was on shift tonight, and he stopped with a little exclamation of frustration. He'd have to drop by the station instead. He turned to go, but registered that, although Max's car wasn't there, Nick's was, and he turned back; the lad must have pulled a sickie, which wasn't like him. Peering through the glass panel in Nick's front door, he realised his son was still up; there was a light spilling down the stairs, and he could see the bathroom door open a crack. Rather than knock, he pushed open the letter box.

'Nick! It's me.' There was no reply, and Tony called louder. 'Nick!' Still no answer. Tony sighed and straightened, then tried the door handle. Surprised to find it unlocked, he still hesitated; he might be the lad's father, but it was still rude to just walk in. Then Bradley's face floated into the front of his mind, cloaking the niggling sense that he was intruding, and he went in anyway.

'You awake? I wouldn't have come if it wasn't...' He fell silent, his words trailing away as he heard a sound that made his heart shrink. Sobbing. Gulping, gasping sobs coming from the bathroom. The row with Max must have hit Nick harder than Tony had realised, and Tony's protective instincts rose as took the stairs three at a time and pushed the bathroom door wider. If Max had hurt his boy...

Nick sat on the floor, leaning against the bath, his long legs cramped up against the wall on the other side of the tiny room. He was dressed only in boxer shorts, and in his right hand he held a Stanley knife. His left leg was a mess. Blood smeared from knee to heel, and ran in rivers down his thigh to soak into his underwear. He looked up at Tony, but the tears that spilled down his face turned his eyes into glassy, unseeing pools.

Tony couldn't speak. His mouth was dry, his throat too tight, and a hundred questions were making it impossible to find one he could bear to ask. Nick – quiet and good-natured at home, laughing and sociable at work; there were old scars on that lacerated leg as well as new cuts. How long? And why?

'Oh, my boy...' He squatted beside his son and reached for the knife. 'Give that to me, lad, come on.'

Nick relinquished the knife without argument; his hand fell open and limp to the floor at his side, and he made no protest either as Tony tore a length of toilet roll from the holder and used it to wipe his son's eyes. The blood was another matter; toilet tissue would have disintegrated into useless mush. Tony ran the hand towel under the cold tap instead, and draped it over Nick's raised knee, hiding the mutilation in an attempt to break the spell of silent hopelessness that held them both.

Tony sat beside his son and wordlessly took his bloodied hand. Only Nick's breathing, hitching as he controlled his emotions, and the dripping water, from towel to linoleum, made any sound.

Eventually Tony had to speak. 'Why?'

'It helps.' Nick's voice was low, hurt. 'Makes me think...' he lifted his free hand in a vague wave, '...in other directions.'

'Other than what?'

'Don't.'

'Nick, please.' Tony grasped the hand tighter. 'I want to help you.'

'You can't.'

'At least let me—'

'I did it for you!' Nick tore his hand free and stood up; the towel fell from his leg, and the dozens of small cuts welled with blood once more. He took a deep breath. 'I killed Ben Cameron's dad.'

Tony sat very still, staring at the blood pooling on the bathroom floor. Had Nick lost his mind? 'I don't get it,' he managed at last. 'I was coming here to tell you... It was Don Bradley.'

'His orders, aye. But not him.'

'I don't... Wait, what do you mean, you did it for me?' Tony shook his head, suddenly frightened that Nick was starting to make sense. 'I had nothing against him back then.' He took a bath towel and draped it around his son's shoulders. 'Come downstairs, let's talk about this properly.'

In the front room Tony put on a low-watt side light, and the two of them sat side by side on the sofa. Blood was starting to soak through the towel, but Nick paid it no attention. He was shivering, and tears were standing in his eyes again, but somehow he got the whole story out.

'Duncan Wallace never trusted Bradley. We'd only just moved here in ninety-three, and I was still new to the force, but I was mates with Ben Cameron. So when Wallace needed someone, he came to me. Told me nothing, except that Mr Cameron – Dougie – was worried he was being targeted by someone, and that his business was at risk. I was to keep an eye on him, and if anything happened to him, Wallace would have my hide. And my career.'

'I still don't—'

'But when Wallace died, all bets were off. His protection of Cameron was over. Bradley told me about you, Dad. Told me what I'd have to do to protect you now.'

'Protect me?'

'Don't come the innocent! I *know*!'

Tony was mystified, and growing worried again. 'Just what is it that you think you know?'

'Bradley told me how you were part of the robbery at the Spence estate. That *you* were the one I'd been protecting Cameron against! And that now Wallace was gone Cameron was scared stiff, and planned to shop you.' He said the only way to protect you was to get rid of him.' Nick's voice thickened, and he lowered his head. 'I didn't want to, Dad. It was the hardest thing I'd ever done, but if you'd gone to prison, as a copper—'

'Stop!' Tony stood up, his heart racing. 'I was *never* involved in that robbery. We were living in Glasgow back then, for crying out loud!'

'It's only a four-hour drive,' Nick pointed out. 'And you knew people here, even back then.'

'Aye, well I never knew Duncan Wallace, or any of his cronies! And I certainly never threatened Dougie Cameron. Are you seriously telling me you *believed* that oily bastard?'

'Of course I did!' Nick pulled the towel closer around himself. 'I thought I was saving your life.'

'How could you have thought that of me?'

'Dad, I was *twenty*!'

Tony pulled his trembling son to him. He'd been a child. He must have been so torn... He felt his own tears burn.

'You've gone all this time thinking I was a thief? And *corrupt*?'

'You were still my dad. The fact that you were so straight... It made sense, that you were covering something up.'

'And you never mentioned it to your mum or Maddy?'

'How could I?'

'And now?'

Nick slumped, looking wretched. 'Now I believe you. Of course I do. I always think clearer after...' He gestured to his leg. 'But Bradley said you'd go down for the original crime as well as perverting the course of justice... Your life wouldn't have been worth that!' He snapped his fingers, and Tony flinched.

'So you killed an innocent man.' He spoke slowly, trying to get the words to make sense.

'I didn't think he was innocent, not at the time.' Nick dragged his bloodied hands through his hair. 'I just thought it was one unholy mess, and your life was at risk from what Dougie could do to you. It was a straight choice, and not a hard one.'

'How... How did you manage it?'

There was a long silence, and Tony felt sicker and sicker as he waited. Finally Nick spoke, and he sounded almost robotic. 'First I tried to run him down. A hit and run, you know? He always had music on when he walked into town. But he heard me anyway and jumped into the ditch. So I had to go all the way to the studio.'

He sat up and moved along the sofa. Away from Tony, as if he were trying to disassociate himself. 'Ben had told me about the gun his dad kept on the shelf, and I was going to use it, but Mr Cameron got hold of a chisel and tried to do me with it, so I used that instead.' He rubbed his chest, as if a remembered pain had become a real one. Or he wished it had. He had managed to get his emotions under control now, and although his face still twisted with self-loathing and guilt, his words made all too perfect sense.

'Bradley *was* lying about where he was, you're right. But only because he was off shagging Sarah Wallace. I was supposed to be down south with Ben at a festival, but I cried off. I knew I was going to do it that weekend. I planned it. Thought about it all the time, until it was something I couldn't go back on.'

'Have you been self-harming ever since?'

'Not quite.' Nick lifted the blood-soaked towel and studied his leg dispassionately. 'I was scared, and that felt right. It was exactly what I deserved. Then, when the investigation was closed and I realised I wasn't going to be punished, that's when I started.'

'Cutting yourself.'

'Eventually. Not at the start. I used to pinch and that was enough, but not for long.' He met Tony's gaze. 'You *are* going to turn me in, aren't you? I mean, you have to, now I know you really are the straight-down-the-line one. The one with integrity.'

Tony felt helplessness creeping through him, turning his long-held principles into questions: what purpose would it serve? Who would benefit from it? Was there still a way to convict Bradley of it after all?

He took a deep breath. 'What you were scared would happen to me, if I got sent down... Nick, that'll be *you*. You'll be a target from the moment you're arrested. Before you're convicted, even. I can't put you through that.'

'You'd do it to Bradley; you have to do it to me. You'll hate yourself, and me, if you don't.'

'I'd be killing you,' Tony said bleakly. He rubbed his hands over his face.

'If the alternative is to go on being a prisoner inside my own head,' Nick gave Tony the saddest smile, 'you'd be doing me a favour.'

The words went through Tony like a shard of ice, and he found a few words, somehow, to get them past this moment of mutual devastation. 'Let's just wait, and talk tomorrow when we're clear-headed.'

He sat in silence, his mind turning over and over, finally understanding Nick's guilt and why he sought such extreme measures to mute it; the conflict was like a pain in his heart. Could he condemn a police officer to a life of terror in prison? Could he really destroy his own life, a life built on honesty and honour, to save a guilty man? He looked sideways at Nick; head bowed, blood drenched, his knuckles white, and he closed his eyes.

Integrity be damned, this was his son.

Maddy watched as different emotions crossed her father's face with bewildering speed. She'd expected some kind of grim satisfaction when he learned of the manner of Bradley's death, as far as she understood it, but as she told him everything, in a quiet corridor just down from Paul's room, he only looked cheated, angry, and then determined.

'He'll still get what's coming to him.'

'I hope so. I've not found out what they think, yet. Nick will be the one to learn the details, I expect.'

His expression changed again, becoming distant. 'Come outside for a bit,' he said, after a moment. 'I need to talk to you.'

As he put out his hand to take hers, she noticed something dark red crusting his cuticles and flaking at the edges of his nails, and she snatched her hand back. He blinked in surprise before following her gaze, and then shook his head. 'It's nothing to worry about.'

'Is Ben Cameron okay?' she asked sharply, and he looked even more taken aback by that.

'Ben? I have no idea, why?'

'Whose blood is that?'

'It's Nick's. He's fine,' he went on quickly, 'just a little accident at home. Why are you asking about Cameron?'

She relaxed slightly. 'Doesn't matter. Look, what do you want to talk about? I want to stay with Paul, and there's Charis to—'

'It's important, hen. Please.'

She went with him, her distracted mind shifting back to Charis, and hoping Gavin wouldn't keep her waiting too long. He'd get her out today, for sure, and reunited with Jamie, but it was going to be tough to convince the police that she hadn't killed Sarah Wallace. Maddy herself was going to have to confess to having shot the woman through the window, and would likely be sent down for attempted murder; only the fact that she was acting to preserve a child's life might save her, though that was no guarantee either.

But even those dark thoughts were blown away when, in the privacy of a deserted bus shelter, her father told her about Nick, and Dougie Cameron. A chill crept through her at the knowledge of what her brother had done, and, almost worse, that he'd been able to keep it hidden from them for all these years... Even feeling the way she had, after shooting Sarah, she couldn't begin to imagine how it must have felt to kill a man face-to-face. An innocent, terrified man, and with a weapon driven by his own hand.

She took a few deep breaths to steady the shakes that seized her, feeling the cool morning air on her suddenly sweating brow, and sat down on the metal seat. After a while she looked at her father, and then down at his hand.

'Does this have anything to do with that?' She nodded at the blood. 'Did something else happen?'

For a moment he was silent, and then seemed to make his decision. Haltingly, he told her the rest of Nick's story. A vivid flash of memory showed her the way her brother had tugged at his jeans leg to cover the blood on his sock when he'd been playing with Tas, and how she'd teased him about cutting himself shaving. *Picked a scab if you must know...* She felt both ill and desperately sad. How many other excuses had he had to scrabble for, to which she just hadn't paid any attention?

'What will you do?' she asked at last.

'Nothing.' Her father met her eyes with his deeply shadowed ones. 'We're going to have to help Nick through this, because no matter what he thinks, he's *not* going to be eased by going to jail. Not by my hand, and not, I trust, by yours.'

'No,' she said quietly, though still not entirely sure. 'Not by mine either.'

'Nor Mackenzie's?'

'No. Nor his own, if I've got a say in it.'

'Good.' He let out a shuddering breath, and Maddy put her arm around him, decision made.

'We'll protect him as best we can.' She drew back. 'But Alistair Mulholland is still out there, and he's the real threat, especially if he knows what Nick did. The trouble is, we need his gun, to prove neither Charis nor myself killed Sarah Wallace.'

Tony looked at her steadily. 'I've crossed a line now. I've chosen to protect a guilty man, which means I'm no longer the man I was.' His eyes took on a disturbingly dangerous glint. 'Any man who's a threat to my family is fair game.'

Maddy stiffened. 'You can't—'

'Ah, don't mind me.' Tony smiled, but it was brittle. 'Just bravado, that's all. Heat of the moment stuff, you know.'

He kissed Maddy lightly on the forehead, and the smile gradually relaxed into his old gentle one. But Maddy glanced sideways at him as he walked by her side, back into the hospital, and wondered about her close-knit, loving family, and whether she'd ever really known them at all.

Acknowledgments

First thanks must go to my wonderful parents, Anne and Eddie Deegan, for moving to Scotland in 1991, and introducing me to its matchless beauty and drama. They started something then, for sure!

I'm grateful to every single one of my friends and readers who have encouraged me to take this, the first novel I ever wrote (in the early 1990s), and give it a new lease of life in the 2020s; your confidence in me is gratifying, and I hope it's been repaid. Likewise, I would like to thank Rebecca and Adrian at Hobeck, for picking up this story and giving it its chance out in the world.

Finally my thanks to everyone in the huge and supportive writing community, on Facebook and Twitter as well as in 'real' life. Special thanks to Glynis Smy, Deborah Carr, and Christie Barlow, and to everyone in the TSAG. And a big shout-out to the Savvies: the best writers' group on the planet!

About the Author

R.D. Nixon is a pen-name of author Terri Nixon, who has been publishing historical drama and mythic fantasy novels since 2013. The initials belong to her two sons, who are graciously pretending not to mind.

Terri was born in Plymouth, UK. She moved to Cornwall at the age of nine, and grew up on the edge of Bodmin Moor, where her early writing found its audience in her school friends, who, to be fair, had very little choice. She has now returned to Plymouth, and works in the university's Faculty of Arts, Humanities and Business. She is occasionally mistaken for a lecturer, but not for long.

Hobeck Books - the home of great stories

We hope you've enjoyed reading this novel by R.D. Nixon. To find out more about R.D. Nixon and her work please visit her website: **www.rdnixon.com**

If you enjoyed this book, you may be interested to know that if you subscribe to Hobeck Books you can download a free novella *The Macnab Principle* by R.D. Nixon, exclusive only to subscribers.

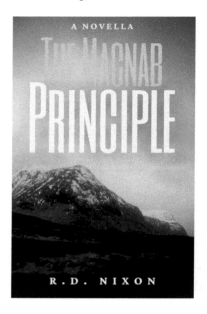

There are many more short stories and novellas available for free too.

- *Echo Rock* by Robert Daws
- *Old Dogs, Old Tricks* by AB Morgan
- *The Silence of the Rabbit* by Wendy Turbin
- *Never Mind the Baubles: An Anthology of Twisted Winter Tales* by the Hobeck Team (including all the current Hobeck authors and Hobeck's two publishers)
- *The Clarice Cliff Vase* by Linda Huber
- *Here She Lies* by Kerena Swan

Also please visit the Hobeck Books website for details of our other superb authors and their books, and if you would like to get in touch, we would love to hear from you.

Hobeck Books also presents a weekly podcast, the Hobcast, where founders Adrian Hobart and Rebecca Collins discuss all things book related, key issues from each week, including the ups and downs of running a creative business. Each episode includes an interview with one of the people who make Hobeck possible: the editors, the authors, the cover designers. These are the people who help Hobeck bring great stories to life. Without them, Hobeck wouldn't exist. The Hobcast can be listened to from all the usual platforms but it can also be found on the Hobeck website: **www.hobeck.net/hobcast**.

9 781913 793357